Praise for
A MEDAL OF H

"A real page turner. This is a powerful and fast moving book of the compelling tales of the behind-the-scenes action, the joys and pitfalls of Olympic greatness. A story of courage, generosity and compassion. The quality of the dialogue and intricacy of the plot will keep you on the edge of your seat. *A Medal of Honor* is a true delight filled with excitement, plot twists and even a sprinkle of romance. Highly recommended!"

-The Master Skier
(North America's Leading Nordic Racing Publication)

"It's a good read, well-written and compelling."

-CBS Sports

"As you read this story your heart will pound and your fingers will fling the pages so you can keep up with the excitement Morton creates."

-The Dartmouth Bookstore

"A wonderful story about Olympic competition, about biathlon, and above all, about human courage, generosity and compassion."

-Lowell Thomas, Jr.
Former Lt. Governor of Alaska

"[Morton] weaves a tale of strength versus weakness and good versus evil, in which the seduction of winning at all costs is a constant temptation. It is full of excitement, camaraderie, fun, and romance. Like a World Cup competitor, this story hops around the globe and visits exotic winter sports venues."

-Nordic Skier
(Newsletter of the Nordic Skiing Association of Anchorage, AK)

"I loved it. Couldn't put it down. I plan to use it for my Sports Literature class."

-High School English teacher

"*A Medal of Honor* is an engrossing, fast-paced read. Morton touches on several themes including behind-the-scene Olympic politics, drug use in Olympic competition, ethics of winning, motivation, guilt, friendship, honesty, patriotism, and the struggles of becoming an adult."

-Vermont Sports Today

"It's a page-turner, a lovely book."

-Vermont Public Radio

"Rather than explaining his sport, Morton dramatizes it. Immersed in the heat of competition along with the book's hero, a reader comes away with a real appreciation of biathlon. Far from glorifying the Olympics, Morton reveals the stresses of competition and the unrealistically high expectations. He approaches the subject of illegal performance enhancement head-on."

-Valley News
(W. Lebanon, NH)

"*A Medal of Honor* is a true delight filled with excitement, plot twists and even a sprinkle of romance. Highly recommended."

-AXCS News
(American Cross Country Skier)

A MEDAL OF HONOR

An Insider Unveils
the Agony and the Ecstasy
of the Olympic Dream

A MEDAL OF HONOR

An Insider Unveils
the Agony and the Ecstasy
of the Olympic Dream

John Morton

Discover History LLC
New York

First published in the United States by Bookpartners, Inc.

First Discover History LLC printing, December 2005

Library of Congress Cataloging-in-Publication Data

Morton, John, 1946-
 A medal of honor : an insider unveils the agony and the ecstasy of the Olympic dream
/ John Morton.
  p. cm.
 Summary: "Recounts the travels, training and competitions of Matt Johnson as he
competes in the sport of Biathlon (cross country skiing and rifle marksmanship). The
story involves Matt facing the dilemma of unethical competitors and culminates in a
fictional Winter Olympics in Cortina and Anholtz, Italy"--Provided by publisher.
 ISBN-13: 978-1-929401-04-8 (pbk.)
 ISBN-10: 1-929401-04-3 (pbk.)
 1. Winter Olympics--Fiction. I. Title.
 PS3563.O88355M43 2005
 813'.54--dc22
                          2005034689

Original Cover design by Richard Ferguson
Original Text design by Sheryl Mehary

Second Edition Cover design by David Spaidal
Maps Illustrated by Amy DeLardi

Discover History LLC
P.O. Box 527
Bronxville, New York 10708 USA

Map and Photograph Credits

The author and publishers would like to take this opportunity to thank those companies, organisations and individuals around the world who graciously gave their permission to reproduce the maps in this book. Thanks go to: DeLorme, for the maps in chapters 1, 2, 3, 4, 5, 6, 9, 11, 14, 18, and 19; the Nordic Skiing Association of Anchorage and Land Design North for the Anchorage map in chapter 7 and the Kincaid Park trail map in chapter 8; Biathlon Ruhpolding for the trail map in chapter 10; Lillehammer Olympiapark AS for the trail map in chapter 12. The maps for chapters 13 and 15 are © Tele Atlas NV and reproduced by permission of Tele Atlas NV. The maps for chapter 16 and 17 are courtesy of Mapgraphic and Biathlon Antholz.

Front cover photograph courtesy of the US Biathlon Association, Christian Menzi / Menzipics; Jay Hakkinen of Kasilof, Alaska, in action at the World Championships, March 2005, Hochfilzen, Austria. Jay won the World Junior Championship in 1997; in 2005 he was America's top biathlete.

Back cover photograph of John Morton courtesy of John Griesemer.

In loving memory of my wife Mimi,
and to all Olympians;
coaches, administrators, and athletes
who resist the pressures
to win unethically,
and who play by the rules.

Preface to First Edition

This book is a work of fiction. The main characters and events of the story were drawn from my imagination. Any similarity to actual people or historical events is unintended, with the following exceptions. The sites described in the novel, Anchorage, Ruhpolding, Lillehammer, and Antholz routinely host major Nordic skiing competitions similar to those described in the book. Occasional reference is made to well known, Olympians in an effort to add authenticity to my fictional Winter Games in the Italian Sud Tirol. And sadly, from my experience at dozens of major international competitions, including six Winter Olympic Games, the insidious problem of illegal performance enhancement is all too real.

John Morton
December 1997
Thetford, Vermont

Preface to Second Edition

When the first edition of *A Medal of Honor* was printed in the spring of 1998, I had expected a readership limited to cross country skiers and biathletes. As a first time novelist, it was extremely gratifying to be greeted instead by a much broader reading audience. People were generous in reaching out to tell me how absorbed they became in the story, but also wanted to share their thoughts about the more serious underlying ethical issues raised in the book.

Perhaps most rewarding has been *A Medal of Honor* being incorporated into high school curriculums. Teens who rarely finish reading any books were engrossed in the novel, surprising both their parents and themselves. It was a privilege to be invited into classrooms filled with enthusiastic teens bursting with perceptive and challenging questions.

I wish I could say that in the seven years since *A Medal of Honor* was first published, the problem of illegal performance enhancement had been resolved. Unfortunately, doping scandals at the 2001 Nordic World Championships, the 2002 Salt Lake City Winter Olympics, the 2002 Sydney Summer Olympics, the Tour de France, Major League Baseball, and elsewhere confirm that the problem still exists. What remains unknown is whether there are more cheaters or whether there are simply more cheaters getting caught. However, it is also true that the International Olympic Committee, the US Olympic Committee, the recently established World Anti-Doping Agency, and other prominent sports governing bodies are finally getting serious about catching and banning those who refuse to play by the rules.

Much of the action in this novel takes place in real towns and sports centers around the world ranging from remote native villages in the Alaskan wilderness to some of the major cities in Europe. Because many of the stops in Matt's travels are obscure, this edition includes maps so that readers may follow his journey more easily.

Finally, I am happy to report that Matt Johnson's story does not end with *A Medal of Honor*. I hope you will enjoy chapter one of the sequel, *The Heroes of Muju* which can be found at the conclusion of this book.

John Morton
December 2005
Thetford, Vermont

Acknowledgements

This book was a team effort. The following people suffered through early drafts of the manuscript, providing valuable advice and encouragement: James Bandler, Kate Carter, Max Cobb, Joni Cole, Jay Davis, Anne Donaghy, Peggy Fogg, Carol Hayes, Alex Kahan, Rea Keast, Nancy Kendall, Joe Medlicott, Jessica Morrell, George and Megan Morton, Shirley Morton, Sam Osborne, Ruff Patterson, Ken Rundell, Dr. Bob Rusfvold, John and Anne Scotford, Rosemary Shea, Steve Williams, and Jed Williamson.

I am indebted to Bob Delfay for his generous support, and to Lyle Nelson whose enthusiasm is as contagious now as it was twenty years ago when we raced together.

Also by John Morton

Don't Look Back

Table of Maps

Table of Contents

The Heroes of Muju

The most important thing in the Olympic Games
is not to win but to take part,
just as the most important thing in life
is not the triumph but the struggle.

Baron Pierre de Coubertin
Founder of the modern Olympic Games

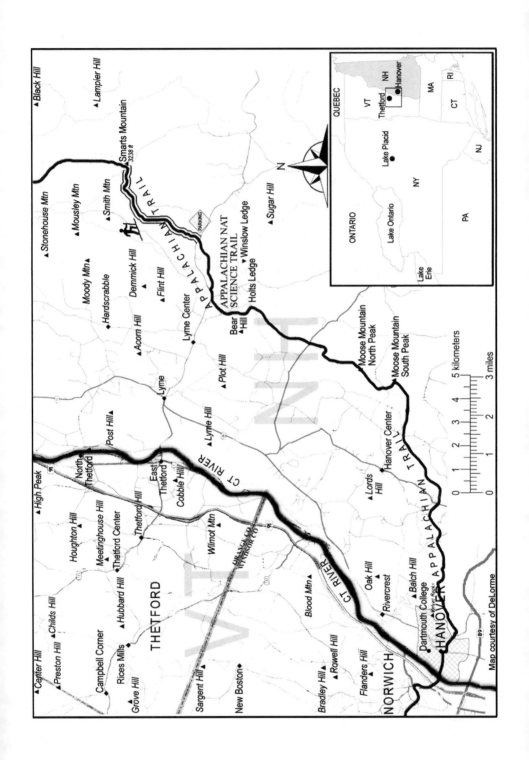

Map courtesy of DeLorme

A Secret Victory

1

Driven by ambition that he couldn't control, Matt Johnson pushed his way up the mountain, his pulse pounding and sweat stinging his eyes. It wasn't just the throbbing sound; he could actually feel the blood surging in the carotid artery of his neck and at his temples. His calves felt like frayed steel cables about to snap. His sweat-drenched palms kept slipping, adding aggravation to exhaustion. Out of habit he concentrated on his breathing, inhaling through his nose, exhaling through his mouth, long, deep lung-filling breaths of air.

Ahead, the trail was booby-trapped with roots and rocks, countless opportunities to trip, fall, and even break an ankle. After months of training he'd learned to anticipate every footstep, avoiding the snags and mud holes. He had also learned long ago that small, vertical steps required less energy than long stretches.

If he were running from a grizzly, Matt could not have pushed himself any harder. He was red-lining, sustaining his heart rate at the highest level possible. Demanding more of his body would produce total collapse a few hundred meters up the mountain.

"Stop the pain," cried an inner voice, "back off, no one will ever know. The Olympics are a fantasy made for television." He ignored the voice, pushing away all thoughts, a discipline that had become more difficult since his father's death.

There was nothing remarkable about Matt Johnson's appearance. In shorts and running shoes, he looked like an ordinary teenage athlete, just under six feet tall, lean and muscular, but without the dramatic definition of older men who spent hours lifting weights.

Smarts Mountain was a twenty-minute drive across the Connecticut River Valley from Thetford, Vermont, where Matt had lived for most of his eighteen years. It was not spectacular compared to the peaks of the western United States, but Matt woke to the sun rising over Smarts every day, and he had come to think of it as his mountain. He'd lost track of the number of times he'd climbed it: first riding on his father's back, then trudging along with his mother and sister, more recently running, pushing his heart rate dangerously close to its maximum of 198 beats per minute.

To distract himself from the pain, Matt pictured the Dartmouth skiers whom he'd idolized as a kid, legends who could run Smarts in under an hour. More than once Matt and his family had been on the mountain when the Dartmouth team charged by, sweating and out of breath, but still laughing and teasing each other. Matt had learned the names of the Olympians: Glen Eberle, Willie Carow, Erich Wilbrecht, and Carl Swenson. Occasionally, tucked in the train of lean bodies, Matt had noticed Leslie Thompson and Nina Kemppel, both veterans of several Winter Olympic Teams. They were so strong that training with the men seemed perfectly normal.

As he slogged across the rocky saddle leading to the summit, his pulse drowned all other sounds and his legs moved only by memory. He staggered on, pushing through the young balsams, finally reaching the steel tower at the peak, where he bent over, gasping for air and fumbling with the tiny button on his digital watch.

59:47!

"All right!" he yelled to the surrounding evergreens. "First time under an hour!"

Matt surveyed the stretch of valley before him as he pulled a water bottle and an orange from his fanny pack. Stiffness was already invading his thighs so he kept moving, shaking his legs and stretching the aching muscles. He drank the water and peeled the orange out of habit, carefully removing the thick skin in one continuous spiral. He succeeded, and smiled at another small victory.

As he ate the orange and recognized familiar landmarks below, he chuckled at the irony. He had just reached the most important milestone in his athletic career, and not another soul knew about it. There were no cheering fans, no proud teammates slapping him on the back, no sports writers asking him how he felt. He was totally alone with his accomplishment. It was his own private victory, and that was just fine.

Well, maybe he wasn't totally alone. Looking out over the forested landscape, he wondered if somehow his father was a silent witness. Matt felt the familiar anxiety that had marked so many of their interactions and still occurred since his father's death. Feeling that customary lurch in his gut, Matt asked himself for the thousandth time if he'd ever think of his dad without some accompanying misgivings. There had been good times, of course. Matt remembered how proud he had been when he was twelve and his dad decided it was time to teach him marksmanship. He remembered the thrill of hunting trips for partridge or deer, and how he'd learned that coming home empty-handed was not a failed expedition as long as he tried his best.

Matt smiled, thinking of their first biathlon competition at Bretton Woods in New Hampshire when he was fourteen. He had relentlessly pestered his dad to let him compete, who at the last minute had relented and then entered the race himself. Both Johnsons shot well, thanks to their hunting experience, but Matt was surprised by how well his dad skied. That spring, they bought a second-hand biathlon rifle from a retiring National Team member, and agreed to shoot together a couple of times each week.

Michael Johnson was a brilliant if unforgiving rifle coach. Matt had never been clear on the details of his father's past, but he knew his dad had been assigned to the Biathlon Training Center at Fort Richardson, Alaska, when he went on active duty in the army. Matt's father had been born in Anchorage, and skiing and hunting were second nature to him.

But something had happened in Alaska that his parents refused to talk about. Sometime before the 1972 Winter Olympics in Sapporo, Michael Johnson had been sent to Vietnam. He flew medevac helicopters for two and a half years and apparently returned home a different man. Matt had seen old pictures of his parents in Alaska; proudly hauling king salmon from the Kenai River, smiling from the summit of a rocky peak, clowning with friends at a backyard barbecue.

But the father Matt knew rarely laughed and seldom smiled. He was like a man who always had a toothache, or some pain that no medicine could cure. Matt suspected that his father's missed chance to compete in the Olympics, coupled with the horrors of war had killed a spirit that was fragile underneath all the surface steel.

Because they both enjoyed hunting, skiing, and climbing mountains, Matt had fond memories of his dad, but these good times came with a price. As a boy he always worried that he never measured up in his father's eyes. During the annual deer hunting ritual, Matt eventually dreaded taking a shot for fear it wouldn't be a clean kill, and his father would fly into a rage. Skiing, Matt could beat his peers by two minutes, but his father's only comment would be about Matt's sloppy technique on a particular uphill. Even when they hiked together in the woods, his dad's impatience was obvious when Matt was slow to identify a tree or shrub.

But all those memories, fond or painful, were eclipsed by the memory of Chuck Stevenson, Thetford's part-time constable, pulling into the driveway as the Johnsons finished dinner on a stormy evening last September. Chuck was the most easygoing town cop in history, occasionally catching kids drinking in the parking lot at a school dance, or busting some "leaf peeper" from New York for doing fifty through Thetford Center. But his face was gray as he stepped from the cruiser into the September rain.

It had been Matt, his mother, and his sister Annie at the table; Michael Johnson had telephoned earlier to say he'd be late for dinner. He was working a forestry job for a land trust in Peterborough, marking trees for a long-overdue thinning. Fall was a busy time for Matt's dad; he often left the house before dawn and was seldom home by dark.

So there was nothing unusual about the three of them eating dinner without him, and nothing unusual about Matt and his younger sister squabbling over whose turn it was to do the dishes. Their mother was about to intervene, but then the headlights pulled into the driveway. Matt assumed it was his dad until he heard his mother gasp as she headed for the door. Through the window, he saw Chuck, standing in the rain, twisting his hat in his hands, while the cruiser's headlights burned a tunnel through the downpour.

Seconds later, his mother stepped back into the kitchen, pulling on her coat, her face drained of color. Her appearance stopped their bickering.

"Your father's been in an accident. I'm going to the hospital with

Mr. Stevenson."

Matt and Annie stood in the silence, too bewildered to ask questions before she whisked out the door and climbed in the squad car. Matt cleared the table and began to fill the sink as Annie peppered him with questions.

"What do you think happened?"

"I don't know, car accident, I guess."

"He'll be okay, won't he?"

"I imagine. He's good about wearing his seat belt."

Matt envisioned scenarios: the pickup truck sliding off the rain-slicked road, maybe rolling a couple of times, his dad banged up, taken to the hospital for observation. Chuck Stevenson would likely bring his parents home in a couple of hours. Or maybe his dad was really hurt: a broken leg, some facial cuts from flying glass, maybe even something serious like a broken back. Matt dreaded how ticked-off his father would be if he was forced to wear a cast; autumn was the prime time for tree marking.

Broken bones were as far as his imagination took him. Hell, his dad had survived a tour flying medevac choppers in Vietnam! Although Michael Johnson never talked about the war, Matt knew his dad had been shot down a couple of times and had seen enough combat to earn a Purple Heart, three Air Medals and a Silver Star. He'd be okay; banged up maybe, but okay.

It was late and the rain had stopped when finally a car pulled into the driveway. Matt and Annie had remained in the living room, trying to do their homework, but unable to concentrate. As an old Ford pulled up, the two teenagers went out on the porch. The smell of the rain and the dead leaves unmistakably signaled autumn. They were surprised that it wasn't Chuck and their mom, but Aunt Sarah and Uncle Jim who stepped from the car.

Sarah's face was streaked with tears and mascara. Stumbling up the steps, she grabbed Annie in a desperate embrace. "Oh you poor kids, you poor kids."

Uncle Jim put his arm around Matt and gently herded everyone into the house.

"What's going on?" Matt asked, an ominous emptiness gnawing in his gut.

Sarah threw a desperate glance at Jim, who ran his hand through his thinning hair and paced across the living room, mumbling, "Jesus… Jesus…Jesus.…"

Before he could answer, another vehicle swung into the yard, then the front door banged open and three people burst into the kitchen. Had she not been wearing a coat that he'd seen a hundred times, Matt would never have recognized his own mother. Her hair was a wild tangle, her face distorted in agony, and she shuffled as if she'd suddenly grown old. Two women that Matt didn't know guided her up the stairs to the bedroom. Before the door closed, Matt heard her sob, "They wouldn't let me see him. Why wouldn't they let me see him? Why…?"

Relatives and neighbors congregated in the kitchen. Annie was crying steadily, a kind of backdrop to the constant stream of visitors. Headlights continued to sweep the yard as more people crammed into the house. Everyone seemed to be watching Matt and his sister from the safety of the kitchen.

The bile churned in his stomach as Matt's fear turned to anger. Why were these people taking over their home? Why hadn't they let his mother see his dad? *What the hell was going on?* Why were they treating him like a little kid and not telling him anything?

Then he spotted the silver hair and gentle face of his grandfather pushing through the crowd.

"What happened, Gramps? Where's Dad?"

"Come on, you two, let's go up to your room."

His grandfather's voice was steady and the grip on Matt's elbow was firm as the old man directed the two teenagers to Annie's bedroom at the end of the hall. Annie sobbed even louder as he closed the door. He pulled his grandchildren into a strong embrace and spoke quietly, "There's been a terrible accident. Your dad went off the interstate into a bridge abutment. He died in the ambulance before they could get him to the Medical Center."

As the old man spoke, he squeezed them even tighter, but at first Matt couldn't comprehend the words. Died on the way to the hospital? That was impossible.

Matt was shaking his head, mumbling "No…no… no…no…," when he felt the old man's grip tighten.

"She's going to need you, Matt. You've got to be strong for her. I've never seen her so broken up, not even when Gramma died. This is going to be a tough one, and you've got to be strong for her. You understand me, Matty?"

The days following the accident were blurred in his memory. For almost a week his mother rarely left her room. Matt had grown accustomed to his mother's strength; it was she who usually bore the brunt of his father's moods and tantrums and usually managed to keep the family buoyed with her patience and optimism. The mother who locked herself in her room, who was hollow-eyed and ghostly was like a stranger. Although he heard her sobbing through the door, he was afraid to go in. There was an endless stream of relatives and neighbors, talking in whispers and glancing with concern toward her bedroom. The refrigerator was jammed with unfamiliar pans, platters and bowls, but it was usually Matt and Annie huddled together who ate the meatloaf and macaroni salad.

For weeks, the Johnson family appeared to be sleepwalking through their lives. Gradually they settled into a routine, but of course everything was different. Matt immersed himself in schoolwork and sports, but Annie floundered, ignoring her school assignments and hanging out with troublemakers. By November their mother had returned to her teaching job at Thetford Elementary, although there were still times when she emerged from her bedroom with her face swollen and eyes red from crying.

The winter following his father's death broke snowfall records in New England. A powerful Nor'easter hit over Thanksgiving, the temperature stayed cold, and deep snow blanketed Vermont. Never before in Matt's memory had there been such excellent skiing so early in the season. Matt stepped up his biathlon training. It might have been his way of dealing with the tragedy. It might have been an attempt to finally live up to his father's expectations. And his grueling training routine certainly was fueled by the devastating rumor that was circulating Thetford that his father's car wreck had not been an accident, but suicide. Whatever the reason, Matt approached his training and racing with an intensity that bordered on obsession.

His efforts paid off when his results in local biathlon competitions during January and February attracted the attention of the National coaches, and Matt was invited to the National Championships in Lake Placid in early March. Although the United States Team members were obligated to attend the Championships, the event was scheduled so late in the season that it meant little to the top competitors. The experienced biathletes had all peaked for the Team tryouts in December, where racers were selected for the Biathlon World Championships in Europe. Most of the National Team members were raced-out and jet-lagged by the time they straggled back to Lake Placid in March.

Matt, on the other hand, was driven to succeed. The snow was cold, the waxing uncomplicated, and the wind calm; perfect weather for shooting. Matt skied surprisingly well compared to the exhausted National Team Juniors, and he out-shot most of them. He didn't finish in the medals, but he caught the attention of the National Team's head coach, Vladimir Kobelev, a recent emigrant from the unraveling Soviet sports dynasty.

On the shooting range during the final Championship race, as Matt brought down all his standing targets, Kobelev turned to the team's program director, Stanley Reimer.

"This kid Johnson, he's not so bad. Where he's coming from?"

"Vermont, I think."

"Who coaches him?"

"No idea. Why?"

"He shoots good. The skiing…well, he will get stronger. But good biathlon shooting, maybe you must be born with that? You invite this Johnson to June testing camp…yes?"

"What are you talking about, Vlad? Our Junior Team is already chosen. What do you think those tryouts in December were all about? We got a dozen kids with international racing experience, for chrissakes."

"Stanley, the American Biathlon Federation paying me, how do you say, big bugs for coaching, da? I telling you, invite this kid to June camp."

By the third week in April, with the competitions behind him, Matt had slacked off his training routine when he received a letter from Stanley Reimer.

American Biathlon Federation
2002 Church Street
Burlington, VT 05401
(802) 862-3008

Mr. Matthew Johnson
Rural Route 2, Box 7
Thetford, VT 05075

Dear Matthew:

I'm contacting you at the request of Vladimir Kobelev, head coach of the United States Biathlon Team, to invite you to our annual spring training camp to be held at the Lake Placid Olympic Training Center, the second week of June. The focus of the training camp will be the most comprehensive physiological testing ever administered to American biathletes.

Although our national training squads for the coming Olympic season were named in January, based upon a series of tryout races, Coach Kobelev was impressed by your performance at the National Championships and asked me to offer you the opportunity to participate in the testing camp. Your room and board during the seven day camp will be provided by the United States Olympic Committee, and the American Biathlon Federation will reimburse you for travel expenses.

I must reiterate that our National Team for the upcoming season has already been selected and that this invitation represents nothing more than our ongoing effort to identify and recruit promising athletes for the future. If you choose to accept this invitation, please contact the ABF office at your earliest convince to confirm your participation.

Sincerely,
Stanley Reimer
National Program Director

The invitation came as a complete surprise, and Matt resumed training the day he received the letter. He worked on his shooting, but his top priority was physical conditioning: running, lifting weights, and hiking, especially up Smarts Mountain.

Standing on the abandoned fire tower, after achieving an important goal, he tried to quell the familiar churning in his stomach. He wondered if his dad would have been proud of him, not only for making the summit of Smarts in under an hour, but for earning an invitation to the Biathlon Team's testing camp. The stakes of the game had just risen. Participating in the Winter Olympics was no longer a childhood fantasy fueled by his father's broken dream. The National Team coach wanted to see how Matt measured up. Nothing was going to get in the way of his big opportunity. He'd seen what his father's tarnished dreams had done to their family. Failure was not an option.

He took a last look at the distant mountains, headed down the stairs, and jogged across the forested summit. As Matt eased down the steep granite slabs, he overtook an Appalachian Trail through-hiker he had sprinted past on the way up, staggering under the weight of a towering pack.

"You're making good time," Matt encouraged, skirting around the hiker. "You'll be in Georgia before September."

"We'll see. Hey, what the hell are you doing, training for the Olympics or something?" the heavily burdened hiker shouted after Matt.

"Yeah," Matt called back over his shoulder, "That's exactly what I'm doing."

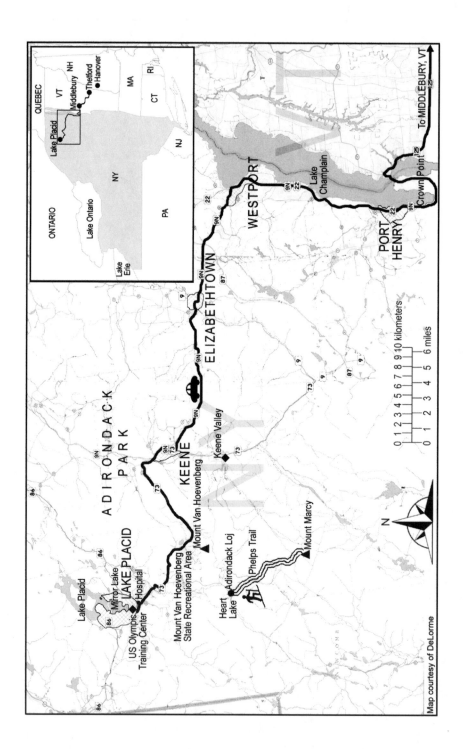

Map courtesy of DeLorme

Agony and Ecstasy

2

Lake Placid lies nestled in the Adirondack Mountains less than 100 miles from Matt's home in Thetford. It was a warm summer morning when Matt left for the training camp. Dense fog shrouded the valleys, but cresting Sharon Hill, Matt emerged into brilliant sunshine. Driving along, he was trying to block out the parting scene with his mother. He was sure that the mother he once knew would be thrilled with his trip to Lake Placid. But that mother was gone. Was she expecting him to fill his father's shoes? To put his dreams on hold and provide some kind of father figure to Annie?

He stopped for gas in Middlebury and wondered again if he'd made the right decision. In September, at the time of his father's death, Matt had been immersed in the college selection process. He'd narrowed his choices to four schools with good ski teams: Bates, Dartmouth, Williams, and Middlebury. He had counted on improving his SAT scores in November, but with the chaos surrounding his dad's death, that hadn't happened. As things shook out, he was accepted at Bates and Middlebury. He was about to accept Middlebury's offer when Stanley Reimer's letter arrived in April. Over his mother's protests, he deferred admission for a year and declared that he intended to make the Olympic Team.

An hour later, as he drove up out of the Keene Valley into the mountains surrounding Lake Placid, the forest gave way to pastures and the skyline was dominated by the twin towers of the 1980 Olympic ski jumps. Moments later he pulled into the parking lot of the Olympic Training Center.

Entering the reception area, Matt felt like he didn't belong, as if "greenhorn" or "rookie" was stamped on his forehead. The walls were covered with Olympic posters, skis, skates and even a bobsled, all depicting past Olympic glories. The receptionist asked pleasantly, "May I help you?"

He cleared his throat. "I'm Matt Johnson. I'm here for the biathlon training camp."

The woman reached for a folder marked, BIATHLON. "Johnson, Matthew J., Thetford, Vermont. You were with us for the Biathlon Nationals last March weren't you, Mr. Johnson? Then you know the drill. Fill out these forms, then I'll assign you a room and issue a key."

There were pages of rules, and a comprehensive health evaluation, listing more medical problems than Matt knew existed. As he struggled down the list, he was distracted by a striking blonde, her running shorts and tee shirt barely concealing her firm muscles and sensuous curves. He could feel himself blush as she approached.

"You must be new here," she said brightly.

Matt's response came out as a croak. The blonde grinned and leaned over Matt's medical form.

"You're healthy, right?"

He nodded.

She helped herself to his pen, "No chronic bed-wetting, kidney stones or emphysema? Then just draw a line down the column like this, turn the form over, do the same on the back. You haven't tried to commit suicide in the last six months, have you?"

Matt shook his head.

"Good, then just sign here, date it, and you're done."

She handed his pen back to him, but Matt couldn't stop staring. He emerged from his trance long enough to scribble his name on the form.

"Matt Johnson. I remember you from the Nationals. You shot really well."

"Thanks. You're on the National Team, aren't you?"

"Yeah, I'm Trudy Wilson from Tahoe, California. I've been on the team since just after Lillehammer. Scoot over and I'll help you fill out the rest of these damn forms. This Code of Conduct thing just says you won't put snakes in other athletes' beds or drop your pants at some press conference."

Matt was having trouble concentrating on the forms. Never before had he been so close to such a beautiful woman. It was like sitting next to a model who had just stepped off the pages of the *Sports Illustrated* swimsuit issue.

"This is your parking permit. You do have a car, don't you?"

"Pickup…I've got a four wheel drive pickup."

"I love trucks! Just fill in the license number here, and describe where you parked it. This is the USOC press office bio sheet. List your best national results, coaches, hometown newspaper…You know, the usual."

Matt paused, wondering if his results at last spring's Nationals were worthy of mention. Trudy noticed his hesitation and slid the form to the bottom of the pile, "It's not important anyway. Those press sheets are really for figure skaters and swimmers. Biathlon doesn't get much press in this country.

"Now this last one, the Drug Statement; you don't fool around with drugs, do you? Good! If you smoke a joint at a party, then three weeks later pee in the cup at a biathlon race, they can tell you where the stuff was grown! And I hear through the grapevine that the USOC is close to perfecting a new test. You've got to tell them in advance, even if all you're taking is aspirin and vitamins."

Matt looked the form over and signed it.

"All right, let's give Sylvia these forms and grab some lunch. There's a meeting at two."

Matt returned to the receptionist still astonished that this beautiful creature had befriended him moments after he entered the Training Center. The woman at the registration desk issued him a room key and a plastic ID card for the cafeteria. He thought about retrieving his gear from the truck, but Trudy grabbed his arm and led him around the corner.

The cafeteria was crowded and noisy. Athletes and coaches greeted each other as they worked their trays past the impressive salad bar, an appealing array of fresh fruit, a sandwich counter with cold cuts and cheese, and finally the hot entrees, rice, potatoes, and pasta. As Matt followed Trudy through the line, she introduced him to several other athletes, whose names he promptly forgot. A color TV suspended from the ceiling filled the room with the latest news of the world from CNN. There was so much going on that when they reached the end of the serving line, Matt realized he had piled on his tray three times what he normally ate for lunch.

Trudy introduced him to more athletes as they threaded their way through the tables, but she purposefully led him to an empty booth. She chatted enthusiastically as they ate. He was beginning to make a dent in the mountain of pasta, when a tall, bearish man, his bearded face wrinkled from years in the sun, stopped at their booth.

"Ah, Vermont Johnson …, so you are here! I am Vladimir Kobelev, National Team coach."

Matt struggled to stand, but the table in the booth made it difficult.

"Sit…Sit…." Kobelev commanded, forcing Matt down with a hand on his shoulder. "Two o'clock we having team meeting for explain schedule of training camp. This, mainly physical testing camp, you understand? How was springtime training for you, Johnson, good? *Harasho?*"

Matt swallowed nervously, "Yes sir, it was pretty good."

"Well, we finding out how good soon enough!" With a wave Kobelev lumbered off to greet another athlete.

After lunch Matt retrieved his gear from the truck and headed down the long hall to his room. The door was ajar, so he knocked and pushed it open with his beat-up rifle box.

"Come on in."

A young man with white-blonde hair and intense blue eyes was lying on one of the beds. He pushed himself up on his elbows as Matt entered.

"Hi, I'm Matt Johnson," Matt said, recognizing the other biathlete from the National Championships.

"Yeah, I remember you. I'm Heikki Lahdenpera from Duluth. You almost kicked my butt at the Nationals. How'd you learn to shoot like that?"

"My dad was on the Biathlon Team back in the sixties. We used to shoot together quite a bit when I was a kid."

"Well, my grandfather was in the ski troops in Finland, and my dad's done biathlon for years in the Minnesota National Guard; but they never taught me to shoot like that. Shit, if you ever learn to ski fast, you'll be a real threat."

"Yeah…well, I guess that doesn't happen overnight."

They talked as Matt unpacked. For the past four years, Heikki had been the top American junior biathlete. He would turn twenty in the fall and compete for the first time as a senior. But he assured Matt he wasn't worried because he had finished among the top six men in the country for the past three years.

At 1:45 they locked the room and headed down the hall for the meeting.

There were almost thirty athletes gathered when Kobelev looked at his watch and nodded to a small man wearing a suit and tie. One of the athletes muttered, "Stan the Man," which generated smiles, as the national program director walked to the front of the conference room.

When he reached the table, Stanley Reimer faced the athletes. "Welcome back to Lake Placid! I hope you're all fit, rested, and ready for the Olympic year. This testing camp marks the start of our preparation for the World Cup circuit and more importantly, the Olympic Games. We have only thirty-two weeks to prepare for what will probably be the most significant opportunity of your lives. Coach Kobelev believes we are finally capable of putting an American biathlete on the winner's stand at the Olympics, and I can tell you he'd better be right or our funding from the USOC will evaporate during the next quadrennial."

Reimer glanced at Kobelev who was standing in the back of the room, his arms crossed over his massive chest.

"As you know, the purpose of this camp is physiological evaluation.…"

"I can't wait to donate my pound of flesh," someone behind Matt whispered.

"What was that, Mr. Edwards?" Stan glared at Roger Edwards.

"Oh, I was just saying that I could hardly wait for the muscle biopsy." There were groans throughout the room.

Stan continued, "Most of our time this week will be devoted to testing. We've put together packets for you with schedules, necessary forms, pages for your training logs, and a sheet to write your suggestion for a team mission statement."

"Don't inconvenience the medical people, the coaches, and your teammates by being late to a scheduled appointment. Now as I pass out these packets, let me introduce our favorite team doctor, who was just approved by the USOC to be our official team physician at the Olympics in Italy, Dr. Mary Manheimer."

Cheers erupted from the athletes as a woman of average height with short brown hair, dressed in a conservative blue skirt and white blouse, walked confidently from the back of the room.

"Thank you, Stanley." She smiled warmly at her audience. "I hope you know how happy I am to be going with you to Italy. I know that some of you have been training for many years for this chance. The purpose of this camp is to make certain that you are in the best possible physical condition."

"The ABF and the USOC have planned the most comprehensive series of tests ever administered to American biathletes. You've heard rumors about the exotic medical support for the Russian athletes and the former Soviet Bloc countries. Well, the testing here this week will be as extensive as anything your rivals from Europe will receive. The data we collect will give your coaches valuable information about your physical preparation, so they can make appropriate revisions to your training program between now and February."

"Some of these tests are exhausting, others are painful, but I can assure you that each test is necessary. Believe it or not, there are some tests we decided not to include. You won't be getting rectal exams, for example."

There was a collective sigh of relief from the athletes.

The doctor continued, "Now, most of you have met Topper Henderson, the Director of the USOC's Human Performance Testing Lab."

An athletic, gray haired man wearing an Olympic Team polo shirt, smiled and waved casually to the athletes.

"Topper will be supervising all the physiological tests: the treadmill, the Cybex, lung capacity, and balance. I'll be updating your physicals, doing the blood work, giving you an eye exam, checking body fat, and getting the muscle biopsy."

"The Olympic Committee has also assigned our athletic trainer for the Games. He will help us with the testing, then rejoin the team in November at West Yellowstone and remain with us through the Olympics in February. He's on loan from Penn State. I'd like you all to meet Roosevelt Brown."

As Dr. Manheimer pointed to the rear of the room, Matt turned toward the blackest African American he had ever seen. The trainer was not more than five feet ten inches, but his chest and biceps strained his USOC polo shirt. When Brown smiled, his brilliant teeth made his dark skin seem almost blue.

The doctor continued, "Rosie has worked for the USOC at two National Sports Festivals. This will be his first Olympics. Please introduce yourselves to him and fill him in on biathlon."

Stanley Reimer thanked Dr. Manheimer and the meeting continued. The rifle coach, Sergeant Tadeusz Jankowski, gave the standard safety briefing and outlined the shooting schedule for the week. Matt remembered Jankowski from the Nationals and liked him. When Stan offered the lectern to Coach Kobelev, the Russian waved from his position against the back wall and grumbled, "Too much talk, time for get to work."

With that, Stan ended the meeting and the athletes filed out. As Matt followed Heikki through the door, he noticed Trudy fluttering her long lashes and rolling a blonde curl on a graceful finger.

Matt caught his roommate in the hall, "Hey, what's with Trudy anyway?"

Heikki looked at Matt with a grin, "Some body, huh?"

"I'll say, but what's the deal? Seems like she adopted me thirty seconds after I got here."

Heikki smiled knowingly, "Yeah, it's always like that. Her nickname is the 'Praying Mantis.' The female praying mantis attracts a mate to fertilize her eggs. But as soon as the old boy's done his duty, his new love bites his head off. Trudy lures her next victim with that magnificent body, then whammo, she dumps him. She's tried to make it with every guy on the team, except of course Brett Adams, who's such a straight arrow he's convinced he'd go straight to hell if he looked at a *Playboy*. I bet Trudy's been in the sack with some of the coaches! Watch your step."

As they reached the room, Heikki searched his pockets for the key. Matt had the sudden urge to make a telephone call. He retraced his steps to the pay phone near the entrance of the cafeteria, and dialed home. After several rings, his mother answered, but she sounded cool and remote. He had hoped to share his excitement with her of being a part of the training camp, but it was clear from her voice that she needed him in Thetford. After two awkward pauses, he ended the call, angry that she could make him feel miserable for just being away a week.

Matt quickly settled into a simple routine: physical tests, workouts, meals and sleep. He and Heikki got along well together. Although they never compared test scores, they were both happy to turn out the lights by nine each night.

Matt's physical exam with Dr. Manheimer took longer than usual because it was her first chance to talk with him. After nearly an hour, the doctor reviewed her notes, "Well then, I guess the only thing we have left is the blood test."

Matt began to feel light-headed. His face felt cold. Dr. Manheimer noticed his reaction and smiled, "Don't panic, I can get them all from the same stick."

"I've never liked needles," he confided. His mouth had become strangely dry.

"That's not unusual. Give me your arm, let's see, here's a nice vein. Make a fist."

The distinctive smell of the alcohol hit his nostrils as she scrubbed the cotton swab on his arm. There was a snap of plastic and she skillfully removed the syringe from its protective cover....

Disoriented, Matt looked up into her smiling face as it slowly came into focus.

"So...you're a fainter. I guess you warned me. Good thing you were sitting down. Well, we're all done. Just make sure whenever you get blood work done in the future that you're sitting down!"

Matt slumped in the chair as the room continued to spin. A cotton ball was taped to the inside of his elbow, and several vials of blood rested on Dr. Manheimer's desk.

"Still light-headed?" she asked. "You just sit there until you feel steady."

Matt was one of a dozen athletes scheduled to meet Kobelev on the high school track in downtown Lake Placid. The big Russian watched carefully as the athletes stretched their tight muscles. Matt mimicked the National Team members since he had never been too conscientious about stretching when he trained on his own. Apparently, Kobelev took stretching seriously.

The coach's instructions were brief, then he broke them into two groups. Each group would run an interval ladder: a 220-yard sprint, followed by a recovery jog, a 440 and another recovery jog, a half mile and a jog, a mile, and then back down the ladder. While the first group was jogging their recovery lap in the outside lanes, the second group would run its interval. Kobelev and Jankowski would record each athlete's time for each interval. Matt had been assigned to the second group, so he watched with interest as the six athletes in group one lined up for their first sprint. At Kobelev's command, they blasted around the corner and down the backstretch of the track. Seconds after the last runner passed Jankowski, Kobelev shouted, *"Groupa* two, *Pashlee,* let's go!"

The coach raised his hand for Jankowski to see, then abruptly dropped it as he shouted, "GO!"

Matt was surprised by how fast the others took off. Tony Morgoloni was several strides ahead of Brett Adams before the rest of the group came out of the turn. Hugging the inside of the track, Sandy Stonington pulled away while Matt drifted out to the second lane. Down the stretch, Morgoloni continued to open an impressive lead on Adams. Although Matt held nothing back, he couldn't even catch Sandy. The only person to finish behind him in the second group was tiny Jenny Lindstrom, a few strides back.

Matt didn't have time to feel sorry for himself. As he jogged in the outside lane, the first group raced around the track on its 440. The second group's 440 was similar to its first sprint; Morgoloni grabbed the lead from the start, while Matt fought it out with Stonington and Lindstrom to keep from being last. When they reached the mile run, Jenny started to fade, while Sandy and Matt gained on two other runners.

As they jogged the warm-down lap after their final sprint, Sandy smiled at Matt, "Well, Rookie, you and me aren't much for natural speed, but pretty damn consistent."

Sandy was the top female competitor on the American team since the Albertville Olympics, the first Winter Games open to women biathletes. She had devoted her life to the sport, living at the Olympic Training Center and traveling to training camps and races most of the year. She was the only American to consistently score World Cup points in biathlon, and would be trying for her third Olympics. She was the most widely recognized member of the United States Team, and could have negotiated lucrative sponsorship contracts, but she avoided the press and dreaded public appearances. At thirty-four, retirement was not far away, but she claimed that her best races were yet to come.

Matt had heard the name Sandy Stonington for years. He couldn't remember ever being out-raced by a girl. Hell, she wasn't a girl, she was a middle-aged woman, almost as old as his mother! He glanced at her strong, tan face glistening with sweat. She seemed to read his mind.

"Don't worry about it, kid. I've never been in better shape. Remember, the team isn't picked by running on the track. I saw the way you shot at the Nationals last spring. If you shoot like that in the tryouts, you're going to scare some of the big boys right out of their socks."

"Tryouts? The way things are going here, I won't even be invited to the tryouts," said Matt, voicing his discouragement.

"You're here because Kobelev wants you here. He's convinced we're never going to win until we shoot better. So hang in there, and don't be so hard on yourself."

The next time Matt saw Sandy, he scarcely recognized her. He was scheduled for a treadmill test and reported to the lab early to familiarize himself with the procedure by watching another athlete be tested. Sandy, dressed in nylon shorts, running shoes and a jog bra, was standing on the large treadmill. Her upper chest and abdomen were dotted with small, patches attached by tiny black wires to a transmitter that hung on a web belt.

She wore a helmet-like contraption, complete with a rubber mouthpiece, connected to a flexible plastic hose. The hose led to a large machine with an impressive array of instruments, digital readouts, and a computer printer poised over a stack of perforated paper. Roosevelt Brown was checking each electrode connection as Topper Henderson reviewed the testing procedure.

"I know you're a pro at this by now, Sandy, but I want to remind you of our hand signals. When I ask if you can hang in there for another thirty seconds, give me a thumbs up if you're okay, wag your hand if you're not sure, and give me a thumbs down if you've had it. Let's try the mouthpiece. All right? Now the nose clip. Okay, let me turn on the analyzer. Looks good. You all set, Sandy? Connections all good, Rosie?"

"All set, Topper. She's ready to rock and roll."

Sandy winked at Rosie.

"Oh yes! The woman loves me. I knew she couldn't resist my charm."

Sandy rolled her eyes at Topper and nodded.

"Enough, Romeo! Start the treadmill. Here we go, Sandy."

For the first five minutes Topper and Rosie were relaxed, occasionally walking over to explain aspects of the test to Matt.

The nose clip, mouthpiece, and hose allowed the machine to measure the volume of air the athlete inhaled and exhaled during the test. The machine also analyzed the air content, and determined how much oxygen the subject took in, transported to their muscles and used during hard physical exercise, as well as how efficiently they disposed of carbon dioxide. The electrodes monitored pulse beat. The printouts of the collected data determined the subject's anaerobic threshold, critical information for the coaching staff.

Topper looked back at Sandy, who seemed to be running effortlessly in spite of the contraption on her head. He motioned to Rosie, who had been increasing the speed of the treadmill every three minutes.

"Rosie, she's a real tough one, blacked out in a test once at Colorado Springs. When we get her up close to her max, I want you to stand behind the track and be ready to catch her."

Over the next eight minutes, they advanced the speed to ten miles an hour, then increased the slope by increments. She was no longer running easily, but was focused straight ahead, sweat pouring from her forehead.

Topper waved Matt over to the test equipment, "Go ahead and cheer, like you would in a race."

Matt felt a little embarrassed, but his first efforts earned a glance from Sandy and a slight nod.

"That-a-way, Sandy. Good running! You're looking strong. Keep it up," Matt tried to keep up a steady stream of encouragement because it was evident that she was finally tiring.

Topper nodded his approval, "Good effort, Sandy. You're going to be happy with these results. Can you give us another minute?"

She pointed a thumb toward the ceiling.

"All right, Sandy! Great job!" Topper said scanning the continuous readout. He signaled Rosie who moved to the rear of the whining treadmill.

"Way to go, Sandy! Can you give us thirty seconds more?"

Her face was bright red and drenched with sweat, but again she signaled with a thumbs up.

"Okay, Sandy, thirty seconds till the next printout, hang in there, great…Oh, shit!"

It happened so fast that Matt almost missed it. One instant Sandy was struggling up the endless hill, the next she collapsed and the moving belt shot her off the back of the machine. Topper lunged for the kill button on the handrail, but not before Sandy piled into Rosie and they fell in a tangled heap on the floor. The rubber mouthpiece was torn free and her lip was bleeding. Several of the electrodes dangled loose. She groaned as Topper pushed Rosie out of the way, and tried to make Sandy comfortable on the floor, "Jesus, I'm sorry, Sandy. I should have known better. Damn, it's just a test, it's not the goddamn Olympics! Are you all right? Rosie, go get Dr. Manheimer! Johnson, grab a couple of blankets."

Sandy stayed on the floor until Dr. Manheimer examined her, then rested on a cot in the corner of the lab before they let her return to her room. While Rosie prepped Matt for the treadmill test, pinching his chest, back, thigh, and abdomen in the ski fold calipers to determine his body fat percentage, Rosie kept replaying the scene, "Damn, I ain't *never* seen that before! That girl just run 'til she passed out. An' you get a look at her numbers? Man, she's in some kind of shape! Hell, I tested some good runners down at Penn State, but I never seen numbers like that from a woman!"

"So do all the really tough ones run 'til they pass out?" Matt asked, still a little queasy from what he'd witnessed. Rosie had begun to abrade the skin on Matt's chest with sandpaper where they would attach the electrodes.

"Hell no! I only seen one other person pass out, and he was so sick with the flu we never shoulda tested him. You run 'til you can't keep up with the machine, then you give us the thumbs down an' we stop it. You just seen something here you probably never going see again. Damn, she's a tough woman!"

Since Matt had not been tested before, it took them awhile to adjust the headgear. He started by walking slowly on the moving treadmill for several minutes until he was accustomed to breathing through the tubes. Finally, Topper asked, "Okay, Matt, you ready to get this rig up to speed?" Matt nodded and gave a thumbs up signal. Running was no big problem, but the mouthpiece was cumbersome and the hoses made him feel claustrophobic.

Rosie announced a speed increase and the treadmill smoothly accelerated. Matt was still running comfortably, but it was no longer a casual jog. The analyzer kept spitting out paper, which Topper scanned with interest. Then Rosie increased the slope. The door to the lab opened and Kobelev walked over to the treadmill. He smiled at Matt and asked, "Okay? All is good?"

Matt gave him a thumbs up, as Rosie announced the next slope increase. Matt was forced to concentrate, he was no longer running easily. It was not as tough as the upper regions of Smarts, but it definitely was no jog in the park.

Topper studied the latest printout, and motioned for Vlad to look over his shoulder. Matt could see Topper pointing to a column of numbers.

"All right, Matt. Feeling okay? Good for a few more minutes?"

Matt gave them a thumbs up. Kobelev grunted with satisfaction.

Rosie cranked the treadmill to a twelve percent grade. Now, Matt visualized the middle section of Smarts and tried to run relaxed. He knew if he began to fight it and stiffen up, he was done for. He chanted to himself, *Relax, relax, relax,* and he imagined the bright sun playing through the overhanging branches on the Lambert Ridge Trail. Lost in that vision, he was only vaguely aware of a new adjustment in the slope. Sweat stung his eyes, and his lips were sore from stretching around the mouthpiece. He was straining to keep up with the carpet whisking beneath his feet. He was afraid he couldn't handle another slope increase.

"Can you give us another thirty seconds?" Topper was yelling.

Matt gave him the thumbs up. He knew he was plodding, no longer running smoothly, but just hanging on. He was having trouble getting enough air through the hose, and the damn nose clip was beginning to ache.

"Harasho, Johnson, good running. You can go longer?" This time it was Kobelev in his face.

Matt gave a wobbly thumbs up and kept running.

"Great job, Matt. Give us thirty seconds more!" Topper was shouting over his shoulder as he studied the printouts.

Matt was beyond the point of responding, he imagined the slope of Smarts and kept running. Suddenly he felt the carpet slow down, and Rosie's strong forearm around his waist.

"You did great, my man, but we already had one crash 'n burn. You're maxed out. You just walk nice an' easy for a couple of minutes 'til your pulse comes back down."

Matt nodded. Topper and Kobelev continued to study the printouts as Rosie disconnected Matt from the wires and headgear. Holding the printout, Topper put a hand on Matt's shoulder, "This is your first VO_2 max test, am I right, son?"

Although Matt's pulse and respiration were returning to their normal levels, he was totally exhausted, "Right, I've never done this before."

"Well, Matt, you had an extremely high result for a first effort. I'll want to review these numbers tonight…and I'd like Rosie to weigh you again just to double check; but I think it's safe to say you have a very good motor. In fact, I'll go on record and predict that if you stay in this sport, you won't encounter many athletes, even in Europe, who have a more powerful engine than you do."

Kobelev was beaming, "Johnson, you are very fortunate. I am knowing not many athletes with VO_2 over eighty milliliters! With this score, even in Russia, many coaches would be interested! But this gift means also great responsibility. Most athletes do not have such natural capacity, so if they are lazy or lack motivation, what does it matter? You may have VO_2 necessary for biathlon champion, but only if you work hard with much discipline. But, enough of this! Now you go for shower, then dinner. Tomorrow you must pass my swimming test."

"I'm not much of a swimmer," Matt responded lamely, "What's swimming got to do with biathlon anyway?"

"Not a swimmer? Well, don't worry, it's not really swimming test, it's mental toughness test. Biathlon, it's a sport mostly about mental toughness."

Walking back to his room, Matt felt both exhausted and exhilarated. As he passed the pay phone he stopped and dialed.

"Hello, Mom? It's Matt."

"Oh, hello, Matt. How are you?"

"I'm fine. Pretty tired right now, I just had a treadmill test. It was really tough, but I think the results were okay. How are things at home?"

There was silence on the line.

"Mom, are you still there?"

"Oh, Matt, I'm so worried about your sister." He could tell his mother was close to tears. "She and the Cahill girls were caught with alcohol at the graduation dance. Chuck Stevenson had to write them up, and they're scheduled to appear in juvenile court. The worst of it is Annie's acting as if it's all a joke. Matt, she's hanging around with some bad kids, and I just know she's going to get into real trouble."

"I'll be home in three days, I can spend some time with her."

"It may be too late for that...."

Although Topper had said it could be misleading to compare the VO$_2$ values of different athletes, everyone in the Training Center heard about Matt's treadmill test.

It was no exaggeration when Matt said he didn't swim well. The next day Kobelev paddled a canoe behind six athletes as they flailed across the deep, cold waters of Mirror Lake. Several times Matt was forced to float on his back to give his aching muscles a break from his clumsy stroke. When the swimmers finally dragged themselves onto the sand at the far end of the lake, Kobelev roared from the canoe, "You call yourselves athletes? That was, how do you say in English? Pathetic! Swim back!"

A couple of the athletes stared at the far shore in disbelief, but Matt remembered Kobelev's comment about mental toughness, and staggered back into the water. The others soon passed him, but midway across the lake, as he thrashed at a breaststroke, Kobelev smiled from the canoe and said, "You are learning, Matthew, you are learning."

The Cybex test was pure torture. Matt followed Tony Morgoloni, who was strapped into the large leather chair like a criminal facing execution. His muscular right arm was attached to a chrome rod which extended out from the chair, making a right angle under Tony's elbow. His hand was fastened with a wide Velcro strap to a metal plate. The Cybex machine evaluated endurance strength through a wide range of motion.

"Hey, let's get on with it," Morgoloni demanded as Matt approached the contraption.

"What's your rush, Morgoloni, you got a hot date tonight?" Topper responded.

"Naw, I just want to get this over with. Anything wrong with that?"

"Nope, we can get started," Topper answered. "Matt, you'll get a clear idea of what happens by watching. Hey, Tony, looks like you've been lifting weights. You've beefed up your upper body since we tested you last year."

"Yeah, I was tired of getting my ass whipped double poling to the finish line. And besides, the girls love it."

"I'll bet. Well, you remember the drill. You reef up and down on that metal arm as fast as you can for five minutes. I'll tell you when to stop."

The instant Topper gave him the signal, Tony began to thrash against the chair's restraints with all his might, pushing and tugging against the metal bar strapped to his arm. As he grimaced with effort, saliva flew from his mouth and the veins on the side of his head bulged. Up and down, up and down, Tony fought so violently against the chair that Matt was sure that the leather restraints would burst. Tony began to shout like a Comanche warrior each time he exhaled. Although only his right arm was being tested, Matt noticed that the muscles of Tony's left forearm, strapped tightly to the massive chair, looked like cables of braided steel.

"One more minute," Topper held up a finger and shouted directly into Morgoloni's face to get the athlete's attention. Matt wouldn't have believed it possible, but Tony fought even more fiercely for the final sixty seconds.

When Topper finally yelled "Stop," Tony collapsed, utterly spent. Matt felt exhausted just watching. During the next forty-five minutes, the scene was repeated three more times, left leg, left arm, and finally right leg. Topper helped Tony release the leather restraints, and the athlete rubbed his bruised wrists as he wobbled to his feet, testing legs that were rubbery with fatigue. Though exhausted, it was clear that Tony was pleased with his effort.

"You compare these results with the ones from last year, you're going to see the biggest improvement of anybody you ever tested, what do you bet?"

"No thanks, Tony, I don't want to take your money. I've seen more than I'd like of this kind of improvement. But I'll tell you something, Tony, those guys aren't competing anymore because sooner or later they get careless and they get caught."

Tony took two quick steps and thrust his red, sweating face an inch from the physiologist's.

"Are you accusing me of using drugs, Mr. Henderson?

"All I'm saying is, I've seen other athletes who put on that kind of muscle, and they do it with steroids. If you're clean, you've got nothing to worry about. If you're not, we'll nail you. Now get the hell out of my lab."

Topper and Morgoloni stood face to face for what seemed to Matt an eternity, until Tony finally jeered, "Asshole," and stormed from the room. As he passed Matt, he taunted, "Let's see you top those scores, Rookie!"

Topper shook his head, "I bet you never suspected there was so much excitement in a physiology lab."

"You really think he's on steroids?" Matt couldn't help asking.

"Tough to say. That aggressive outburst is one of the classic symptoms. But he's always been a fierce competitor."

Matt's Cybex test was the hardest thing he had ever done except attend his father's funeral. At times he was actually afraid that the elbow or knee being tested was about to explode and spray bloody parts all over the lab. He tried to keep in mind that the medical staff was there to help athletes, not destroy them. When Matt finally finished, Topper assured him that his results were average for an athlete of his age, though he hadn't come close to equaling Tony's numbers.

The training camp was nearing its end and Matt was exhausted. Fortunately, Kobelev's dreaded run up Mount Marcy wasn't much different than Matt's training on Smarts. After synchronizing their watches, Kobelev sent the women's coach, Andy Christensen, up the trail to the summit. Half an hour later, giving Andy a decent lead, Vlad started the athletes at one minute intervals. Because Matt was new to the group, he was one of the first men in the starting order.

He wasn't far up the mountain before he began passing other early starters. He was pleased that only two National Team men overtook him before the summit. Back at the Training Center when Vlad posted the results, Matt was happy to see that he had finished fifth, ahead of half the National Team men.

The day before the camp ended he got a message to report to Dr. Manheimer's office. When he knocked at the door, he found Vlad and the doctor going over paperwork on her desk.

"Ah, Vermont Johnson, how you are doing this day? Tired and sore from running up mountain? No? *Harasho!* Maybe I make you biathlete after all. Maybe…Dr. Manheimer must give you two more tests, then we are finished with testing. After you are going home, we study results and maybe invite you to November, on-snow camp in West Yellowstone. But first, two more tests."

Matt's head was spinning at the thought of skiing in Montana for the entire month of November. It seemed too good to be true. The Russian nodded to Dr. Manheimer and left the room. The doctor called after him, "Oh Vlad, if you see Tony Morgoloni, please ask him to stop by. He missed his appointment for the blood tests."

"Matt, I want to talk to you about your blood. I've just received the results from the samples we sent off earlier in the week. There's no cause for alarm, but there are some findings we should discuss. The lab reports show that you have a rare blood type. Most of us fall into four major groups: types A, B, AB, and O. What is not widely understood is that human blood is actually made up of hundreds of factors, which in healthy individuals are in a constant, but delicate, state of balance. The four major blood types actually represent general groupings of those hundreds of factors, rather than four specific chemical formulas. Are you with me so far?"

"I guess so," Matt couldn't help wondering where this biology lesson was headed.

"The lab results show that your blood is AB Negative, by far the smallest of the four main blood types. This in itself is not a problem because hospitals keep an adequate supply of all four types on hand. However, your case is complicated by an unusually high concentration of a particular protein, which, in effect, could cause your body to reject normal AB Negative blood. Yours is not a totally unique situation, but it is rare. There is not enough research to indicate whether this condition has any effect, either positive or negative on your day-to-day health. The only real concern is the possibility of serious ramifications if you ever require an emergency transfusion."

"What do you mean?" The doctor had Matt's undivided attention.

"Well, let's say for example, you were involved in a serious accident and lost a considerable amount of blood. In the emergency room they would preform a quick blood typing to determine what to give you. If you were seriously hurt, or happened to be in a particularly busy emergency room, there is the possibility that they might not notice the unusual protein spike, and immediately begin transfusing you with AB Negative."

"So, what's wrong with that?" Matt asked.

"Because of the protein spike, it is likely that your body would reject the transfusion, your liver might shut down and your kidneys could be irreparably damaged before anyone realized what was wrong. Left unrectified, the situation could be fatal."

"Wow!" Matt stared at the doctor.

"But that's a worst case scenario. I've filled out a medical information card for you to carry in your wallet. Now that we're aware of the condition, it will be a permanent part of your biathlon medical file.

Here is a form to send to the Medic Alert company. They make necklaces and bracelets with important emergency medical information inscribed on them."

"I'm not much for jewelry," Matt responded.

"Then order a necklace and use the medallion for a key chain, or keep it in your pocket as a good luck charm. Any questions?"

"Nope, I guess not. I'll fill this out today."

"Good, now Coach Kobelev has asked me to administer two more tests. The first is just a simple vision screening. Actually, he mentioned your fine shooting, and he's curious to know if you have especially strong eyesight. If you'll just sit over here and face that wall, while I turn out the lights...."

"What was the other test he wanted?" Matt asked.

"We'll get to that in a couple of minutes," the doctor responded.

The eye exam confirmed Vlad's observation that Matt had better than average eyesight. After Dr. Manheimer finished explaining the results of the test, Matt asked, "What does this mean in terms of biathlon?"

"Practically speaking, it means that in poor light, late in the afternoon or on a cloudy day, for example, you will probably see a more distinct bull's-eye than many of your competitors."

"Great! What about the other test?"

"What do you know about fast twitch and slow twitch muscle fiber?" she asked.

"Not much," Matt admitted. "I guess sprinters have fast twitch and marathon runners have slow twitch."

"Right," the doctor smiled. "What about biathlon competitors?"

"Probably slow twitch, a 20K distance event takes about an hour."

"Ah, but in a biathlon race aren't you constantly sprinting and recovering, charging up the hills, then resting on the downhills? You even get four rest stops in that 20K race you mentioned, two of them lying down!"

Matt looked puzzled.

"Coach Kobelev has a theory. Most Americans consider biathlon an endurance sport, and therefore most of the athletes drawn to biathlon have a preponderance of slow twitch muscle fiber. But he believes a sprinter, someone with more fast twitch fiber could be trained to compete in biathlon. The sports medicine people in the former Communist countries have been selecting young sprinters, athletes with natural speed, and training them for endurance sports like biathlon. We can't give muscle biopsies to entire classrooms of junior high students as the Communists used to, but Vlad believes it's helpful to know the muscle composition of the athletes he's training."

"Muscle biopsy?" Matt didn't like the sound of it.

"That's right, it will be your last test. Come with me, we'll do it in Topper's lab."

Matt followed the doctor down the hall to the physiologist's testing lab. Both Topper and Rosie were waiting next to the Cybex chair. Roosevelt Brown smiled as Matt entered the room with the doctor.

"All right! My man! You're here to give us our pound of flesh, right? Just slip off your warmups, then come on over and make yourself comfortable in my Lazy Boy."

Dr. Manheimer gave Rosie a severe look, and he became instantly contrite. She led Matt to the chair where he reluctantly sat down. He did not have fond memories of that chair.

Topper began strapping him in as Dr. Manheimer continued, "Matt, this is not a pleasant test, but I assure you the significance of the information we gather far outweighs the discomfort."

"Why do I have the feeling this is going to hurt me a lot more than it's going to hurt you?" Matt asked.

That earned another smile from Rosie, "See, I told you folks, this rookie's smart."

Dr. Manheimer was still serious, "Matt, muscle biopsies are painful procedures. We can't give you a local anesthetic to deaden the pain because that might invalidate the sample we remove."

"Remove?" As they were talking, Topper and Rosie strapped Matt tightly into the chair, restraining his arms and legs then securing a wide Velcro band across his chest.

Dr. Manheimer had moved to a small rolling table holding chrome instruments, glass bottles and cotton swabs. She began to rub a plastic bag of ice cubes on Matt's thigh, midway between his knee and his hip. "Matt, this won't take long. I'm going to take an instrument about the size of a slender ink pen and jab your thigh. Once I have the instrument positioned, I will extend a tiny blade which will slice a small cube of muscle tissue, then I withdraw the blade and the sample back into the instrument. Finally, I remove the instrument from your leg. Any questions?"

Matt was trying desperately to think of some convincing reason why he shouldn't donate his muscle tissue, but his mind was focused on the silver instrument.

Dr. Manheimer wasn't waiting for an answer anyway. With deliberate, professional motions, she soaked a gauze pad with alcohol and briefly rubbed the numbed thigh. It was strange for Matt to watch her, yet feel nothing on the skin of his leg. In one confident motion she picked up the slender instrument, and without hesitation, stabbed it deep into his thigh.

"YEEOOW!" Matt's howl filled the room. Topper watched intently, but Rosie turned his head away with a grimace. Dr. Manheimer seemed oblivious to the intense pain she was inflicting. She spoke in a steady voice, as if she were teaching a class: "Good penetration, now we extend the blade…that's it…retract the sample…okay…and now the instrument, there! So, Matt, that wasn't so bad was it?"

Matt didn't respond. His forehead felt clammy and the room began to spin. Topper leaned forward to shake Matt awake, but the doctor interceded. "He's a fainter. It's just as well. Let's get a triceps sample while he's out, then I'll give him a shot of Demerol for the pain."

Matt regained consciousness as Dr. Manheimer plunged the biopsy instrument deep into the back of his left arm. He couldn't imagine any information so valuable that a responsible coach would put his athletes through this kind of torture. Then Dr. Manheimer jabbed him with yet another needle. "This will take the edge off the pain. Just don't operate any heavy equipment or table saws until tomorrow. You'll feel pretty dopey tonight."

Hobbling down the hall, he felt like he'd been in an accident. He opened the door to his room, and was surprised to find it dark. He expected to see Heikki packing or listening to his Walkman. Reaching for the light switch, Matt caught a hint of perfume. A woman's voice commanded, "Close the door." He did as he was told. He could dimly make out a silhouette reclining on his bed.

"What's going on?" He asked, groping for the light switch. Trudy Wilson smiled at him from across the room. She was wearing the distinctive red, white, and blue National Team warmup suit. A rolled bandanna held back her golden hair. She wore lipstick and eye shadow, unusual since the women seldom bothered with makeup during training camps. Again, Matt caught the scent of her perfume.

"How you doing, Matt? Those biopsies are a bitch, aren't they?" She swung her legs to the floor and sat facing him on the edge of the bed.

He couldn't help noticing that her jacket was partially unzipped, revealing an expanse of deeply tanned skin.

"Where's Heikki?" was the only thing he could think to say.

"He's meeting with the Sarge and Vlad to go over summer training schedules. They won't be finished for more than an hour. I knew you'd be hurting after the biopsy so I thought I'd stop by to offer a back rub," she patted the bed. Matt hesitated, his conflicting emotions compounded by the dull pain of the biopsies and a numbing fatigue from the week's demanding schedule.

Trudy noticed his indecision and laughed as she stepped toward him. "You really are a rookie," she said playfully, taking his hand and pulling him toward the bed. "I'm not going to attack you or anything."

She helped him ease the tee shirt over his painful left arm, and began to knead the taut muscles of his shoulders as he lay face down on the covers. Her strong fingers expertly massaged the stress and tension away and he felt himself growing sleepy.

"Feel better?" She purred.

"That's great," he mumbled. "But I don't think I can stay awake."

"You've got to stay awake a little longer. Roll over."

Gingerly, because of his throbbing wounds, he rolled onto his back, struggling to focus on the striking young woman kneeling next to him. She unzipped her jacket and slipped it off. Then she stood, and stepped out of her warmup pants. She was totally naked.

Matt couldn't breathe, "Uh, Trudy…I don't know…I mean…."

"Relax, Rookie, you made the team! It may not be official for awhile, but Kobelev likes you and that's what counts. You set a new record on the VO_2 test! Now, I want to see if you have as much endurance lying down as you did on that treadmill!"

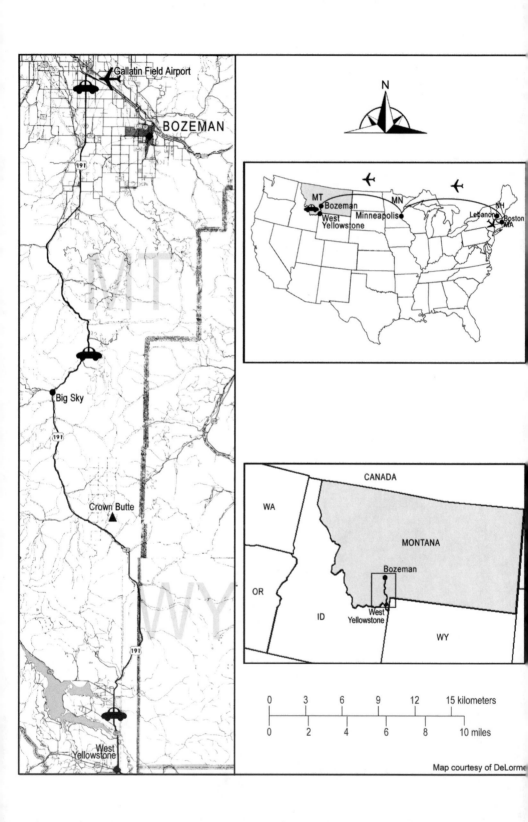

Gallatin Field Airport

BOZEMAN

191

Big Sky

191

Crown Butte

191

West
Yellowstone

N

MT
Bozeman
West
Yellowstone
MN
Minneapolis
NH
Lebanon
Boston
MA

CANADA

WA

MONTANA

Bozeman

OR

ID

West
Yellowstone

WY

0	3	6	9	12	15 kilometers

0	2	4	6	8	10 miles

Map courtesy of DeLorme

Big Sky Country

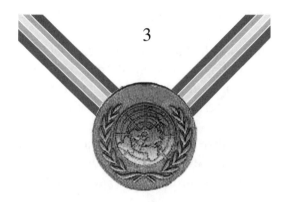

3

Trudy was right about Kobelev. The next day as Matt hefted his backpack into his pickup, the coach came striding across the parking lot. He was carrying one of the ABF's official rifle boxes. The bright aluminum reflected the sun, and the distinctive red, white, and blue team logo was impressive on the side of the case. Still several cars away, Vlad shouted, "Matthew, Matthew, before you are going, I have small gift. This, for you."

He held out the rifle box and smiled when Matt noticed that it had already been inscribed with his name and address.

"But…I thought these were for the National Team."

"This is true, but you have special, old Anschutz. It shoots very good in cold, *da?* We must protect these old treasures. Besides, I'm thinking you will be National Team soon enough. Now Matthew, you must have good training this summer; lots of hiking and roller skiing, some strength training, and plenty shooting. In November, I see you in West Yellowstone. Don't forget, bring plenty warm clothes!"

It was not an especially good summer for Matt. First of all, the weather was abnormally wet. Although his boss, Elmer Blake, was supportive of Matt's need for a flexible schedule at the landscaping business, all too often it was pouring rain when Matt planned a distance roller ski or a hike in the mountains.

That might have been tolerable, if only Matt had been able to stay in touch with Trudy. He had written to her several times, but received no response. Summoning his courage he called twice, only to talk to her answering machine.

The Johnson home had never been a peaceful haven when Michael Johnson was alive, but now it seemed that bickering and arguments dominated their time together. Matt's mother and Annie were embroiled in what could only be described as a battle of wills. From Matt's vantage, it looked like Annie was winning. Try as he might, he couldn't reason with her or get her to realize that her new friends were essentially heading for trouble or jail. Summer evenings were punctuated with a screen door slamming and his mother's shrill, "Annie, get back here!" But she never did.

On November third, Matt's mother drove him to the Lebanon airport. It was 5:45 A.M. and there was no line at the counter for the Northwest flight to Boston. Matt and his mother stood awkwardly in the waiting area until it was time for him to proceed through the security check. As she reached to give her son a hug, and he bent to kiss her cheek, he noticed her eyes fill with tears. It had been more than a year since Michael Johnson's death, but it still tore him apart to see his mother cry.

"Please don't cry, Mom."

She forced a smile and blew her nose, "I'm sorry, I can't help it. I've come to depend on you so much this past year."

"Mom, I have to do this. I'll call a couple of times a week. Tell Annie if she doesn't behave, I'll kick her butt when I get home." He stepped out into the damp November chill. At the base of the folding stairs to the aircraft, he glanced back at the terminal. His mother hadn't moved. He risked a hesitant wave, but she stood like a frail statue as he stooped to enter the small plane. His stomach was in knots.

Making his connection in Boston was no problem, but Minneapolis was thronged with busy travelers. He walked for what seemed like miles from the red to the gold concourse, arriving at the departure gate just as his flight was announced. Six other students in faded jeans and ski jackets hoisted their packs to their shoulders, and chatted casually as they boarded the plane. Two hours later the 727 taxied to the arrival gate at the

Bozeman airport.

"Matt, Matt Johnson, over here." The energetic voice belonged to Jimmy Clark, the young biathlete who had traded his competitive aspirations for the position of team manager. Jimmy had dreamed of going to the Olympics, but when it became clear his prospects of making the team were dim, he became a tireless "go for," quickly becoming indispensable to the coaches and athletes. In fact, Jimmy's informal job description earned him the nickname, "Gopher," and it was used with such respect by the athletes that Jimmy had adopted it, even signing team notices and memos.

"So Matt, how was the flight?" Without waiting for an answer he rattled on, "The van's outside. Start hauling your stuff, while I track down a couple of cross-country skiers I promised to take to Yellowstone." Jimmy jogged off through the baggage claim area in search of his other passengers.

Gopher gave an informative monologue as they skirted Bozeman and headed south on U.S. Route 191 toward the Gallatin Canyon. The young athletes listened, but their attention was riveted to the spectacular sight of the sun dipping on the western horizon. By the time they stopped for gas at the turnoff to the Big Sky ski resort, the sunset had faded and a fine snow was falling. They passed into Yellowstone Park twenty miles later, near Crown Butte.

"There's been snow up on the plateau for a couple of weeks, but a storm last Wednesday dumped enough to groom the trails in town. It's been great skiing since then. There's still some work to do before the biathlon range is in shape. I hope you brought plenty of warm clothes, it's been...Oh, Jesus!"

Gopher jerked the steering wheel left and the van lurched, before starting into a lazy four-wheel skid across the glazed pavement. Matt grabbed the armrest, and glimpsed a dark shape outside his window in the swirling snow. In spite of Gopher's frantic efforts, the van continued its graceful spin across the highway. After what seemed an eternity, Gopher yelled, "Here we go," and the van burrowed, rear end first into a wall of white. All five of the athletes sat motionless in the eerie silence, mindful of the pounding in their chests.

Matt spoke first, "What the hell was that?"

Gopher was shaking, "Elk. The snow drives them down from the mountains. People are killed here every winter colliding with them. Jesus, we're lucky! We didn't even crunch the guardrail."

Gopher was the only one who could open his door, so the others followed him out over the driver's seat. Though well off the pavement and buried up to its windows on the passenger side, the van appeared undamaged. As the others surveyed the vehicle, Matt was mesmerized by the majestic animals fearlessly striding across the pavement, their massive antlers held high. Unlike the white tail deer back east, which would have bolted at the first hint of human intrusion, these massive elk seemed oblivious to the highway and the skiers.

When Gopher's shaking subsided, his optimism returned. "I think we can get this van out of here. Penny, you've driven in the snow, haven't you?"

"Sure," the cross-country skier answered.

"Get your gloves on boys, and let's try to shovel this thing out."

After a few minutes of scooping the packed snow from around the tires, the four men pushed while Penny eased down on the accelerator and steered the van back onto the shoulder. Watching for headlights through the falling snow, Gopher turned the van around and they continued through the pass to West Yellowstone. For several miles they crept slowly and stared out frosted windows at the large shapes that slipped through the darkness like a strange army taking up positions for an impending battle.

In the silently falling snow, the village of West Yellowstone was a picturesque ghost town. A few streetlamps illuminated log storefronts and wooden sidewalks. Gopher dropped the cross-country skiers at the Three Bears Lodge, across from the abandoned train station. The Three Bears was the prime location in town and the United States Ski Team had staked it out years earlier.

In contrast, the Biathlon Team had been relegated to the worn but venerable Stage Coach Inn, which had seen its glory soon after Teddy Roosevelt popularized America's first National Park. It was several blocks away from the ski trails, and was largely closed down for the winter.

Matt risked a question that had been gnawing at him since he left New England. He tried to sound casual, "Hey Gopher, is Trudy here yet?"

Jimmy Clark gave Matt a long, careful look before answering, "Naw, Matt, she's driving from Lake Tahoe…should be in sometime tomorrow. Why do you ask? She didn't get to you in Lake Placid, did she?"

"Heck, no! We just talked. I wrote her a couple of letters over the summer, but never heard back. I was just wondering."

"That's typical, Matt. She's a tremendous athlete. Hell, if it weren't for Sandy, Trudy'd be our top finisher. But she's ruthless, and plenty of guys on the team have scars to prove it."

Gopher helped Matt with his gear and led him to his room, far down a hall decorated with Native American artifacts, deer heads, and antique paintings of the natural wonders of Yellowstone.

"You'll be staying in 149. Tony Morgoloni will be your roommate, but he doesn't arrive until tomorrow night." Gopher watched Matt's face for a reaction.

"How'd I get so lucky?" Matt asked.

"Well, I'm afraid you're low man on the totem pole right now. The National Team guys refuse to room with him, so you're the man. At least you've got a day to stake out your territory. When he shows up, just don't let him browbeat you. He's not a bad guy really, he just plays by different rules."

"The Snake," as he was called by other members of the team, had grown up in Brooklyn, New York, and discovered biathlon on a high school field trip to the Olympic Training Center. He was attracted to the sport because of the shooting and he thrived on competition. His only objective was to win, and he never worried too much about how.

His nickname was the result of a tryout race in which he cut nearly a kilometer off one of the ski loops. An official spotted him and Tony was disqualified, but he remained unrepentant. After all, he grew up in a place where the only mistake was getting caught.

Although Matt was tired from his long day of traveling, his body was still on Eastern time, so he was wide awake by 4:00 A.M. He struggled to get back to sleep until 5:30, then gave up and dressed for a morning run. The snow squeaked under foot and the frigid air bit his nostrils as he jogged under the streetlights. Twenty minutes later, he stretched in front of the Stage Coach, a thick layer of frost covering the chest of his warmups and stiffening his eyelashes. The thermometer next to the entrance registered minus twenty-eight degrees Fahrenheit.

When he joined the other biathletes in the dining room for breakfast he recognized most of them from Lake Placid. There wasn't much conversation, since the athletes were still groggy from stumbling out of bed only minutes earlier. But as the line moved slowly past a serving table loaded with steaming oatmeal, whole grain toast, jams, yogurt, scrambled eggs, home-fried potatoes, and pitchers of fruit juice, a strong hand squeezed Matt's shoulder and a cheerful voice boomed, "So, Vermont Johnson, what are you thinking of cowboy country?" Vladimir Kobelev looked like he'd been up for hours.

"Well, I haven't seen too much of it yet," Matt replied.

"But you see a little on morning run, *da?* You like this weather, a gift to Montana from my former home in Siberia?"

"I guess it's not so bad if you're dressed for it. I'm not wild about shooting prone in temperatures like this though."

"No problem," responded Vlad. "Only easy skiing for few days, then if still cold weather, we shoot at midday when light is best and temperature is warmest. But you keep running in morning; good for stretching, good for routine, most important, good for mental toughness."

As Matt found a vacant seat at a table of athletes, Sergeant Jankowski stood to make the morning's announcements. Everyone was expected to show up in warm clothes ready to shovel, rake, paint targets, and generally get the range in shape for the training camp. Kobelev added that after working on the range, the athletes should explore the trails at a comfortable pace. He warned about going fast when first getting on snow, and of the dangers of training at altitude, although it was evident that most of the athletes had heard his talk before.

Although the temperature was below zero when Matt reached the shooting range around ten, the bright sun had warmed the snow-covered landscape considerably. The coaches were shouting and joking as they worked, happy to be in winter conditions once again. Since they were on Sergeant Jankowski's turf, the others deferred to his instructions. The Sarge looked warm in military issue bunny boots, heavy wool pants and an olive drab Alaskan parka, complete with a wolverine ruff on the hood. Vlad worked happily in a faded blue sweater with CCCP in tattered white letters across the back. He carefully graded the firing line with an iron rake and sang Russian arias in his rich baritone. He was the only one working without hat or gloves.

Sandy Stonington and two other women were spray-painting the metal targets. Burl Palmer, the team's authentic cowboy from Durango, Colorado was raking the firing line under Vlad's watchful eye. During a momentary pause between solos, Burl spoke up, "God damn, Vlad, but you sure can sing! Them Rooskie songs ain't bad, but don't you know any

Garth Brooks?" Vlad stared at Burl as if he hadn't understood a single word, then launched into another Russian classic.

Ragnar Haugen, the old man of the national team at age thirty-six, stood in front of the firing line, shoveling snow onto the shooting positions. He was from Trondheim, Norway, and attended the University of Wyoming on a skiing scholarship. He had won the NCAA cross-country title all four of his undergraduate years, while also getting top grades as an engineering major. Matt knew that Ragnar would be trying out for his fourth Olympic Team, and although the rumor mill suggested the transplanted Norwegian was too old, he still shot well.

Back at the Inn around one, the range workers hurried to the dining room as the kitchen staff began clearing. The athletes who had avoided the work detail had already eaten, except for Oliver Wainwright, who had miscalculated his escape. As the coaches headed for the soup and remaining sandwiches, they looked at Oliver but said nothing.

Ragnar, though not officially the team captain, was aware of his stature as the senior athlete, and confronted Oliver in typical Scandinavian fashion, head-on.

"Wainwright, why aren't you helping on the range this morning."

"Aw, piss off, Ragnar. I didn't come out here to rake and shovel, I came out to ski and shoot. If this organization is so screwed up that the coaches and athletes have to do the manual labor, so be it. But I've got better things to do with my time."

Before Ragnar could respond, an insistent buzzing caused Oliver to reach inside his team jacket and withdraw a cellular phone. With practiced efficiency, he unfolded the instrument, placed it to his ear, and spoke into the mouthpiece.

"Wainwright here," he barked, as he marched from the dining room.

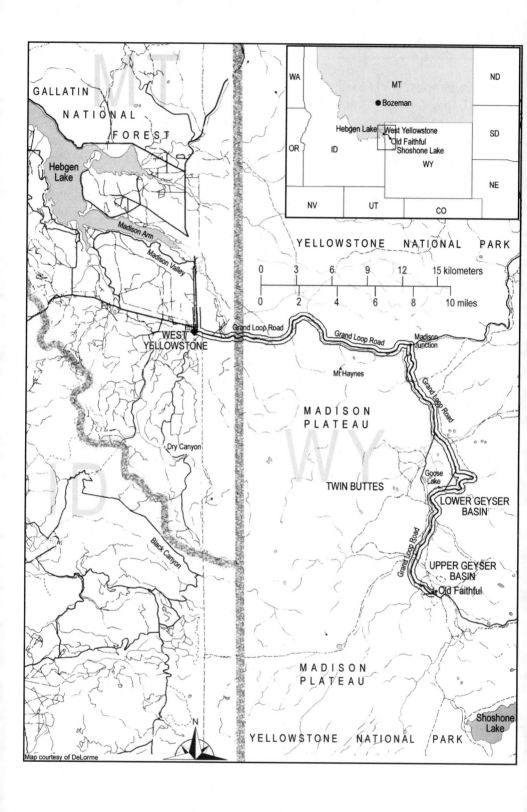

GALLATIN

NATIONAL

FOREST

Hebgen
Lake

Madison Arm

Madison Valley

WEST
YELLOWSTONE

Grand Loop Road

Grand Loop Road

Madison
Junction

Mt Haynes

MADISON
PLATEAU

Grand Loop Road

Dry Canyon

TWIN BUTTES

Goose
Lake

LOWER GEYSER
BASIN

Black Canyon

UPPER GEYSER
BASIN

Old Faithful

Grand Loop Road

MADISON
PLATEAU

Shoshone
Lake

YELLOWSTONE   NATIONAL   PARK

N

YELLOWSTONE   NATIONAL   PARK

0   3   6   9   12   15 kilometers

0   2   4   6   8   10 miles

WA

MT

●Bozeman

ND

OR

ID

Hebgen Lake   West Yellowstone
              Old Faithful
              Shoshone Lake

SD

WY

NE

NV   UT   CO

MT

WY

ID

Map courtesy of DeLorme

Old Faithful

4

It took Matt a few days to settle into a routine. He got up quietly at six each morning to stretch and run, careful not to wake his roommate. He often saw other shapes in the predawn darkness, but his fellow early risers seemed to enjoy their solitude, so Matt ran alone. After breakfast, the morning workout usually involved shooting, often combined with interval skiing. Following lunch most of the athletes slept for an hour or so, then headed back out for a distance skiing workout at 2:30. The evenings were reserved for lectures, video analysis of skiing and shooting, or group discussions about team dynamics, goal setting and relaxation techniques.

Gopher's prediction about Tony Morgoloni turned out to be right on target. Matt staggered back from a two-hour distance ski, to find Snake rearranging the room. Matt caught his roommate off-guard and commanded, "Put that stuff back where it was, Tony." Although the Snake had earned a reputation as a scrapper, he was barely five feet, nine inches, despite the cowboy boots he habitually wore. He shrugged and began replacing Matt's belongings.

There was little friction following that first encounter; in fact it seemed that Tony was making an effort to cultivate his roommate's friendship. Matt still considered Tony unpredictable, but he assumed that might stem from growing up in New York City.

Tony explained that for the past several years, athletes eager to break the monotony of the training schedule skied the fifty kilometers from West Yellowstone to Old Faithful in a single day. The event had become such a tradition that most of the competitors and even a couple of coaches took part, some skiing in, while others rode a snow coach to the geyser and skied back out.

Tony continued that for the past five seasons a handful of hard-core biathletes and cross-country skiers attempted the 100 kilometer round trip. The unpredictable weather had forced a few cancellations, so the informal honor roll of those who had finished the Old Faithful round trip was still exclusive. Tony confided that the rivalry between the cross-country skiers and the biathletes had stimulated sizable bets on the outcome of the tour. Participants who planned to ski both ways each kicked in $25.00. Other team members fattened the pot by betting on a particular athlete.

"The rules are simple," Tony continued. "Each athlete has to carry his own gear: food, water, and dry clothes. Everyone starts together at the West Yellowstone park entrance, skis to Madison Junction, where there's a half-hour rest stop, then on to Old Faithful for a one-hour lunch break. After lunch, it's every man for himself for the fifty kilometers back to the West Entrance. The first guy back wins the pot."

"Ragnar Haugen has taken home the cash for two of the past three years. Had to cancel once 'cause there was a wind chill of seventy degrees below! We keep the betting quiet so the coaches don't get pissed off, but Ragnar won $475 last November. I figure it'll be over $600 this year."

Jesus, Matt thought, *six hundred bucks for a glorified workout.* He certainly could use that kind of money. The tryouts in Anchorage would cost a bundle, if he was invited. That $600 might cover the plane ticket. Of course he'd have to outlast Ragnar, but hell, Haugen was almost forty! Matt told the Snake he'd think about it.

That evening at supper, Matt found himself seated with Burl Palmer, Roger Edwards and Heikki Lahdenpera. Roger and Burl were teasing each other, as always, when Paula Robbins and Trudy Wilson approached.

"Well, you children certainly seem to be enjoying yourselves. Mind if we join you?"

"Heck no, girls. Glad to have ya." Burl spoke for the rest of the table.

Since arriving in Montana, Matt had found no opportunity to talk with Trudy alone. She had been cordial, but there was no indication of the fireworks he remembered from Lake Placid.

"So what's going on?" Trudy fluttered her long lashes at Burl.

"Just the usual. You know, arguing about what awesome studs we are, an' how you girls is just dying to get your hands on us!"

"Dream on, Cowboy!" Trudy responded.

"Be honest now, Trudy, you've had the hots for all of us one time or another. I even saw you making cow eyes at the rookie here in Lake Placid. The poor pup didn't know what the hell hit him." Burl looked at Matt in mock seriousness.

Trudy dismissed Matt with a shake of her golden hair, "He's a rookie all right! He's the only guy I've ever seen who fell asleep when I took my clothes off!"

The table erupted in wild hoots and guffaws. Matt could feel his face burn, as he concentrated on his spaghetti. Eventually, the conversation shifted to another topic and he was spared further embarrassment.

Two days later when Morgoloni reminded his roommate about the Old Faithful pool, Matt pulled out his wallet and handed over his bet.

"All right, kid! You got style. I don't remember any other rookie with the *cajones* to join the pool in his first season at Yellowstone! You making me proud."

"You're in the pool, aren't you, Tony?" Matt asked as his money disappeared in Morgoloni's pocket.

"Sorry kid, all entries are secret. You'll find out at Old Faithful."

On Wednesday, Matt noticed the sign-up sheet for the tour into the Park. Stan Reimer had reserved the snow coaches, conventional twelve-passenger vans modified to travel on tracks, like a Snow Cat. Some of the athletes would ride in to Old Faithful, eat lunch at the visitor's center, then ski back to West Yellowstone; while those who had opted to ski from town to the geyser would take the snow coaches back out of the Park.

Thursday was Thanksgiving, a light training day. For those with no other plans, the Stage Coach put on a delicious holiday spread. Since Tony was away, after Matt stuffed himself with turkey and potatoes, he went back to his room and dialed home. He had kept his word about calling twice a week, but it was becoming increasingly difficult. He could barely get a sentence out before his mother would begin sobbing; and if Annie got on the phone, it was only to argue. They didn't display any interest in his training, and Thetford seemed like a different lifetime. After the call, he lay on his bed, wracked by frustration and guilt.

The room was dark when Ragnar's knock on the door awakened him.

"I see you're skiing into the park tomorrow.Maybe you're thinking about going both ways?"

"I don't know, it sounded like a good break from the training loops. I was hoping to see some animals," Matt responded.

"Oh, we'll see animals! But you must be ready for anything: sometimes wind, sometimes wicked cold. You can't imagine how hungry you get after seventy, eighty kilometers, so bring all the food you can carry. Also dry clothes: Polypro, warmups, socks, extra hat, gloves, maybe even a down vest if you got one."

"You'd need an expedition pack to haul all that stuff," Matt observed.

"You break a pole or a binding, you gonna be damn glad you got all that stuff."

As Ragnar reached for the door, Matt called to him, "Hey, Grandfather, thanks for the advice."

Ragnar turned with a smile, "Look, Rookie, you keep up with the Ol' Grandfather tomorrow an' you going to do okay."

A handful of athletes were at the dining room when it opened at 7:00, but Sandy was the only woman among them. There wasn't much talking, just a serious interest in the huge pot of oatmeal and the pile of bananas. At 7:30, while the athletes were cramming oranges and Power Bars into their backpacks, Kobelev stood in the doorway and surveyed the scene.

"You listen me! Skiing 100 kilometer in one day is good workout for springtime, *after* competition season. We having time trials next weekend. For biathlon we must be thinking intervals now, not over distance. Next week I need racehorses, not plow horses! Besides, big snowstorm coming after lunch, skiing through new snow for fifty kilometers is too much. Are you understand me?"

The athletes shifted uneasily. No one answered Vlad. Matt was confused. Snake had mentioned that the betting was kept secret from the coaches, but this was the first indication that the coaches actually disapproved of the round trip. Matt hated to get crosswise with Kobelev, but $600 for a day's skiing seemed like easy money. Finally, Vlad broke the awkward silence himself, "You Americans, you have no discipline! No respect for coach."

Kobelev left the room shaking his head. The athletes put on their windbreakers, hefted their packs, and headed for the exit. They walked the three blocks to the impressive West Entrance, a gateway built of huge pine logs appropriate for the world's first national park. The biathletes joined eight cross-country skiers stretching in the sunrise, two women and six men. The cross-country women were happy to see Sandy Stonington, and the three of them chatted enthusiastically. With the five biathletes, the expedition consisted of thirteen skiers.

Everyone deferred to Ragnar. He put his skis on the snow and cinched up his backpack. "It's eight o'clock," he announced.

"An' we ain't getting famous standing here," added Burl.

The experienced Norwegian launched into his powerful, skating stride down the snow-packed road into the park. The others fell in behind. As they left the West Entrance they enjoyed nearly ideal conditions; cold dry snow, a wide, groomed trail, and a beautiful pink dawn. The rising sun even promised to push the temperature above the single digits by mid-morning, a warm November day by Montana standards.

An hour into the tour, someone shouted, "Elk!" They spotted a herd of about twenty of the large animals on the far side of the river, their jaws grinding methodically, jets of vapor escaping their nostrils. The elk seemed to be posing for tourists, heads held high in profile with massive antlers sweeping back over powerful shoulders.

Half an hour later, they reached Madison Junction. Ragnar leaned his skis against the building and announced, "We take thirty minute break for warming up, use the toilet, and have some food."

Matt joined the others inside where they sat on the floor. He pulled off his sweaty windbreaker, and rummaged through his backpack for food. Sandy Stonington dropped to the floor next to him, and began massaging her quads.

"So how you holding up, Rookie?" The strong features of her face were flushed from cold and wind.

"Great! Kind of surprised Ragnar's not setting a faster pace. This doesn't seem too tough."

"Don't let him fool you. If you're planning to do the round trip, remember you're not a quarter of the way there yet. Ol' Ragnar'll still be skiing the same pace at sunset. You doing the whole thing?"

"I was thinking about it. How about you?" Matt asked quietly.

"I'm going to see how I feel at Old Faithful. If I can stay healthy this winter, I think I can kick butt in Europe. I don't want to screw things up by putting myself under today. Vlad's right, you know, this workout's perfect for April, not so smart for November."

Without any fanfare, Ragnar stuffed the remnants of his smorgasbord back into his pack, snugged the lacings of his boots, and started for the door. The others scrambled to follow, pulling on windbreakers and stuffing oranges in their mouths. Soon they made the turn south onto the Grand Loop Road, and began climbing out of the Madison River valley. Two cross-country skiers couldn't contain their impatience any longer, and they gradually pulled ahead of the rest of the group.

After forty minutes of a winding climb, the road entered a broad plateau bisected by the Firehole River and dotted by steaming thermal pools. Matt went close enough to the hot pots to see deep into the turquoise depths, smell the sulfurous fumes, and feel the hot steam on his face.

Like massive black ghosts of a prehistoric time, bison stood passively amid the rising clouds of vapor. The road led the skiers through a herd of the shaggy beasts. To Matt they looked like statues, carefully arranged for the benefit of the tourists.

At the southern edge of the herd, Ragnar stopped the group and pointed toward a depression across the river. The athletes could see several dark, snarling shapes lunge and tear at the carcass of what had been a buffalo calf.

"Coyotes?" asked Sandy.

"Hell no, that there's the Madison Plateau wolf pack," answered Burl. "Remember a couple years back when Fish and Wildlife reintroduced a few wolves into the park? Local ranchers were afraid those wolves would carry off their calves. Well, the ranchers got nothing to worry about. Those wolves got a regular banquet right here in the park. Looks like six, maybe eight in that pack. And there's probably a half-dozen coyotes sittin' back in the trees waiting for the scraps."

"So the wolves don't bother visitors to the park?" Sandy asked as she watched the animals dart in and out of the blood-stained circle surrounding the buffalo carcass.

"Well they sure as hell bothered folks out here a hundred years ago, that's why the early settlers worked so hard to kill 'em all off. I imagine before long there'll be a flap with some stupid tourist, then the rangers will have to relocate the wolves for their own protection."

Ragnar led the group the last few kilometers through the Upper

Geyser Basin to Old Faithful. It was just before noon when they leaned their skis in the racks next to the largest log building Matt had ever seen. As they were staggering inside, the roar of engines announced the arrival of the snow coaches. Stan Reimer was one of the first to climb out, looking odd in a Biathlon Team racing suit and warmups. He chattered to three older men who must have been potential ABF corporate sponsors. Coach Kobelev got out and approached his athletes.

"So, everybody okay? Grandfather, how is your little family?"

Ragnar was flushed from more than three hours of steady skiing. He grinned at Vlad, "No problems."

As the tired athletes filed into the visitor's center, Vlad put a hand on Matt's shoulder. In Lake Placid, Matt had noticed that Kobelev still laced his conversation with Russian words, and that the athletes had picked up on them. The bearded Russian studied the young Vermonter, *"Harasho?"*

Matt smiled, *"Harasho,* I'm fine."

"Okay, okay, maybe you going be biathlete after all," Vlad laughed and led Matt through the door into the warmth of the visitor's center.

There was animated conversation from everyone who had just driven in, but the sweaty skiers, changing out of soaked turtlenecks and burrowing into their packs for food, were subdued by fatigue. Tony Morgoloni slid over to Matt.

"So, how's the kid? I noticed those two Ski Team guys got twenty minutes on you. What gives, Ragnar gettin' soft? Nobody's gonna say anything if you just have your lunch an' hit the trail, the hell with waitin' an hour. We're talking some pretty good cash here, at least $600 bucks for you, not to mention a couple a bets I got on the side."

"Why're you so interested in me? Ragnar hasn't even started to sweat," Matt answered, the fatigue evident in his voice.

"I got news for you. Ragnar, Burl and Brett ain't skiing out. That means you're the man if biathlon's gonna take any money away from them cross-country assholes. So get your shit together, an let's make some cash."

They were interrupted by the loudspeaker announcing the next eruption of Old Faithful. Everyone left the visitor's center and followed the boardwalk to the geyser viewing area. Matt caught a glimpse of the two cross-country skiers sneaking behind the building, skis in hand. He checked his watch. Twenty minutes before he could legally begin his return trip.

The gentle rise beyond the boardwalk looked like a moonscape surrounded by snow. Wisps of vapor rose from gray cracks in the earth, while tiny rivulets of water coursed down the slope toward the spectators, only to disappear back into the ground. An eruption of steam burst from a fissure at the crest of the knoll. As it fell back, a second, stronger eruption engulfed the first. These intensifying pulsations continued for several seconds until a steady, powerful hissing commanded everyone's attention. It was as if a park official in some remote control room was deliberately cranking open a giant valve. A huge volume of steaming water shot higher and higher into the winter sky. The drenching spray from the geyser did not quite reach the boardwalk, but the skiers were engulfed in a warm, sulfurous mist.

"Hey, we've got to get a team picture while it's still blowing its top," someone shouted.

Stan officiously arranged the athletes until he and the honored guests were surrounded by the National Team in front of the geyser. He ordered Matt, and two others who were not outfitted in the flashy United States uniforms, to step out of the picture.

Four minutes until Matt could leave. Reimer had everyone else restrained on the boardwalk in front of the towering plume of steam. Matt made his decision. He ducked into the visitor's center, quickly retrieved his wet clothes and took a long drink from the water fountain. He hefted his pack to his shoulder and slipped out of the building through the service entrance. Keeping the visitor's center between himself and the geyser, he waded through the deep snow until he reached the packed exit road. He bent to snap his bindings onto his boots, and skied powerfully away from the collection of log buildings. By skating in a low crouch, he was concealed by the high snowbanks.

Within minutes, Matt was surrounded by the rising clouds of the Upper Geyser Basin. The buildings at Old Faithful were no longer in sight. He glanced back and saw no other skiers behind him. His escape gave him a sense of exhilaration similar to the final moments at the end of a race when he knew he was winning. The food and rest at Old Faithful had revived him.

He scanned the broad basin ahead for the dark specks which could be his rivals. Half an hour later, Matt noticed a fine-grained snow, falling almost imperceptibly from the gray overcast. This won't amount to much, he thought. It could snow all day like this and not add up to four inches.

Then he noticed that it was accumulating fast enough to obscure the tracks of the skiers ahead, and it was cutting down his visibility. More than once he was certain he spotted the two skiers rhythmically bobbing in the distance, but each time he poured on the coal to catch them, he was forced to throttle back without success.

After an hour of skiing, the euphoria was gone. He had to admit that it was definitely snowing harder. He was pushing new-fallen powder with every stride. Skiing with his head bent into the steadily falling flakes, his heart nearly stopped as he slid past a huge shape covered with snow. The buffalo stood like a frozen statue in the storm as Matt skated past. His pulse pounded as he threaded his way through the silent herd, which must have taken to the packed roadway in anticipation of the oncoming storm. Occasionally, a massive, snow-covered head with bulbous eyes and fearsome horns would slowly turn as Matt skied past. He had the eerie feeling he had slipped into a strange prehistoric world, unchanged for centuries.

By the time he negotiated a route through the herd, Matt was exhausted. The snow was coming hard, a curtain of countless flakes which cut the visibility to a few feet. His clothing was soaked through. The new snow even stuck to the top of his skis, making each stride a chore. If he'd had any kick wax, he would have abandoned skating and plowed through the powder using the old kick and glide technique.

Matt had run out of blood sugar in long workouts before, so he recognized the symptoms. His face felt clammy, his legs were weak, and he was light-headed. Then he noticed the snow around his legs reached half way to his knees. He studied his boots and skis buried in the deep snow for several minutes before realizing he had skied off the road. Confused, he stood in the deathly quiet of the all-encompassing falling snow, and became conscious of his uncontrollable shivering.

It was fear that finally roused him out of his pre-hypothermic stupor. He knew he had to get warm and eat or he'd be in serious trouble. He stumbled in an effort to kick-turn in the deep powder and follow his tracks back to the road. The storm had created a virtual white-out, totally obscuring the tracks he had made just moments earlier. He plowed through the light fluff, increasingly frantic to find the road.

As he pushed on, disoriented by the blizzard, not even the tips of his skis were visible under the deep blanket. He slogged through the powder until the ground disappeared beneath him. He had skied over the bank of a creek, tumbled fifteen feet down, and landed in a tangled heap of skis and poles.

"Sonofabitch!" He cursed as he struggled to his feet, but not before one foot and both hands were soaked in the frigid water. Fumbling with his poles and bindings with wooden fingers, he noticed an ancient spruce a few yards upstream. The exposed roots formed a network of rafters that supported a heavy cornice of snow. He released himself from the bindings and dragged his gear toward the natural snow cave. He rammed the skis and poles into a drift, then crawled under the shelter. His hands and feet ached as he fumbled with the plastic slide that cinched his pack.

"Just stay calm. Get warmed up, then have something to eat. It'll be okay," he muttered through chattering teeth.

After what seemed like hours of concentrated effort, Matt struggled out of his wet clothes and pulled on dry gear from his pack. He layered the down vest under his windbreaker, then massaged the circulation back into his feet and stuffed them into the empty backpack. Considering his predicament, he was surprised he didn't feel worse. He wolfed down his remaining sandwich and a bottle of Exceed. *Thank you Ragnar, for making me pack all this stuff.*

As he finished the last bits of a chocolate bar, the shivering began to subside. The tiny hollow beneath the exposed evergreen roots was completely out of the wind and provided shelter from the falling snow. He knew that trying to plow through the new accumulation would be suicide. His only option was to sit tight, try to stay warm, and wait it out. He had heard stories about hikers in New Hampshire's White Mountains getting caught out after dark and dying of exposure before sunup. But in a snow cave, with a little food, Matt figured the real challenge would be staying awake until the storm blew over.

His Timex Ironman gave off a faint green light as he pushed the button and read 4:38. He knew he wasn't going anywhere in the dark, so he concentrated on how to stay awake for fifteen hours. He began by thinking of home, wondering what his mother and sister were doing. He found he couldn't entertain thoughts of home because it only made him worry whether his mother was still depressed and if Annie was skipping school. Then images of Trudy Wilson appeared in his mind. Had she just been teasing him in front of the other guys, or was she disgusted with him for falling asleep?

His thoughts drifted to his father. Boy, would he be pissed for this screw-up! Maybe it was the army training or perhaps the years in Vietnam, but Matt's dad had no tolerance for careless mistakes. The painful memory of Matt's third deer hunting season surfaced, when he was sixteen. It was opening day. He and his dad had driven to the top of Houghton Hill and were waiting for sunrise to begin tracking the big buck they knew was up there, when Matt discovered he had forgotten his ammo. Without a word, Matt's father drove home and dumped him in the yard. They didn't hunt together again that season.

When he finally allowed himself to check his watch, he was surprised that it was after 8:00. His thoughts returned to his father. There was so much Matt had never understood. He knew his father loved him and was dedicated to the family. It was clear he was devoted to Matt's mother. Although he often displayed his violent temper, he never lifted a hand against Matt or his sister, unless of course they deserved it. He wasn't a drunk like some other Vietnam vets Matt knew.

But his dad seemed incapable of having fun. Even when they went fishing, or hunting, or skiing, he forced Matt to perfect his skills, exhorting him to practice endlessly, to never settle for second best. Matt knew he was lucky that his dad was such a good teacher, but he never remembered a word of congratulations for a job well done. Sometimes he wondered what made his dad tick. What had he been like when he was Matt's age, or when he had first met his wife. Did hauling wounded and dead bodies out of a jungle expose something frail that had always lurked there? Or had his missed opportunities fed a rage that grew over the years? If Matt didn't have any answers now, how would he find them? His mother seemed determined to keep his father's secrets.

I'll show him, Matt thought. Making the Olympic Team might have been a pipe dream last spring, but I'm not that far out of it. If I can get to Anchorage and shoot well, I know I can be on that team. My old man may have been one of the best before Sapporo, and he got screwed by the tour in Vietnam, but he never competed in the Olympic Games, and by God, I'm going to!

Sometime after midnight he vowed to stop checking his watch every five minutes. He wracked his brain, inventing diversions to keep himself awake. He listed his classmates at Thetford Academy and predicted what they all would be doing in five years. That led to his plans for five years hence, and he visualized biathlon races in Europe where he skied fast, hit all the targets, and finally stood proudly on the winner's podium.

He was yanked back to reality by what sounded like a low growl outside the overhang. He focused on a spot in the dark about ten feet beyond his skis. He could see nothing, but his whole being told him something was out there. His pulse throbbed in his ears. He thought he heard another sinister growl, but the snow absorbed all sound, and his own pulse was deafening. Then he remembered the ski poles, just beyond reach outside the overhang and he lunged at the poles. One fell away, but he snatched the other, and huddled back under the roots. Holding the long, carbon fiber pole by its grip, he glared into the blackness and listened once more to the ominous silence of the falling snow.

Another deep growl; he hadn't imagined it! He slashed the ski pole into the dark. There was a yelp as Matt felt the tip strike something solid, but soft.

"Get out of here! Go on!" He was shaking again. He could taste the bile in his mouth. For interminable minutes he held the slender pole ready, but there was no more growling. Finally, he lay the pole across his lap, and leaned back against the frozen ground.

Later, he became aware of his own shivering and the distant sound of a vehicle engine. The snow had blown in around the tree, and Matt was completely entombed. Using the ski pole, he broke a hole through the drift, and was surprised to see the gray sky of dawn. It had stopped snowing, it was light enough to ski, and he even had a little food left. He had slipped a bottle of Exceed under his vest to keep it from freezing, and now he drank it all. He gnawed a frozen peanut butter sandwich and found a small package of M&M's he'd forgotten in his pack.

With food in his stomach, even the grim task of working his feet back into the frozen ski boots didn't seem hopeless. He crawled out from under the overhang. The remnants of the storm clouds were backlit by gentle pastels in the east. His skis were still standing, but it took several minutes of wading through the thigh-deep fluff to locate his second pole. As he climbed to the top of the bank, he spotted a Snow Cat engulfed in a cloud of powder, roaring across the basin. The frozen world sparkled in the brilliant orange sunrise.

It took Matt several minutes more to plow his way to the freshly packed road. His feet were cold, but once on the groomed surface, with the rising sun breaking free of the mountains, he settled into a long, skating stride, and soon warmed up. The packed powder was magical in the dawn, and Matt had the broad basin entirely to himself. Aside from cold feet, he felt fine. He wondered if the two cross-country skiers had made it out to

West Yellowstone before the storm.

Thirty minutes later he had begun the long descent to Madison Junction when a snow coach overtook him from behind.

"Jesus H. Christ, Johnson, what in the hell do you think you're doing? We thought you were frozen solid by now. Stop skiing, for chrissakes," Stanley Reimer was leaning out the passenger window, yelling over the roar of the tracks.

"I'm okay. I'm going to ski on out," Matt shouted back to the program director as the powerful vehicle kept pace. They crossed the Madison River bridge, then Matt turned left at the junction on the road leading to the West Entrance.

"Stop skiing, goddamn it. Get in the van," Stan the Man's face had taken on a deeper shade of crimson. Matt looked over at the vehicle, and for the first time noticed Vladimir Kobelev in the back, his arm casually draped over the adjoining seat, and a smile on his face. Vlad was enjoying the show.

"Listen, dammit, stop skiing and get in this freakin' van right now, or I'll kick you off the team."

"I didn't know I was on the team," Matt called back, and watched Kobelev's smile broaden. "I'll ski on in." Reimer glared at him a few seconds longer, then closed the window, and the van roared off to the west.

It was almost noon when Matt hobbled back to the Stagecoach. He was dead tired, fiercely hungry, and hadn't felt his toes for the past hour. His hat, gloves and windbreaker were stiff with frozen sweat. His face was cold and his eyes seemed full of sand from lack of sleep. His quadriceps just above the knees were so tight they threatened to cramp with every step. He crabbed his way up the stairs of the Stagecoach, hobbling sideways. Staggering down the hall toward his room, he met three National Team members on their way to lunch.

"Jesus, Matt, you okay? Where the hell've you been?"

"I'm all right, I just skied back from Old Faithful," he mumbled, afraid if he didn't get to his room quickly he'd fall down.

He dropped the skis and poles on the floor, pushed open the door to his room, and collapsed on his bed. Tony Morgoloni, engrossed in cleaning his rifle, sprang to his feet.

"Sonofabitch, Rookie, you look like death warmed over. I thought the coaches went to haul your sorry ass outta there. Where the hell'd you spend the night?"

"Snow cave, and I skied all the way out this morning. Did those two Ski Team guys make it?"

"Hell, no. We picked 'em up at that trailer in Madison Junction yesterday."

"So did anyone make it all the way out?"

"Shit no. I guess you're the only one dumb enough to even try in a storm like that. You're goddamn lucky to be alive."

"I know, but at least I'm $600 richer."

There was a long silence.

"Right Tony? If I'm the only one who skied the round trip, I win the pot."

Tony's ferret-like eyes shifted around the room. Then he cleared his throat, "Hey, Matt buddy, I'm sorry about this, but the bet was on finishing in one day. You did a hell of a job, stayin' out there all night, but you gotta finish on the same day to win the pool. I'm sorry, Rookie, but rules is rules."

"What're you talking about? What happens to the pot if nobody makes it out in a day?"

"Hey, sorry kid. Nobody twisted your arm to enter the pool. You're not that much of a woodchuck. Any time you bet on something, you take a risk. I run the pool, if there ain't no winner, I make a profit, simple as that."

"You son of a-bitch…." Matt willed his exhausted body off the bed, but before his feet touched the floor, Tony was poised, his right fist cocked next to his ear. The punch came so fast Matt didn't have time to blink. A wall of flashbulbs blinded him, then it became dark.

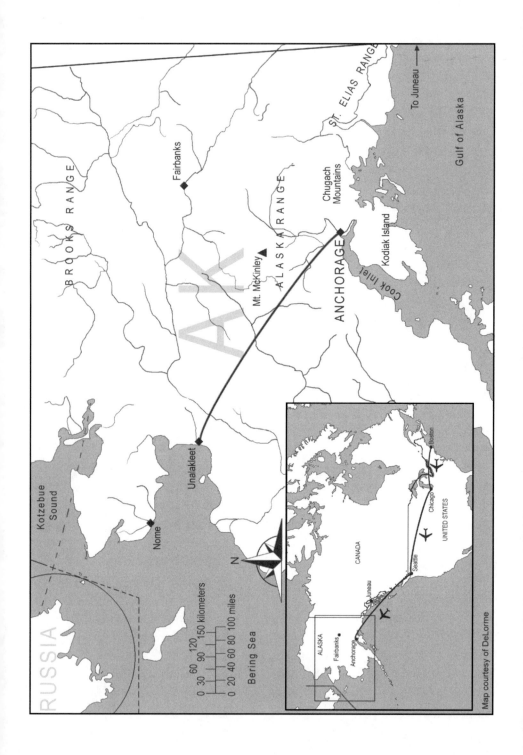

Rough Landing

5

Matt awoke with a swollen cheek and a throbbing pain in his feet. He carefully removed his socks and surveyed his damaged toes. He had frost-nipped his extremities before, even lost a couple of toe nails; but he had never seen such a colorful array of blood blisters and swollen skin from one workout.

After an initial inspection, Rosie and Gopher bundled Matt off to the West Yellowstone Medical Clinic.

"Well, son," the doctor announced, "the good news is, you'll be keeping all your toes. The bad news is, you're not going to be skiing for awhile."

"How long?" Matt asked.

"Hard to say. If you keep them clean, avoid infection, and most important don't get them cold again; a month to six weeks."

Matt had suspected the upcoming time trials were out of the question; but the doctor was suggesting the Olympic trials in Anchorage, more than four weeks away, were also in jeopardy.

After the doctor swabbed the blisters with disinfectant and wrapped the damaged toes, Gopher, Rosie and Matt drove back to the Stagecoach.

"How you feeling, Rookie? Looks like they hurt pretty bad." Rosie asked.

"It stung like hell when they were thawing out, but now there's only a dull ache. I'm just ticked I can't race in the time trials."

"Yeah, that's a bummer," Gopher responded. "Your skiing was really coming around. I think you've got Oliver worried."

Matt smiled, "On the Rendezvous loop a couple of days ago, I wasn't paying attention and skied up on his tails. He about chewed my head off. Then he missed three shots standing when we got back to the range. I think he's a head case."

"You got that right! How'd you shoot after harassing Oliver?" Gopher asked.

"Hit 'em all."

"Figures." Jimmy smiled. "By the way, you better steer clear of Stan the Man. He's mighty pissed. I guess he had some explaining to do to the Park Service. When Rosie told him about your feet, Stan ordered me to get you on the next flight east. I checked, and everything's booked, but he's on the warpath. Vlad tried to cool him off by saying we can use help on the range during the races, but I wouldn't give Stan anything else to complain about if I were you."

The next day, bundled up in most of the clothes he'd brought west, Matt was at the shooting range with a clipboard. He watched as the National Team members zeroed their rifles, tested skis, and prepared for the first biathlon competition of the season. It was an ideal Montana day: clear, cold, and not a breath of wind.

Kobelev had cornered Matt the day before and explained his assignment. "I must watching the shots through the scope, but is also important to have range times of best athletes, you understand? From dropping ski poles down, 'til picking them up, how many seconds it takes for shooting? Impossible to time everyone, but you record so many as you can, especially the best ones. And make notes if somebody look to you very good, or another guy is slow and sloppy. This good time for you to watch and learn. You have good boots? *Nyet?*"

Kobelev led Matt to a locked room in the Stagecoach where the team's equipment was stored. Rummaging through piles of racing uniforms, warm-ups and parkas, Vlad finally uncovering a pair of heavily insulated sno-pacs, the coaches' model with extra thick, felt liners.

"If you working for me on range, you must have proper boots. Try them. *Harasho?* Okay! You helping coaches paint targets after breakfast, then take range times during race." He patted Matt's shoulder before locking the storage room.

"You know, Matthew, I remember men in Novosibirsk who would risk their lives for boots like this! You Americans, you can't imagine...." He shook his head as he lumbered down the hall.

Matt stood in the brilliant West Yellowstone sunshine, the sharp mountain air turning to vapor with every breath as he waited for the competition to begin. Tony Morgoloni was prancing from one competitor to another jabbering nervously. Oliver Wainwright was trying to choose among his six new pairs of racing skis. The experienced competitors recognized this as Oliver's basic psych-out technique. He wanted everyone to be aware that he already had his six new pairs of Rossignols, while the other athletes managed on last year's equipment until after the trials in Anchorage. Once the team was selected, the suppliers scrambled to sign on the racers who were chosen to go to the Olympics.

The race was a kaleidoscope of color and action. Once the competitors, who left the starting gate at thirty second intervals, began arriving at the range, Matt was fully engrossed in his job. Two hours evaporated before he knew it. Although many of the top competitors overlapped each other on the firing line, he recorded at least two range times for everyone. His observations were revealing. Both Ragnar and Sandy seemed to approach the shooting range casually; relaxed and poised. Sandy easily beat Trudy in the women's race, while Ragnar had the best shooting among the men. Burl Palmer out-skied Ragnar by a few minutes, which earned the cowboy from Durango first place overall. Oliver was third in spite of a misunderstanding with a range official, who he accused of interfering with his approach to a firing point.

Kobelev was pleased with the notes Matt handed him after the racers headed back to the Stagecoach.

"So Matthew, what are you seeing on range today?"

"I was surprised that Ragnar and Sandy came in so slowly," Matt answered.

"Ah, excellent! There are times on the trail when you must throw away caution, you must attack each hill like it is your last. But as you approach the shooting range, maybe 100 meters out, you become a marksman, poised and disciplined. On trail, there are days when you ski faster, maybe even with less effort. But on range, in a big race you *never* do better than your training. You shoot only so good as your discipline. Sandy and Ragnar, they are not slow on the range, they know what they're doing."

On the second day of competition, the temperature was warmer but it was snowing hard. Everyone was soaked, and even with a sheet of plastic covering the clipboard, Matt had difficulty reading the stopwatch and recording times on the sodden start list. The races were held according to a sprint format, which meant that the athletes skied penalty loops for missed shots.

Sandy and Trudy were well ahead of the other women while Oliver, Burl and Brett Adams led the men. Tony Morgoloni missed four of his five shots standing, and complained to a range official that the heavy snowfall obscured the targets.

While Tony charged up and down the range complaining, a young racer from Bozeman slowly but confidently hit four for five. The range official gave the Snake a patient smile and walked to the far end of the firing line to reset the girl's target. Morgoloni tore off his racing bib and stormed into the army tent where the athletes stored their warmups.

That evening there was a frenzy of packing. In a team meeting after dinner, Kobelev outlined a training plan that would carry them through the Olympic trials in Anchorage.

Stanley Reimer was determined to say something inspirational. Oblivious that the athletes were exhausted from a month of hard training and anxious to get back to their packing, he rambled on until he finally realized he was about to lose his audience, then he wrestled a heavy cardboard package to the table and announced, "Before we head our separate ways for the holidays, I want everybody to sign these team posters."

"Aw, Stan, not now, it'll take an hour," someone protested.

"Not if we assembly line it. We only have a hundred this time. I've got to send them out to suppliers and board members before Christmas. Grab a marker, and let's start passing them along."

As the grumbling athletes approached the stack of posters, Burl Palmer and Andy Christensen edged toward the door.

"Where the hell do you think you two are going?" Stan yelled.

"Get your asses over here!"

Matt didn't know what to do. Since he wasn't a National Team member, he assumed that he was free to leave, but he didn't want to aggravate Reimer further. He stood confused, while the other athletes grabbed markers and dragged chairs to the table. As the colorful team photos began circulating, Matt noticed that Stan's signature already appeared in the prime spot on the poster.

"What the hell are you gawking at, Johnson? This is for National Team members. See if Gopher needs any help packing the team gear."

Matt's mother and sister were waiting at the small terminal in Lebanon. Despite the tensions in their little family, he hadn't realized how much he had missed them. He'd always pictured his mom as a vibrant, energetic woman, but standing in the late November overcast, she looked small and frail. He could see she was fighting back the tears as he dropped his backpack to give her a hug, and he felt embarrassed when she clung to him hungrily. Holding his mother in an awkward embrace, for the first time he entertained the idea that his father had killed himself. Why else would his mother's decline be so dramatic? But then the questions and doubts that he'd held at bay for over a year swarmed into his head: How could Michael Johnson leave them? Hadn't he known that despite his moods and rages they needed him?

As they drove home, Annie peppered him with questions about the other athletes and for details about the Old Faithful tour. His mother drove on in silence, occasionally shaking her head.

The next morning, Mrs. Johnson arranged a checkup with Dr. Arneson, a family practitioner across the river in Lyme. After carefully inspecting Matt's feet he reassured her that her son would make a full recovery. Dr. Arneson contacted a friend at the Dartmouth Athletic Department and arranged for Matt to use the college swimming pool during December. Dr. Arneson told Matt that running and roller skiing would be impossible for a while; but swimming, weight lifting and shooting would keep him reasonably fit until the tryouts.

Five days before Christmas it snowed, dropping enough fresh powder for skiing at the higher elevations. Matt had learned about a Forest Service road on the crest of the Green Mountains only an hour from Thetford. His toes, though still sensitive and pink with new skin, were no longer painful in his ski boots. When he reviewed his training log on Christmas Eve, he realized that in spite of the frostbite and the fickle Vermont weather, he had maintained nearly the training volume Coach Kobelev had recommended.

When Matt joined his mother and sister for the Christmas Eve candle light service at the Congregational church on Thetford Hill, he was flooded by images of his father's funeral. He remembered his grandfather helping his mom into the church as she leaned on him heavily, pale and hollow-eyed. Matt and Annie had followed behind. The church had been packed. Not until they were seated in the reserved seats of the first pew, had Matt noticed the flag-draped casket. The red stripes and the deep blue field of the flag seemed to vibrate with intensity. All through the droning ceremony that was supposed to bring comfort, Matt couldn't tear his eyes from that flag.

He tried to imagine his father lying beneath it, but he didn't know if combat veterans were buried in their military uniforms or in business suits. Years earlier, when Matt and Annie were playing in the attic, they had discovered the dusty army uniform; complete with tarnished brass insignia and rows of faded service ribbons. Their dad had flown off the handle at the time, even though they put the uniform right back where they had discovered it. When Matt was in the attic again a few weeks later, the uniform was gone. At the funeral Matt's thoughts wandered back to the morning in the attic. Was his dad mad because of pride in those medals and the time he served? Or didn't he want to remember those months spent in Vietnam?

The minister had talked of Michael Johnson's service to his country and his love of the outdoors. The choir sang "A Mighty Fortress" and "Amazing Grace." When Matt thought the service was nearly over, the minister asked if anyone had memories of Michael Johnson they wanted to share.

"I got something I want to say." A huge, bearded man stood in the rear of the church. He seemed awkward in a dark suit that was too tight through the chest and exposed his thick wrists.

"Mike Johnson mighta got messed up in 'Nam, but he was a damn good forester. I worked a bunch a woodlots with him, an' he was always fair to us loggers, an' he was always fair to the landowner."

The bearded logger's words gave others the courage to speak, and for thirty minutes, friends, neighbors and acquaintances shared memories of Michael Johnson. Men with weathered faces and glistening eyes, standing in the back of the church, talked about his courage flying the dangerous medevac missions in Vietnam. Three men stepped forward, and one by one acknowledged that they owed him their lives. Matt listened with wildly conflicting emotions. He was proud of what these men were saying about his dad, but it bothered him that strangers knew more about his father than Matt did himself.

The congregation closed the Christmas service with "Silent Night" and Matt was jarred back to the present.

Though the memories were still painfully vivid, the funeral had been fifteen months ago. In two days Matt would leave for the Olympic trials in Anchorage. He remembered how his father's eyes had come alive when he spoke about Alaska. Matt had loved his dad's stories of the wild adventures during the Fort Richardson tour. There was a hair-raising encounter with a grizzly bear while on a fishing trip, ski plane landings high on Mount McKinley and helicopter "missions" to peek inside the rumbling cauldron of Redoubt volcano.

As Matt anticipated his trip to Alaska, he could picture his father's smile, which in life, he saw rarely.

On December 26, Matt's mother and sister drove him to the airport. Although the Johnsons had left Fort Richardson soon after Matt was born, the stories, faded photos and Christmas cards from old friends made Alaska seem real to him. He was excited to be headed north, but he dreaded saying good-bye. His mother had tried to keep up a pretense of normality through the holidays, but Annie was rarely home and the tensions between them boiled over every time his sister left the house refusing to disclose her plans or answer her mother. After West Yellowstone, his mother conceded that Matt was going to pursue the Olympics, so she refrained from openly trying to discourage him. But it was obvious she struggled through his absences and counted the days until his return.

Now she seemed to be pulling herself together as she faced his leaving. "Matt, have a good trip. I hope you do well in the races. And remember what Dr. Arneson said about refreezing your toes. Annie will help you with your stuff, I'm going to wait here in the car. I can't stand many more of these airport good-byes."

"Come on, Mom, it's only seventeen days this time, and I'll be seeing some of your old Alaskan friends." Matt's effort to cheer his mother failed. She swallowed hard and the tears began to flow.

"I'll call after every race," he promised. She nodded, but her eyes stared straight through the windshield at the dirty snowbank.

"I love you, Mom." The only response was a tightening of her jaw as the tears coursed down her cheeks. He suppressed a sigh as he walked toward the terminal. After all, he was going to have to leave home some day. Would she be crying if he were heading off for college?

The airports in Boston and Chicago were thronged with holiday travelers, but Matt's flights left on schedule. Departing Seattle on the final leg of his journey, he was assigned a window seat. The plane climbed to the east through thick clouds. When they emerged from the overcast, Matt looked out at the massive, snow-covered flanks of Mount Rainier. He could make out rock formations, trees, and hanging snowfields. As they rose beyond the huge white pyramid, Matt recognized other West Coast giants poking their shoulders above the gray blanket of clouds: Mount Adams, the shattered summit of Mount St. Helens, and beyond that, Mount Hood in Oregon.

It was ninety minutes later when Matt glanced out the window again. The cloud cover, which had shrouded Seattle, was gone and the setting sun painted a thousand snow-covered peaks an unbelievable pink. Scores of indigo fjords snaked inland between rock cliffs and ice falls. There were no roads and no towns; just vast reaches of snow-covered mountains and dark blue water. Matt had never imagined such mountains. He concentrated on individual summits: smooth wind-blown cornices, jagged rock outcroppings, sheer faces that soared thousands of feet.

As the jet followed the Gulf of Alaska northwestward and the St. Elias mountains fell behind, Matt spotted huge, rounded mountains to the northeast. The snowcapped crags of the coastal mountains were now purple in the last rays of the setting sun, but the snow-covered giants inland still reflected the bright pastels of dusk. Unable to contain his curiosity, Matt asked the passenger behind him, "Is that McKinley?"

"Naw, the one on the left's Sanford, the one on the right's Mount Blackburn. They're only 16,000 feet, Denali is over 20,000. We may get a peek in a few minutes as we approach Anchorage. This your first time to Alaska?"

"I was born in Anchorage. My dad was stationed at Fort Rich, but we moved to Vermont when I was a year old. My folks used to talk about Alaska a lot though."

The Alaskan passenger pointed out the window, "There, that's a pretty good look at the rooftop of North America. Foraker is on the left, the little bump in the middle is Hunter, and that big beauty on the right is McKinley, but most of us up here call it by it's original name, Denali."

Matt had never seen anything more spectacular. The sky was still a brilliant spectrum: orange, to pink, to purple, to nearly black overhead. The frozen landscape below was shrouded in a deep violet shadow, but the summits of Foraker and Denali still caught the dying sun. They rose boldly from the foothills and forests to totally dominate the panorama. Matt remained transfixed by the impressive view until the aircraft began its final approach to Anchorage International Airport.

He again was met by Jimmy Clark, but this time Gopher was in a rush, "Grab your stuff, Matt, Stan's scheduled a team meeting that starts in ten minutes. We can just make it!"

A rental van was idling at the curb, and after loading Matt's ski bag, rifle box, and backpack, Jimmy pulled out into the traffic.

"We'll be staying at the Baranof Inn," Gopher announced. "Nothing fancy, but it's only a short drive to Kincaid Park, and the food's great. Just leave your stuff in the van. We'd better head to the meeting."

Stanley Reimer was addressing a large gathering of athletes as Matt and Gopher slipped into the room. A few heads turned, and a couple of greetings were whispered.

"Hurry up and find a seat, will you?" Stan commanded.

He continued with a long list of administrative details related to the tryouts: van routes to and from the competition site, training schedules, Olympic Team selection procedures, a review of the corporate logo regulations, and a list of public appearances which the athletes were expected to attend.

He wrapped up his rambling announcements with a flourish, "Most of you know that this team had its origins here in Alaska. Even after the Training Center at Fort Richardson was closed, Alaska has continued to provide the National Team with top competitors, thanks to the efforts of one man. We are privileged to have with us this afternoon, John Miller."

Sitting near the front was a man whose weathered face was largely concealed by a flowing mustache and a bushy, gray beard. His unruly hair had been matted by a thick balaclava, discarded on the floor next to his seat. His heavy pants were held by wide suspenders worn over a faded wool shirt. A hooded, army surplus parka was draped over the back of his chair. When the applause subsided, Miller stood awkwardly and turned to face the athletes.

"Welcome to Alaska! We're mighty proud to be hosting these tryouts, and to have you all here. As Mr. Reimer said, I run some programs for kids out in the bush. Since you folks have almost a week before the races begin, I asked Mr. Reimer and Coach Kobelev if I could recruit a few volunteers to help with three clinics out in the Interior. You'll see a part of the state seldom visited by tourists, stay with Native families, and you'll inspire some kids who are really excited about biathlon. I have a chartered plane leaving tomorrow for Unalakleet on Norton Sound. We'll work with about forty kids there tomorrow afternoon. The next morning we'll fly to Shaktoolik for another clinic, then finally on to Koyuk for the Regional Championships."

"Isn't it a little early in the season for championships?" an athlete interrupted.

As John Miller smiled, the furrows on his face deepened and his eyes scanned the audience. "I don't know about you folks from the Lower Forty-Eight, but my kids have been on snow since September. They're ready for the Regionals. In fact, a couple of 'em are ready for these tryouts!

"Your first race is a week from tomorrow. I'll have you back here by Wednesday night. So…who's interested?" The only hand to go up immediately was Sandy Stonington's. Tony Morgoloni studied the ceiling. Oliver Wainwright scribbled notes in his day planner. Burl Palmer mumbled, "What the hell," and raised his hand, followed by Brett Adams.

"Anybody else?" Miller pleaded.

"How many do you need?" Stanley asked.

"I had hoped for half-a-dozen. If we could have three more with Sandy, Brett and Burl, it would be great."

Stan scanned the room full of competitors, "Okay, folks, the following athletes are volunteering to help the ABF with these clinics: Edwards, Lindstrom, and…." Stan's gaze fell on Matt and a smile creased his face, "and Johnson. You enjoyed the wilderness so much in Yellowstone, you're going to love this trip!"

Matt's pulse shot up. He didn't know whether to be excited about visiting the three remote villages, or angry that Stan the Man was trying to undermine his chances to do well at the tryouts. Declining wasn't an option in the packed conference room. He was reassured by Sandy's confident smile.

Miller continued enthusiastically, "Thanks a lot. You can't believe how excited these kids will be to see you. Let's get together for a few minutes after this meeting and I'll outline tomorrow's schedule."

Burl turned in his seat to face Matt, "No sweat, Rookie. This trip will be fun. Hell, we'll have an advantage by being out of the pressure cooker for five days. Oliver and Snake will have everyone wound so tight by next Saturday, they'll be shooting each other instead of the targets!"

Matt had been awake for an hour when John Miller knocked on his door at 5:00 A.M.

"Breakfast in thirty minutes! Bring your gear, we'll head over to the airport at six."

The athletes ate quietly, then boarded the Baranof shuttle to the airport. Miller led them out of the terminal into a predawn deep freeze reminiscent of West Yellowstone. In front of a freight hanger sat a silver tail-dragger right out of the history books. Matt remembered a plastic model he had built back in grade school of the Douglas DC-3. As Miller led them to the plane, a man in the back of a pickup truck was struggling with their skis and rifle boxes.

"It's about time! Help me get this stuff loaded so we can get outta here."

In spite of the bitter cold, his insulated flight jacket hung open and a baseball hat emblazoned "Southeast Asia War Games — Second Place" perched above his bright red ears.

"Couple you kids hop in the aircraft an' pile this gear aft of the door."

In a few minutes the athletes and all their baggage were on board. The plane had no interior paneling or insulation. Matt could touch the aluminum framework and the thin metal skin of the plane. Cables and hoses threaded through openings in the bulkheads from the cockpit to the tail. The seats were canvas benches on aluminum tubing running the length of the fuselage. The seatbelts were a random assortment, scrounged from an automotive junkyard. The cabin windows were scratched to an opaque white.

A center aisle led steeply to the cockpit where the pilot and co-pilot's seats faced the sky. John Miller stooped through the hatch and announced, "Welcome aboard Alaska Bush Air Service. Your captain for today's flight is Joe O'Donnell. I'll be in the right hand seat, so you'd better hope nothing happens to Joe."

"Our flight time to Unalakleet today should be three hours, depending on the head winds. If there's anything we can do to make your flight more enjoyable...."

"Aw, cut the crap, Miller. It'll be at least two-and-a-half hours, but it won't be much more, since we've only got fuel for three. Stay in your seats and keep your belts buckled unless you want to be peeled off the ceiling when we land. If you gotta use the head, clean it after you finish. If you're gonna get sick, use the barf bags; nothing I hate worse than puke in my airplane. It'll warm up a little back here once we get airborne."

Roger Edwards joked, "Is this relic going to make it? I saw one of these in the Smithsonian."

In one stride Captain O'Donnell was face to face with Edwards, "Listen wiseass, this aircraft has flown combat missions for longer than than you've been alive. She dropped commandos within walking distance of Hanoi, and she rescued fighter pilots out of Laos. Beyond that she's carried the mail, medical supplies, and color TV sets to every bush village in interior Alaska since I bought her in '72. You are goddamned privileged to set foot in this aircraft. You got that?"

"Yes, sir." It was the first time Matt had seen Roger without a comeback.

"Joe, let's get this bird in the air," said John Miller, trying to defuse the confrontation. O'Donnell pointed at Matt, and turned toward Miller.

"This is the kid, isn't it?" John Miller nodded. The pilot held out an oil-stained hand to Matt. "I knew your dad in 'Nam. We flew together out of Di An, bringing ARVNs into Cambodia, then hauling their sorry asses out of there when the NVA kicked the shit out of 'em. Did you know your ol' man had four birds shot out from under him in one day! Shit, if it hadn't been a covert operation they woulda written him up for the Medal of Honor. He saved my ass more than once, I'll tell ya. Sure was sorry to hear you lost him. I woulda been back for the service, but I didn't hear about it 'til it was over. Hell of a pilot."

Matt didn't know what to say. Covert mission? This new information was another piece of the puzzle. But what did it mean? Who was Michael Johnson? If he was so brave, why couldn't he stick around for his wife and kids? Being a family man had to be easier than getting shot at. O'Donnell slapped him on the shoulder, "Well there's a buncha Eskimo kids in Unalakleet that're so excited you guys are coming out, they're probably peeing in their mukluks right now. We better get airborne."

Soon after O'Donnell and Miller climbed to their seats, smoke belched from the engine cowlings and the three-bladed props labored. Finally, the engines caught and their deafening roar drowned all conversation. The plane bounced and jolted as it taxied for takeoff. O'Donnell leaned on the throttles, the tail rose, and in seconds they were flying.

The noise and vibration were numbing, but as O'Donnell had promised, the cabin grew warmer. After an hour, John Miller came back to check his passengers. It was too noisy to talk, but Matt gathered they were flying into strong headwinds and the trip would take three hours. Below them lay endless coniferous forests, broken only by frozen rivers and lakes. There was no trace of human habitation; no roads, no bridges, no towns.

Matt was dozing when a deafening alarm wrenched him awake. In the cockpit he saw O'Donnell's face, bathed in the red glow of a blinking warning light. Both the captain and John Miller were concentrating intensely on the windshield and the instrument panel. Matt peered out the cloudy window and noticed that the starboard prop wasn't turning.

Miller shouted from the flight deck, "Hold on. We're going to crash!" Matt wondered how Miller was so easily heard over the roar of the engines, then he realized the only sound was the annoying wail of the alarm. O'Donnell struggled with the steering yoke as Miller ducked low and covered his face with his arms. There was a sickening crunch behind Matt's back. Out the corner of his eye, he saw the top of a spruce spiral above a jagged tear in the wing. He was jerked off the canvas bench and doubled in half by the seatbelt. The first crunching sound became a deafening, metallic roar and the plane lurched violently as it hit. The cabin was filled with the screech of tearing aluminum as a fierce jolt rocked the fuselage around him. Matt saw his teammates tossed like dolls. He could see their mouths screaming, but nothing was audible over the hideous rending of metal. The web netting restraining the baggage broke free as rifle boxes, ski bags, and backpacks slammed forward, forcing Roger

Edwards into the air and driving him into the cockpit.

It took Matt several seconds to realize that the plane had stopped. He felt cold air rushing into the cabin. Where the windshield had once been, a spruce branch swayed as the wind began to fill the cockpit with snow.

Sandy clutched her hand over her right eye, the side of her face streaming with blood. Burl Palmer was doubled up in his seat, buried under a heavy ski bag. Brett Adams cradled his left wrist, then bent forward and retched all over his shoes. Jenny Lindstrom sat bolt upright, her face the color of the windblown snow. Roger had disappeared under the heap of baggage that barricaded the cockpit.

As if in a trance, Matt surveyed the littered interior of the old airplane. Something warm was running down his neck. As he touched the sticky, matted hair at the back of his head, he spotted his ski hat across the cabin. Even before he checked his palm, he knew it was covered with blood. At the same instant, a thought raced through his mind: *plane wrecks often catch on fire!*

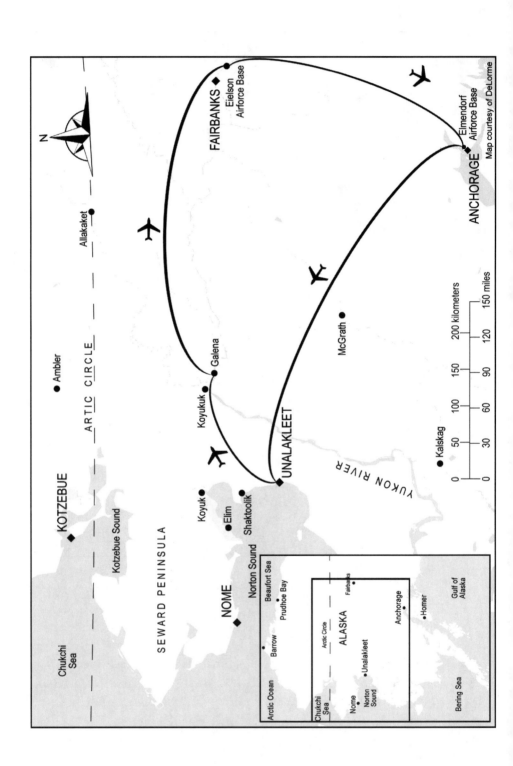

Map courtesy of DeLorme

Stranded

6

The crash site was strangely quiet. Red warning lights throughout the fuselage blinked in a garish rhythm, but the alarm Klaxon was now silent. A moaning came from the jumble of baggage that jammed the doorway to the cockpit. John Miller rocked forward and back in the co-pilot's seat. Captain O'Donnell was hunched motionless over the steering yoke.

"Sonofabitch." A heavy ski bag and a backpack crashed to the floor revealing Burl Palmer. "I ain't been this roughed up since I got stomped by Widowmaker at the Denver Stock Show! Anybody hurt?"

He looked across at Matt, "You don't look so good, Rookie." Matt pointed at Sandy and Brett. "Get your seat belt off and help me get 'em out of here."

Burl moved to Jenny and unfastened her belt.

"Matt, see if you can open the door."

Although the thin aluminum skin of the fuselage was dented and torn, the rear hatch pushed open when Matt released the lever. He peered out and saw a powerful truck plowing through stunted evergreens, red lights flashing as it roared through the snow. Burl helped Jenny to the door just as two Inuit men in heavy parkas ran toward the plane. They reached to help when Burl and Matt handed her out. The smaller of the two men removed his coat, revealing a Seattle Seahawks sweatshirt. He wrapped Jenny in the parka and led her to the ambulance.

Burl walked Sandy to the door. It was awkward getting her to the ground because she refused to take her hand away from her eye. "I'm okay," she said, "but Roger's hurt bad. I saw a rifle box hit him in the back."

Two members of the rescue squad helped Sandy to the ambulance, while an older man in a heavy parka peered into the plane, "You boys all right?" His weathered face displayed no emotion. "I'm Eben Oksoktaruk. We'll get you to the health clinic right away."

Oksoktaruk motioned to Matt, "Hop out. My wife will take a look at you in the truck. She's a nurse."

Matt dropped to the snow, and the big Native Alaskan hoisted himself into the plane. "William, we're going to need a couple of backboards," he shouted.

Burl and Oksoktaruk released Brett from his seatbelt and guided him to the door. Then they began to remove the tangled mass of baggage that buried Roger Edwards. He was breathing but unconscious, his left leg sprawled at a severe angle. The Inuit grabbed Burl's arm, "Help me get my wife in here. William, we need you and Martha up here right now! Elizabeth can take care of the others."

Burl helped the three Alaskans skillfully lift Roger onto a backboard and secure him with straps. They used the same procedure with Joe O'Donnell, whose chest had been punctured, spraying the cockpit with blood. John Miller had facial cuts and was holding his right arm to his chest. Once the Inuit woman had immobilized the arm with bandages, and the litters had been muscled into the ambulance, Miller was able to hobble from the plane.

The back of the ambulance was crowded, O'Donnell and Edwards on litters in the center, the others sitting on benches. They arrived at the modest Norton Sound Health Clinic fifty minutes after the crash.

When the ambulance backed to the rear of the clinic, the doors swung open, and a young doctor in a white lab coat helped the Inuits guide the crash victims into the building. After Edwards and O'Donnell were lifted from the vehicle, the the doctor did not reappear, but Eben led the others to a second examination room. Wrapped in blankets from the ambulance, the athletes sat in stunned silence.

Eben Oksoktaruk unzipped his heavy parka. "It's going to take a while. Our clinic can handle the usual problems, but we don't have the staff for an emergency like this. Dr. Bean is young but he knows his stuff. Elizabeth, would you heat up some tea and soup for these folks?"

Oksoktaruk's wife, who had been assisting the doctor, stepped through a door connecting the two examination rooms. Her pale green scrubs were splattered with blood. She went directly to a cabinet, retrieved a large box of gauze pads, then closed the door behind her without saying a word.

Eben stepped to the cupboard and returned with a handful of gauze. Sandy's hand had not left her face since the crash and the dark blood was drying on her fingers. Eben handed her a wad of pads and she tentatively placed the sterile gauze over her eye. He also passed Matt some of the white pads. Matt held them to the back of his head where his hair was stiff with dried blood.

After what seemed like hours, the young doctor walked briskly into the room. "Eben, we've got to medevac those two out to Anchorage as soon as possible. There's an air force Huey at Galena. They could be here in forty-five minutes. Both the patients are stable for the time being. Can you and William get them back out to the airstrip? I'm going to send Martha with you to keep an eye on things until the air force medics take over. If the chopper can land in this wind, they should reach Anchorage before dark."

Without saying a word, Eben zipped his parka and disappeared through the door to the adjacent examining room. The boyish doctor addressed his patients, "Well, who's next? This is almost as much excitement as we had back in Rochester on a Saturday night!"

He approached John Miller, but the bearded coach insisted he check Sandy first. The doctor introduced himself and checked her bruises before inspecting the injured eye. Reluctantly she withdrew her hand. The young doctor carefully studied the wound from several angles. Her eye had swollen shut and was caked with blood.

"I'm going to have to numb it so I can clean it properly. The laceration through the eyebrow will take a dozen stitches, but I think the eye itself is going to be fine."

Sandy's shoulders sagged in relief and tears spilled from the uninjured eye. "I was so afraid I'd damaged my eye."

"You're going to have a scar there," he said, helping her to the table, "but it shouldn't be too noticeable after your eyebrow grows back."

"I'm not worried about the scar. I was afraid I'd lost my eye, and

I'm too old to learn to shoot left handed!" She looked like she'd been in a street fight; the injured eye was swollen shut and turning a deep violet.

After he stitched Sandy's eye, Dr. Bean turned his attention to Brett Adams, who appeared to have a broken left wrist. The doctor applied an inflatable air cast and gave Brett some medication for the pain. Jenny Lindstrom was next. She was uninjured, but on the brink of shock. Dr. Bean spoke with Elizabeth, who guided Jenny into the adjoining examination room.

Then the doctor approached Matt. He inspected Matt's eyes before turning his attention to the gash on the back of his scalp. "You must have hit something pretty sharp, probably the metal bulkhead. You have a mild concussion. I'm going to give you a wild haircut before I stitch you up. But you certainly haven't fractured your skull, I'm looking at it right now, and it's solid as a rock."

After numbing the edges of the wound, he quickly shaved, cleaned and stitched the injury. Matt returned to his seat next to the wall.

"All right, Coach Miller, last but not least." Miller's right shoulder was dislocated. "John, I'll get you scheduled for x-rays back in Anchorage, but we're going to have to attempt reducing that shoulder right now. If we do nothing, it will definitely require surgery by the time you get out of here. If we're lucky, it might pop back in smoothly and you'll avoid the scalpel later on."

"Sounds okay to me, Doc. I'm not big on hospitals," responded Miller, his voice revealing that he was in great pain.

"I'm going to need a hand from you guys," he motioned to Matt and Burl. They approached the examining table where Dr. Bean gently removed the coach's parka.

"John, I have to put pressure on your arm before I can manipulate it back into the socket. It may pop in quite easily, or it may not. Either way, it's no fun."

"Let's get it done," said Miller.

"Okay, guys, I need you to hold John firmly on the table. As I put pressure on the arm and shoulder, he'll tend to ease toward me to minimize the pain, but you have to hold him firmly on the table. It should pop right back in."

The doctor positioned Matt and Burl, then he gently lifted the coach's injured arm. Miller strained on the table and Matt used all his strength to keep the patient steady as the doctor pulled on the arm, Miller's face contorted in pain. As the pressure increased, he groaned, then there was an audible snap and Miller went limp.

Dr. Bean sounded casual as everyone resumed breathing, "Well, John, we'll still want to have some pictures taken in Anchorage, but it went back in smoothly, which is a good sign." As he was immobilizing the coach's arm, the rear door to the room opened and the three Alaskans entered, shaking snow from their parkas.

"It's really howling out there, but the chopper made it. The other two are on their way to Anchorage, but there sure won't be any commercial flights until the weather lets up," Eben announced.

Looking up, the doctor asked Martha, "How was O'Donnell holding up?"

"No worse. I was afraid we might lose him on the drive to the airstrip, but his vitals were stable. The air force medevac had three corpsmen in the back, and I've never seen such equipment! They thought they could make Anchorage in less than three hours."

"Good! Thanks, Martha. You too Eben, and William. Now maybe we should get these folks someplace where they can rest."

When the athletes entered the waiting room in the front of the clinic, Matt was surprised to see it crowded with Native Alaskans. As John Miller introduced the athletes to the townspeople, Matt was impressed that the crusty Alaskan knew so much about each of the competitors.

Matt was assigned to the Oksoktaruk family, the same couple who had supervised the rescue. A black-haired boy about Matt's age eased to the front of the crowd. Like everyone else, he wore a heavy, hooded parka, of army surplus olive drab. When they stood face to face, the Inuit boy looked at the floor and said shyly, "I'm Thomas Oksoktaruk. I'll show you where we live."

The boy was more animated outside the clinic, and although the wind was whipping the snow horizontally between the buildings, his parka remained unzipped.

"You didn't get hurt too bad?"

Matt had to walk quickly to keep up, "Nope, a few stitches on the back of my head."

In spite of the blowing snow, Matt noticed that Unalakleet was a tiny village, a collection of humble buildings facing the frozen expanse of Norton Sound. There were fishing boats pulled up on the shore, encrusted with ice. Thomas noticed Matt squinting into the wind. "It's always blowing here in town, but we train in the hills about a mile east of here, where it's not so windy."

Like the other homes they passed, the Oksoktaruk's yard was cluttered. A Boston Whaler, buried under the snow, rested on rugged saw horses, and piles of traps and fishing nets filled the corner of the yard. Four fifty-five-gallon oil drums were lined up, one of them with a hand pump installed in the top. Two snow machines were parked near the front steps, one missing its fiberglass cowling.

"Come on in." Thomas led Matt onto a porch which had been enclosed with sheets of plywood. The interior of the house was bright and warm. Music poured from a room in the back. "Mary, turn that down! That's my sister Mary. She's a junior at the new school east of town."

Matt enjoyed his evening with the Oksoktaruks. Conversation ranged from the plane crash to the family's stand on the controversial issue of Bowhead whaling. Matt learned that Thomas' father had served two tours in Vietnam as an infantryman in the central highlands. When he returned to Unalakleet, Eben Oksoktaruk became a village elder and a director of the Bering Straits Native Corporation. The rescue vehicles at the airfield were a result of Eben's National Guard connections. The ski trails and biathlon range east of town were constructed by a Guard engineering unit from Fairbanks during their two week summer training.

Thomas's mother had attended the University of Alaska in Fairbanks, and earned a degree in nursing. Mary was a typical teenager, amazingly similar to Matt's sister back in Vermont.

After supper the family sat in the living room listening to Northwind on the radio. Matt was fascinated. For an hour the announcer read messages to people living in the bush who had no telephones; messages that hinted at the joys and hardships of living in Alaska's remote wilderness.

"To Sally in Koyukuk: Have to stay two more days in Fairbanks, doctor wants to do additional tests. Don't worry. I love you, Burkie."

"To Ronald Farnsworth in Ambler: The replacement gaskets and couplings you ordered for your 1947 Poseidon pump are no longer stocked by the manufacturer. We will conduct a computer inventory search of all the licensed Poseidon dealers in North America in hopes of finding the parts you requested. Should know by this time next week. Ralph at Northern Hydraulics."

"To Megan in Upper Kalskag: Found a Super Cub on wheel-skis. Low hours on rebuilt engine. The guy will trade even for our lot in Homer. Do you want it? Love, George."

The next morning it was still blowing and the temperature had dropped. The biathletes met with John Miller in the entry of the new school. The halls were bright and the classrooms colorful. Miller gave the biathletes a tour of the gymnasium, pool, weight room, gymnastics hall, and the sparkling locker rooms. It was the most beautiful high school Matt had ever seen.

Eventually Miller led the athletes back to the gymnasium. "Our original plan was to conduct biathlon clinics here in Unalakleet, then in Shaktoolik and finally in Koyuk. Obviously, we've had to revise our plans. We can't get a charter in to pick you folks up until the weather improves, but the Alaska Air Guard has a routine training flight tomorrow; Anchorage to Galena, then on to Eielson Air Force Base near Fairbanks, and finally back to Anchorage. Eben is on the phone with Air Guard headquarters to see if they'll divert from Galena to pick us up. We could be back at the Baranof in time for supper tomorrow."

"I could understand if you all wanted to spend the day resting in bed. I don't feel so hot myself. But I can't tell you how excited these folks are to have you here. Even if we did an informal clinic in the gym this afternoon, they'd be very grateful."

Burl Palmer spoke up first, "Hell, might as well. We can't dance and it's too windy to throw stones."

The athletes set up waxing benches, video monitors, blackboards, and posters designating the different stations. Even before the kids began to arrive, Matt noticed several adults quietly entering the gym and sitting in the bleachers. Just after two, as John Miller welcomed the school children to the gym, Matt counted more than sixty adults in the stands.

As Miller was explaining how the young athletes would rotate from one station to the next, they heard the whine of two-cycle engines and dogs barking outside. One of the adults looked out the window and announced to Miller, "It's the folks from Shaktoolik!"

The gym door opened and more than two dozen Inuits, their faces red from wind and cold, entered the large room. After the heavy coats came off and Miller restored order, the clinic got underway.

At 4:30, Eben Oksoktaruk asked for everyone's attention, "As many of you know, we had planned to have a big potluck in Koyuk after tomorrow's clinic. Because of the accident, John and the athletes won't be going to Koyuk, but instead will be heading back to Anchorage tomorrow. We thought we might as well have the potluck here tonight.

The ladies have been working all afternoon. Everything's ready over at the community center. I hope you're hungry!"

The kids led the charge, grabbing their coats as they sprinted for the doors.

"Thomas, you and John lead the biathletes through the line. Don't let them miss the muktuk. They won't get any back in Anchorage." Eben was warming to his role as master of ceremonies. Thomas led Matt down the length of the table. There were casseroles, vegetables, breads, and desserts similar to a buffet served at a church supper in Vermont, but also an array of distinctly Alaskan dishes. There was a smoked salmon more than three feet long, its beautiful flesh a deep, dark orange. A large tray of caribou meat, sliced paper thin, and another plate heaped with roast goose looked tempting. Near the end of the table was a platter piled with square chunks of white meat with a thick black skin. Thomas smiled as he loaded a chunk on Matt's plate.

"What's that?" Matt asked as they found a place to sit.

"Muktuk, it's a traditional Inuit treat. Great for energy in the winter," Thomas answered.

"What's it made from?" Matt asked his host.

"Whale blubber, pure fat. Like I said, great for energy."

As the assembly was finishing their meals, Eben Oksoktaruk stood to make another announcement.

"We have a lot to be thankful for. Even though several people were seriously hurt in the plane crash yesterday, it could have been much worse. Joe O'Donnell and Roger Edwards made it through the night okay."

"In spite of the accident, we had an excellent clinic today, and now this wonderful potluck. Some of us were thinking the only thing that could improve the day would be a little dancing."

His words were scarcely out before the children pushed the chairs back, creating a large open space in the center of the room. Then they sat cross-legged in a circle, while the adults settled in behind the children. Someone dimmed the lights. Eben, two other men and an elderly woman, dressed in elaborate parkas and delicately beaded mukluks, stepped to the center of the room. Two of the men carried large hoops, covered by taut animal skin. They sat in the circle, while the white-haired woman, stooped with age, remained standing. The drummers began to beat the skin drums with long, thin bones, filling the room with a rhythm that Matt felt as well as heard. The seated Inuits joined in a low, pulsating chant, while the woman stamped in time to the music and sang a high solo part.

When she finished, the audience bowed in appreciation. A man from Shaktoolik danced next, adding more elaborate steps. His story was about hunting caribou. Other dancers followed, mostly grandparents. The persistent throbbing of the drums and the deep chanting of the singers had almost put Matt to sleep when the lights came on and people reached for their coats. John Miller gathered the athletes for instructions, "You can head home from here with your hosts, but be packed and ready to leave tomorrow morning. Someone will pick you up at 8:30. Thanks again for a great clinic this afternoon."

Matt grabbed his coat and followed Thomas into the bitter cold. Walking along, it took him a moment to realize that something was different. Then he noticed it was calm; there was absolutely no wind. The snow squeaked loudly under foot and dogs barked in the distance, but otherwise all was silent. They looked up. Beyond the smoke from the houses, on the dome of the frozen sky, vibrant sheets of pastels danced and shifted like a curtain in the wind.

"Wow, I've seen the northern lights back in Vermont, but never like this," Matt said.

"Yeah, this is a good one. We often have one color, but it's rare to see all these colors together. The elders say the aurora is a good omen for the future."

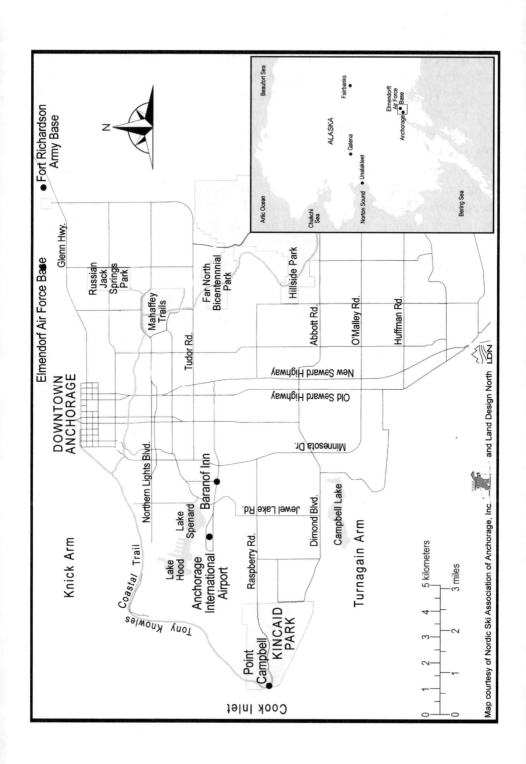

Map courtesy of Nordic Ski Association of Anchorage, Inc. and Land Design North

Celebrities

7

Because John Miller was bringing five of his top competitors to Anchorage for the Olympic Trials, there were more townspeople at the airstrip to see the biathletes off than had met their arrival. Thomas Oksoktaruk was the most experienced of the group, having been on the Junior National Team. Lacking money for travel to the tryouts, Thomas had remained in Alaska for the past two seasons. He would be a dark horse, adding unpredictability to the Olympic Trials.

As the Oksoktaruk family said their good-byes, Eben pulled something from a pocket inside his parka. Unwrapping a piece of cloth, he produced two straight shafts, eighteen inches long, the width of a finger in diameter, and handed one to Matt and Thomas. Matt studied the gift. It appeared to be bone or ivory. Thomas' face broke into a broad smile. Eben explained, "These are called oosiks. You saw them used last night for the drumming. They are the bone found in the sex organ of a bull walrus. We believe the oosik carries great power. They will bring you boys good fortune. It's our way to thank you."

They loaded the Herkie quickly. The athletes simply walked up the ramp that formed the rear door to the airplane's large cargo bay. After a short hop to Galena where two pallets of cargo were off-loaded, there was a longer flight to Fairbanks. An hour later the pilot banked and descended across the Cook Inlet on his final approach to Elmendorf Air Force Base near downtown Anchorage. Although the plane landed at 4:00, the sun was below the horizon and the lights of Anchorage blazed as the biathletes were met on the tarmac by an air force bus.

It took thirty minutes to negotiate the commuter traffic leaving Elmendorf and rush hour in downtown Anchorage. When the bus pulled into the Baranof Motor Inn, Matt was exhausted but relieved to be back at the team's headquarters. The athletes shuffled off the bus, each hauling a backpack or rifle box into the brisk air. Immediately, they were surrounded by an insistent, shouting crowd.

"What's your name, son? Were you hurt in the crash? How does all this affect your chances to make the Olympic Team?" The speaker was an overweight, middle-aged man. A ball-point pen was poised above a spiral-bound steno pad.

Matt stared at the reporter, confused.

"Jesus, Harry, give the kid a break, he's probably still in shock." The second guy was younger and taller. A heavy case hung from a broad strap over his right shoulder. A cord from the case led to a microphone in his left hand, which also held a sheet of paper. He held the paper to his face, "Let's see…you must be Burl Palmer, or Brett Adams, or Matthew Johnson?"

"Matt Johnson," was the only response Matt could muster.

"Ah, okay, Matt! I'm Rodney Hammerfest with KYAK Radio Sports. I wonder if I could ask you a couple of questions?"

Before Matt could respond, someone in the crowd shouted, "There's Sandy Stonington. Oh, my gosh!"

Sandy had waited in the bus while the other athletes disembarked, hoping to slip through the frenzy unnoticed. There were gasps as she stepped from the bus and her swollen, distorted face was illuminated by the halogen lighting.

"Sandy, Sandy, over here! Is there any permanent damage to your eye? Isn't that your shooting eye? Will you be able to…."

"Hold it, hold it, that's enough!" Although Matt couldn't see him amid the crush of reporters, he recognized the shrill voice of Stanley Reimer. "No more questions out here. Let the athletes get off the bus and inside. We have the Kodiak Room set up for a press conference. I know some of you are working against deadlines, so if you'll cooperate we'll do our best to get your interviews. Now please, let the athletes through!"

"Sandy, did you think you were going to die?" one reporter couldn't resist.

"Please!" Stanley shouted in the direction of the question. "We have refreshments waiting for you in the Kodiak Room. The press conference will begin in fifteen minutes."

Stanley stepped forward, grabbed Sandy by the elbow, and pushed her through the throng. Matt and the other athletes were abandoned as the reporters pushed to get through the large glass doors of the Motor Inn. Like a school of tropical fish, the reporters milled aimlessly in the lobby until they were directed to the Kodiak Room.

A young Asian woman behind the reception desk held up a fistful of room keys. Burl Palmer and John Miller left the other athletes with the gear to handle registration. When they returned, Burl issued the keys and John explained, "The girl at the desk will watch our stuff until it can be delivered to our rooms. Stan's instructions are to clean up, and return to the Kodiak Room for the press conference. Oh, and wear your white National Team sweater."

Matt took his key and headed down the hall with his rifle box. He could feel his stomach beginning to churn. Maybe it was hunger, or maybe it was his usual fear of aggravating Stan the Man. Matt had been involved in the plane crash, so he assumed Stan wanted him at the press conference, but since he wasn't a member of the National Team, he had no team sweater.

Matt stopped in front of room 128 and was pleased to see Thomas Oksoktaruk, equally loaded down, stop in the hall behind him.

"You in here, too?"

Thomas nodded.

"Great! I was praying they wouldn't stick me with the Snake again."

Thomas nodded knowingly, "I roomed with him a couple of years ago. Not much fun."

Matt set down his rifle box and slipped off his coat. He had been wearing his knit ski hat since before dawn, and when he threw it on the bed, his hair remained flattened to his skull. He remembered the large patch of shaved skin on the back of his head, bisected by stitches. He reached for the hat and put it back on. "Naw, that looks like hell."

"Don't worry about it, Matt. They're expecting you guys to look banged up. You don't want to disappoint the press."

Moments later, the two roommates were walking down the hall toward the lobby.

"God damn it, I thought I told you to wear a team sweater!" Stan's voice behind them seemed an octave higher than normal.

Matt turned and waited for Stan and Sandy to catch up. Sandy was frowning, but the white team sweater emphasized her deeply tanned face. It also highlighted the rainbow of colors spiraling from her swollen right eye. The row of stitches formed a neat line from her eyelid to her forehead.

"Oh, it's you," Stan snarled. "Jesus H. Christ, do I have to do everything myself? Sandy, you and the Eskimo head down to the press conference. Tell them I'll be there in a couple of minutes. Johnson, come with me."

Stan unlocked the equipment storage room, pawed through boxes until he found a large team sweater, tossed it at Matt, and barked, "Let's go, you can put it on while we walk."

As they entered the Kodiak Room, the glare of bright lights was blinding. Sandy was engulfed by a crush of reporters and cameramen, jostling for position. Stan sprang into action, pushing through the group, "Thank you, thank you for coming. Now if you'll all just take a seat, I'll get the athletes up front here and we can field your questions."

Once again, Stan held Sandy's elbow and directed her through the crowd. The journalists followed, filling the chairs facing a long table at the end of the room. The camera crews flipped off their lights and scrambled to reposition their equipment.

Matt was listening to Reimer's insistent, "Take your seats, please, find a seat and we'll get started," when a strong hand gripped his arm. He turned to see Vladimir Kobelev, whose weathered face showed concern. "Matthew, *Harasho?* You are okay? How is the head?"

"It's not bad. Pretty good headache and a punk haircut, but that's about it. Have you been to see Roger?"

"*Da, da,* of course. Must be he is recovering quickly, he teases the nurses without rest. I'm sorry for this circus, but Stanley must promote biathlon while the press is interested. We will talk later."

"Okay, Vlad."

Once the athletes joined Stan at the head table and the journalists were seated, Reimer stood to address his audience. The high intensity lights flashed, video cameras whirred, and pens scribbled as Stan reviewed the events of the previous days, plowed through an overview of the ABF's grass roots development program, and continued with an explanation of the Olympic biathlon events.

"Excuse me, Mr. Reimer. We'd like to ask the athletes some questions before we file our stories."

Somewhat crestfallen, Stan sat down.

"Sandy, I'm Betty Moerlein from the *Anchorage Daily News*. Do you think your injury will prevent you from competing in the Olympic Trials?"

Sandy looked steadily at the reporter through her good left eye. "The doctor in Unalakleet didn't think there was any damage to the eye itself, but because of the swelling I can't tell for sure. We still have five days before the first race and I'm optimistic the swelling will go down by then. One thing's for certain, it could have been a lot worse."

"Miss Lindstrom, I'm Eric Erickson from the *Minneapolis Star Tribune*. Can you describe for us what went through your mind when you first became aware that the aircraft was crashing?"

Jenny Lindstrom shrank from the glare of the harsh lights as the cameras whirred. The color drained from her cheeks, "Ah...Ah...I don't remember much except Roger crashing into the bulkhead under the baggage. Then I remember seeing Sandy's face covered with blood. It was awful." Her shoulders began to tremble and she covered her face with her hands. The cameras zoomed in for close-ups. Matt noticed Stan suppressing a smile. Vladimir Kobelev pushed his way through the journalists to the front of the room, scowling at Stan as he approached the head table. Then the big coach lifted Jenny from her seat and guided her from the room.

Stan recovered quickly, "I'm sorry, folks, she's obviously still upset about the accident, and Coach Kobelev is very protective about...."

"I have a question for Burl Palmer," a voice said. "We understand you weren't hurt in the crash, while Roger Edwards and Brett Adams appear to be out of the trials, if not for the whole season. How do their injuries change the lineup of the Olympic Team?"

"What the hell kind of a question is that?" Burl glared at the reporter.

"Well, this year's Biathlon Team is expected to be the most competitive we've ever sent to Europe. The two casualties on the men's side must change the tryout picture. I just want to know what you think."

Burl was visibly angry. "I haven't thought about it at all! Brett,

Roger and I have been on the team together since the Lillehammer Games. We've roomed with each other at dozens of World Cup events. We didn't know for more than twenty-four hours after the crash whether Roger would live or die. And you're thinking the first thing through my mind is how much better my chances are of making the Olympic Team?"

Stan was on his feet, flapping his arms, "That's enough, Burl! I'm sorry, sir. You understand that the athletes are under considerable stress from their ordeal."

"Sandy, Beverly Schmidt from *Sports Illustrated*. Let me change the subject if I might. With the Olympics a few weeks away, there is renewed speculation about the use of illegal drugs during major international events. How much doping goes on at the Winter Olympics?"

Sandy thought a moment before answering. "I believe that unethical performance enhancement routinely takes place at major events. In some cases the doping occurs months before the Olympics; the use of steroids during off-season training, for example. A second problem in endurance sports is blood doping."

"Could you explain that?" The reporter interjected.

"I'm not an expert, but it involves withdrawing a unit of blood weeks before a major competition, then reinfusing it before a major event. In the meantime, the athlete's body has reestablished a normal blood level, so the additional unit just before the big race is like turbocharging a sports car. There's no foolproof method to test for blood doping, and the performance advantage in distance competitions can be dramatic.

"How much of this stuff goes on?" the writer asked.

"It's impossible to tell," Sandy continued, "but I suspect the bigger the event, like the World Championships or the Olympics, the greater the temptation. These days a medal can mean hundreds of thousands of dollars in endorsement contracts. I don't think anybody really knows how much cheating goes on. But I can tell you it's discouraging as hell to be racing well in World Cup events, then at the Olympics find yourself two minutes behind a dozen competitors who haven't beaten you all season."

Beverly Schmidt almost shouted, "Are you saying that there are dozens of biathletes who are doping illegally at the Olympics?"

"No, I'm not," Sandy answered firmly. "I said it was impossible to tell. Most athletes peak for the big races like the Olympics, and every so often someone can have an inspired race. But I'm also convinced a significant number of competitors cheat. What is a significant number?

If I place fifth in a big race and two women whom I've beaten all season finish ahead of me by blood doping, then two is a significant number."

"I think I should add something here," Stan was on his feet. "The International Olympic Committee has been vigilant in its efforts to protect the purity of the Olympic movement. There have always been those who would win at all costs, but as soon as a form of unethical performance enhancement is uncovered, the IOC moves quickly to ban its use and penalize those who seek an unfair advantage. There are many reasons why the world's best athletes occasionally fail to achieve their goals. Sometimes in their disappointment it's easy to cast the blame on a situation which is impossible to evaluate. I'm afraid Sandy exaggerates the problem. In the past two decades, at literally hundreds of international biathlon competitions around the world, only a handful of athletes have tested positive for illegal drug use. I just don't think we have a drug problem in biathlon. Now we have time for one more question."

Stan smiled benevolently at Sandy. "Whatever you say, Stan," Sandy mumbled. Matt could hear the fatigue in her voice.

"One last question for Sandy. I'm Vickie Chang, *Women's Sport and Fitness* magazine. Sandy, I see on your bio sheet that you'll be thirty-five soon and this is your third Olympics. Do you ever feel like you've put your life on hold while you've been competing; you know, marriage, a family, a career?"

"For the best part of a decade I've been one of the top ten women in the world at what I do," Sandy answered. "Unfortunately, it doesn't happen to pay very well. But just because I haven't won an Olympic medal or had my picture on a Wheaties box, doesn't mean it's been a waste of time. I'll quit racing when I'm no longer progressing and when I don't enjoy it any more. Besides, I might not be cut out to be somebody's wife or somebody's mother."

"Well, thank you, Sandy!" Stan was back on his feet. "We can always count on Sandy Stonington for a candid answer. Why don't we wrap this up now?"

Matt was relieved to be rooming with Thomas. They both preferred reading to watching television or arguing obscure points of skiing technique. Matt drew five small dots on white athletic tape and stuck the tape at eye level on the back of the door as a dry-firing target.

Matt believed in dry-firing and soon had Thomas believing in it, too. Each night, they took turns aiming at the black dots, growing accustomed to the smooth, metallic sound of operating the precision bolt, pausing for the dot to settle in the rifle's front aperture, and then the crisp snap of the firing pin on the empty chamber.

On Monday evening, before the first tryout race, the Kodiak Room was filled with athletes, coaches and officials gathered for the first seeding meeting. Stanley Reimer opened the meeting by thanking the organizing committee for their hard work and warm hospitality. Then he turned the meeting over to Alan Hostatler, the chief of competition.

"It's my pleasure to welcome you to the Biathlon Olympic Trials here in Anchorage. We are proud to have you in our city, and proud to send those of you who are successful on to Italy and the Olympics."

"There are some aspects of racing in Anchorage that may be new to you. First of all, the open bolt policy will be in effect and will be enforced! In other words, keep the bolt of your rifle open at all times, except when it's on your back. We don't want any accidents."

"We also have some local ground rules regarding the moose. In spite of the volume of recreational skiing and competitions hosted at Kincaid, we have had surprisingly few encounters with our shaggy friends. That's not to say the potential doesn't exist. Here's how we deal with the situation. During your events, we will have checkers stationed at all the trail junctions and areas where the moose hang out. If a moose actually obstructs the course, and a racer is delayed, the checker will record the incident and the racer's final time will be adjusted. Any questions?"

Hostatler was followed by another volunteer who read a detailed weather report promising a perfect day for racing on Tuesday: clear skies, calm winds, and temperatures well below freezing. The athletes grinned at each other. The volunteer went on to mention, however, that a low-pressure system was approaching Anchorage from the North Pacific, bringing snowfall and the possibility of high winds.

Then Dr. Mary Manheimer addressed the athletes. "Those of you who have competed in previous Olympic Trials know that the USOC requires doping control after each of our tryout events. We will test the top three finishers and a competitor selected at random. If you are to be tested, you will be met at the finish by a medical steward who will escort you to the doping control room. Have a teammate take care of your equipment, because the testing can take an hour or more."

"Your medical escort will accompany you to our doping control room, where Roosevelt Brown and I will be waiting. There will be plenty of soda, juice, and water to drink. As soon as you can produce a twelve-ounce urine sample, you will be accompanied into the rest room and observed as you give the sample. Then Rosie and I will guide you through the process of dividing your sample into A and B containers, labeling, sealing, and finally packaging the two samples."

"When all the samples for the day's events have been gathered, Rosie and I will deliver them to the airport. The samples will be shipped by commercial airliner to the USOC's West Coast testing lab in Los Angeles, where the A samples will be analyzed. We will receive the results before breakfast on the day following the race. In the unlikely event of a positive test result, we will inform the coaches and the athlete in question. The athlete must then authorize the testing of the B sample. Do you have any questions?"

Vladimir Kobelev wrapped up the meeting with some final instructions for the athletes. "Most of you participate in team selection before. This is nothing new. We are having two sprints and two distance races. You must count three results. Everybody understand? Anybody has questions? *Harasho!* Do your best."

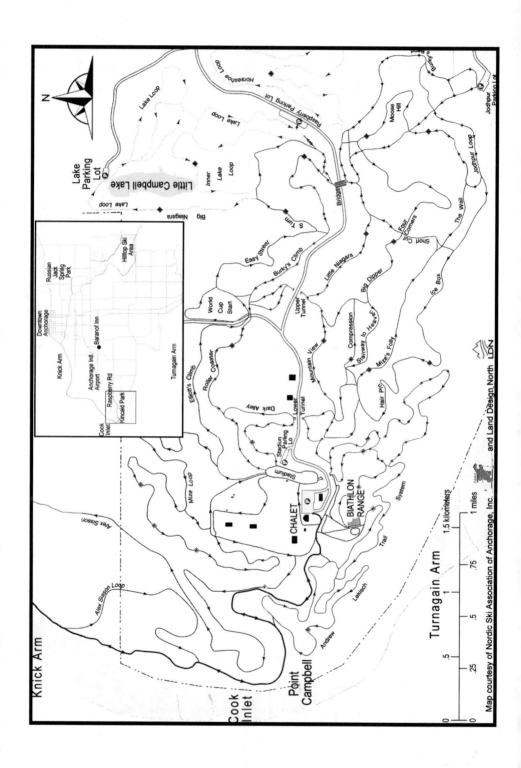

Map courtesy of Nordic Ski Association of Anchorage, Inc. and Land Design North, LDN

Sabotage at the Trials

8

At 6:30 on the morning of the first tryout race, when Matt headed out for a jog, the stars were still bright overhead. Forty minutes later he entered the dining room as some of the women, dressed in their Lycra racing suits, were leaving. Trudy Wilson had her blonde hair woven into a braid, her striking good looks skillfully enhanced with makeup.

"Oh, Matt," she gushed. "Wish me luck! I'm so nervous. There'll be reporters and even TV crews out there today. I'll probably ski into the range and pee my pants!"

She wrapped her arms around Matt and planted a warm kiss on his lips. Then with a wink, she pranced from the dining room. Matt watched her go, trying to recover his composure. Trudy had already pulled the Lycra racing bib over her tight racing uniform. Matt smiled, anticipating the excitement she would generate when she skied onto the shooting range.

As he approached the buffet table, Matt noticed Sandy smiling at him. The swelling around her right eye was subsiding, but the rainbow on her cheek had intensified.

"Hey, you'd better watch out, Rookie, or Trudy's going to have you for lunch!" Sandy was wearing blue jeans and an Albertville Olympics sweatshirt. Matt grabbed a bowl of oatmeal and orange juice and joined Sandy in the otherwise empty dining room.

"Yeah, I know. She's so good-looking it's scary. I'm too much of a woodchuck to tangle with a girl who moves that fast."

"She's not a bad kid. I've roomed with her on a couple of trips. She had a real tough childhood; an alcoholic father who abandoned her when she was six. I think this constant flirting is all about a need for approval. You watch yourself, though. She's left a trail of broken hearts, and she's after you."

"Thanks for the warning, but I think I'm already history. Hey, aren't you racing today?"

"Nope, I figured I'd give the eye a couple more days to recover. The stitches come out tomorrow."

"But that means you count the final three races. You won't have one to throw out."

"Right, but that shouldn't be a problem, as long as they don't cancel one of the last three races. Anyway, I'm thinking ahead to the World Cups in Europe. I don't want to burn out here and be a basket case when we're across the pond."

"Well, I guess I'd better go wax my skis." Matt picked up his bowl and juice glass.

"What're you using?" Sandy asked.

"It sounds like it's going to stay cold enough for Start Green, or Rex Green."

"Yeah, except that Kincaid is nearly surrounded by water. If I were racing today I'd give Rex Blue a try. It might slide better in the higher humidity."

Matt thanked her for the tip. He inspected the thermometer every day, but he never considered the humidity. Waxing was not a complicated process for Matt, because he had only two decent pairs of race skis. In West Yellowstone some of the athletes spent hours preparing their skis. Matt's dad had taught him to keep it simple, partly because the new fluorocarbon waxes were obscenely expensive, and partly because focusing on a limited selection taught him to learn the gliding capabilities of each wax. Matt ironed his first choice, Start Green, on his newer skis, and out of respect for Sandy, tried Rex Blue on his second pair.

At eleven, Matt claimed a seat in Gopher's van for the fifteen-minute ride to Kincaid. The air was cold, the sky crystal clear and the Chugach Mountains loomed brilliant white. There was little conversation in the van as each athlete focused on his own thoughts.

When the parking lot for the Nordic Center came into view, someone exclaimed, "Jesus, look at the cars! You think they know there's a biathlon race here today? Maybe they got it confused with figure skating." There were groans of agreement, but when the athletes entered the chalet to stash their backpacks and rifle boxes, they were surrounded by eager spectators. Kids clamoring for autographs was a totally new experience for Matt. Several media people recognized him from the press conference and interviewed him while he prepared his rifle and loaded his clips.

He finally escaped when the early starters from the women's race returned to the lodge, ruddy-faced and sweating in spite of the cold. As he approached the finish area, he spotted Trudy surrounded by reporters and a film crew. Even when exhausted she looked glamorous.

Sergeant Jankowski assigned Matt a zeroing target, but suggested he ski a loop to warm up since the range wouldn't reopen for another twenty minutes. Matt carefully placed his rifle in the rack on the firing line, double-checking to be certain that he left the bolt open. Then he took off his warmup pants and headed out on the hilly loop marked with red flags. His skis felt great. It was hard to miss with Start Green in cold snow.

When he returned, the range was open for zeroing. He retrieved his rifle and glanced at Jankowski who was waiting at his spotting scope.

"Shoot on number four, lower target," Jankowski shouted after checking his clipboard. Matt took his time easing into the prone position, pounding dents into the firm snow to stabilize his elbows. He systematically checked the limp range flags. The shooting stadium at Kincaid faced northeast. As an afterthought, Matt glanced at the bright noontime sun, low over the Chugach Mountains to his right. He remembered his dad mentioning that a click into a bright sun was good insurance, so he pulled his cheek off the stock and carefully twisted the windage adjustment knob clockwise until he heard the metallic snap.

His dad had also taught him another trick from the old days. After Matt had been shooting for three years, his dad explained that the relatively consistent setting on his sights represented Matt's normal zero. He might change those adjustments for weather conditions or changing light, but after each race he returned the sights to his normal zero. To make the zero easier to spot at a glance, Matt's dad carefully painted a delicate red stripe of fingernail polish across the graduated scales of the sights. A quick glance at the red stripe and Matt could tell if he had made a prior correction.

By taking a click into the sun, Matt offset the red stripe on the horizontal scale slightly. Satisfied with the adjustment, he wiggled back into his prone position and confidently squeezed off three shots with a crisp cadence. Then he rolled to his left side and looked back at the Sarge.

"Damn, that's a nice group! Did you take a click into the sun?" Matt nodded. "Well, those three are interlocking, dead center. Don't touch a thing!" Matt smiled and got to his feet. "You shoot like that in the race, Matt, and you're going to steal some old timer's place on the Olympic Team."

"Thanks, Sarge, I'll see what I can do."

Matt felt optimistic, despite having drawn starting position number one. In a sprint competition, entrants often gambled by racing into the range full speed, hoping to hit all their targets in spite of a skyrocketing pulse. Every miss meant a trip around the 150M penalty loop, which was not only physical punishment, but was psychologically grueling. If a top contender approached the range and spotted a rival skiing penalty loops, it could inspire them to shoot clean. Skiing round and round while other racers shot clean and returned directly to the course was seriously demoralizing to the penalized athlete.

As race time loomed, the range became a storm of activity. Most of the men were clambering for target assignments so they could zero their rifles. Coaches squinted through scopes and shouted sight corrections. The press had captured sound bites as the women finished, and then followed the racers to the chalet to warm up. Now the reporters and photographers were regrouping at the range to cover the men's event. There were hundreds of spectators strung along the range and the trail and lining the difficult climbs.

Matt returned his old Anschutz to the rifle rack at the rear of the range and opened the bolt. He checked his watch to be certain he had enough time to ski the green loop before the start. His skis felt fast, but he switched to the second pair so he could at least tell Sandy he had tried them. The snow was cold and dry, the air temperature still in the low twenties, but the second pair seemed surprisingly fast. As he cruised the loop, imagining how he would take each turn during the race, the skis seemed even quicker. By the time he returned to the range, he was struggling to decide which pair to choose.

With only a few minutes remaining before the start, he skated to a gentle downhill not far from the stadium. He scratched a mark in the snow with his ski pole, aligned his boots to the mark, and began a gentle glide down the incline. He made another mark in the snow where he came to a stop. He skated back up the hill and repeated the process twice. Then he switched to the first pair, waxed with Start Green. He repeated the glide test. No question, the Rex Blue that Sandy recommended was better!

He could hear the starter warning the early racers, so he returned to the range. Stashing his warmups and extra skis next to a snow fence, he retrieved his rifle and checked his clips.

"Five minutes 'til the start. Numbers one, two, three, four and five, you should have your skis and rifles marked, and be in the starting pen," the announcer barked. There was a jostling at the entrance to the pen, but the big number one on Matt's chest did wonders.

"Okay, number one, right up here, we don't want you to miss your start," a volunteer took Matt's rifle, handed it to a second official who weighed the trigger and applied a bright orange sticker to the stock, indicating that the rifle had passed the safety check. In the meantime, the first official inspected Matt to ensure that his skis and poles conformed to international rules, and that any corporate logos on his racing uniform were within the international guidelines. The official smiled at Matt as he scribbled on his skis with a dark blue marker, "Well, son, no danger of disqualification from violating the corporate sponsorship rules. But if you race well here, you'll have some trademarks on that suit before February. Have a good race."

"Number one in the gate, number two on deck, then three…" the voice on the loudspeaker continued. "Ladies and gentlemen, in just a moment we will start the first men's competition of the United States Olympic Biathlon Team Trials. We have sixty-seven racers today, representing eighteen states from across the nation. Six of these men will be chosen in the best three out of four competition to represent the United States at the Winter Olympics next month in the South Tirol region of Italy."

"The first competitor on the course this afternoon is Matthew Johnson from Thetford, Vermont. Matthew had strong results at the Nationals last spring in Lake Placid, and is one of several non-National Team athletes invited to compete in these tryouts. He is eighteen years old… and hey, how about this, Matthew was born right here in Anchorage!"

That announcement drew a cheer from the crowd and Matt smiled back, trying to conceal his nervousness. He slid into the chute. The starter, bundled up like Santa Claus, placed a mittened hand on Matt's shoulder, "So, born in Anchorage. Your folks must have been in the military. Fifteen seconds!"

"Yeah, my dad was a chopper pilot at Fort Rich."

"Well, in that case, welcome home! Ten seconds…. You have fun out there today. Five…four…three… two…one…GO!"

The official withdrew his hand as Matt leaned on his poles and accelerated down the starting ramp. The trail was lined with spectators waving small American and Alaska state flags. They hollered as Matt skated from the stadium. Soon he was powering up the first long climb, and he could feel the familiar throbbing in his head and neck. He wondered if he'd started too fast, or if he was just pumped up by the excitement. He'd find out soon enough.

His skis felt fast, but he wouldn't know for certain until he skied alongside another racer. The red loop was the most challenging at Kincaid. Matt had to concentrate to pick the fastest line on the downhills and to maintain his momentum on the climbs. He was only vaguely aware of the heavily bundled checkers at trail junctions. Soon he rocketed down the roller coaster descent toward the far point of the red loop, then rounded the airplane turn and began the long climb back up the ridge. Although the trail was nearly flawless, he almost fell twice after catching a ski on a frozen clod of snow left by a moose.

When he reached the top of the ridge he was heaving and gasping. He braced for the tricky S-turns leading toward the range. The fast, technical descent was not a rest. Then there was half a kilometer of gradual climb back to the stadium.

As he began climbing to his first prone shooting, the trail was lined with screaming spectators and he could feel adrenaline coursing through his body. He skated to the firing line and another cheer rose into the frozen air. Swinging the rifle off his back, he was acutely aware of his heaving chest. He had definitely come in too fast. He dropped and rammed his elbows into the cold snow. Through the sights the target was bouncing more than usual. He closed his eyes and took three deep breaths.

He was remotely aware of cheering as another competitor skied to a firing position. Okay, enough screwing around, got to shoot 'em, he thought, as he took up slack on the trigger. The sight picture looked good…

CRACK.. As the aperture settled, the sight picture cleared. "Damn!" The first target hadn't fallen! That shot felt good in spite of the high pulse.

He concentrated on the second target, took a breath, relaxed, waited for the rifle to settle and squeezed…Crack! "Shit!" Another miss. "That one felt okay, too!"

He lifted his cheek from the stock and glanced at the wind flags. Still calm. He took more deep breaths and banged deeper dents in the snow for his elbows. Another skier passed behind him. A shot split the air followed by shouts from the spectators.

He settled on the center bull, a breath, good sight picture, squeeze, CRACK…."What the hell, *another* miss!" He heard a low "Ouuuuuh" from the crowd.

He rolled from his stomach to his left side to inspect his sights. The nail polish stripe confirmed the adjustment he had made zeroing. He glanced back to where the coaches were standing and spotted Sarge staring back at him. Jankowski shrugged his shoulders and turned up the palms of his mittened hands. Matt rolled back into position.

Now the other athletes were coming into the range steadily, at least two were firing, and from the crowd's cheering, they were hitting targets. Matt focused on the fourth black disk and squeezed off the shot. Nothing changed in his sight picture, still a row of five black dots! He tried to suppress the panic rising in his throat. *Settle down,* he reminded himself, *even one hit saves a trip around the loop.* He shifted his position and squeezed off the last shot. CRACK….

As he scrambled to his feet and fumbled for his ski poles, he stared at the five black dots on the target line. His face burned with embarrassment as he skated to the entrance of the penalty loop, which was surrounded by wildly applauding spectators. The volunteer at the entrance held up a gloved hand with all fingers extended and shouted, "Five loops. Number one has five loops."

It seemed like Matt was on the loop forever. Other athletes came and went for one or two loops, but Matt kept skating around and around. After his third lap, the people along the fence seemed embarrassed and ignored him, favoring racers with fewer penalties.

Finally, he finished his fifth lap and skated back to the course. After an eternity on the penalty loop he was struggling. Other competitors passed him.

He forced himself to be optimistic. The skis still felt good. Other guys were bound to have problems shooting standing. Five penalties might not be hopeless if enough other guys also had trouble.

He approached the range for standing with three other competitors. As he steadied the sights on the bouncing bull's-eye he forced his mind to forget the horrible memory of the five prone targets left unscathed.

He breathed, settled the rifle into his shoulder, and took up slack on the trigger. CRACK! *Right down the pipe!* He resisted the temptation to pull up his head and check for the hit. He settled the sights on the second bull, and was relieved to notice white where the first target had been. "Breathe, relax, squeeze, let it settle…" CRACK…The black dot remained.

"Sonofabitch, that one was good, I know it was. Why the hell aren't these targets falling?" He could tell from the clamor that the others had finished and left the range.

He shuffled a little on his skis to bring the third bull into his natural point of aim. "Steady…. Don't hold too long…looks good…." CRACK! Another miss. "Damn, what am I doing wrong?"

The fourth shot was yet another miss, and Matt was so disgusted he almost threw the final shot away. But training and discipline took over, he settled into position and hit the fifth target. Matt felt humiliated. Never before had he shot so poorly. His two standing hits actually made things worse. After shooting prone he fantasized about faulty mechanical targets, but the two standing hits confirmed that the targets were not the problem. Only pride kept him from skiing to the fence and taking off his racing bib.

This wasn't a bad race, this was a disaster, and at the Olympic Trials! When he finally left the penalty loop for his last segment of skiing, he was emotionally crushed and physically spent. The hills seemed endless, and he struggled to keep from stumbling.

Cresting a steep rise, a voice behind him screamed, "TRACK!" Matt was so startled he actually jumped off the snow. When he recovered his balance, he glanced back to see Tony Morgoloni, looking ferocious.

"I said 'track' you asshole, get the hell out of the way!" They were both gliding fast enough to crouch into aerodynamic tucks. Matt stepped to the right margin of the groomed trail, giving the Snake plenty of room on the left. But when it became clear that Tony was not going to overtake him on the twisting descent, Matt dropped into a tuck, and immediately pulled away. Seconds later, the hill bottomed out. Matt carried his speed smoothly through the transition and well up the long climb to the ridge. He heard Tony's frantic breathing behind him, and again skated to the side of the trail to let the Snake pass.

Hunched over like a troll, Morgoloni attacked the hill. Pulling even with Matt, he snarled, "Asshole." As he whipped his poles forward for the next stride, he swung his right arm wide and slammed Matt in the left shoulder, almost knocking the younger skier to the snow.

Matt forgot about his disastrous shooting and charged after the Snake, but Morgoloni easily pulled away. Damn, I've never seen anyone ski uphill so fast, Matt thought.

He was ready to settle things with Tony once and for all. The Snake had knocked him cold and sleazed $600 from him after the West Yellowstone tour. Now he was throwing punches on the course. Matt charged through the finish line, gasping for breath and scanning the exhausted racers for Morgoloni.

The Snake was at the end of the equipment check area, slinging his rifle back on. As Matt headed for a confrontation, an official grabbed his shoulder. "Whoa, hold on here. We've got to check your rifle, son."

Matt paused as the officials tested his trigger and inspected the chamber for live rounds. "Okay, number one, you're clear. How'd it go today?" Matt struggled to be polite, "Pretty grim, lots of trouble on the range."

"Too bad. But maybe you worked the bugs out in the first one. You still got three more chances. Good luck on Thursday."

"Thanks."

With his rifle returned, Matt looked for Morgoloni. He spotted the Snake surrounded by reporters who were scribbling in their notebooks. A TV cameraman was pushing other athletes out of the way so he could get a better angle on the Snake. Tony was beaming. His face was still red and beaded with sweat, but the fierce intensity Matt had seen on the trail had given way to confident charm. Matt knew there was no chance of confronting Tony now, so he tried to calm down as he took in the scene.

Matt moved to retrieve his warmups and heard Morgoloni's voice over the clamor, "Hey, Rookie! Tough day on the range, huh? Looked like you owned the penalty loop. Welcome to the big leagues, kid. And you'd better watch yourself on the trail or you're going to get run over!"

Other competitors were finishing and the pen was congested with exhausted athletes. Matt wanted to get away from everyone. He left the finish area and walked over to the shooting range for his warmups. He spotted Sergeant Jankowski in the coach's box, packing his gear. Jankowski motioned Matt over.

"I don't know what happened, Sarge. I've never shot that badly before in a race. I feel like packing up and heading home."

"Let me take a look at your rifle, Matt."

Matt swung the Anschutz off his back and handed it over the fence to the rifle coach.

"Where'd you learn the old fingernail polish trick?" The Sarge was inspecting the sights on Matt's rifle.

"My dad showed me. He learned it in the Biathlon Unit when he was stationed up here. He said the nail polish would let me tell at a glance where I was, relative to my zero."

"Your dad was right! It's a great trick and can save the day when wind conditions vary. But there's one disadvantage. When I zeroed you before the race, you took one click right into the sun, correct?"

"Yup, and you can see the slight break in the line of nail polish, showing I'm one click off my normal race zero."

"Okay! Because you were the first competitor in the race to shoot prone, I got a good look at where your shots went. Do you have any sense of where you lost them?"

"That's the crazy part, Sarge, they all felt okay. I had a good position, and figured when I squeezed them off, they were hits. I thought it might have been a target malfunction."

"There's nothing wrong with the targets. Every one of your misses was out the top at twelve o'clock. Even the three standing shots you missed were out the top. Now look at this," Sergeant Jankowski held Matt's rifle between them, the sights just below their faces. "Look carefully at the elevation adjustment knob." Matt stared at the rifle. Everything looked okay, he had made no elevation change from his normal zero, the stripe of nail polish was straight and unbroken. He looked at Sarge in confusion.

"You took one click right, and that's on. But you didn't change the elevation from your normal zero, correct?" Matt nodded. "How many clicks to one complete revolution of the adjustment knob?"Jankowski asked.

"Well," Matt thought out loud, "these are the old sights so there would be ten clicks to a complete revolution."

"And how far would those ten clicks move the strike of the bullet at fifty meters?" asked the Sarge.

"I think twelve clicks moves the bullet the diameter of the prone bull," Matt answered.

"Right!" The Sarge was getting excited. "And if you were zeroed before the race, then added ten clicks up, where would your shots go?"

"They'd go out the top, I'd miss the prone bull by half the diameter of the scoring ring."

"Right again, and that's just where your shots went! Now look at these sights again."

Matt took the rifle from Jankowski and studied the sights. "Jesus, Sarge, the elevation is up ten clicks from my normal zero!"

"That's right, Matt. At a glance, the fingernail polish lines up, so it looks like the elevation is right on your zero, but in fact you are one complete revolution high!"

"But Sarge, I never made this sight correction. I can't remember a time when the wind was so bad I had to take ten clicks in one direction."

"Oh, I know, Matt. You didn't make that change at all. Somebody else made it for you. Somebody who's been around this sport for awhile, who desperately wants to make the Olympic Team, and is afraid that you are going to hurt his chances."

Matt was stunned. Jankowski was saying that another athlete had sabotaged his sights to take him out of the running for the Olympic Team. He remembered the endless publicity about the Tonya Harding/Nancy Kerrigan scandal during the winter of the 1994 Olympics in Lillehammer. But there was so much money at stake in figure skating; unless you were a self-promoter like Oliver Wainwright, nobody made any money at biathlon. There wasn't much to gain except a pile of Olympic Team uniforms and a trip to Europe. In fact, most American biathletes went into debt pursuing their sport.

"After you zeroed, Matt, what did you do with your rifle?" Jankowski continued.

"Well, let's see…I put it in the rifle rack over there and skied the green loop to warm up."

"So you were out skiing for fifteen minutes and the rifle was here on the range while dozens of other athletes were zeroing."

"Yeah, that's right. Damn, Sarge, is there anything I can do about this, file a protest or something?"

"I'm afraid not, Matt. We have no idea who tampered with your sights. But, it's not all bad. For starters, he tipped his hand early. Nobody, not even Ragnar is a sure bet for this team. The cheater could have waited for the third or fourth race, and could have pulled his dirty trick then. Now we know what he's up to, even if we don't know who he is. For the remainder of these tryouts, don't let that rifle out of your sight! And another thing, Matt, remember that properly zeroed, all of the prone shots and at least four of the standing, would have been hits.

"Don't bother looking at today's results, they'll just get you discouraged. Your Olympic Trials start on Thursday and you need three good races to make it. Now let's forget this race and focus on the next three."

"I'll try, Sarge. I guess it's a relief to know that I'm not shooting that badly."

"Matt, you can be a world class biathlete. Now kick ass in the next three races, and brush up on your Italian!"

Matt took a dry shirt from his backpack, then pulled on his warmups. He swung the rifle to his back and headed out on the green loop for a warm-down. It was beautiful skiing. Even though he was still disappointed by his performance, it was a relief to know his shooting hadn't gone out the window.

It was dark when Matt caught Gopher's last van back to the Baranof. "Tough day on the range, eh, Rookie?" Jimmy Clark had been around athletes long enough to pick up on their moods.

"Yeah, I'll say."

"I've never seen you shoot like that before. What happened, Olympic fever?"

"I'm not sure, but I don't think it will happen again. Sarge got me straightened out."

"He's a damn good shooting coach. You know he goes to Camp Perry every summer on the all-guard team and usually wins? He's been one of the top small-bore shooters in the country for years."

"Yeah, I learned that today. Hey, how'd it come out? I haven't seen any results."

"Well, the Snake hauled butt. He won by over thirty seconds, even with two loops. Oliver was second, Burl third, Heikki just nipped Ragnar for fourth, and Oksoktaruk surprised everybody by sneaking into sixth. You were pretty far back. I guess you probably know that."

"Yeah, I got dizzy on the penalty loop. But Thursday's another day."

"You said it, Matt. And this is biathlon! Anything can happen... and it usually does."

Back in his room at the Baranof, Matt congratulated his roommate.

"So Thomas, you've got to be happy with sixth place."

"You bet I'm happy. There's a bunch of guys who can do okay when the conditions are great, like they were today; fast skiing and no wind. I was surprised to end up sixth. But you know Matt, I think I can do better, especially if we get some bad weather, real Alaskan cold or a good stiff wind off the inlet. What happened to you?"

Matt told Thomas the whole story, finishing up with Jankowski's instructions never to leave his rifle unattended.

"Damn, Matt! I'd heard rumors of that happening years ago, back in the '72 tryouts, but I thought it was ancient history. I'd better keep an eye on my rifle, too. Thanks for telling me."

"No problem, I just wish I could catch the guy doing it," Matt answered.

On Thursday Matt was up for his run at 6:30. As he stepped through the glass doors of the Baranof, he was almost blown back inside. The wind was whipping the falling snow into wild eddies. Matt headed across the parking lot, running from one circle of light under the high street lamps to the next. When he returned to the room, Thomas was ready for breakfast. Matt had never seen his shy roommate so energized.

"You wait, Matt. You won't believe the whining you'll hear today. But remember, they can't postpone because they've already made airline reservations for Europe on Tuesday. And they can't cancel because Sandy Stonington needs the three races to qualify. You can be pretty sure they'll have the events as scheduled. So everybody else can piss and moan about how unfair it is, and we'll just go out there and make the Olympic Team! Hell, biathlon's a winter sport! Anybody who can't handle a little wind and snow ought to join a bowling league."

As the Alaskan predicted, there was a lot of talk at breakfast about canceling or at least postponing the race. Oliver Wainwright approached Stanley Reimer talking loud enough for everyone to hear, "You know, Stan, this is bullshit if the conditions don't improve by race time! The whole purpose of these tryouts is to pick the best possible Olympic Team, and any idiot knows that's impossible if the wind is howling and the snow is blowing so hard you can't see the freakin' targets."

"That's a decision for the jury, Oliver, you know that," Stan responded.

"Don't give me that shit, Stan. They're responsible for conducting the competitions, but the ABF is responsible to the USOC for a fair selection procedure that places the best American athletes on the team. It's a crapshoot, Stan, and you know it."

Kobelev had been listening to Oliver's outburst. "Wainwright, you waste too much energy on politics! Maybe we race today, maybe not. But I tell you, Olympic biathlon competitions don't always have beautiful, sunshine day. At Sarajevo in '84, we plowing through almost one meter, new powder snow. But you know what, they gave out medals anyway! Somebody won, even in that blizzard. That's biathlon, always different. Maybe tryout in bad weather shows who is ready to race in any conditions."

"Aw, you guys are nuts. I don't know why I waste my time talking to you," Oliver turned and left the dining room. Thomas Oksoktaruk smiled at Matt over his bowl of cereal.

It was a totally different scene at Kincaid Park. There were deep sculptured drifts across the access road and the air was thick with swirling snow. Matt couldn't tell if it was actually falling, or just continually whipped into the air by the wind. When Matt and Thomas reached the range to zero their rifles, they noticed the range flags lashing around the compass. It was still snowing hard enough to limit visibility, but didn't completely obscure the targets.

The roommates approached Sarge who had set up his tripod and was about to attach the spotting scope. "I'll bet you eager bucks are after zeroing assignments. Since you're the first two here, I'll give you a hint. Take a careful look at the flags and tell me what you see."

Matt answered first, "They're blowing all over the place, not from any one direction."

"That's right, Matt. But what else do you see?"

All three studied the snow swirling within the earthen berms that formed the sides and rear of the range. Finally, Thomas spoke up, "It doesn't seem to be blowing as hard in the center of the range as it is at the edges."

"Thataboy! You kids might have some promise after all. The berms cause the wind to act like a whirlpool. If you pick a shooting position near the edge during the race, chances are you'll be dealing with stronger winds. If you pick firing positions nearer the center, it may be more consistent. I wouldn't be surprised, on a day like today, if you'll have to make sight corrections for each stage of shooting. Don't be afraid to do that. Okay, Oksoktaruk, you shoot on target eight, Johnson you shoot on six."

From the moment the starter released his shoulder and yelled "Go," Matt felt isolated in his own world, as if he were the only racer. Due to the heavy snow, there weren't many spectators. The storm continued throughout the competition, enfolding Matt in a quiet world of falling white. He was pleased when he passed other skiers, but because the visibility was limited and everyone was wearing some type of eye protection, it was hard to recognize his fellow competitors.

At the bottom of the depression on the red loop, as he tucked through the transition, he sensed a dark shape on the left edge of the trail. As he began skating up the long climb to the ridge, he noticed a heavy, musty smell. It had to be a bull moose. He risked a quick glance over his shoulder, but all he saw was falling snow.

Each time he came in to shoot, Jankowski gave him a slight nod and bent to look through the scope. Matt was careful to check the wind flags as he slipped into position, and each time he made a sight correction. His view of the target was blurred by the falling snow, but he settled into a good cadence, confident that his zero was dead on.

He shot clean for the first three stages, fifteen hits for fifteen shots, and as he entered the range for the final stage of standing, adrenaline pumped through his veins. Again, he adjusted his sights for the wind, controlled his breath, and settled into position. He hit the first three. Sonofagun, he might just shoot clean in this race! His thoughts jumped ahead to blasting around the final loop and finishing in a blaze of glory, high on the results sheet, a redemption from Tuesday's disaster. He rushed the fourth shot and moved to the the final target. Too quickly. The fourth black disk remained visible through the snow. "Damn," Matt swore under his breath, "I rushed it! I had it in the bag and I blew it."

Then his left leg began vibrating from fatigue and accumulated lactic acid. He dropped the rifle to his waist, took a couple of deep breaths, and tried to shake the fatigue out of his legs. He brought the rifle back into position and aimed at the final bull's-eye, which appeared to be dancing all over the hillside. He was conscious of holding too long, but the sight picture just wouldn't settle down. Finally he yanked the trigger as the bull wobbled though the sights. The shot went off, but the target remained. "Damn," Matt swore again as he swung the rifle to his back and skated from the range.

He was angry at himself for blowing what had been close to a perfect day of shooting; but he also recognized that a two-minute penalty was probably not bad for such stormy conditions. He skied the last loop hard, knowing that he'd done well. He powered up the final hill, through the finish line and coasted to a stop. The officials helped him get the rifle off his back, unfastened the bindings from his feet, and wrapped him in a blanket.

"How you doing, fella? Pretty tough conditions out there today. You all right, or do you need a hand getting to the chalet?"

"I'm okay. Just whipped. I can make it." Matt retrieved his gear, pulled on a warmup jacket and headed toward the chalet to change clothes and get something warm to drink. He was soaked from the falling snow, and once he stopped skiing, he quickly became chilled. It wasn't until several minutes later, as he was changing out of his wet racing suit that he looked at his soggy number sixteen, and realized that there weren't fifteen other athletes who had finished ahead of him.

Although he was anxious to see the preliminary results, Gopher was headed back to the Baranof, so Matt collected his gear and jumped in the van.

"So how'd it go this morning, Rookie?" Gopher was upbeat as usual.

"Hard to tell, but at least it went better on the range. I hit eighteen out of twenty."

"All right! Way to go, Matt! The word I got was, lots of guys were having trouble on the range. If you only missed two, you might be in there today."

As Matt staggered out of the van in front of the Baranof, several women were waiting for their ride to Kincaid.

"Matt, you look terrible!" Trudy Wilson squealed as Matt struggled to slide his ski bag out from under the seats of the van. "How'd you do?"

"Hard to say. There weren't any results posted when I left. I shot okay but it was snowing so hard I couldn't tell about the skiing." As Matt freed his ski bag, the women began loading their skis and backpacks in the van.

Matt took a long, hot shower, cleaned his rifle then fell asleep. It seemed only moments later when he was awakened by a key in the lock and Thomas staggered in, soaking wet. The Inuit's face showed no expression as he leaned his ski bag in the corner and dropped his pack on the bed. Matt studied his roommate for some clue of how the race had gone for him. For several seconds they stared at each other without speaking, no emotion on Oksoktaruk's distinctive face.

"Well?" Matt couldn't stand the tension. The Alaskan's broad features broke into a smile that made his eyes virtually disappear.

"We were *awesome!* I told you some of those wimps were going to cave in because of the weather." He pulled a wet, wrinkled paper from his backpack. "These are unofficial, and there are a couple of protests, but check 'em out."

Matt scanned the soggy results. Ragnar Haugen first, Burl Palmer second, Heikki Lahdenpera third, Thomas Oksoktaruk fourth.... "Damn, Thomas! Fourth! That's great!"

"Keep going," Thomas said.

"Wainwright fifth, Johnson sixth!" he stopped reading and stared at his roommate.

"I told you, buddy, we're back in the hunt! You put together two more races like this one and you've got a good chance."

He checked the results again and discovered that no one had out-shot him. Then he looked up at Thomas and smiled.

"I wondered how long it would take you to notice that," Thomas beamed. Matt was ahead of Tony Morgoloni, who had finished eighth.

"Sonofagun, I out-shot him by three minutes, but he finished only twelve seconds behind me!" Matt was studying their times.

"Hey, that's biathlon. Skiing fast won't cut it, you've got to shoot straight, too. I'll bet the ol' Snake isn't too happy," Thomas was gloating.

Matt and Thomas slept late Saturday morning, the women's turn to start first. As Matt left the lobby for his run, the women were piling into Gopher's van. Sandy gave him a nod as she climbed into the vehicle. She had led the women's field by more than two minutes in the distance race on Thursday, and was now considered a sure bet for the Olympic Team. "Have a good one," Matt called to her as she disappeared into the van.

The sky was a fluorescent pink behind the Chugach Mountains as

Matt jogged the access road to Anchorage International Airport. It was going to be another spectacular day; bright sun, three feet of fresh powder, and calm winds. Matt felt confident about his shooting and was rested from the day off on Friday.

Later when Gopher dropped off the men, the parking lot below the chalet was full, and the area in front of the building was packed with spectators. Inside, the bright lights of TV cameras illuminated a corner, and by craning over the heads of the media people, Matt could see a small dark-haired woman holding a microphone in front of Trudy Wilson. Trudy smiled and tilted her head, casually shaking her blonde hair as she listened to the TV commentator. A heavy newspaper reporter, standing in front of Matt, finally gave up dancing on tiptoe, and turned to leave.

"Jesus, she's gorgeous! If she were a skater, she'd be headed directly to Hollywood after the Olympics," the reporter said.

"She'd love that! Who do you write for?" Matt asked as the reporter pushed past.

"Me? I'm sportswriter for the *Fairbanks Daily News Miner.* Who'er you?"

"Matt Johnson. Did Trudy win it today?"

The reporter looked back over his shoulder, "Who, her? Naw, she was second. Sandy Stonington won it by over two minutes! Can you believe that? A 7.5K race by more than two minutes! She shot clean and skied like a rocket. But nobody can find her — she disappeared — so everybody's drooling over the beauty queen here." Matt abandoned the interview and went in search of a quiet corner where he could prepare for his race.

The announcer was pulling out all the stops for the large, weekend crowd. "And next on the course is number five, Matthew Johnson, from Thetford, Vermont. Matt had tough luck on the range last Tuesday hitting only two of ten targets. But he seems to have straightened things out, since he missed only two targets in Thursday's 20K. Matt is eighteen years old and a graduate of Thetford Academy. Fifteen seconds 'til the start for Matt Johnson. Wish him luck folks! Ten seconds…five…four…three…two…one…GO!"

The crowd cheered as he skated out of the starting area, "Heya, heya, heya!"

"Okay, Johnson, let's go!"

"All right, number five, ski fast and shoot straight!"

"Way to go, Vermont! Hang tough!"

The sunlight was so bright that Matt had trouble focusing as the trail went from the brilliance of the new-fallen snow to deep shadows under the dense spruces. He skied in to shoot prone with confidence and nailed the targets, five for five. He was superstitious about looking at the penalty loop, but out of the corner of his eye, he thought he saw at least two competitors skating frantically around the oval.

On the green loop, he skied by himself. He never saw anyone ahead, and no one overtook him. As he approached the range for standing, he tried to suppress the thought that it was "make or break" time. As he coasted to a firing position, he reminding himself to take the shots one at a time, keep a steady cadence, and not to rush the last one. His position felt good although he was unnerved by how steady the sight picture appeared. But he knew enough not to fight it. He squeezed off the first three shots, all hits, somewhat quicker than his normal cadence. He began to worry, remembering the final two misses on Thursday. He took a deep breath, forced the thought out of his mind, and remembered, *Don't think, just shoot.*

He squeezed off the last two shots, hit them both, and whooped as he snatched his poles and scrambled from the firing point. As he left the range, he heard the announcer, "Number five, Matt Johnson, has just finished shooting offhand, zero penalties! Johnson is the only competitor at this point in the race to avoid the penalty loop."

Matt knew that all the hotshots were in the final seed and had not yet shot, but that was okay. Shooting clean was a big boost any time it happened, especially at the Olympic Trials. As Matt charged up the first hill of the red loop for the second time, he felt thankful for the early start number. The hill was deeply rutted, and the snow collapsed under each powerful stride.

He could see a National Team uniform ahead fighting the deep ruts. Matt concentrated on being light and quick, and before the crest, he pulled abreast of the other skier. It was Oliver Wainwright. Matt was still energized by the shooting and his momentum carried him past Wainwright at the crest of the hill.

"Come on, Oliver, let's go after 'em," Matt yelled as he powered past the older racer and compressed into a tuck for the long downhill ahead. Matt didn't look back, but as the roar of air passing his ears increased, he barely caught Oliver's response, "This sucks!"

Holding a tight tuck, his eyes watering from the speed, he was slow to adjust again to the bright sunlight, but then he glanced ahead and saw the trail obscured by a dark wall. He was going too fast! There was no way to stop. "Jesus!" A bull moose was standing squarely in the trail on the outside of the turn. Reacting purely by instinct, Matt took one desperate skating step to the inside of the turn, carved deeply into the soft snow, and fought the centrifugal force that pulled him toward the moose. He tucked even tighter, and by some miracle shot past the moose within arm's length of the massive animal. His speed carried him through the transition and a few strides up the following ridge. As the momentum dissipated, he rose out of his crouch. His legs were shaking and his pulse thundered. He struggled to get a breath. Matt hesitated to look back, afraid the bull might be charging up the hill after him, but a terrified shriek forced him to turn his head.

"HO–LY…SHEE–IITT…!" Matt saw the mature bull moose in full profile. It had turned sideways, looking back up the trail to where Oliver had thrown his skis into a frantic slide-slip in a desperate effort to stop. At first the moose seemed curious, but then it dropped its massive antlers and took a step toward Oliver. Matt could hear the moose exhaling through wide nostrils, a loud "whoosh" that left no doubt that Oliver was in trouble. Head lowered, the animal took another deliberate step toward the terrified athlete.

"Sonofabitch, help…HELP!" Oliver screamed.

Matt had been moving up the hill away from the moose when he realized Oliver had nowhere to go. Matt shouted, *"Hey…Hey, go on, get out of here!"* Then he whistled, as loud as he could. The moose swung its massive rack around and stared in Matt's direction. Matt waved his arms and ski poles, yelling and whistling. The moose appeared confused. It swung its head first in one direction, then in the other, undecided which way to charge.

A snowmobile crested the rise. It slowed slightly as it overtook Oliver, who slid his skis out of the machine's path. A passenger on the Skidoo stood, and pointed an aerosol air horn, and the hollow was filled with a deafening howl as the snowmobile charged the bull.

If the animal had been undecided before, it no longer was after the arrival of the snowmobile and the air horn. Majestically, it turned and, raising its long, double-jointed legs above the deep snow, trotted back into the trees. Even after the bull was out of sight, and the official had let up on the wailing horn, Matt could hear branches snapping as the massive animal plowed through the forest.

"Okay, boys, let's get back to racing," the official on the snowmobile said. "We're going to have a lot of traffic through this dip pretty soon and we don't want any pileups."

"Sonofabitch, I could have been killed! That thing was charging! You guys are freakin' nuts racing out here with these monsters everywhere," Oliver was still in shock.

"Naw, we been watching that one all week. He won't be back for a while. Now you better get going. We got a checker on the ridge who's got you two on a watch, so you'll get credit for this little, authentic Alaskan adventure. Just don't tell the other racers or they'll all want a mid-race rest like this. See ya at the finish." The snowmobile roared through the dip, past Matt.

"This whole lash-up is nuts. I don't know why I stay with this sport. It's insane...."

Ignoring Oliver's complaints, Matt took off. Another skier rocketed down the hill and through the hollow, but Oliver scarcely noticed. The new skier was Burl Palmer, and Matt hung in behind him, letting Burl set the pace up the long, tough climb to the ridge. Then downhill. Matt fell behind, but not out of sight. He was able to stay with Burl on the final climb to the range, where Matt peeled off to the finish as Burl headed for the firing line.

In the finish area, waiting for his rifle to be checked, Matt watched Oliver ski into the stadium, still mumbling, "This whole state is bullshit. I mean I almost got trampled by a goddamn moose in the Olympic Trials, for chrissakes!"

There were scowls from the spectators as Wainwright skied by, and one young mother clapped her mittened hands over her daughter's ears.

Matt retrieved his gear and headed for the chalet to change into dry clothes. After a cup of hot soup, he went out to ski a cool-down loop. Thomas Oksoktaruk was approaching the chalet from the range. "Hey, Matt, let me get changed, and I'll go with you."

"Let's do the green loop," said Matt firmly.

"Had enough fun on the red loop for one day?" Thomas said with a grin.

"How'd you hear about that already?"

"I checked in with John Miller after the race. He said all the officials were talking about the bull on the red loop. They were laughing about Oliver, but also saying that number five must have brass balls to ski under the nose of a big bull."

"Brass balls, nothing! I never even saw him 'til it was too late. I couldn't stop, so I went for it. I was lucky as hell."

"Well, don't let on! The other guys are convinced you aren't afraid of anything."

By the time the two friends returned to the chalet, the unofficial results had been posted. Burl, Ragnar, and Heikki had taken the top three positions, but the next three, Oksoktaruk, Morgoloni and Johnson, had finished within ten seconds of each other. Matt was pleased to again be among the top six, that magical number of athletes to be selected for the Olympic Team. But Thomas sounded a note of caution, "Yeah, these are decent results for us, but unfortunately the times are so tight, the points won't be any good."

The final seeding meeting took place after supper in the Kodiak Room as usual. The weather report was not promising. The temperature had been dropping, and after a clear night, predictions called for a daytime high on Sunday that would not reach zero. Stanley Reimer outlined the options if conditions were simply too cold to compete, "The men's 20K is scheduled to start at ten. We'll have someone at Kincaid by seven, checking the temperature every half hour. The Competition Jury will meet at nine and again at nine-thirty. As many of you know, international rules require a decision by the jury if the temperature is lower than minus four degrees Fahrenheit. If it doesn't warm up to minus four by ten o'clock, our first option is to delay the start for an hour, perhaps two. We can't delay longer than two hours or we'll run into problems finishing the women's race before dark. If I were competing tomorrow, I'd bring a good book and be prepared to spend some time waiting."

When Matt stepped outdoors for his morning run the cold was penetrating. He remembered the warning from the doctor in West Yellowstone; the next time he froze his toes, he could lose more than skin and toenails. As the sun finally peeked over the Chugach, the temperature began to rise. On a notice board in the chalet at Kincaid the readings were recorded:

7:30 A.M. ... -34° F

8:00 A.M. ... -34° F
8:30 A.M. ... -31° F
9:00 A.M. ... -26° F

The Competition Jury met at nine and postponed the men's start until eleven.

9:30 A.M. ... - 20° F
10:00 A.M. ... -16° F
10:30 A.M. ... -12° F

"Okay, Matt, let's go zero our rifles," Thomas was bundled in his warmups with a heavy earband under his hat and old wool socks pulled over his ski boots.

"Why? It's never going to make it to minus four degrees in half an hour."

"You're right! It won't get up to four below, but we'll race. I told you, they can't postpone because of the airline tickets, and they can't cancel because their top woman needs a third start. Pull some socks over your boots, and stuff another one down the front of your pants and let's get ready to kick some butt."

Thomas was a prophet. The race started one minute after noon, exactly a two-hour delay. Oliver Wainwright and Tony Morgoloni complained loudly and threatened to protest the results, but the Technical Delegate assured them that all the rules had been followed. When Oliver pressed the TD for an actual temperature reading at the start of the race, the answer he got was, "The jury has determined it is safe to race." He added that Wainwright and Morgoloni were under no obligation to participate; they each had three good finishes, and they could sit out the final race if they chose.

Matt was grateful for the fourth event. If he could manage just one more strong finish, he might have an outside chance of making the team. Oliver had been circulating point totals which he calculated on his laptop computer. Counting the three previous races, Matt was hopelessly out of it. But Oliver also printed a ranking based on the best two of the previous three competitions. Matt was surprised to see that he was solidly in seventh place, only a few tenths of a percentage point behind Oliver himself. If Matt cleaned his targets, skied the race of his life, and if someone on the list ahead of him had trouble, it was possible he could move up to that critical sixth position.

When the early starters left the gate at twelve, it was too cold to really appreciate the beauty of the day. Matt skied a loop in his warmups and was amazed how Thomas' trick of pulling old socks over his boots kept his feet warm.

The race itself was much like the previous 20K, except this time he could see more of the other competitors. After his first prone shooting, where he hit five for five, Matt remembered another bonus that might tip the scales in his favor. Although Anschutz .22 caliber rifles were the world's undisputed leader for accuracy, there had been problems with some of the biathlon rifles in severely cold temperatures. The Central Europeans rarely experienced these mysterious difficulties, but the Scandinavians, Russians, Canadians and Americans all had documented a strange expansion of the shot groupings in sub-zero weather. It might have been luck, or more likely his father's savvy about firearms, but Matt's old Anschutz had never misbehaved in the cold.

Although his toes stayed warm, Matt realized too late that his fingers were getting cold. He had missed only one target in the first ten when he approached the range for second prone. He rocked into position, unaware that his finger was on the trigger. The rifle recoiled and a burst of snow erupted about fifteen feet in front of the firing line.

"Damn," he said, and withdrew his finger from the trigger guard until he had solidified his position. He bolted the rifle to eject the wasted shell casing, then let the rifle settle onto the second black bull. He meant to take up slack, but the rifle barked again, this time hitting metal, but missing the scoring ring. Only then did Matt realize he had lost feeling in his trigger finger. He took his right hand off the pistol grip and thrust it under his left armpit. Within seconds he felt the tingling pain that he remembered so well from Yellowstone.

He breathed deeply, forcing himself to remain calm. He reasoned, *If I waste two minutes warming my hand, but hit the rest of these targets, I'm still a minute ahead.* Soon he could feel his finger again. He rolled back into position and smoothly hit the remaining three targets.

The last two loops were tough. Because of the severe cold, the snow was like skiing on sand. During his final stage of standing he could barely keep his legs from vibrating out of control. He was grateful to hit four out of five. He pushed hard on the final lap, his only goal to reach the finish line. He knew he was running low on blood sugar, but if he could just hang tough for the final few kilometers....

At last the stadium appeared and he skated through. He had always avoided finish line theatrics, but his legs began shaking so violently he couldn't stay upright. A first-aid volunteer instantly had a blanket around him, and called for help.

Matt couldn't remember how he got from the finish line to the chalet, but eventually he was lying on a cot in the rear of the building. Around him other athletes were moaning in pain, rocking back and forth on the cots. A volunteer offered Matt a cup of steaming broth, which he accepted gratefully.

"How are you feeling, son?" A tall, gray-haired man with glasses sat next to Matt on the cot.

"I'm okay. This soup hits the spot. I just ran low on blood sugar."

"That and the early stages of hypothermia; we see quite a bit of that up here. How'd the race go for you?"

"Hard to tell. I didn't shoot as well as I did in the first 20K, but I imagine some other guys had trouble on the range, too. I guess I couldn't have expected much more."

"Well, I hope you make it. Now I've got to go keep an eye on some of your teammates. I'm afraid we've got some pretty serious cases of hooter freeze. You'd think anyone who lies down in the snow every day as part of his sport, would invest in a pair of wind-panel briefs or a fur-lined jock. You sit tight here until you warm up. You're dehydrated, so keep drinking water all afternoon."

Before Matt could thank him the tall volunteer was moving down the row of cots checking on other athletes. Then Matt saw the wide, smiling face of Thomas Oksoktaruk approaching through the gathering crowd in the chalet. "Hey, Matt, what're you doing in here? You all right?"

"Yeah, just ran out of gas. Your advice about the socks saved my life, though. Feet stayed warm and nothing froze in my pants like these guys," he turned his head toward the other cots where athletes were clutching their groins and rocking methodically in pain.

"Let's catch a ride back with Gopher. I got your skis and warmups from the range."

After a hot shower and a late lunch Matt felt better, though still close to exhaustion. His roommate however, seemed to be running on jet fuel.

"Thomas, how can you be so fired up after racing a 20K in weather like we had today?"

"What weather? This was a great day for racing, plenty of snow and no wind. Heck, only one day in ten is this good for biathlon back in Unalakleet! Besides, I think I made the team!" Thomas grinned so broadly he looked like a billikin, the small ivory charms the Inuits carve for good luck.

"How do you know?" Matt asked.

"I got a look at Oliver's printout after three races. I was sitting in fourth then, and I don't think anyone moved ahead of me."

"You don't know how I ended up, do you?" Matt asked, almost afraid to hear the answer.

"I didn't see any results, but I think you did okay. Seems like you were fighting it out with Oliver and the Snake for sixth place. You didn't clinch it today, but you didn't give it away either. I'm betting there will be less than a percentage point separating the three of you after totaling your best three races."

The roommates spent the rest of the afternoon packing. Thomas was experienced enough to know that nothing was certain in a tryout series, but he was quite confident that when the Olympic Team was named at the awards banquet, he would be on it. He was also sensitive to his friend's disappointment. Matt had not really expected to make the team, especially after the disastrous first race. But with each subsequent competition, the flicker of hope burned brighter. Matt had been convinced that if he could just pop a great race on the final day, he would be able to move up into that elusive sixth position. But he was afraid the four-minute penalty in the final 20K was simply not good enough. Matt would wait until the team was officially announced, of course, but he was pretty sure he'd be headed back to Vermont.

The Kodiak Room had been transformed into a festive banquet hall, draped with patriotic flags, banners, and balloons. The room was crowded with exuberant people, most with ruddy, wind-burned faces. Matt had become so accustomed to seeing the officials in heavy parkas and thermal boots that he didn't immediately recognize them in tweed sport coats and neckties.

The athletes, distinctive in their white team sweaters, mingled with the guests. Thomas Oksoktaruk sought out John Miller, but his old coach couldn't protect him from the crush of Alaskan well-wishers. Matt almost forgot his own disappointment as he was caught up in the congratulations for his friend. The dignitaries began to assemble at the head table and the athletes, volunteers, and guests gathered on the main floor. Matt found a vacant seat with John Miller, Thomas, and several skiers from the Bering Strait Biathlon Club.

"Mind if I join you?" Sandy Stonington leaned across the table toward John Miller.

"Of course not! We'd be honored!" Miller introduced Sandy around the table to the Alaskans.

As dinner was being served, Stan Reimer took the microphone and began what promised to be a long and tedious evening of speeches. First he thanked the dozens of volunteers, the corporate sponsors, and the officials. Then he asked various Alaskan dignitaries to help him hand out the awards. The prizes were widely distributed among the men: Ragnar, Burl, Heikki, Tony, Oliver and Thomas all received medals. But in three of the four women's events, the only variation was Sandy's margin of victory over Trudy Wilson and Kate Anderson. Each time her name was announced, Sandy jogged from the rear of the banquet hall and jumped to the platform, ignoring the stairs. For her third gold medal, the audience rose to their feet and cheered until she returned to her table.

Finally, long after the dessert plates had been cleared, dozens of volunteers had been recognized, and several corporate sponsors had been acknowledged, Stan paused behind the microphone. The banquet hall grew quiet. "Ladies and gentlemen, it is now my pleasure to introduce to you the athletes who have accepted the challenge, who have dedicated themselves tirelessly to the pursuit of this one magnificent goal, America's Olympic Biathlon Team! Will the athletes please come forward when their names are called, and remain with me on the platform. From Rochester, New York, participating in her third Olympic Games, Sandy Stonington!"

The audience rose again, cheering and clapping loudly. Sandy hopped to the platform, waved to the crowd, and endured a clumsy kiss from the Program Director. Returning to the microphone, Reimer continued, "From Lake Tahoe, California...." A squeal of delight interrupted the introduction. The audience turned see Trudy Wilson negotiate a route down the middle of the banquet hall between tables and chairs. She was the only athlete wearing a dress, its low-cut neckline and sculptured bodice showcasing her stunning figure. She took her time getting to the podium, where Stan met her with a warm embrace, while the other women watched with bemused tolerance.

"From Bozeman, Montana, a junior at Montana State University, Kate Anderson." More clapping and cheering as Kate joined Sandy and Trudy on the platform. "From Bend, Oregon, our refugee from the United

States Cross-Country Team, Paula Robbins!" Stan waited until Paula joined her teammates on the stage. "From Minneapolis, Minnesota, bouncing back from that terrifying accident in Unalakleet, Jenny Lindstrom!"

"And finally, from Alaska's own Anaktuvuk Pass, making her first Winter Olympics Team, Emily Livengood." Matt could see Emily blush through her smooth, dark skin, but she smiled at John Miller as she started for the podium, walking straight and tall. The audience was back on their feet chanting, "Emily…Emily…Emily.…" As she joined the others on the platform, Matt glanced across the table at John Miller. Tears filled the crusty coach's eyes and threatened to spill over his sunburned cheeks.

"And now, joining this impressive group of women," Stan was smiling directly at Trudy, "it is my pleasure to introduce the Men's Olympic Biathlon Team! From Burnsville, Minnesota, earning an astonishing *fourth* trip to the Winter Olympic Games, Ragnar Haugen." The applause was nearly as deafening as it had been for Sandy and Emily. "From Durango, Colorado, biathlon's own rodeo king, Burl Palmer."

Someone shouted, "Yeee Haaa.…" above the clapping, as Burl sauntered to the stage in blue jeans and alligator boots. "From Duluth, Minnesota, America's authentic Laplander, Heikki Lahdenpera." Matt watched the white-blonde head negotiate a course through the seated guests toward the front of the room. "And from the unlikely location of Brooklyn, New York, the United States Biathlon Team's token urbanite, Tony Morgoloni."

The applause was polite, but restrained, and there was no cheering. If Tony noticed, he gave no clue. The Snake acted as if he had just won the Olympic gold medal. Matt glanced over at Thomas. The Alaskan gave the faintest hint of a smile, and produced a long thin object which he placed on the table between them. Matt recognized it as one of the oosiks Thomas' father had given them on their departure from Unalakleet.

Stan was relishing the spotlight, "And now, from that bustling metropolis…of…Unalakleet, Alaska.…" Pandemonium erupted again. The audience was on their feet chanting, "Tommy…Tommy…Tommy.…"

As he pushed his chair back, Thomas rolled the oosik across the table so that Matt had to react quickly to prevent it from falling on the floor. The cheering intensified as Thomas joined his teammates behind the podium. It took several minutes for Stan to be heard over the applause.

Matt noticed that his pulse was pounding and he was having trouble breathing. It seemed to him the temperature in the banquet hall had risen to about ninety degrees.

"And the final member of the Men's Olympic Biathlon Team...." Matt held his breath. "from the cradle of liberty, Lexington, Massachusetts...Oliver Wainwright the third! Ladies and gentlemen, please join me in applauding our Olympic Biathlon Team!"

Matt stood along with everyone else. In a way, he was relieved it was over. He'd never had a serious chance anyway. He had to admit it would have been a colossal long shot. Hell, some of these guys had been competing at biathlon for longer than Matt had been on skis! Unnoticed among the applauding audience, Matt succumbed to a selfish thought: *I just hope none of the men wins an Olympic medal, because I want to be the first, and it's going to take me four more years.*

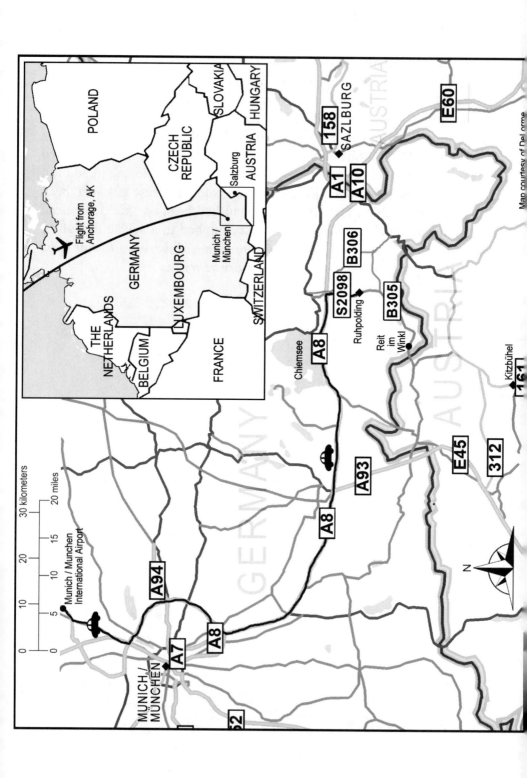

Map courtesy of DeLorme

Biathlon, German Style

9

It was evident immediately that the athletes who had made the Olympic Team were quite different from their less fortunate counterparts. Once the applause subsided, many in the audience, which included officials, volunteers, and journalists, worked their way toward the raised platform and the beaming team members. Only the athletes who had failed to make the team remained at the dinner tables.

Those who hadn't made the team, including Matt, sat in confusion, wondering what to do next. Matt knew he could congratulate Thomas when he returned to their hotel room. He could probably catch Sandy, Ragnar, and Burl at breakfast in the morning. After an intense week of racing, and the emotional strain of coming so close yet falling short, Matt was exhausted.

He had an open plane ticket back to New England. Maybe if he phoned the airline he could make connections to fly home tomorrow. He wondered briefly if Middlebury would let him enroll for the second semester rather than deferring the whole year as he had originally planned. Skiing the local biathlon races back home for the remainder of the winter didn't seem exciting any more.

John Miller and a couple of his Inuit kids were the only others remaining at the table. Matt noticed that Miller had been studying him, ignoring the boisterous activity at the far end of the banquet hall. Matt said, "I think I'll head back to the room and finish packing." John smiled sympathetically and watched Matt leave.

The hotel room seemed empty without Thomas. Matt was acutely aware that everyone else was still celebrating in the Kodiak Room. On his airline ticket envelope he found the listing for Northwest reservations and dialed the toll-free number. It took several minutes, but eventually he learned there was a seat available on a flight leaving Anchorage at 8:45 A.M. for Minneapolis with connections to Boston, and finally to Lebanon, New Hampshire. His mother wouldn't be thrilled about the 11:35 P.M. arrival, but he knew she would tolerate the inconvenience to have him back home.

He began packing his dirty clothes around the skis in his ski bag. He disconnected the carrying harness from his rifle, withdrew the bolt, and gently nestled the Anschutz into the protective foam of the new aluminum rifle case Kobelev had given him. Fumbling through his backpack, he felt the long, thin oosik, Eben Oksoktaruk's gift. He withdrew it with a wry smile. Maybe it only brought good luck to Inuits, he thought, as he laid it carefully on the foam rubber next to his rifle. Then he closed and locked the case. Within a few minutes, he was packed. He called the front desk to check if he could catch an early shuttle to the airport.

It was after ten when the door opened and Thomas entered. He was hauling a large tote bag, decorated with the colorful logo of the United States Olympic Team. In his other hand he held a fistful of paperwork. Matt sat up in bed. "Nice going, Thomas! I'm really glad you made it. You sure called it right about the weather."

"Yeah, I got lucky. If there had been calm winds and sunshine for all the races, I probably wouldn't have made the team. But I put in my time. I trained as hard as most of those other guys. I'm sorry you didn't make it, Matt. Did you see the results? You were only two-tenths of a percentage point behind Oliver! Totaling your three races, two-tenths is probably less than one missed shot!"

"I know you're discouraged, but think back to last March at the Nationals. Did you ever imagine that by January you would be seventh in the country? And remember, you're the top junior by a mile. Your results here put you on the National Team for sure. Some of the older guys will retire after Italy. You have a great chance for the next Winter Olympics in

Korea."

Matt felt better after Thomas put it all in perspective. "What's all the paperwork?" Matt asked his roommate.

"More forms to fill out; press releases, clothing size charts, insurance policies, medical update forms, and the Olympic Team Code of Conduct. Then there are all these letters of congratulation addressed to 'Dear Olympic Team Member' telling us how proud they are that we made the team. Looks like dozens of politicians and all the employees of Coke, Jeep, and Visa have 'been with us every step of the way.' Funny, I don't remember any of them being with me while I trained my butt off in Unalakleet for the last two years!"

"What's in the bag?" Matt asked.

"Oh, you'll love this. Take a look at our 'sundries bag.' It's products provided by official Olympic Team sponsors." Thomas unzipped the heavy nylon bag and emptied the contents onto his bed. Both athletes studied the pile of loot that overflowed to the floor. Thomas began to inventory the products as he picked them up and returned them to the travel bag. "Well to start with, you've got your official Olympic Team shampoo, one bottle for dry hair, one for oily hair and one for normal hair. I'm surprised they gave us all three. I'm sure I must have filled out a hair condition form somewhere along the line."

Matt smiled at his roommate, who had become more animated than ever before.

"And here we have several varieties of skin cream and body lotion — this one's got vitamin E, this one's with aloe. We'd better lock the door and turn out the lights. As soon as Trudy checks through her sundries bag, she'll be fetching you to give her a complete rubdown. 'Course maybe you wouldn't mind that at all."

"I'm ancient history. She's got the hots for Rosie these days."

"I see…" said Thomas. "Just as well, I'd say. Hey, look at this camera! And here's a year's supply of M&M's and Snickers! Check out all these coupon books for McDonald's. I'll have to use these up before I get back to Unalakleet. Kinda ironic, we work our butts off for years, eating rice, spaghetti, salad and fruit. Then when you finally make the Olympic Team, they give you a year's supply of Snickers bars and fifty dollars worth of gift certificates at McDonald's."

Toward the bottom of the pile Thomas uncovered a heavy plastic bag filled with brightly enameled trading pins. There seemed to be hundreds of corporate sponsor pins: Coke, Visa, Xerox, Jeep, and dozens of others. Then Thomas found a smaller bag with USOC pins, among them a few large, heavy pins that featured the Italian Olympic symbol, the words United States Olympic Team, and below that, in bold letters, BIATHLON. Thomas studied the pins carefully, separating the various styles into different piles. Matt noticed there were few of the large biathlon pins. Thomas selected a pin from each pile and handed them to Matt. "I want you to have these. Once the pin trading frenzy begins in Europe, they'll all disappear. I feel good knowing my first trades were with you."

"But I don't have anything to trade back," Matt said. "Oh, wait a minute, maybe I do." He hopped out of bed and went to the dresser where he retrieved the oosik which Thomas had left at the dinner table.

"Oh, that's right, I left it in the banquet room. Thanks for rescuing it," Thomas said brightly.

Matt was up the next morning at six, but he decided to skip his pre-breakfast run. He quietly moved his gear into the hall and dragged it to the lobby. Then he gave his room key to the desk clerk and checked out. He was the only customer in the dining room when the doors opened. During the tryouts, Kobelev, Jankowski, and three or four athletes had always been waiting at the door for the breakfast buffet at 6:30. Matt suspected even the coaches had celebrated last night after the banquet.

He finished his oatmeal, returned to the lobby for his gear, and headed to the van at the front entrance. Even though he was more than an hour early for his 8:45 departure, there was a line at the Northwest ticket counter.

After checking his bags and receiving his boarding passes, he followed the long concourse to departure gate B-12. He found a seat in the waiting lounge and dug his copy of *Lonesome Dove* out of his day pack.

He was engrossed in Captain Call's cattle drive when a familiar voice jolted him back to the present, "There he is! Johnson, Matt Johnson! What the hell're you doing, trying to sneak out of here!" Stanley Reimer was out of breath. Matt's heart jumped as he struggled to remember some foul-up that would bring Stan the Man chasing after him in the Anchorage airport. Then Matt noticed Vlad, who, like Stan was breathing hard, but was smiling broadly.

Several passengers waiting to board the flight had been distracted by Stan's noisy arrival. Matt was bewildered as the two biathlon officials collapsed in seats beside him.

"Let me catch my breath. Damn! I'm glad we made it in time." Beads of sweat formed on Stan's forehead and his breathing was rapid. Kobelev's face was full of color, but his breathing was almost normal as he smiled. Matt glanced nervously at the line of passengers, who were disappearing through the boarding gate onto the airplane.

"I'm going to have to board my flight pretty soon," Matt explained.

"No, you're not! That's why we ran our asses off to catch you. You're not leaving on this flight. You're not flying out until tomorrow."

"But I called last night and got reservations back home today."

Kobelev's smile broadened, "But maybe you not going home! We are coming to tell you that you make Olympic Team! You going tomorrow with us to Germany!"

Matt heard Kobelev's words, but at first their meaning didn't register. "What do you mean I made the Olympic Team? You named six men and I was seventh."

Reimer glanced furtively around the deserted waiting lounge. The ticket agent looked at Matt and called over, "Sir, you'll have to board now."

Matt stood, but Stanley shouted to the agent, "He won't be taking this flight."

Vlad nodded and Matt sat back down. Stanley spoke in a quiet voice, "We have been concerned for some time about Tony Morgoloni. As you know, he's a scrapper, and that's good in a tough sport like biathlon. But Vlad noticed during training camp that Tony had gained a surprising amount of muscle mass, and was even more confrontational than usual. At the testing in Lake Placid last spring, Vlad was almost certain that Tony was using steroids. But the USOC has not yet endorsed unannounced, off-season drug testing, so our only chance to catch him was here at the tryouts."

"Fortunately, the Olympic Committee has developed a new testing method that is much more sensitive. We requested the new protocol for our tryouts, and caught Tony flat-footed. With the old procedures he probably would have slipped through, but the new spectrometer nailed him. We learned of his positive test result late last night after the banquet. We had to inform Tony so that he could authorize the analysis of the second urine sample. Those results, which confirmed the first test, were phoned to us less than an hour ago. We had to make sure Tony understood his rights before we could officially remove him from the team and come looking

Vlad was still smiling. "Congratulations, Matthew. You make Olympic Team, how do you say, fair and square. For a time another athlete is ahead of you by cheating, but now we have it right. Come, we have uniforms for you back at hotel."

As they drove back to the Baranof, Matt felt like he was in a dream. Half an hour earlier he had been headed home, his future uncertain. Now he was on the Olympic Biathlon Team and would soon be headed for Germany! It was too good to be true! But another question nagged at him: Would his mother be able to hang in without him while he traveled to Europe?

The sky above the Chugach range radiated the brilliance of the approaching sunrise. As they entered the lobby, Vlad put his arm around Matt's shoulder, steering him down the corridor toward the dining room. "We talk more over breakfast."

As the they entered the dining room, Sandy Stonington and Burl Palmer, who happened to be facing the door, stood and began clapping. The other athletes and coaches spotted the new arrivals and they also stood, adding to the the the uproar.

"Ladies...and...gentlemen...," Burl Palmer gave his best impersonation of the announcer at the Denver Stock Show. "It is my distinct pleasure to introduce to you Matthew Johnson, from Thetford, Vermont, the youngest member of this year's Olympic Biathlon Team."

As the biathletes left their tables to greet Matt, he was embarrassed to notice the other guests and even the waitresses clapping. Matt's teammates shook his hand or slapped him on the back. The women hugged him, all except Emily Livengood who stood shyly on the fringe of the group. As Sandy embraced Matt, she whispered in his ear, "I knew you could make this team!" Trudy Wilson hugged him tightly, and planted an aggressive kiss on his mouth. There were hoots and cheers from the other athletes and Matt felt his cheeks burn.

When the celebration subsided, Matt sat with Stan, Vlad, Sergeant Jankowski, Andy Christensen, and Jimmy Clark. He listened as the coaches planned the afternoon workout, transportation to the evening's potluck at the Nordic Ski Club of Anchorage, and arrangements for the team's departure to Europe.

When it finally registered that he really had been named to the Olympic Team, Matt called home. He had called after the banquet and his mother was relieved he would be headed back. Now, when Matt felt more joy than he had in years, his mother was reserved about his success. As Matt enthusiastically described the scene at the airport and listed their destinations in Europe, his mother interrupted, "How long will you be gone?"

"Early March, I guess. The Olympics aren't over 'til the end of February." There was a deathly silence on the line. "Mom, are you still there?" Five thousand miles away, he thought he heard two faint sobs before the line went dead.

On Tuesday the coaches tried to reestablish a sense of routine, but with only limited success. The morning workout at Kincaid was typical, but the athletes were so energized, it was hard for anyone to concentrate. The afternoon was a frantic jumble: checking out of the Baranof, hauling baggage, and waiting. The team assembled in the departure lounge as Stanley double-checked the tickets, passports, and rifle permits.

Finally, their flight was called. They found their seats, stowed their carry-ons and settled in. To reduce the effects of jet lag, Dr. Manheimer handed out a sleeping pill to each athlete. Some team members were going to wait for the in-flight meal, then go to sleep, but Matt wasn't hungry. He took the pill, reclined his seat, and pulled a blanket over his head. It was hard to believe that yesterday he had been a disappointed Olympic hopeful heading home to Vermont. Today, he was a member of the United States Olympic Team on his way to World Cup races in Germany and Norway, and then on to the Olympics.

As the powerful whine of the jet engines induced sleep high over the Yukon Territory, Matt wondered if his dad would have been proud. Matt had never been sure what his dad was thinking. They had spent many hours shooting together; he must have loved biathlon. But his dad had also been sullen or angry whenever someone mentioned the Olympics. He might have thought Matt's making the team was terrific or maybe he'd resent the fact that Matt had passed him by. Oh well, he'd never know. He was going to show them all that this wasn't a wild goose chase drawing Matt away from home where his mother and sister needed him. He was going to make them proud.

"Matt, wake up! Put your tray table down for breakfast." It took Matt several seconds to get oriented. He had slept soundly for almost six hours as the jet traced its route from Alaska to Europe over the frozen wastes of the Arctic. Rosie Brown was elbowing Matt awake.

Soon the drone of the engines changed pitch as the jet began its descent. They penetrated the clouds above meticulous fields and clusters of cream colored buildings with red tile roofs. Matt saw narrow roads lined with neat rows of hardwood trees, leafless in the bleak January cold. The ground was bare except for the remnants of snowdrifts at the edges of the fields.

The earth grew closer, and Matt realized he was gripping the arm rest of his seat so tightly his knuckles were white. Rosie broke the tension by slapping a large hand on Matt's knee. Matt whipped his face from the window to see concern on the trainer's expressive features, "It's okay, Rookie. This plane ain't no leftover from World War II, and there ain't no howling blizzard down there. You already had all the flying excitement you gonna have."

The Munich terminal was a stark, modern design, primarily white panels and glass. Matt had the impression of a futuristic hospital rather than an international airport. He realized that for the first time in his life he was surrounded by signs and posters, all written in a foreign language, and he didn't understand a single word.

Matt followed the other athletes to passport control, and by paying attention, figured out what was expected of him. When the German official nodded, Matt approached the booth and passed his new passport through the slot in the thick glass.

Because of the mountains of baggage that accompanied the team, it was exhausting work clearing customs. After what seemed like hours, Jimmy Clark met them at the automatic doors leading out of the terminal. Although there was no snow in sight, the air was cold and the sky was a gray overcast. Gopher directed them to a parking area where a towering purple bus idled quietly. In spite of the cold, five musicians in *lederhosen,* knicker socks, and traditional alpine hats stood next to the bus playing Bavarian music. With notes floating around them, loading the vast cavern under the bus became more of a party than a chore.

Before the packing was finished, two passengers jumped down from the bus. A handsome, blonde athlete in a stylish maroon jacket shouted to Ragnar. He was followed by a lean, silver-haired man, who stepped down carefully and approached Kobelev with reserved dignity. Matt couldn't hear the greetings over the "oom-pa-pahs..." of the musicians, whose knees were pink from the cold. Heikki Lahdenpera, who was helping Matt load the baggage, explained that the Americans would be sharing the bus to Ruhpolding with the Norwegian team, which had arrived from Oslo earlier.

All the baggage stowed, the driver locked down the panels and the Americans climbed aboard. Matt had never seen such a luxurious machine. The seats were upholstered in a beautiful, soft fabric which contrasted with the exterior color scheme. Every four rows a small television hung from the ceiling. The huge side windows were spotlessly clean, providing a panoramic view.

The Norwegians had taken seats in the rear. As the Americans boarded, there were good-natured greetings and joking. The old timers on the United States team worked their way back, shaking hands and slapping shoulders.

"*Fee fawn,* Ragnar! You not competing *again* this year? Is the American team so weak they must have Norwegian grandfathers racing for them?"

Ragnar responded in Norwegian, which Matt couldn't understand, but his answer caused the Scandinavians to roar with laughter. The athlete who had jumped off the bus to greet Ragnar dragged him to a vacant seat toward the rear.

Sandy Stonington worked her way back, smiling and shaking hands. When she reached a reserved, older Norwegian athlete, they embraced and Sandy dropped into a seat next to the woman. As Trudy Wilson moved up the aisle, the Norwegian men greeted her with low wolf whistles and a subdued chant, "Tru...dy, Tru...dy, Tru...dy." The Californian relished the welcome like a movie star, smiling, blowing kisses, and winking. There was pushing and shoving to make room for her.

Burl Palmer was midway down the isle when he shouted, "Damn, we luck out an' get us a bran' new bus for a change, but by the time we get our gear loaded, it already smells like moldy wool and sardines!"

There were hoots and boos from the Norwegians until a voice rose above the clamor, "Ya, sure cowboy. How come the bus now smells like cowshit? Burl, maybe you forget to check your boots before you leave Colorado." More laughter all around.

Matt was following Thomas feeling self-conscious as the greenest rookie on the bus. Emily Livengood and Jenny Lindstrom had already slipped quietly into seats in the front. Oliver was also seated near the front, his laptop computer unfolded and illuminated.

Thomas turned to Matt and said, "Let's sit here." Matt stuffed his day pack in the overhead rack, then settled next to the window. They had claimed the last vacant seats in the middle of the bus, where Americans and Norwegians were evenly distributed. Thomas turned to the aisle and spoke to a couple of the Norwegians he knew from a previous trip to the Junior World Championships.

Matt twisted in his seat, taking the opportunity to study the Norwegian team. Any one of them could have been a fashion model or a movie star. Most had the classic Scandinavian blonde hair and blue eyes. The women were beautiful in a natural, wholesome way. None appeared to wear makeup, in contrast to Trudy, who looked like a painted doll in comparison.

Near the back of the bus Matt noticed a striking Norwegian girl who stared confidently back at him. He was embarrassed that she had caught him gawking, but she was so good-looking he couldn't pull his eyes away. She epitomized traditional Scandinavian beauty, a healthy outdoor glow to her tanned face, golden hair held back by a colorful ribbon, and unflinching, bright blue eyes.

Soon they were underway and an efficient-looking woman stood next to the driver, holding a microphone. In accented English she welcomed the athletes and coaches to the Ruhpolding World Cup. She told the athletes that although the ground was bare in Munich, there was plenty of snow in Ruhpolding. The organizers realized how important it was for the athletes to inspect the course upon arrival, so registration at the Sport-Hotel would be expedited, a light lunch would be waiting, and the bus would be ready to transport them to the newly renovated biathlon center immediately after lunch. She went on to explain that at 19:30 all the teams would participate in a torchlight parade through the village, followed by a welcoming ceremony hosted by the mayor of Ruhpolding.

When the woman finished, she sat down and the conversation among the athletes resumed. Matt watched the countryside slip past, manicured fields, picturesque villages nestled around impressive church spires, more stucco buildings with tile roofs. The flat terrain near Munich gave way to rolling hills dotted with the remnants of earlier snowfalls.

As the bus left the Autobahn and turned onto a smaller road twisting through the hills, the silver-haired Norwegian stood with the microphone at the front of the bus. "American friends! I am Ole Per Rognstad, Team Leader of Norwegian Biathlon. Your esteemed coach, Mr. Kobelev, has allowed me to speak to you along with my athletes concerning plans for this afternoon." Matt noticed that the athletes from both countries were silent, giving Rognstad their complete attention.

"We will arrive shortly at the Sport-Hotel and each of you will be assigned a roommate and issued a key. You may bring the rifles to your rooms, but the skis should be left in the basement. After eating, you must change into training clothes, bring rifle and skis, and be on the bus by 13:00. Do you have questions? Good! Thank you for listening to an old Viking."

Soon the the towering bus pulled off the road, up a narrow driveway and stopped in front of a comfortable hotel which seemed to have grown in stages up the hillside. A small grandfatherly man was waiting on the front steps and greeted each athlete. Matt was glad to learn that he and Thomas were again sharing a room. Although it was small, they had a breath-taking view of the village of Ruhpolding.

Within minutes, Matt and Thomas had unpacked and were beginning to assemble their rifles.

"Hey, Matt, maybe we should grab lunch now before it gets crowded. We can come back and finish with the rifles before one."

Matt agreed and they headed to the dining room. There were several varieties of bread and rolls, a large tray of cheeses, a similar tray of cold cuts, a huge tureen of steaming soup, and the biggest wooden bowl he had ever seen filled with fruit. Matt couldn't help wondering what a normal meal was like if this qualified as a light lunch.

As Matt and Thomas headed back to their room to change for the workout, four of the Norwegian women approached them in the hall. The Americans stood aside to let the women pass. The fourth in the group was the girl with the ribbon in her hair. She smiled at Matt and said casually, "So! You boys have eaten already? I hope you've left something for the rest of us." She was down the hall behind her teammates before Matt could respond.

When Matt glanced at his roommate, the Alaskan was grinning. "You know her, Thomas?"

"Her name is Grete Dybendahl. She was Junior World Champion a few years ago. I think this is her first year as a senior. She speaks great English, and she's no wallflower. At the farewell party following the Junior Worlds two years ago, she dragged me onto the dance floor and wore me out!"

Back at their room, Matt and Thomas changed into their ski clothes, finished assembling their rifles, and retrieved their skis from the basement wax room. It was a short, scenic drive through the village, which was thronged with winter vacationers, then into a gap in the mountains to the west. The valley was narrow and Matt was surprised when the bus eased into a parking lot crammed with vehicles of every description. The mountains were so steep that the valley floor was already in shadow, although it was early afternoon.

Biathletes in brilliant Lycra skated past them on the trails. The coaches and older athletes shouted greetings to those already training. Matt soon learned that the shooting range was actually a stadium with the target line situated against the steep, western mountainside. Fifty meters toward the center of the valley was the firing line, and behind that a fenced area for coaches. A broad expanse of snow gave athletes access to the trails. Beyond the groomed trail, overlooking the shooting range, a terraced slope served as a grandstand. Though it was only a training day, Matt noticed dozens of spectators watching the athletes. At the top of the slope, an impressive building ran the length of the range. Huge glass windows provided a commanding view of the stadium. Matt assumed the building housed offices for the race organizers, the jury room, a VIP lounge, and a press center. The roof of the long building was bristling with flag poles, each one bearing a colorful, national banner. The fences that lined the sides of the shooting range and the hillside beyond the targets, were covered with advertisements, only a few of which Matt could understand: Fischer Skis, Audi, and Lowenbrau. Bavarian music, complete with yodeling, flooded the stadium from powerful speakers.

Matt and Thomas followed the Norwegians to the back of the stadium, where they found dozens of identical doors leading under the facility. Each door was designated with a small national flag and the three letter abbreviation of the country. At the end of the building they spotted the Stars and Stripes.

"You know, Matt, during our Olympic Team outfitting next month in Garmisch, they'll quiz us on these flags and abbreviations." Thomas glanced at the long line of flags gently flapping in the light wind.

"You're kidding!" Matt responded.

"Better get studying. The USOC doesn't want any ignorant, ugly Americans speaking to the world media in Antholz."

Behind the door marked by the American flag, Matt and Thomas found a small but efficient wax room. There were racks on the walls and overhead to accommodate dozens of cross-country skis, a standing rack in the corner for rifles, shelves where Andy Christensen was stacking the team's wax supply, and two sturdy work benches. Oliver and Sandy were already scraping travel wax from their skis. Sergeant Jankowski, rucksack over his shoulder and spotting scope in hand, was headed out as they entered. "We've been assigned lanes twenty-three and twenty-four. I'll zero the women first, then you guys, beginning about 1500. That's three o'clock for you civilians. Get your skis on and go inspect the loops."

In spite of the language barrier, the trail map of the race course was easy to understand. The biathlon range was located at the base of a rocky spine which separated two narrow river valleys. The World Biathlon Union had settled upon a standardized color code for course maps throughout the world. Regardless of the event — distance, sprint, or relay — the competitor's first skiing loop was always marked with red flags or signs. After returning for their first prone shooting, the athletes then headed out on their second loop, always marked in green. After shooting standing, they skied the third loop, always marked with yellow flags or signs. Only three loops were necessary for the sprint races and the relays, but in the distance races, the final two loops were marked with blue and brown, respectively.

Matt and Thomas decided to ski the red loop first, as they would in Thursday's race. The trails generally climbed up the narrow valleys, then turned and descended back to the stadium. The crusty snow was worn and rutted by the more than two hundred athletes who had arrived for the event. Many were cruising in warmups, inspecting rather than skiing hard. The Germans and Ukrainians, however, were carrying their rifles and appeared to be racing.

"Why're they hammering like that the day before a race?" Matt asked Thomas.

"Maybe having a time trial to see who races tomorrow."

"I sure don't feel like going fast after that plane flight," Matt responded.

"You'll feel better tomorrow. Remember, these guys didn't fly all night to get here. They've probably been training on this course all week."

Rather than gently descending back to the range, the course made two abrupt climbs which were carved into the side of the mountain. Even shuffling in their warmups, they were soon winded. As they surveyed the valley below, a German woman powered up the hill, wheezing and panting.

"Damn," said Matt, "this course won't be any walk in the park."

They followed the German biathlete down the hill, hugging the mountainside. The groomed surface, in the shadow most of day, was hard and fast. Matt's eyes watered as he rocketed behind Thomas. When the trail approached the valley floor, it hooked sharp left. Thomas wasn't ready. He threw his skis on edge, but he scraped across the firm surface and disappeared over the bank. Following Thomas had given Matt an instant's warning, but it wasn't enough. He cranked on his skis with all his might, but made it only a few meters further before rattling off the course.

Fortunately, the snow was deep, and the saplings below the trail forgiving. Wiping snow out of his eyes, Matt glanced at Thomas, digging himself out a few meters away. The Alaskan was unhurt, but disgusted that he had fallen. The snow was deep enough to make getting untangled difficult. Thomas grew more frustrated, swearing loudly. When he finally got free of his ski poles, he threw them up the bank toward the trail.

Several minutes elapsed before the Alaskan wiped the snow from his face and noticed Matt standing silently a few meters away. Matt grinned. Finally, Thomas smiled back, "You, too?"

"Hey, Nanook, you know I'd follow you anywhere!"

"Well, we've had our token fall for Ruhpolding so we shouldn't have any problems in the races. Let's check out the green loop and see what surprises they have for us there."

Back at the Sport-Hotel, dinner was even more impressive than lunch. Although he was famished, Matt was fooled by the European customs. By the time the main course arrived, he was stuffed with soup, pasta and bread. The coaches and team leaders were at the seeding meeting, so there was a relaxed, playful atmosphere between the Norwegian and American athletes. When Matt noticed Grete Dybendahl smiling at him from across the room, he risked a self-conscious smile back. Her golden hair shimmered and her face was radiant from spending the afternoon in the cold. The Norwegians wore their team sweaters, the traditional snowflake pattern in white on dark blue, with elaborately embroidered collars and cuffs.

At 1915 (Matt was still getting the hang of European time), the athletes again boarded the bus. Although they had been instructed what to wear, Gopher, in the absence of the coaches, was forced to send Trudy and

Kate back for their team hats.

The village of Ruhpolding looked like a fairy tale brought to life. The narrow, twisting streets were festive with banners. Warmly clothed tourists lined the parade route and teenagers in Bavarian costumes carried placards and national flags representing the participating teams. The Finns were dressed in their distinctive blue and white, and the French team wore large floppy berets, the Russians were impressive in luxurious fur hats.

An athlete signaled to Matt from the Russian group. At first, Matt assumed the compact skier, whose high cheekbones seemed chiseled out of birch, must be gesturing to someone else, but the determined Russian made it clear he wanted Matt. As Matt tentatively approached, the Russian thrust out his hand, and displayed a dazzling smile, thanks to a solid gold front tooth.

"My name…Popov, Dimitry." Matt shook the Russian's hand as he studied the distinctive Tartar features and the golden smile. Although Popov was several inches shorter than Matt, the Russian's handshake was crushing.

"I'm Johnson, Matt."

"My home, Novosibirsk, Siberia! My sports trainer, former times, Vladimir Kobelev, now trainer for American team."

"Oh, Vlad! Yeah, he's our National Team coach."

"Da…da.… You are liking Kobelev?"

"You bet, Vlad's great! The team's improved a lot since he began coaching in the States."

"Okay! Kobelev my trainer, my friend. Now Kobelev you trainer. It must be Popov and Johnsonmatt is friends also!" Popov's smile grew even brighter as he pounded Matt on the shoulder.

"Moment!" The Russian took off his huge fur hat and released the strings that held the ear flaps. He folded down the fur, revealing a sparkling assortment of colorful trading pins. "Johnsonmatt, you choose!" It was more a command than an invitation. After studying the selection, Matt pointed to a large pin with the Olympic rings and a biathlete on the flag of the Russian Federation.

"Harasho.… Russia Olympic Biathlon," Dimitry seemed to approve of Matt's choice. Matt dug into his pocket and withdrew the pins he had received from the USOC. Using an index finger to sort through the options, Popov expertly selected the rare United States Olympic Biathlon pin. The gold tooth flashed again as the Russian attached the United States pin to his coat. Matt followed Popov's lead and put the Russian pin on the chest of his United States parka. They completed the transaction with another handshake. This time Matt was ready for the punishing grip of the Russian. Popov laughed, "Johnsonmatt, *par Rooskie…mya drug,* in English…my friend!"

As Matt returned to the American delegation, officials were distributing small torches to the athletes.

"Hey, what was that little conference with the Russians all about?" As usual, Oliver had an edge to his voice.

"The guy with the gold tooth, his name's Dimitry Popov. He wanted to trade pins," Matt answered.

"I know who he is, for chrissakes! He's won half a dozen World Championship medals as a junior," Oliver responded impatiently. "Now that the Soviet sports machine is history, Valeri Vassiliev in cross country and Popov here are Russia's best hopes for hardware in Italy. And if you believe the rumors, Vassiliev is over the hill. What'd Popov want?"

"He asked how we liked Vlad. Sounds like Vlad used to be his coach in Novosibirsk."

Officials were walking among the assembled teams, lighting the small torches. Moments later, the procession got underway. Though the Americans were far back in the order, Matt could hear the distinctive Bavarian marching music from the band leading the parade. Holding the torches, the athletes formed a river of light as they marched through narrow streets lined with rosy-cheeked spectators. Flags and banners fluttered from the buildings. Small children bundled in snowsuits waved tiny, red, yellow and black flags of the host country.

At a park near the center of town, the teams assembled facing a stage decorated with more banners. The music continued as the teams squeezed into the open space. Then the speeches began. At first Matt tried to listen carefully, but the German was unintelligible, and even the English translation was difficult to decipher over the loudspeaker.

As Matt surveyed the crowd, two small girls held out pens and note pads, their eyes pleading. Matt pantomimed writing, and they nodded vigorously, pointing to Sandy. Matt tapped Sandy on the shoulder and nodded toward the eager German girls, their note pads outstretched over the fence. Sandy smiled, eased back to the fence and signed their autograph books. Instantly, more kids appeared determined to get Sandy Stonington's autograph.

After greetings from the mayor, the chief of competition, and the president of the World Biathlon Union, a representative from the German Olympic Committee moved to the microphone. The athletes were stamping their feet and swinging their arms to keep warm. Trudy Wilson noticed the cluster of autograph seekers and slipped from the front of the delegation to join Sandy. She smiled as kids passed their autograph books over the barrier. Her smile faded as the children pointed insistently at Sandy. Scowling, Trudy returned to her place behind the flag bearer.

Finally the speeches ended, the band played a closing march, and Kobelev shepherded his flock back to the bus. Matt flopped into a seat across the aisle from a Norwegian, who pointed at Matt's Russian biathlon pin. "So you have done business already with the Russians! Since we are in the same hotel, you must also have a Norwegian badge." He withdrew a small Norwegian Olympic team pin from his pocket, and presented it to Matt. Matt offered his handful of pins to the Norwegian, who selected one.

Back at the Sport-Hotel, Kobelev conducted a team meeting in the dining room. He reviewed waxing, race strategy, and shooting in front of a large crowd.

"Finally, we setting goals for tomorrow's competition. I not forgetting we arrive in Europe only twenty-four hours before first race. Also, you just finish difficult selection procedure in Anchorage, eleven time zones different from Ruhpolding! So…tomorrow we will not be at our best. Still, this is World Cup, and results here will tell how many start positions we have at Olympic Games in Antholz. Even if you don't feel strong on your skis, you can still hit all the targets and be happy with your result. I promise, before we race in Lillehammer, you will feel very strong."

Thursday dawned clear and cold. The Americans were groggy as they stumbled into the dining room for the breakfast buffet. The Norwegians, dressed in blue-and-red racing suits looked even more intimidating than they had on the bus from Munich. They were awake, alert and eager to compete. Matt felt drugged, and desperately wanted to go back to bed.

The ride to the biathlon stadium was quiet. It was a distinctly different atmosphere than the animated conversations that had previously filled the bus. Their arrival at the race site was delayed by a traffic jam near the parking lot. Attendants in fluorescent yellow vests directed motorists onto a huge field which had been cleared of snow. There were hundreds of Mercedes and BMWs in rows so straight they could have been positioned by engineers. A steady stream of spectators in bright ski jackets filed from the parking field over a pedestrian bridge to the biathlon stadium.

When the athletes stepped from the bus into the cold air, the excitement was tactile. Matt retrieved his skis from under the bus and headed toward the shooting range. One of the parking attendants, holding a small radio to his ear, halted the Americans and Norwegians by stretching his arms wide so they couldn't pass. Two other attendants quickly removed a rope barricade which had protected a prime space in the crowded parking lot.

Matt expected an ambulance with lights flashing, but instead, eight, bright red Audi Quattro station wagons swept in like a formation of fighter jets. Although most automobiles were covered with a film of dirt from the sanded roads, the Audis gleamed as if driven directly from the factory.

When all eight had pulled in, smiling members of the German Biathlon Team emerged to the enthusiastic cheers of the spectators. In matching warmup suits, the Germans unloaded their rifles and skis from the flashy cars as the visiting athletes resumed their trek to the stadium. Matt noticed the black leather seats and the logo of the German Biathlon Federation tastefully emblazoned in yellow and black on the driver's doors. Just below the window, each car was personalized in German script with the driver's name.

Bavarian music echoed to the cliffs of the narrow valley and back across the shooting range. Although it was two hours before the first race, the viewing stands behind the range were filled. Concession booths seemed to be everywhere, and the cold air was rich with the smells of coffee and grilled sausage. Although the stadium was bathed in early morning sunlight, the shooting coaches slapped their hands to keep warm. Clouds of frosty vapor obscured their faces, then dissipated. Matt had never seen so many spectators at a biathlon race. He was reminded of homecoming weekend at Dartmouth every October, when the town of Hanover overflowed with enthusiastic football fans.

Some competitors were identifiable by their uniforms: the Swedes, dignified in white with tasteful blue and yellow trim, the Finns in bright blue with white accents. The Italians had royal blue warmup jackets with green and red trim, but their racing suits resembled an explosion at a paint factory. There were dozens of racers who wore colorful variations of a standard Adidas suit. Many of these competitors looked older, the women with leathery faces from years spent outdoors, the men sporting beards or days of stubble. There were short, powerful Japanese and Koreans sporting the brightest colors and shiniest fabrics of all.

The range was a crush of anxious athletes trying to zero their rifles as coaches shouted sight corrections in dozens of languages. Out on the ski trail, Matt forced his concentration back to the race. He was cautious on the descent that had given him trouble the day before. Thankfully, the grooming equipment had replaced the boilerplate with skiable, packed powder.

In a large, fenced area, he stretched with the other early starters. An official handed him a plastic shopping bag identified with his start number. Matt was instructed to put his warmups in the bag which would be waiting at the finish line. As the announcer called the start numbers, racers charged out on the course at thirty second intervals, the crowd chanting its approval.

A compact, muscular racer in the red, white and gray of Canada placed his shopping bag next to Matt's.

"Quite a scene, eh Yank?"

Matt looked at the Canadian, "I guess! I'm not used to this much excitement about biathlon. The only spectators we get for races in the States are a few parents and friends of the competitors."

"Yeah, it's the same in Canada. Here in Germany the only sport more popular on TV is soccer. You're new this year, what's your name?"

"Matt Johnson."

"Joe Albertson, Pinawa, Manitoba. Just remember, Matt, these Europeans put their pants on one leg at a time, just like we do! Ski fast and shoot straight!"

Matt could hear the electronic countdown; "beep...beep...beep... BEEEEPPPP." Albertson skated down the ramp, engulfed by the throng of cheering spectators.

Then it was Matt's turn. As his number was called and he moved toward the chute, he turned toward a frowning athlete who followed him in the start order. "Have a good one," Matt said trying to conceal his nervousness. The grim athlete just stared, his unshaven face totally devoid of expression.

Then Matt was under way, the cheering of the crowd deafening in his ears. Heading up the valley on the red loop, he had the sensation that he was watching himself race, rather than actually racing. He was conscious of his pulse, of riding a flat ski, and of stretching for a long glide with every stride.

He made the turn at the far end of the loop, passed a Korean, and roared around the difficult turn without problems. Matt could hear the staccato crack of rifles and the roaring crowd as he approached the range for his first prone shooting. He was deliberate settling into position and took extra time establishing his natural point of aim. When he began to shoot, the cadence was brisk and assertive. The five metal plates fell without hesitation. As he scrambled to his feet and swung the rifle to his back, he glanced at Jankowski in the coach's box. The Sarge was all smiles and gave him a thumbs-up with his mittened fist.

Matt skated out on the green loop wondering if he should feel so strong. Vlad had cautioned that they would be tired and jet-lagged, but Matt was exhilarated. If his shooting held together and he didn't run out of gas on the last loop, he was confident his first World Cup effort would be a good one. He went into the fast downhill on the green loop in a tight tuck and passed another racer as he glided far out on the flat that led back toward the stadium.

His approach to a shooting point for standing was disrupted by the competitors entering and leaving the range. After slamming to a stop to avoid colliding with a German, Matt skated to a firing point, dropped his poles and slipped out of his carrying harness. He loaded, settled into position and waited for the bull's-eye to begin its controlled wobble through his sights. The first shot surprised him, but the next four followed as predictably as the beat of a metronome. Five for five standing!

The yellow loop was the easiest of the three. Matt cruised confidently, knowing he was on the way to a good result. A growl and the clatter of skis over the tails of his own jerked him back to reality. He jumped to the edge of the groomed surface as the stubble-faced racer thrashed by. Number nineteen had made up the thirty-second start interval, but appeared on the verge of collapse. His sunken eyes stared vacantly at the track ahead. His unshaven face was deathly pale, and a dangling beard of foaming mucous obscured his mouth and chin. He wheezed like an ancient locomotive as he struggled past.

Matt had expected to be tracked. He had planned to let the faster

Europeans go past while he concentrated on good shooting. But nineteen was clearly struggling, so Matt fell in behind and matched the other racer stride for stride. Matt felt his breathing deepen and his pulse escalate a level.

They entered the range together for the second stage of prone shooting. Number nineteen coasted to firing point seven, Matt slid into number six. They loaded and dropped into position simultaneously. Matt knew he should ignore everything except his targets, but he could see the stubble-faced athlete from the corner of his eye. Their first shots echoed across the stadium together, but Matt pushed his cadence slightly, and beat his rival with the four remaining shots. He scrambled to his feet confident he had hit all five, and couldn't resist checking the target to the right of his as he snatched his ski poles from the snow. Five black dots! The grizzly guy had missed them all!

Matt was hunched low, skating hard and fumbling with his pole straps as he passed Jankowski. He smiled at the Sarge expecting to see a big thumbs-up in return, but the Sarge seemed to be studying the sky. Wheezing behind him brought Matt back to the skiing. He fought it out with racer nineteen on the blue loop, but led by a stride when they entered the range for their final stage of shooting.

As he loaded his rifle and shifted position, Matt realized that the competition with the sullen racer had taken its toll. He could feel his left leg begin to vibrate uncontrollably. His first shot was a miss. He dropped the rifle to his knees, took a couple of deep breaths, and started again to build his position. Ignoring the first target, he settled on the second and squeezed the trigger. Hit! The remaining three fell smoothly with a steady cadence. Jankowski nodded as Matt scrambled past, determined to catch number nineteen on the final loop. Damn, Matt thought, the Sarge seemed pretty reserved. One miss in my first international 20K isn't bad. If I can hang on for the last few kilometers, the skiing should be okay, too.

He worked hard on the brown loop. Although he had nineteen in sight most of the way, Matt couldn't reel him in before the finish. The young American coasted through the line, exhausted but confident he had raced well. After he caught his breath he skated over to the racer who had out-skied him. Matt held out his hand, "Good race, you were skiing well."

The stubble-faced athlete stared at Matt, shook his head and bent to retrieve his warm-ups from a plastic bag. Ignored by his unfriendly rival, Matt headed through the maze of fencing to the wax rooms. Because he had been the first American starter, he knew it would be a while before the coaches could talk with him about the race.

The women were preparing for their start. Sandy looked up from her rifle, "So how'd it go, Rookie?"

"Not bad! Those downhills aren't nearly as rough as they were yesterday. That crowd sure is a rush! No trouble telling when the Germans are hitting their targets!"

"How were your skis?" Sandy asked.

"Fine. The guys who passed me didn't blast by on the downhills, they just out-skied me on the uphills."

"How'd you shoot?" Sandy's concentration returned to the rifle in her lap.

"Pretty well, I missed one, second time standing," Matt answered.

Sandy looked up, and the others in the wax room stopped what they were doing and stared at Matt.

"You shot one minute penalty in your first World Cup race! Damn, Matt that's terrific!"

"Yeah, I'm psyched! I guess I'll change my shirt and go ski a little." Matt put his rifle in the rack, changed out of his wet turtleneck, and headed back outside.

"Hey, I'll be cheering for you. Go fast and have fun," he said to the women as he left the wax room.

"Thanks, Matt. Nice going!"

Matt headed out on the course to watch the late starters. He was impressed by their strength and their flawless technique. He cheered for Ragnar, Heikki and Burl, when each skated past. As the last of the male competitors struggled toward the finish, Matt was drawn into a crowd of coaches, racing in from the far reaches of the course to congratulate their athletes. Kobelev and Christensen were not part of the group, but when he reached the range, Matt saw Jankowski pouring himself some coffee.

"Hey, Sarge, whadaya know?" Matt was sure Jankowski would be pleased by his shooting.

"Ah, Matthew Johnson…rookie biathlete in his first international competition! Well, my boy, as the saying goes, we've got good news and we've got bad news. How's about I give you the good news first?"

Matt got a sinking feeling in his stomach. It was obvious that Jankowski wasn't kidding. "Okay, Sarge, what's the good news?"

"Well, Matt, your zero was perfect and you hit everything you aimed at, except that first shot on your second stage of standing. That one got away out the top."

"Yeah, about eleven o'clock, I knew that. What's the bad news?"

Jankowski reached across the fence and held Matt's shoulder, "You cross-fired, second prone. You hit all five targets, but you were firing from point number six, and you shot at target five."

Matt was dumfounded. "What?"

"I think you got so wrapped up racing that Bulgarian, number nineteen, that you settled in on target five instead of six, and shot 'em all."

"Damn, Sarge, are you sure?"

"Oh yes, Matt, I'm sure. You had one hell of a race going there, best American for sure, probably top fifteen overall. But that's biathlon! Everybody out here can play 'if only' all afternoon. Remember what I said first, you hit what you aimed at, and not everyone can do that. We all have lapses of concentration, and you're certainly allowed one or two on your first trip to Europe. Now go ski a little more and cheer for our girls."

Matt skied across the range in a stupor. He hadn't entertained any fantasies about a medal, in fact, he hadn't even thought about final results; but he was convinced he had done well in his first international competition. Jankowski had burst that balloon. Matt was guilty of one of the dumbest, most obvious oversights in the sport, shooting the wrong target. Instead of an impressive one minute penalty, he had six.

He skated past the official bulletin board where athletes and coaches jostled for a glance at the preliminary results. As Matt scrolled down through the pages tacked to the plywood, he noticed that no American had broken the top twenty. Ragnar was 35th, Burl, 38th. Heikki was listed in 49th position, and Oliver was tied for 72nd place with a Japanese racer. Thomas finished 83rd, and Matt was 123rd, listed on the final page of the results, eight places from last.

The numbers blurred for a minute and he realized that he felt completely drained. He shuffled out to the course and cheered the American women up a tough hill. Then he staggered back to the wax room and collected his gear. Desperate to be alone, he found the bus, climbed aboard, and fell asleep in the deep purple velour.

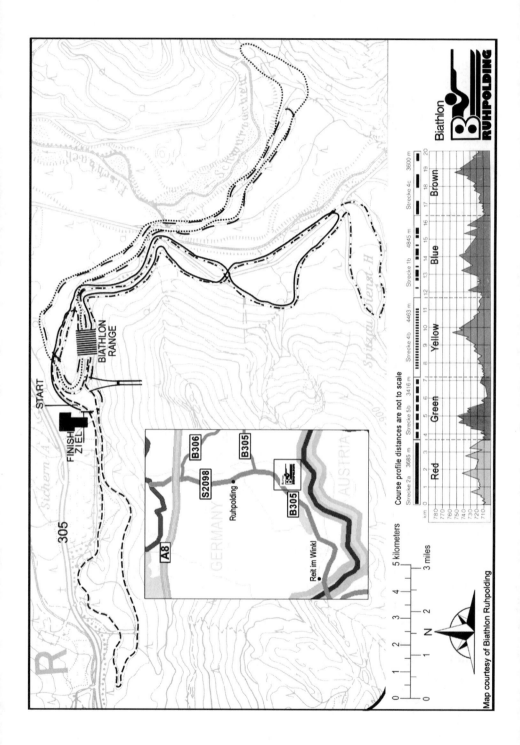

R

305

START

FINISH
ZIEL

BIATHLON RANGE

Sichern A

Fischbach

Schönauer Bach

Spitzquienst. H

A8

S2098

B306

Ruhpolding

B305

GERMANY

AUSTRIA

B305

Reit im Winkl

5 kilometers

3 miles

N

0   1   2   3   4   5

0   1   2   3

Course profile distances are not to scale

km   0   1   2   3   4   5   6   7   8   9   10   11   12   13   14   15   16   17   18   19   20

Strecke 2a   3685 m   Strecke 5b   3416 m   Strecke 4b   4463 m   Strecke 1b   4845 m   Strecke 4c   3600 m

Red   Green   Yellow   Blue   Brown

780
770
760
750
740
730
720
710

Biathlon
RUHPOLDING

Map courtesy of Biathlon Ruhpolding

On the Job Training

10

The atmosphere at the Sport-Hotel Thursday night was subdued. Kobelev's athletes had performed as he had predicted. Most were physically spent before they were halfway through the race. Sandy was the exception. In spite of a two-minute penalty on the range, she finished ninth overall, one of the best World Cup results ever for an American. She was quietly pleased with her race. "I'll take it, considering the jet lag and the tryouts, but I hope I feel stronger by Lillehammer."

Trudy Wilson had skied extremely well and broke into the top twenty for the first time. She was thrilled, and recounted to her teammates a lengthy analysis of her race, disappointed that there were no American reporters in Ruhpolding to cover the United States Team.

The men were especially quiet. They knew Vlad was right and their results would improve, but it was no fun finishing in the back of the pack, especially when Sandy and Trudy had done well. Matt tried not to sulk, but he felt so embarrassed he wanted to hide in his room. Thomas helped a little.

"Hey, Matt, lighten up! Cross firing, or some other stupid mistake is a kind of initiation to the big leagues. In my first Junior World Championship I messed up the color sequence of the loops. I skied red, yellow, green instead of red, green, yellow. Disqualified! And ask Heikki about his relay tag at the Junior Worlds in Minsk! We were fighting it out with the Swedes for the bronze!

"No, on second thought you'd better not ask him; he's still pretty touchy about that one. He was skiing the anchor leg and was so excited, he coasted out of the tag zone before I could reach him. Another disqualification. Probably cost us World Championship medals! So don't feel like the Lone Ranger. We've all been there. Besides, you shot well."

Friday morning the Ruhpolding biathlon complex was bustling with activity. Coaches had set up speed traps on several of the downhills, and their athletes coasted through the electronic timers to compare waxes and base structures. The shooting range was a three-ring circus: coaches shouting sight corrections, athletes scrambling in and out of position, flags fluttering in the gentle breeze, and the staccato CRACK of rifles, all accompanied by robust oom-pa-pahs pouring from the loud speakers.

In the wax room, Sergeant Jankowski gave the athletes their zeroing schedule and target assignments. Trudy was still basking in the glow of her success, Sandy was quietly self-assured, and Matt had begun to rebound from his disappointment.

"Okay, gang, we're on twenty-one and twenty-two this morning. We'll zero the ladies first since you gals race first tomorrow. After I confirm your zero, ski a loop at race pace and shoot a five-round group prone with a good pulse. You guys get lost until about 10:30. I'll work with the rookie last, since he may need both lanes." The Sarge delivered the last line with a big grin.

"Ouch! Sarge, you'd better be nice to the rookie or he ain't going to give you credit for being his shooting coach when he starts winning races over here," Burl Palmer reprimanded Jankowski with mock severity.

"Damn, that's right, Cowboy! Matt, you won't forget to mention me when you're featured in *USA Today,* will you?"

Trudy purred from the back of the wax room, "Sarge, if you want your picture in *USA Today,* you'd better be nice to *me.*"

"Trudy, there's nothing I'd like more, except it would ruin my marriage, I'd go broke paying alimony, and before long you'd run off with that Italian stud who's been chasing you the past two seasons."

The small room erupted with hoots and wolf whistles. Heikki forced his way through his teammates in search of Trudy, imitating the passionate Italian, "Oh Truuu…dee, you are *magnifico!*"

"Shut up, Heikki! You're just jealous because Luigi kicks your butt every time you race!"

"Okay, folks, we could discuss Trudy's love life all day, but it's time to get out there and launch some lead down range. Andy and Gopher have the speed trap set up at the far end of the green loop. Get out there sometime this morning and test your skis."

Matt and Thomas skied together, checked their wax through the speed trap, and returned to the range on Sarge's schedule. The Russians had been assigned lanes nineteen and twenty. At one point Dimitry Popov and Matt were shooting side by side. As they finished a five-shot sequence, Popov flashed his golden smile and stepped toward the American. "Johnsonmatt, you must shoot new Vostok! Very good gun! Popov will try hitting targets with your old Anschutz — how do you say in English — antique?"

The Russian held out his flashy rifle to Matt. The stock was a bright blue, molded fiberglass, the barrel and action brilliantly chrome-plated. Matt's scarred wooden stock looked pitiful by comparison, and his carrying harness was held together with duct tape. They swapped rifles and Popov immediately dropped to the prone position to fire five rounds at a paper target while the Russian shooting coach had his eye glued to his scope.

Matt shouldered the fancy Vostok and bolted a round into the chamber. He was so accustomed to the silky smoothness of his old Anschutz, the balky mechanism of the Russian rifle caught him off guard. He fumbled with the bolt before it locked. Matt shot his five bullets, finally operating the hesitant bolt smoothly on the last shot.

Popov was inspecting Matt's old rifle. "So, Johnsonmatt, this gun is good?"

"Yeah, it's old, but the action is smooth and it shoots well in the cold."

"*Da…da…,*" Popov reluctantly returned the Anschutz, then broke into another sparkling smile. "You like Russian Vostok?" He rapped the garish blue pistol grip, which sounded hollow. "Stock, how you say, fiber-carbon, very strong!"

Later, Jankowski pulled Matt aside. "Congratulations, Rookie, you've arrived!"

"What do you mean, Sarge?"

"What do you suppose that rifle swap with Popov was all about?"

"I don't know. I met him before the parade Wednesday night. I guess he wanted to show off his new rifle."

"Nope. His coaches were studying the results of the 20K and noticed that some snot-nosed American kid they'd never seen before, hit nineteen targets in his first international race. That Russian coach recorded every shot Popov took with your rifle, and I'll bet he's never had such a tight group with his fancy Vostok. They know you can shoot from yesterday's results, and today they confirmed you have an accurate rifle. When you gain some experience, you're going to be a threat to them!"

Matt couldn't tell if the Sarge was being serious, or was just trying to reestablish his self-confidence after the cross-firing incident.

Saturday was a postcard winter day in Bavaria; clear blue sky, plenty of dry powder snow, and a bright sun. There were even more spectators at the biathlon stadium than on Thursday. Because the women were racing first, after Matt confirmed his zero and coasted through Andy's speed trap a few times, he went back to the wax room, where the activity was frantic with coaches, waxing technicians, and the female athletes scrambling through last-minute preparations.

Matt wandered from the wax room to the front of the stadium, where he watched some of the early starters shoot. Cheers from the huge crowd erupted as an athlete approached the range. The tumult subsided while the athlete got into position. As the first shot echoed across the valley, the crowd roared back to life. If the shot scored and the black dot was replaced by white, the spectators yelled in unison. If the athlete missed, and the black target remained, the crowd released an ominous, "Ooooooh...."

Matt realized after watching a few of the women that his pulse was rising from pure excitement. He went back to the wax room to prepare for his start. He was vacillating between optimism and pessimism. He loved the festive excitement: the crowds, the music, and the foreign competitors, but he was still ashamed of cross-firing, and dreaded screwing up again.

Matt started early in the order, as he had in the first race. He quickly learned that the sullen Bulgarian was not the only intense competitor. Other athletes grunted once, and if Matt didn't immediately yield the track, they clambered over the tails of his skis to race past. Matt had the feeling that for many of these biathletes, a poor result represented a lot more than a personal disappointment.

He approached the range for his prone shooting, determined not to foul up. As he unslung his rifle, he double-checked the number of the firing position and the number above the target. Then he dropped into position, established his natural point of aim, and just before squeezing off the first round, rechecked the target number. By the time he finally pulled the trigger he had held his breath too long, his sight picture had become fuzzy, and the shot missed at three o'clock. He knew exactly what had gone wrong, took a breath, got back into his cadence and hit the remaining four targets.

There was plenty of company on the penalty loop so Matt didn't feel overly self-conscious. Returning to the course, he tried to ski his own race instead of thrashing to keep up with the Europeans who tracked him. Matt had just dropped his poles on the snow to shoot standing when Dimitry Popov slid to a stop on the next firing point. Because they were both right-handed, Matt was no more than an arm's length from Popov's back. He was impressed by how smoothly the Russian slipped out of his carrying harness and settled into the standing position. Matt remembered being distracted by the Bulgarian, so he rechecked his target number, took a breath, and let the wobble settle into a predictable pattern.

Popov got the first shot off and the crowd roared. An instant later Matt's old Anschutz barked, and the crowd roared again. A second shot by the Russian, another roar from the crowd. An answering shot from the American, another cheer. The two athletes and the spectators were entwined in a tight rhythm: a shot, a cheer,… another shot, another cheer. With Popov setting the pace, the two competitors nailed the first eight targets at an impressive cadence. As the Russian bolted the Vostok for his final shot, the flashy rifle jammed and Popov fumbled with the mechanism. Subconsciously, Matt had been waiting for Popov's last shot. When it didn't come, he glanced over at the Russian. By then Popov had the Vostok down from his shoulder and was struggling to free the jammed cartridge.

Matt recognized his chance, looked back through his sights, and aggressively jerked the trigger. The sudden movement pulled the rifle off target even as the bullet left the muzzle, and although the black disk began to fall, it hesitated and swung back up. A miss, followed by a deep "Ooooh …" from the spectators. Matt cursed himself for rushing the shot, grabbed his poles, and skated for the penalty loop. As he left the range, he noticed his poles, and skated for the penalty loop. As he left the range, he noticed that Popov was fumbling for his final .22 bullet in the snow.

The American had barely reached the entrance to the penalty loop when he heard a shot from the range and a roar from the crowd. As he rounded the far turn of the 150M loop, Matt looked up to see Popov hammering out of the range toward the yellow trail. For a moment, Matt had visions of catching the Russian and battling out the remaining kilometers to the finish; but by the time Matt cleared the penalty loop, Popov was nowhere in sight.

Matt skied the final three kilometers with several other competitors, but he never saw the Russian until he coasted under the banner marking the finish line. Flushed and animated, Popov was surrounded by coaches and spectators who were leaning over the fence. Dimitry laughed and gestured as he pulled on his warmups, his golden smile flashing in the sunlight. He noticed Matt getting a warm drink, and nodded to his American friend, never pausing in the animated monologue he was providing to his admirers. Matt was about to walk over and congratulate the Russian when a hand grasped his elbow.

"Start number twenty-two. You name is Johnson, Matthew from Ooo–Ess–Ahh…?"

Matt turned to see a race official wearing a white bib with a bright red cross in the center. "Yeah, I'm Matt Johnson."

"Herr Johnson, you are selected by random for doping control. When you are ready, you must with me to medical room. We suggest you have also with you an official from your team. I must ask you now to sign this form, confirming that you have been properly informed." The official looked at his watch. "I must stay with you until you report to the medical room, and we must sign in there not more than sixty minutes from now. Do you understand?"

Matt was intimidated by the formality of the official, who seemed to be taking his job way too seriously. "Yeah, okay, I understand. Where do I sign?"

The form on the clipboard was in German, and as far as Matt knew, he might be confessing to smuggling machine guns into Munich. He told the official that he had to take his skis and rifle to the team's wax room. The official nodded and followed. The wax room was vacant. It was evident that the coaches and other competitors had left in a hurry before the race.

"I guess I'm ready," Matt told the official.

"You will have a coach or team leader with you?"

"I forgot." He reached for the radio hanging from the ski rack. "This is Matt in the ski room, can anyone hear me, over?"

"Roger that, Rookie, this is the Sarge on the range, over."

"Sarge, I've been picked for doping control and I'm headed to the medical room with one of the officials. He says I should have a coach with me, but there's nobody here at the wax room, over."

"Got a good copy on that, Rookie, you're headed for doping control. I can get to Stan from where I am, so somebody will meet you at the medical room. Good luck filling the cup! This is the range…out."

He followed his German escort beyond the stadium into the medical building, then down a hall, and finally into a room that appeared to be a lounge. There was a table that displayed the paraphernalia of urine sample collection: clear plastic cups, small glass bottles, foam-lined mailing containers, and the plier-like device used to seal the jars. A matronly medical technician in a starched lab coat sat behind the table, guarding the testing materials. She looked more fearsome than a Doberman.

The room was crowded. Dimitry Popov was accompanied by two burly Russian coaches. There were two muscular German competitors, each attended by a coach. Finally, there was an Italian woman who looked tired, frustrated, and on the verge of tears. Her coach, a small man with wavy black hair and a deeply tanned face, was engrossed in a magazine.

"Johnsonmatt! At first World Cup you are selected for doping control! Perhaps next time you will be tested because of competition result!" Popov approached Matt, but paused next to a large plastic cooler, his hand above the heap of ice. "What you like for drinking, Johnsonmatt, beer or apple juice?"

"Ahh…apple juice, I guess. Thanks, Dimitry."

"No problem, juice is okay, but beer is better. You will see. Fabiana, you drink beer or juice?"

The Italian girl scowled at the gregarious Russian. Her coach looked up, an expression of pained boredom on his face.

"See, Johnsonmatt, Fabiana drink only the best Italian wine, so now she can't pee. She sit here all day. Come on, Fabiana, drink a good German beer with Popov!"

The Italian grimaced at the Russian and resumed studying the floor. At that moment, Mary Manheimer burst into the room, flushed and breathing hard in her heavy team parka. Atilla the Hun in the white lab coat glared at the latest arrival. "Hi, Matt. Tough luck last shooting. Those first four shots were terrific. Hey, isn't this the fellow you were shooting against?"

Matt nodded, "Dr. Manheimer, this is Dimitry Popov from Novosibirsk. Vlad used to be his coach." Popov flashed his most sparkling smile as he shook hands with the American doctor, "How do you do you! Your speciality is sports medicine?"

"No, internal medicine. I volunteer my time to the team because I enjoy working with our athletes."

Popov had been sipping his German beer, but when Dr. Manheimer finished, he drained the bottle and nodded toward the medical technician, "Now, I must go fill the cup, but I hope she's not the one to watch!"

Matt and Dr. Manheimer smiled as Popov confidently approached the table and helped himself to a plastic cup. He grinned at the woman in the lab coat. She scowled back and barked, *"Moment!"* Then she rose and disappeared through a door. She returned with a thin, balding man who also wore a white lab coat.

"So, you are ready to provide the necessary sample," he said timidly. "I am Herr Dr. Rötsch. I supervise the doping control for the race committee and for the World Biathlon Union. You may have a coach or a team official accompany you while you make the test."

"Da…da…," I make this test many times. Where is WC?" Popov's coach stood and followed the athlete and the doctor out of the room.

"What's that all about?" Matt asked Dr. Manheimer.

"Well, ever since the use of illegal performance-enhancing drugs became a problem at major international sporting events, athletes, coaches, and I'm embarrassed to say, even medical doctors have become more sophisticated in their ability to manipulate the system. The person who met you at the finish line has never left your side until he delivered you here, right?"

"Yeah, that's right," Matt answered.

"Well his job was two-fold. He was responsible to make sure you arrived here within an hour of finishing, that you didn't just take off and claim that you hadn't been informed. Secondly, he was watching to be sure you didn't take any masking agents which could conceal a residue of drugs in your urine. Remember when Vlad warned you never to take a drink from someone you don't know? There have been cases where a drink from someone you don't know? There have been cases where innocent athletes have accepted tainted fluid after a race, which then showed up in their drug tests."

"Finally, here at the doping control, the World Biathlon Union supplies a representative to actually observe the athletes as they provide their samples. That became necessary when it was discovered that unethical athletes were filling the sample cups with urine they smuggled in plastic bags under their clothes."

"But why did Popov's coach go along?" Matt asked.

"For two reasons. First of all, in some countries, the athletes are under such pressure to win that they resort to illegal performance enhancement without the knowledge of their coaches. The Russian coach may be trying to keep his athlete honest. But in this case, considering the historic rivalry between the Russians and the Germans, I suspect Popov's coach wants to be sure the German doctor doesn't tamper with Popov's urine sample."

"Are you going to watch me pee?" Matt was getting nervous.

"No, I don't have to. I trust you. Just be damned sure you don't let anyone else handle your urine sample after you've filled the cup. To be candid, Matt, since you were randomly selected, there is little reason for anyone to tamper with your results. When you start winning races over here, that's a different story."

The door to the lounge opened and Popov emerged proudly holding the clear plastic cup filled to the brim with bright yellow urine. He displayed it to the others in the room as if it were vintage wine, then approached the table where the glass bottles and packing cases waited in neat rows. Herr Dr. Rötsch began to explain the procedure for dividing the sample and sealing the glass jars.

"*Da...da...*, I know...I know! Doctor, I have done this many times before," Popov mumbled as he confidently poured the urine from the plastic cup into two identical glass bottles. Then he placed metal lids on the bottles and crimped each tight with the special pliers. He held the bottles up-side down to demonstrate that they were tightly sealed. Both the German doctor and Atilla nodded their approval. Popov taped a coded label over each metal lid. The doctor watched carefully, and nodded when Popov had properly sealed both bottles. Then the Russian athlete gently nestled each bottle into the case, zipped it, and snapped the end of the zipper into a plastic lock with an audible *click*. He checked to be sure the package.

He nodded formally to the doctor and announced, "So…. Finished! All is good?"

The doctor seemed resigned, "All is *normal*. You are free to go."

Dimitry once again illuminated the room with his golden smile, "Good-bye, friends! Maybe today I am not first on the course, but still I am the best pisser! Good luck, Fabiana! Have a beer or you will miss the relay tomorrow!" The Russian and his coach opened the door and disappeared down the hall.

One of the German athletes stood and picked up a plastic cup from the table. His coach rose to follow.

"Excuse me, Dr. Rötsch?" Matt was surprised by Mary Manheimer's assertiveness. The German doctor jumped like a frightened rabbit. "If I'm not mistaken, the Organizing Committee is required to provide a medical official of a different nationality than the athlete being tested."

The German doctor's bald head glistened with sweat. The coach intervened, "We have a doctor appointed by the World Biathlon Union. He does not represent a country, he represents the WBU."

Mary Manheimer stood up, "I'm sorry, but I disagree. The reason we must subject our athletes to these inconvenient and humiliating doping controls is that unethical competitors and coaches will break the rules to win. The WBU protocol was carefully established to provide checks at every step of the procedure. A German doctor and a German coach observing the collection of a urine sample from a German medal winner is a serious breech of the WBU's protocol."

The coach's face turned deep crimson, the muscles and veins visible in his neck. He towered over Dr. Manheimer, trying to intimidate her. "Are you suggesting, Doctor, that the German team is cheating? Are you attempting to create an embarrassing international incident? Perhaps you had better consult with your Chief of Delegation before you open, how do you say, such a worm can!"

Dr. Manheimer stood her ground, relaxed and confident, "Herr Kirchner, it is you who mention cheating, not me. I simply pointed out that the WBU protocol for doping control clearly states that the doctor supervising sample collection must be from a different nation than the athlete being tested. You know perfectly well that two doctors, from different nations, are assigned by the WBU for this very reason."

"Doctor, you are correct of course," the German coach turned on the charm. "But unfortunately, Dr. Leitner from Austria was taken ill, and was unable to travel. Therefore we must overburden Dr. Rötsch, whom you have met."

"These things happen," Dr. Manheimer responded brightly. "The intention of the WBU protocol could still be maintained if I stood in for the missing Dr. Leitner." She smiled past the towering coach toward the two German athletes, who were obviously nervous. "Of course if your boys are too modest, I'm sure this capable Italian coach would serve in my place."

The Italian looked up, understanding that he had become part of the discussion. Kirchner cast a disdainful glance at the Italian, scowled at Mary Manheimer and roughly pushed the athlete through the door. Atilla the Hun sat stone-faced at the table as if nothing had happened. The Italian coach shook his head, mumbled to his athlete, then looked at the Americans. "Germans," he said, as if that explained everything.

"What's going to happen now?" asked Matt, fearing the international incident Kirchner threatened. Mary Manheimer smiled, "Not a thing. I could file a protest with the WBU, but it's such an 'old boy network' nothing would come of it. At least he knows he'd better watch his step because he's being watched."

"Do you think they're cheating?" Matt asked.

"I don't know. I hope they are beyond that now. But Kirchner is a career biathlon coach originally from East Germany. There was always speculation that the East Germans were doping, and when the two Germanys unified, secret records revealed that those suspicions had merit. Many in biathlon were surprised when Kirchner emerged with the head coaching position of the unified German Team, since there was pretty solid evidence that he, at the very least, knew about the doping violations on his old East German Team."

The first German athlete returned with his sample in the plastic cup, and the frowning coach motioned to the second German racer, who sprang to his feet, grabbed a cup, and bolted down the hall. As the door closed, Kirchner scowled at Mary Manheimer, who smiled back innocently.

The German athletes followed the same procedure as Popov, dividing the urine sample into two bottles, sealing, and then packing them into protective mailing cases. Then the athletes followed their coach out the door without another word.

Matt finished his apple juice.

"I think I'm ready," he said quietly to Dr. Manheimer.

"Good. Just be sure you don't give your sample to the doctor or anyone else after you've filled the cup."

Matt selected a plastic cup then followed Dr. Rötsch down a spotless hall to the men's rest room. The doctor motioned toward the row of urinals against the wall and said simply, "Please." Then he stepped to the side and watched intently. Matt had urinated hundreds of times in public rest rooms when other men were present, but never before had he been studied during the process. A wave of panic began to crest. What if he couldn't pee with this doctor watching him? He tried to stay calm, ignore the German, and concentrate on the plastic cup. Finally, he gained control of his anxiety and a bright, yellow stream arched into the cup. There was another moment of panic when Matt realized the cup was about to overflow and pour all over his hand. At the last instant, he moved the cup aside and finished into the urinal.

The German doctor led him back to the lounge where Dr. Manheimer helped him through the tedious process of dividing, sealing, labeling and packing the samples. When the procedure was finished, the two Americans returned to the invigorating Bavarian afternoon outside.

Relays were scheduled on Sunday; women at 1030, men at 1300. Because it was an Olympic year and most of the participating countries were trying to prepare their athletes before the Games, the Ruhpolding organizers amended the World Cup rules, and permitted unofficial relay teams along with the official entry from each nation. Vlad assumed all of his athletes wanted to race, so he organized make-up teams with the Norwegians. Kobelev's eyes sparkled with excitement as he explained the details of the relay start to his athletes.

"We are only in Europe a few days, not yet recovered from Anchorage, and already you have promising results! My coaching friends have noticed your progress, and some already have anxious. They say America is huge country with many peoples and great wealth. What chance has a small country like Poland, Austria, or Romania if the United States decides to excel in biathlon? Even Russia sees you as a possible threat. So, congratulations! You earning the respect of even the strongest biathlon nations."

"She–it, they just know we're going to kick their asses by the time we get to Italy," Burl Palmer drawled.

"Maybe you right, Cowboy," Vlad smiled, "and relay is best place to show them. Every nation has individual champions, but true test of a strong national program is relay. Tomorrow, all of you race and we look at these results when we deciding who competes in Olympic Games." He went on to explain the women's start order and lane assignments.

"Now the men. Heikki, you want to scramble?" Vlad asked the white-haired Finn.

"Sure, if it's okay with the other guys." Everyone nodded their approval.

"For the men, we are fourteenth in Nation's Cup, so you start in lane four, second row. After hundred meters you are free to skate out of your lane, so you try to move up with lead pack. Oliver, you skiing second, Burl, third, and Grandfather, you going last."

"Uh, Vlad?" Oliver interrupted, his voice rising testily. "I'd rather ski third."

"What difference, second or third?" Vlad barely concealed his impatience.

"Hell, no difference to me, Vlad," Burl responded, defusing the tension. "If the corporate whiz kid wants to ski third, no problem."

Vlad continued, "Johnson, you starting right behind Heikki. After meeting, you and Thomas talk to Norwegians about team order, but I want you to start."

"Okay, Vlad." Matt had little experience skiing relays, and virtually none skiing the lead-off leg. But if Vlad wanted him to start, he knew enough not to question the coach's decision.

Although Sunday was gray with a low overcast threatening snow, the biathlon stadium was thronged with spectators. Because the men didn't compete until 1300, Matt and Thomas were handed a radio and sent to the steep climb on the red loop. They waited with the coaches, listening as the cheering bystanders followed the race through the forest below. Finally, competitors appeared through the trees and began skating up the long, steep hill. Matt and Thomas were so caught up in the action that they forgot to report the race details over the radio. A German girl led a train of about a dozen racers and Kate Anderson was hanging tough in fifth or sixth place.

By the final leg, the Russians had moved up to challenge their former teammates from Belorussia who were gaining on the Germans, the Norwegians, the French and amazingly, the Americans. Twelve seconds separated the top six teams as they approached the range through a frenzied crowd to shoot standing.

Moments later, when they passed Matt and Thomas on their final lap, the German was in the lead followed by Norway, but Sandy Stonington was closing in on second place. As she hammered up the difficult hill, focused on the Norwegian racer ahead of her, Matt recognized the fierce concentration that she'd first shown during the Lake Placid treadmill test.

"Range, this is Johnson. It's going to be close! Sandy's in third, but the Russian and the Belorussian are gaining…over!"

Moments later they heard the muffled roar of the appreciative crowd. Thomas smiled, "Well, it sounds like the Germans won it!" Then their radio crackled, "Son of a gun, she did it! Sandy held off the Russians in a sprint to the finish! Our women just won a bronze medal in a World Cup relay!"

The scene in the wax room was pure jubilation. Kobelev engulfed the women in classic Russian bear hugs, kissing them on each cheek. The competitors, though flushed and sweaty, were euphoric. Photographers jockeyed for position. Stanley Reimer was in his glory, surrounded by journalists who scribbled notes, and TV crews thrusting microphones in his face as the video cameras rolled tape. Someone produced a large American flag and the four women stood together with the Stars and Stripes draped across their shoulders.

"So, the women show us the way!" Vlad announced. "Now is time for the men! Sergeant Jankowski already is waiting on the range for zeroing. Heikki and Matt, be sure you are not late for your start."

Matt was among the first competitors in the relay start area. The lanes had been set across the outrun of the jumping complex. Because it was wide enough for only ten tracks, a second start line had been marked in the snow five meters behind the first, and further back, a third. In the Nation's Cup standings for the men, Russia was first, followed closely by Germany. Italy was third and Finland was assigned to lane four. The American team was fourteenth in the standings partly because their budget hadn't permitted participation at last spring's World Cups or the pre-Christmas events. They would line up in lane four, five meters behind the Finns. Matt wondered if that was why Vlad had selected Heikki to scramble, as he watched the biathlete from Duluth chat with Finland's lead-off skier in his native language.

As Matt tried to shake the tightness from his thighs, he noticed that the sullen Bulgarian from the 20K was starting in lane three, just behind the Italians. As they warmed up in the parallel tracks, the Bulgarian made eye contact and Matt nodded back. The Bulgarian showed no reaction as he glided past less than a meter away.

At the five minute warning, the athletes began to strip off warmups and adjust their pole straps. Vlad held their rifles as the two Americans removed their jackets and straightened their Lycra bibs.

"So, you are ready?" The tension in the air was like lightning before a thunderstorm. Vlad, however, seemed energized by it. "I tell you, boys, there is nothing more exciting than starting a biathlon relay! Your first job, stay out of trouble; protect your equipment. But if you have problem, Andy is over the bridge with extra poles and skis. Second, stay in the train. Relax for the first skiing loop. You will be surprised that the leaders don't go faster. But when you arrive at range for prone shooting, the race really begins! You can't imagine how fast the leaders will shoot. After that it's, how you say in English, balls-to-wall!"

In their brilliant racing suits, the athletes were fidgeting like thoroughbreds as the starter shouted final instructions in German. A dozen officials were stationed in the gaps between the starting lanes, their arms outstretched to restrain the competitors until the gun went off. Matt noticed the valley was strangely quiet. He had become so accustomed to the music, the crackle of firing on the range, and the cheering of the crowd that silence seemed ominous.

The gunshot rang into the stillness, the athletes surged down the tracks, and the stadium exploded with the screaming of thousands. Within seconds, Heikki opened a ten meter gap. Matt panicked. He'd been caught flat-footed at the start and was in danger of being the last competitor out of the stadium!

In desperation, he heaved on his poles for the final meters of the prepared tracks. Ahead of him snow was flying as the leaders entered the skating zone and thrashed for position. To his right a racer caught a tip, and spun 180 degrees. He struggled to turn around, but tripped another competitor and they both sprawled in the soft snow.

As Matt zig-zagged avoiding the pileup, he drew abreast of the Bulgarian. The trail narrowed as the competitors approached the overpass. The course was wide enough for two racers to skate side by side, but as they approached the incline, their pace slowed and there was jockeying for position. A Frenchman and a Swede surged by on Matt's right, jamming him closer to the Bulgarian. Once the Swede passed, Matt skated back to the right, giving the Bulgarian enough space for the steep climb. Matt thought the determined competitor would explode into the opening and push ahead, but the Bulgarian held back.

Hell, if he's not going for it I will, Matt thought, throwing his weight onto his left pole. The instant the pole began to bend under Matt's strength, the Bulgarian's right ski slashed out like a scythe cutting grain. The edge of the ski hit Matt's pole six inches above the basket and the delicate shaft shattered. Matt collapsed in a heap on the steepest section of the overpass and was trampled by the skiers behind him. Frantic competitors fired by adrenaline clambered to get around the obstacle, but the tangle of skis and poles made the pileup worse.

Although Matt had seen the Bulgarian use his ski like a weapon, in the chaos of the moment he didn't comprehend the impact of his treachery. Even after he struggled to his feet and started skiing again, he was hampered because his left pole was six inches too short. He finally stumbled to the crest of the bridge in last place, far behind the leaders who were disappearing through the trees. He was overwhelmed by frustration, embarrassment, and fury at the Bulgarian.

Accelerating down the far side of the overpass, Matt spotted Andy Christensen running beside the track, a ski pole in his outstretched hand. Matt wiggled his hand from the grip of the broken pole, and snatched the replacement.

"Tough luck, Matt. Remember, everything can change on the range. You've got three other guys counting on you!"

In spite of Andy's encouragement, the race was a total loss for Matt. He was never able to gain on the other teams, and by rushing on the range, he missed more targets than he should have. He staggered through the finish line firmly in last place and coasted to a stop clinging to his poles, his legs quivering. A volunteer threw a blanket around his shoulders, snapped open both bindings, and led him through the fence.

"Come! You must rest and drink something," said the volunteer in a thick German accent. After clearing the equipment check, Matt shuffled to the refreshment table and helped himself to a plastic cup of tea and a handful of orange slices. He sipped the steaming liquid, remembering that identical cups had been used for the urine test.

By the time Matt hauled his rifle to the wax room and changed into dry clothes the second-leg skiers had already shot standing and were skiing their final loop. A large electronic scoreboard listed the current standings of the relay teams. Only six teams were displayed at one time, and Matt was not surprised to see that USA#1 and USA/NOR were not listed among the top six. A battle raged between Germany and Russia for the gold, Italy was third, Sweden fourth, Romania fifth, and the Czech Republic sixth.

Then the scoreboard cycled down the list and listed the United States in eighth place! Burl had moved up two places since Heikki had tagged him. If Oliver and Ragnar both had strong races, they had a chance to remain in the top ten. Matt was sure Vlad would be happy with those results for their first relay in Europe.

Burl handed off to Oliver in eighth place and in spite of fierce competition, Wainwright held on to his position. The final leg developed into a barn burner as the Italians pulled ahead of the Russians and challenged the Germans for first. Eight seconds separated the top three teams as they headed out for the final skiing loop. The race for the medals was so intense that few of the frenzied fans noticed when Ragnar Haugen quietly pushed the Americans from eighth to seventh place, then battled Romania for sixth.

It was a dead heat for first place between the hosting German team and the Italians, who edged out the Russians by less than a meter. The stadium fell silent, the fans uncertain whether their favorites had won the gold or were robbed at the line. Then the scoreboard displayed the top three teams, Germany, Italy, Russia, and the stadium exploded. Fans hugged each other, waved German flags, and clanged cow bells. They scarcely noticed Sweden cross the line for fourth place, the Czechs, a minute later in fifth, and Ragnar Haugen several strides ahead of Romania for sixth.

The Americans were on the scoreboard! As additional teams finished, the board would cycle down the order, but every few seconds it would return to display the top six relay teams in the world, and the United States was on the board. Matt's vision blurred as he blinked back tears, his emotions warring between pride in his teammates and disappointment in himself.

Again the athletes assembled in the small park in the center of Ruhpolding, led by local children in Bavarian costumes. In the hours since the final racer crossed the line the officials had checked, and rechecked the results. As the mayor once again addressed the competitors, volunteers circulated through the park distributing packets of results.

In the individual races, the top ten finishers were called to the stage in reverse order. The Americans cheered loudly as Sandy was recognized for ninth place in the 15K.

When Dimitry Popov was introduced to receive his bronze medal in the sprint race, Vladimir Kobelev slapped him on the back as he jogged forward. Returning from the stage, Popov accepted the congratulations of the United States biathletes. His gold tooth flashed as he shook hands, the World Cup medal hanging from a wide ribbon around his neck. He held the medal out to Matt, who took it in his hand, surprised by its weight. The gregarious Russian slapped Matt's shoulder, "Johnsonmatt, in you first World Cup you are learning very much! For me, I am competing five years internationally before I taking home medal. I thinking, for you it will not be five years!"

The Americans cheered again when Sandy, Trudy, Kate and Paula were called to receive their bronze medals for the relay. The four United States women huddled together on the platform. On the silver medal step, the four Norwegian women looked as if they had been cast for their parts in Hollywood. Grete Dybendahl's face was radiant as she smiled and waved to the crowd.

After the ceremony, the athletes were instructed to follow their guides to the town hall for the World Cup banquet. The Rathaus was a beautifully restored fortress in the center of Ruhpolding. The town offices were located on the upper floors, but the ground level was a large hall which had been filled with tables.

There was good-natured shouting and gesturing as athletes recruited friends from other countries to join their tables. When the Americans stepped into the hall Trudy was surrounded by fawning Italians, who whisked her to the far side of the room. Matt saw Sergeant Jankowski talking with two heavy men in dark sweaters, who led him to a table of Polish athletes.

In the crush, Matt lost his roommate. Eventually he spotted Thomas and Emily Livengood sitting at a table of Japanese athletes. The Norwegians and Swedes filled a corner of the hall with laughter, and Matt could see Ragnar and Sandy in the center of the commotion. As he started in that direction, a firm hand stopped him. Matt was dazzled by the smile of Dimitry Popov, his two bronze medals still hanging from his neck. "Johnsonmatt, you must dinner with us, our trainer commands it!"

With an expansive gesture Popov pointed to Vladimir Kobelev who was engrossed with a former colleague now coaching the Russian National Team. Kobelev looked up to see Matt and Dimitry. *"Da...da...da...,"* Matthew, you sit. I introduce you my friends from Siberia!"

Matt sat next to Popov, flattered that the Russians had invited him to join their table. He was concentrating on Popov's thickly accented English, when someone slipped into the chair on his right. He turned to see Grete Dybendahl, smiling mischievously. She leaned past Matt to speak to Popov, "Dimitry, the Norwegian boys sent me to make sure you Russians have plenty of beer. Then maybe you'll tell them your training secrets."

Popov angled for a better view of the Scandinavian corner. The waitresses, dressed in elaborate Bavarian dirndls, were distributing heavy steins of foaming German beer among the gathering. In answer, Popov stopped a waitress, grabbed a stein, and stood on his chair. One of his teammates knew what was coming and shrilled a deafening whistle. The hall fell silent as athletes looked up from their conversations. Popov raised the heavy stein, sloshing beer on the table.

"I make toast! First to organizers of Ruhpolding World Cup for the best event of the tour." There were cheers across the room, and those who held steins raised them. "Next, I make toast to host team, Germany and for fine results here in Ruhpolding! I hoping you understand, we not will be so easy for you next month in Italy." More cheers, catcalls and a smattering of boos.

"Finally, I toasting our friends from Norway who send to us Norse ski-goddess Grete Dybendahl! We accept your gift of international friendship and bring Grete home with us to Russia!" Popov raised his stein and drained it in one continuous pour to the raucous applause of the other athletes.

The dining room staff served a traditional Bavarian feast of veal, boiled potatoes, and sweet red cabbage. The beer steins were replenished as soon as they were emptied, and a local band filled the hall with songs and yodeling. When the meal was finished, the tables were cleared and the furniture stacked in the back of the hall. The German athletes flooded the dance floor followed by others from Austria, Switzerland, and Poland. Then the experienced folk dancers pulled novices from the audience. Koreans, Canadians and Australians, unfamiliar with the steps, were awkwardly bobbing and hopping to the music.

Matt had no intention of participating until Grete grabbed his hand, "Come, we must dance!"

Matt felt clumsy, but Grete guided him through the steps, and soon he was dancing smoothly, enjoying being close to her. The band played a polka and the dance floor was a whirling mass of athletic dancers.

When the band finally took a break, the sweating, red-faced athletes left the dance floor. Some lined up at a counter where women in dirndls were filling beer steins as fast as the carved tap handles would permit. Other athletes headed for the door of the Rathaus and the parking lot beyond, where they cooled off in the winter air. Grete led Matt to the stairs. "I must go to the Sport-Hotel to finish packing. We go by bus to München at 5:30 in the morning."

"Whoa! Nothing like an early start! We're staying here to train for a few days before heading to Lillehammer."

"I know. I talk already with Ragnar. You are flying to Oslo on Wednesday. Our team will not come to Lillehammer 'til Monday the twenty-sixth. But my home is in Gjøvik, only one hour from Lillehammer, so maybe I come to the Birkiebineren stadium before the others arrive. I look for you there, okay?"

"That would be great! I watched everything I could on TV during the '94 Games; but to actually race in Lillehammer…, I'm stoked…, I mean, really excited! I'll walk you back to the Sport-Hotel if you like," Matt offered.

"That would be nice, but our team leader has reserved the bus. He will check to make certain we are there, or we get into trouble. You stay with your friends and enjoy the party. I see you in Lillehammer next week." She disappeared through the tall, oak doors into the cold Bavarian night.

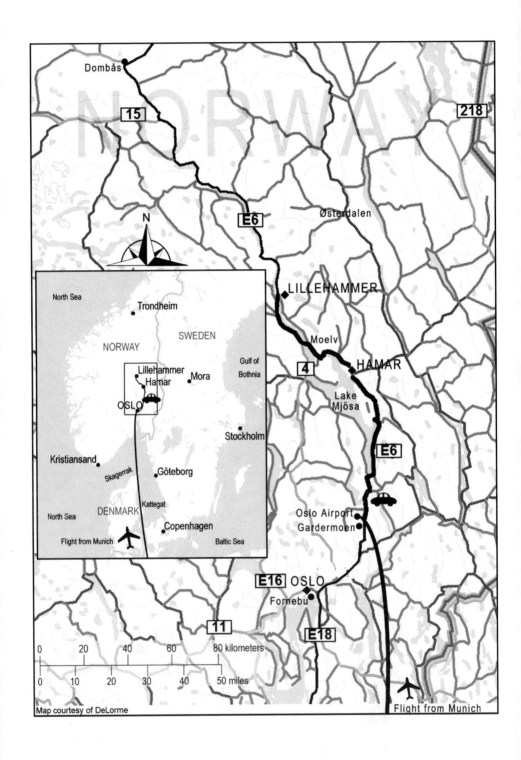

Dombås

15

218

Østerdalen

E6

N

LILLEHAMMER

Moelv

4

HAMAR

Lake
Mjösa

E6

North Sea

Trondheim

SWEDEN

NORWAY

Lillehammer

Mora

Hamar

Gulf of
Bothnia

OSLO

Stockholm

Kristiansand

Göteborg

Skagerrak

Kattegat

North Sea

DENMARK

Copenhagen

Baltic Sea

Flight from Munich

Oslo Airport
Gardermoen

E16 OSLO

Fornebu

11

E18

Flight from Munich

0   20   40   60   80 kilometers

0   10   20   30   40   50 miles

Map courtesy of DeLorme

Culture Shock

11

The flight from Germany to Norway was uneventful. As they approached Oslo, Matt could see the runways of the old airport, Fornebu, to the south of the city. They were flying into the new Oslo Airport at Gardermoen, 50 kilometers north of the city, which would make their bus ride to Lillehammer almost an hour shorter than it would have been from Fornebu. Like the airport in Munich, the new Oslo airport was stark, efficient and spotlessly clean, though the light colored wood detail throughout the building gave it a warm and distinctively Scandinavian feel. Matt noticed that many of the customs and immigration officials were attractive young women, who were friendly and helpful, unlike their stern counterparts in Germany.

The bus was loaded and threading its way through the busy streets of Oslo by 1530. As they climbed the gentle hills behind the city heading northeast on Highway E6, Matt was encouraged by the deep blanket of snow covering the fields and forests. In Hamar, Ragnar pointed out the illuminated shape of the Olympic Speed Skating Arena, known as the Viking Ship, because it resembles the overturned hull of the ancient wooden boats used by early Norwegians to cross the oceans.

At Moelv the bus crossed Lake Mjösa then continued north on the western shore. Matt caught a glimpse of Lillehammer, its cheerful golden lights reflected in the dark water. There was no doubt they were approaching the site of the 1994 Olympics. Bathed in spotlights on the hillside above the village, the breathtaking ski jumps were beacons to skiing enthusiasts everywhere.

The bus crossed the lake on another bridge, drove into a short tunnel and emerged in the narrow streets of Lillehammer. The driver skirted the business district and climbed the hillside east of town. Ahead loomed the massive roof of Håkon Hall, the Olympic ice hockey arena, with the twin ski jumps towering in the night sky beyond. Matt was swept by the sense that they had just arrived at the heart of Nordic skiing.

The bus pulled into the Birkebeineren Lodge, a squat rambling building with rustic wooden siding and a thick frosting of snow on its massive roof. The interior was warm and comfortable, the aged pine paneling glowing with a golden hue. The walls were decorated with ancient, handmade skis and carved farming tools. Photos and paintings on the walls depicted Nordic skiers, either racing or perched high on a mountainous overlook. The lodge felt like a clubhouse for ski worshippers.

The buffet dinner was basic: boiled potatoes, beef stew, salad, bread and butter. Matt was satisfied because he preferred straight-forward, no nonsense meals. He liked having all his food in front of him from the start, that way he knew how much to eat.

Matt had abandoned his morning runs in Ruhpolding because of jet lag and accumulated fatigue. But he was awake by 6:30 in Lillehammer and eager to see the town. After fumbling for his training clothes in the dark he walked to the lobby and out the main door. Ragnar, Heikki and Sandy were stretching in the parking lot.

"Okay, Rookie! You're just in time. You want to go uphill first to see the Olympic facilities or down to the village?" Ragnar assumed the role of tour guide.

"The jumps and the ice rink." Matt answered without hesitation.

"Good! That's where we go this morning. Tomorrow we run down through town." Ragnar led them through a labyrinth of residential streets bordered by four-foot snow banks.

They emerged on an open hillside; the town and lake below, the towering ski jumps on their right, massive Håkon Hall directly ahead. The athletes jogged around the huge arena and the smaller practice rink, Kristin Hall. As the sun was brightening the sky over Lillehammer, Ragnar led his teammates diagonally up the hillside to Lysgårdsbakkene, the ski jumping complex. Matt decided that the ski jumps at Lake Placid and Ruhpolding paled in comparison. Unlike Lake Placid, where the concrete towers dominate the skyline, the Lysgårdsbakkene jumps are carved into the hillside. The broad expanse of the landing, a huge, cresting wave, awed the biathletes. Matt, who had spent much of his life on skis, could scarcely imagine the thrill of riding the precipitous outrun, to say nothing of taking flight.

"Ragnar, this Norwegian word *Birkebeineren* is everywhere. I've heard about that race in Wisconsin, then there's the lodge, and the stadium up the road. What does *Birkebeineren* mean in Norwegian?"

Ragnar answered as he ran. "It's a special word with lots of history. *Birkebeineren* means birch legs. In medieval times, people here were so poor they protected their feet from the deep snow by wrapping their legs with birch bark. The infant prince, Håkon Håkonsson, was rescued by two of these 'Birch Legs' who carried him on skis from Lillehammer to Østerdalen, saving his life and the royal succession. Skiing is much more than a sport to Norwegians."

They returned to the Birkebeineren Lodge and joined their teammates at the breakfast buffet. There was a wide variety of bread, cheese, and steaming hot cereal. Matt determined he would try the pickled fish for breakfast before he left Norway. But not just yet.

For Matt, training conditions in Lillehammer on the days before the World Cup were almost ideal. The weather was beautiful: cold, plenty of snow and no wind. By the weekend other teams were arriving. The Russians joined the Americans at the Birkebeineren Lodge so Matt was reunited with his friend Dimitry, and began to feel more comfortable around Dimitry's hulking teammates. The only other group scheduled to stay at the Birkebeineren was the Norwegian team, but they would arrive a day before the first race, since many of them lived nearby.

At a team meeting after dinner Vlad made an announcement. "You notice we were testing skis all afternoon. We have interesting opportunity. Ragnar, maybe you should tell."

"You guys know I stay in touch with old friends here in Norway. Well, one guy is now assistant coach of the Norwegian National Cross-Country Team. After the Olympics here in '94 we learned that the Norwegians had very fast skis in those competitions because of special stone grinding."

"Alpine ski manufacturers discovered that grinding textures into the base of a ski improved its performance. But that Alpine technology is appropriate for speeds of forty to ninety miles per hour, speeds we never see in biathlon. A couple of craftsmen here in Scandinavia have been tinkering with what makes a cross-country ski go fast. There's this old guy in Dombås, two hours north of here, who spent $40,000 on a stone grinding machine from Germany, took it apart, and rebuilt it for cross-country skis. He won't let anyone in his shop and nobody's even seen the machine. But the Norwegians on the '94 Olympic Team had wicked fast skis!"

"Here's the deal. Kjell Svensberget, who owns the grinder, signed a contract with the Norwegian National Team to stone grind skis exclusively for them, with one exception. Svensberget demanded the right to prepare skis for the American Team if we ever asked. The Norwegians agreed, probably because we aren't a threat to them. We never would have known about this if my old racing buddy hadn't tipped me off. He loaned us some skis that Svensberget prepared. We've been testing them all afternoon, and we don't have anything that will touch them!"

"You didn't test my Rossignols!" Oliver was indignant.

"That's right, Oliver. We concentrated on the team's twelve pairs of wax testing skis, which are usually in the ballpark with everyone's race skis, even your precious Rossignols. Vlad, Andy and I are convinced Svensberget can make all our skis faster, so we are going to take some skis up to Dombås on the train tomorrow morning."

"Well, you can count me out," Oliver was decisive. "My Rossies come from the factory with the best base in the industry. I'll stick with Rossignol's research staff rather than some Gyro Gearloose in the wilds of Norway."

"I tell you, this man's stone grinding is definitely fast. If I am still racing, I having all my skis prepared by him," Vlad's endorsement seemed to balance Oliver's skepticism.

Andy Christensen tallied the skis to be taken to Dombås. Oliver was the only athlete to totally decline the opportunity, but several others listed only two pairs for stone grinding. Matt was in a quandary because he owned only two pairs of racing skis. As Andy approached with the clipboard, Matt noticed Vlad nodding at him. Matt signed up to have both pairs of skis stone ground.

Before dawn the next morning, Matt and Andy dropped Gopher and Ragnar at the station with forty-four pairs of skis in four heavy bags. At almost nine that evening, they returned to the train station to haul the exhausted couriers and their precious cargo back to the lodge. Andy couldn't contain his curiosity, "Well, guys, does the old guy know what he's talking about?"

Ragnar and Gopher were groggy from a long day.

"Well, Andy," Ragnar answered. "We have to see, but I bet they're going to be faster."

"If this guy's stone grinding is so super, why's he doing it for us?" Matt asked.

"When he was our age the Nazis occupied Norway. He and a few friends escaped to the mountains and avoided capture for more than two years. Sometimes they got help from townspeople in the valleys, but mostly they hid in snow caves and ate small animals or birds. They were a real headache to the Germans, sabotaging their vehicles and destroying communications equipment. But according to Svensberget, his little band of resistance fighters never would have survived without help from the Americans. In fact, a United States bomber crew died trying to drop supplies to them in bad weather. This is a small way to thank America for keeping him alive in 1941."

As the van pulled in to the lodge, Gopher asked, "Did they save us any supper?"

"Damn, Gopher!" Andy answered, "You think we'd forget you guys? Actually, the Competition Committee scheduled a coaches' meeting that just broke up. Lots of talk about Olympic qualifying procedures and doping control. I'll tell you what, Mary Manheimer is not intimidated by any of those WBU honchos."

"Anyway, the Russian coaches asked the hotel staff to delay dinner so they could take a sauna. You guys ought to head on down there, it's a scorcher."

There was no hesitation from Ragnar, "Drop your pack in your room Gopher, and grab a towel. I'll see you there in five minutes."

Ragnar's enthusiasm was so contagious, Matt decided to join the two travelers for a sauna.

The floor was a textured tile surrounding a dunking pool in the center of the room. The pool was four feet in diameter, made of smooth fieldstone, and it looked deep. Chunks of ice floated on the surface of the water. A row of recliners lined one wall, three of which were occupied by bathers, their wet bodies glistening and their skin a mottled red.

One of the men was lying on his back, totally naked. He made no attempt to cover himself, and appeared oblivious to everyone else in the room. A second man, towel loosely wrapped around his waist, lay on his side talking to a woman on the third recliner, between the two men. She was also naked, lying on her back with her towel draped casually across her hips. She glanced at the man on her left as he spoke, then laughed out loud.

Matt felt a hand on his elbow as Ragnar directed him to the changing room, "Remember, Rookie, you're in Scandinavia now!" There was an assortment of warmup suits hanging from pegs. Matt's anxiety increased when he noticed that some of the plastic shower slippers were too small to belong to men.

Gopher got undressed, then looped a towel around his waist. Ragnar stood at the door with his towel over his shoulder, "We must go in quickly so it doesn't lose too much heat."

As Ragnar reached for the wooden handle, the door burst open and two glistening female bodies bolted for the ice water. Matt turned to watch the women scamper to the pool and lower themselves into the water, then gasp for air after dunking below the surface. Matt stood transfixed as the first girl rose from her icy dip, streaming with water. She wiped her eyes, ran her fingers back through her blonde hair and stood beside the pool, a classic example of feminine beauty.

"Come on, you get used to that soon enough," Ragnar pushed Matt through the insulated door into the hot room. The cedar-lined chamber was dimly lit and crammed with sweating, naked bodies. Matt's eyes were slow to adjust.

"Okay! Johnsonmatt, *mya drug!* Come! Sit with you Russia friend, Dimitry!"

As Matt peered in the direction of Dimitry's voice, a hand dragged him through the stifling heat. There was a shifting of sweaty buttocks on the wooden benches, and Matt squeezed between two poached, wet bodies. His back burned when he leaned against the cedar boards behind him, his perch was only inches below the ceiling on the third and highest shelf in the small room.

Matt's eyes began to adjust as Popov's sparkling smile illuminated the dim chamber. "So, Johnsonmatt, now you are real Nordic skier! You like sauna?"

"I don't know. It's pretty damn hot!"

"Da...da...da..., hot is good! And pool is very cold. Good for sportsmen. Make very strong in heart!" Dimitry thumped his chest with his fist. Matt noticed that others in the sauna were hunched over in the intense heat, their heads drooped in silence. Popov, however, acted as if he were carrying on a conversation in the dining room.

Matt shifted slightly on the bench. Popov had squeezed him onto the bench although there wasn't actually an extra place. Sensing Matt's discomfort, Dimitry moved a little to give the American a few more centimeters. But on Matt's left side, the leg, hip and shoulder of his neighbor had fused to his in the heat, and then tensed, reclaiming some of the space.

Matt glanced left and met the stony glare of Lyudmila Kulakova, the most successful female biathlete since the sport was opened to women in 1984. She had broad cheekbones, heavy eyebrows and the determined jaw reminiscent of a commune worker pictured on propaganda posters from the former Soviet Union. When she flexed her thigh to defend her space on the bench it was an anatomy lesson. Matt could distinguish distinct muscle groups, taut as steel cables beneath the thin layer of skin.

Their sweat mingled and dripped to the bench below. Matt noticed that his biceps did not have Lyudmila's impressive definition, nor did the rest of his body radiate her undeniable impression of raw strength. Sweat poured in tiny rivulets from her neck and shoulders into her lap. Her chest and stomach were like a man's. Matt could see ribs, and a washboard abdomen. Her breasts, her only remotely feminine feature, appeared sadly out of place on the muscular torso.

Matt had never seen anyone so intimidating. He dared not reclaim his meager space on the bench. In fact, he was beginning to wonder how much longer he could endure the intense heat of the top shelf. He began to pray that someone else would leave, so that he could follow unobtrusively.

His eyes were finally adjusting to the dim light, though they smarted from the sweat. He studied the other bathers in the tiny room. The upper level was mostly Russians and Norwegians. Kobelev was squeezed into the far corner, smiling through the gloom. On the lower, second level, Matt saw his teammates: Gopher, Ragnar, Kate Anderson, and Heikki. On the lowest bench sat three heavy Russian coaches, Trudy Wilson and Stan the Man. Matt grinned, thinking how embarrassed Trudy would be when she discovered her mascara had smudged into dark splotches below her eyes.

Compared to the burly Russians, Stan looked comical. He was thin, and it was evident that his spindly arms and legs had never been exposed to serious exercise. But while most of the sauna inhabitants lowered their heads, or endured the ferocious temperature with their eyes closed, Stan braved the heat and gawked at one naked woman after another. His pallid skin was turning deep pink, but Matt suspected Stan would endure the heat as long as a woman remained in the sauna.

Within minutes of entering Matt was drenched with sweat. Popov chatted amiably in Russian with his teammates. An obvious, unspoken challenge was in the air; no one wanted to be the first to bolt for the ice water pool. Matt fought down panic. He couldn't last much longer. The heat was overpowering.

Mercifully, Trudy broke the standoff. She stood, defiantly facing the other occupants of the sauna, drawing everyone's attention to her perfect figure. In the same motion, she retrieved her bath towel from the bench and deliberately draped it around her waist. "Well, the rest of you can bake your brains all night, but I've had enough."

Stan and two of the Russian coaches were within arm's length of Trudy during her performance, and as she pushed through the door they stumbled over each other to follow. That signaled an exodus. Matt saw his chance and lowered himself to the floor on wobbly knees. Glancing back, he was stunned to see Grete Dybendahl smiling from the top level opposite the Russians. He hadn't noticed her before. Stumbling toward the door, Matt was afraid he couldn't survive another five seconds, yet Grete remained on the top bench, sweating profusely but clearly enjoying herself.

The ice water pool was so painfully frigid that Matt wondered if the freezing pool had ever caused a heart attack. He imagined every cell in his body contracting in panic from the numbing cold. At the same time, it felt delightfully invigorating following the stifling heat. He discovered that after the initial shock, the water actually felt good. He was almost enjoying the pool, even as chunks of ice bumped his chest and shoulders. But soon a numbing ache invaded his feet and he hoisted himself onto the wet tiles.

The recliners were all filled so Matt joined other athletes sitting on the floor, leaning against the paneled wall. He closed his eyes and pressed his hands to the tiles as the room began to spin.

"Dizzy, Rookie?" Ragnar had followed Matt from the pool. "It's normal, especially in a real sauna like this. Your blood vessels must adjust to the temperature extremes. That's why rest is important before you go back in the hot room."

Matt almost choked. He hadn't considered returning to the sauna. It was blissfully relaxing sitting against the wall with his teammates while the room spun. He could hear others splashing in the ice water, but he was so relaxed he couldn't open his eyes.

Someone gently shook his shoulder. He looked up at the playful smile of Grete Dybendahl.

"Come, you get cold sitting here too long. We must go to the hot room again." She turned and led the way to the insulated door, holding her towel casually in her left hand. Matt was enthralled. It was evident that Grete was in excellent condition. She was slim, but muscular. Her arms and shoulders were strong, and she held herself erect. Her torso narrowed to a trim waist and curved gracefully at the hips. Unlike Kulakova, who appeared to be a woman in a man's body, Grete was all woman, although a fit, athletic woman.

The second session in the hot room wasn't as bad as the first experience. There were fewer bathers and the door opening and closing had lowered the temperature slightly. Grete sat next to Matt, a towel draped across her lap, her body reflecting the golden glow of the rich cedar-lined room. Matt struggled not to stare, but it was impossible. She was the most beautiful woman he had ever seen.

"So you take skis to Kjell Svensberget for stone grinding?" Grete leaned closer as if sharing a secret.

"Yeah, he worked on them today." Matt was afraid to look at her.

"You are very fortunate," Grete whispered. "There are many racers in Norway who would pay a lot of money to have Kjell work on their skis, but his contract with the National Team forbids it. There were Norwegian coaches who hoped you Americans would never hear about Kjell and his stone grinder."

"You mean there are Norwegian coaches who are actually worried about us?" Matt smiled at the back-handed compliment. Grete hesitated, "Well, not exactly. These coaches were afraid you would sell your stone ground skis to the Russians or the Germans." She looked contrite for a second, then broke into her smile and gave him an elbow to the ribs.

"Are they really faster?" Matt asked, risking a glance in her direction.

"Especially in new snow. You just wait!"

Grete hopped lightly to the floor, then pushed through the door with Matt close behind. While other athletes splashed in the pool and relaxed on recliners, Matt followed her to a door in the glass wall of the solarium. Opening the door, she dropped her towel and stepped out into the deep, powder snow. She strode purposefully into the frigid night, then turned to face Matt, who remained in the doorway staring in disbelief. Standing in the middle of the snow-filled yard, illuminated by the stars and the glow of lights inside, Grete looked like a mystical Norse goddess. She laughed, stretched her arms wide, and like a tree cut down in the forest, fell stiffly backward into the snow sweeping the light fluff on top of her.

Then Grete hopped up and bounded back toward the building, her body brilliant red with patches of snow sliding down her smooth skin. She grabbed Matt's hand and dragged him into the yard. "Come, come, before you get cold. This is the best!"

"I don't know, Grete, my feet are already…."

He didn't have a chance to finish. Dragging him into the deep snow, she planted her foot, tripped him, and pushed him face first into the powder. He sputtered like a non-swimmer caught in the surf. Laughing and holding him down, she piled fresh snow over him until he was totally submerged.

Finally, she released him and he stumbled back to the building, gasping for air, a numbing ache invading his extremities. Grete was waiting at the door.

"So, what do you think of a real Scandinavian sauna?" Grete asked as she led him toward the lounge chairs.

Matt was still recovering from the intense cold of the snow. Clumps of white were melting out of his hair. He wasn't sure he could talk. "How often...do you...take saunas like this?"

"When I'm home, once a week, Sunday afternoon. In the winter when we are traveling, it is not always possible. Do you like it?"

"I don't know. I think I could learn to like it. Especially with you... You're amazing!"

It seemed only a moment later that she was again shaking his shoulder, "Come, time for our third round."

"Aw, Grete, I don't know. I've had it. I don't think I can stay awake for another round."

"Matt, you must. The third is the best. Come!"

It took a supreme effort, but Matt struggled to his feet and followed Grete into the hot room for a third time. There were six others in the cedar-lined chamber when they found their seats on the top bench. Ragnar and Gopher sat across from Matt and Grete just below the ceiling. A Norwegian athlete and a Russian also sat on the top level. Kobelev stretched out horizontally on the second shelf, and Stanley sat like a shriveled prune on the lowest bench.

Matt tried not to look at the timer, but he couldn't resist. Six minutes! If anyone left, he'd follow, if not he might be able to hold out for six more minutes. Then Grete stepped down from the top shelf. Great! She's leaving, Matt thought! I can follow her out. But she stopped in front of the door and faced the stove. Her towel was wrapped around her waist, a short skirt which emphasized her athletic figure. Blocking the door, she reached for the wooden bucket of water.

"Third time! We throw water on the rocks. Do you approve?" The others in the sauna nodded enthusiastically.

"But there is a rule, no one must leave for five minutes. Do you agree?" Again there were nods from the experienced bathers. Matt tried to suppress his panic as Grete ladled water over the hot rocks on the stove. The water evaporated instantly with an ominous hissing. As she scooped more water from the bucket, the room was filled with the rich scent of balsam.

Like an invisible monster, the scalding vapor curled down from the ceiling and engulfed Matt's head and shoulders. His ears burned, even the hairs inside his nostrils curled. It felt as if a scalding blanket had been thrown over his shoulders. The others had hunkered down, but were enduring the steam without complaint. Matt wondered if he could permanently damage his lungs breathing the boiling vapor.

And still Grete kept pouring on the water! When the bucket was empty, she surveyed the small chamber like a conductor about to bring her orchestra to life. She whipped the white towel from her waist, and flapped it rhythmically above the stove, creating currents which circulated the scalding air from the ceiling down around the bathers like a shower of boiling, forest-scented water. Matt desperately wanted to close his eyes from the searing heat, to slip to a lower bench, to stop breathing. But he couldn't take his eyes off the magnificent woman standing in front of them naked yet composed, her lovely body swaying with every wave of the towel.

Then Grete switched methods. Grasping the towel by a corner, she raised her arm and twirled it like a cowboy spinning a lariat. The spinning towel, inches from the ceiling somehow found more scalding air, and the bathers were once again surrounded by fierce heat.

Ragnar had mentioned that attitudes were different in Scandinavia, but Matt hadn't known what to expect. His head was whirling, not only from the sauna, but from the sight of the remarkable, young Norwegian woman. Grete Dybendahl was unlike any girl he had ever known.

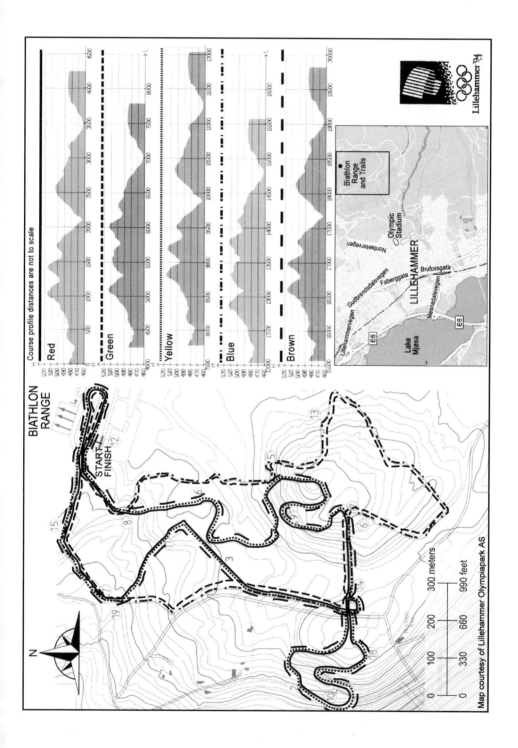

Course profile distances are not to scale

Red

Green

Yellow

Blue

Brown

BIATHLON RANGE

START FINISH

N

Lillehammer '94

Biathlon Range and Trails

Olympic Stadium

Nordsetervegen

LILLEHAMMER

Gudbrandsdalsvegen
Faberggata
Brufossgata
Lillehammervegen
Mesnadalsvegen

Lake Mjøsa

E6
E6

300 meters
990 feet

0   100   200   300 meters
0   330   660   990 feet

Map courtesy of Lillehammer Olympiapark AS

Making Headlines

12

The days before Lillehammer's World Cup seemed to fly by. The shooting range was windier than at Ruhpolding, so Thomas Oksoktaruk wore a constant grin. In Germany, if you survived the rocketing downhills, there was half a kilometer of level skiing as you approached the range, a chance to get your breathing under control and to start thinking like a shooter. In Lillehammer, however, the last 500 meters was a climb to the stadium. It wasn't a gut-busting hill like others on the course, but you knew you were climbing. This hill was a significant bonus for the more experienced competitors. An over-zealous skier might make up valuable seconds on the uphill approach, only to miss his targets because of a pulse beat elevated out of control. On the other hand, a racer who was timid on the climb could lose half a minute each time, more than two minutes in the distance event, a deficit even perfect shooting couldn't erase.

The wind was another factor at Lillehammer. Perched near the edge of the plateau overlooking the Lågen River and Lake Mjösa, the prevailing winds swept up the hillside and swirled within the berms of the shooting range.

Thomas Oksoktaruk insisted that the more difficult the conditions, the better he liked it, because some of the high-strung thoroughbreds would psych themselves out of the race. Matt agreed with Thomas, but he also suspected there were plenty of Europeans like Popov, who welcomed adversity every bit as much as the Alaskan. They would know soon enough. A high pressure system was moving in off the North Atlantic bringing cold temperatures, clear skies, and winds from the west.

Since their evening in the sauna, Matt had been captivated by Grete Dybendahl. Her playful laugh brought sunshine to the cold darkness of winter. She was a mystery to him, a constant surprise.

On Wednesday, the day before the World Cup distance races, Grete seemed uncharacteristically pensive as they returned from the stadium in a bus. "Matt, I like you. Maybe we have more in common than just biathlon. But for me these next days are difficult. Three of us are very close for the last two places on the Norwegian Olympic Team. I must concentrate all my attention on these races. You understand?"

"Sure! It's the same for me. Vlad is looking at these World Cups to decide who races in Antholz. I've got to have strong finishes here to earn a starting spot."

Grete responded, "So we must concentrate on racing for five days, maybe Sunday night we celebrate!" Her smile made him weak.

"Celebrate how? Another sauna?"

Grete laughed out loud, "You like the sauna?"

"I sure liked the one we had Monday night!"

"Okay, we celebrate success at Lillehammer World Cup with another sauna. Maybe with a name like Johnson, I make you into a Viking yet."

With clear skies and cold temperatures, the snow was firm and fast. Andy had aligned the speed trap on a sloping field behind the grandstands, which had been groomed for wax testing. Even though Matt suspected the waxing would be simple, since the air temperature had remained constant; the coaches and manufacturers' reps were going through all the motions, as if each World Cup medal depended on some exotic combination of super-secret, fluorocarbon compounds. Matt knew from painful experience that wax could have a dramatic influence in a race, but the most critical waxing conditions were around the freezing point. The temperature had not risen close to freezing since their arrival in Lillehammer, and was not expected to. Matt was confident that the competition would not be decided by wax unless the weather changed dramatically.

Matt was eager to see how his old Atomics performed after the stone grinding treatment in Dombås. He took several trips down through the speed trap with each pair of skis, unable to detect much difference. He stopped behind Andy, who was recording times on a clipboard, then resetting the timer after every run.

"Andy, I couldn't tell much difference."

"Good call, Rookie. Both pairs were within two-tenths of a second."

"In other words, that trip to Dombås didn't give us the super advantage it was supposed to."

"Whoa, not so fast! Remember, Svensberget told us the improvement would be most dramatic in new snow around the freezing point. And skis get faster the more you wax them. The two pairs that were reconditioned basically have new bottoms."

Matt nodded, "Right, I waxed 'em once last night."

"So even on boilerplate, with only one coat of wax, your reconditioned skis are as fast as anything we've tested today. If you ask me, the skis Svensberget worked on are going to be wicked fast by the time we get to Italy, even better if we get into new snow."

On the shooting range, Sergeant Jankowski was all business. The uphill approach and the persistent wind had resulted in sloppy shooting for the Americans. The Sarge had not yet lost his patience, but everyone could detect an edge of seriousness in his comments.

"Matt, you zero on target eighteen as soon as Oksoktaruk is finished. But remember, zeroing is just a formality if we have winds like this tomorrow. You can count on making sight corrections each time you shoot, maybe even within a five-round string! Now while you're waiting for Tommy to finish, you study those range flags and tell me what you see." The Sarge pressed his eye to the scope, his pencil poised to record each one of Oksoktaruk's shots. After a brief conference with the Alaskan, the coach turned to Matt, "Okay, Rookie, tell me about the wind on this range."

"It's a lot like Anchorage, coming from behind, roughly six o'clock, but squirrely, nothing steady you can count on. The wind flags down the center of the range seem to be flapping in every direction, the ones along the berms seem more steadily downrange, toward the targets."

"Pretty good call, Matt. What else?"

Matt was stumped until Jankowski glanced overhead at the bright winter sun. "Oh yeah, take a click into the sun. I guess at race time that would probably be a click up."

"Thataboy! What else?"

"I think that's about it."

"What about your racing zero? How much does it vary from your zero when you're shooting without a pulse?"

"I shoot high with a pulse, maybe a couple of clicks."

"So what do you figure this uphill approach is going to do to that zero?"

"I'll be coming in with a higher than normal pulse, so I suppose I'll tend to shoot 'em out the top."

"Right again, Rookie. Damn, with all this excellent coaching, you just might turn into a competent biathlete! So, what sight corrections will you put on to be zeroed this morning?"

"One click up for the sun, but four down for the uphill approach, or a total of three down. I wouldn't take any windage, but I'd pick a firing point next to the berm."

"Right. Now remember, Matt," Jankowski concluded, "except for the cross-firing, you might have been twelfth in your first World Cup back in Ruhpolding. If the wind is as squirrely tomorrow, there are going to be good skiers who will make some mistakes on the range. If you use your head, a top fifteen is not out of the question! You might even earn some World Cup points!"

"Okay, Sarge. Oksoktaruk convinced me that difficult conditions are an advantage. It turned out to be true in Alaska. I'm not afraid of a little wind."

"Thataboy. You just keep thinking that way, 'cause I got a feeling you're going to get your wish."

Jankowski's prediction was right on target. When Matt stepped outdoors for his morning jog to the base of the ski jumps, the flags were snapping frantically. He wondered if biathlon races were ever canceled due to high winds.

Later, at the Birkebeineren Stadium, the wind was strong but steady. Word spread among the athletes that the Competition Jury had met to consider a delay, or even cancellation, but so many teams were using the event for Olympic selection that the jury was reluctant to reschedule.

It was announced that the event would begin as planned.

The women were scheduled to race first. Matt stood on one of the toughest hills and cheered during the first laps. Sandy and Trudy appeared to be skiing strong, and Grete was turbo-charged. Late in the race, he skied back to the range to watch the shooting. The large national banners were blowing straight out, their ropes loudly clanging against the aluminum poles. The delicate wind flags which marked the shooting lanes were spinning crazily. Matt grimaced as Sandy missed two on her second prone stage and Grete missed three.

Matt had time to kill before his start, so he found a vacant press booth and stretched out on the carpeted floor. After taking a few deep breaths to relax, he closed his eyes and visualized his race from start to finish. He knew the loops so well he could picture every climb and every turn. He saw himself coming into the range, studying the wind conditions, and making the necessary corrections. He imagined the black disks falling as he shot one after another. He saw Thomas smiling at him from across the range, as the wind whipped the flags. By the time the loudspeaker announced the early starters, Matt had already enjoyed the satisfaction of a successful race, at least in his mind.

He left the press box feeling confident. During the women's race he hadn't noticed the crowd, but as he skated from the starting line wearing bib number fifty-eight he heard the enthusiastic cheering from the Norwegians who lined the trail, *"Heya...heya...heya! Ooo–Ess–Ahh, Ooo–Ess–Ahh!"*

As Matt had anticipated, the convoluted trail was like an amusement park ride. He overtook an Australian who was just starting his third loop. The uphills were as tough as Matt had imagined, but the twisting descents were no problem. The course had been perfectly groomed and the snow was so firm it showed little wear from the women's race.

Soon Matt was approaching the range for his first prone shooting. From the bottom of the hill, he began picturing himself shooting. He powered up the trail in a confident skating stride, but his mind was on shooting.

Breathing hard, he slid into firing point number two. As he slipped his rifle off and clipped the sling to the Velcro cuff on his left arm, he studied the range flags flapping wildly toward the targets. The delicate lane markers gave a different message, as they whipped toward three o'clock.

Steadying himself, Matt had a fleeting memory of his father, from one of the rare times that his dad had mentioned Vietnam. Matt recalled his father talking about night combat missions, and how he was forced to fly by instruments. "Toughest thing I ever did," he said, "You have to totally ignore your normal sensory input and trust those damn instruments, no matter how cock-eyed they seem."

Matt glanced again at the tiny wind flags and added two clicks left on his sights. His position was solid, and although the firing line was bustling with competitors, Matt isolated himself mentally as he squeezed off the first shot. It was a hit! He took a breath, relaxed, aimed, took up the slack…a second hit! With his cadence established, and confidence in the sight adjustment, he hit the remaining three targets in rapid succession.

The green loop went by quickly. The steep climb up the back side of the knoll, perhaps the most extended climb on the course, didn't even seem bad. He returned to the range confident, anticipating his first stage of standing. This time he deliberately skated the full length of the firing line, finally pulling in at point twenty-eight, the last open position on the far right of the range.

He drew deep breaths as he loaded his rifle, but then let the old Anschutz hang limp as he studied the wind. The large national flags high overhead were snapping violently toward the targets, but the small wind indicators at ground level were trying to blow to the left, although they couldn't make up their minds. After a final glance down range, Matt took a click right and brought the rifle up to his cheek. Immediately he felt the wind buffeting the barrel. He knew he couldn't force the shot, he had to relax, wait for his pulse, his breath, and also the wind. He focused on the target, took up the slack in the trigger, let the sights settle back on the bull after a gust, and the shot went off. The black target disappeared. He repeated the routine three more times, the cadence slow and halting because of the wind, but each time the black dot vanished. He was on a roll, and he knew it. One to go! He settled into position. A faint voice in his head warned him to check the wind, but the sight picture looked good, and the shot went off. A miss!

As Matt swung the rifle to his back, he glanced at the tiny wind flags, now blowing steadily to the right. Damn, if only he'd checked before the last shot! One click back to the left would probably have made the difference. He was still shaking his head in frustration as he left the range. Matt's third and fourth stages of shooting were much like the first two. He was even more alert for changes in the wind direction, and when his fourth prone shot caught the edge of the bull, but without enough force to tip the white paddle, Matt readjusted his sights and hit the final target. He knew that two-minutes penalty had to be good shooting in such difficult wind, and that inspired him on his skis.

As he approached the big climb on the blue loop, he spotted Andy Christensen, holding out a plastic cup to him. As Matt skated to Andy, the young coach ran alongside, "Here, Matt, drink this! It will give you some punch for the last loop. You're having a hell of a race, Rookie! Top twenty right now, and best American! KEEP IT UP!"

Matt choked down the contents of the cup between gasps for air as he fought his way to the top of the knoll. It tasted like warm Gatorade. His final standing shooting was right out of a textbook. Again, he settled into a firing point on the far side of the range, carefully checked the wind as he loaded the old Anschutz, patiently waited for lulls before squeezing off the shots, and hit all five. As he grabbed his poles and raced from the firing line, he heard his name over the loudspeaker, amidst unintelligible Norwegian. Jankowski give him a big thumbs up with both hands.

The final brown loop seemed endless. Andy had convinced him that top twenty was possible, but Matt was spent. The steep hills, which he had already skied during the red and yellow loops, now seemed monstrous. The twisting, giant slalom descent next to the inrun of the Olympic jump was deadly. His thighs quivered from exhaustion. But he kept repeating, top twenty…top twenty…, and pushed himself to his limits.

He hammered up into the stadium and skated the long stretch in front of the grandstand that looped back to the finish line. He was vaguely aware of cheering from the Norwegian crowd. Finally, with a desperate double pole, he flew through the finish line. As he coasted to a stop, he felt his knees wobble, and feared he was going down.

A powerful arm held him upright. Matt turned to see Kobelev's animated face, "Matt, you are a biathlete! You shooting today, I think you are the best in the race! Two minutes penalty, in wind like this! This is something that cannot be taught, it is a gift you have. You get stronger, more experience, you can be Olympic Champion!" Kobelev hugged Matt so forcefully, he was almost hoisted off the snow.

Although the finish area was clogged with exhausted athletes and their coaches, it didn't take Matt long to pull on his warmups, and follow Kobelev through the maze of fencing to the wax rooms. As they passed a section of the grandstand reserved for the media, Matt heard his name, "Matt! Matt Johnson, up here!"

He followed the voice and picked out a woman nearly concealed by a heavy down parka, a thick mohair hat and a bright scarf covering the lower half of her face. As he gazed in her direction, the woman loosened the scarf, "Matt, I'm Beverly Schmidt from *Sports Illustrated.* I covered your tryouts in Anchorage. How about a couple questions?" She pushed her way through the other reporters until she was standing next to the fence, her note pad ready.

"How does it feel to be top American in only your second World Cup?"

Matt felt drained, totally out of gas. His wasn't sure if his brain was working properly. "The race isn't over yet, we've still got a couple of guys to finish."

"You finished with only a two-minute penalty, Ragnar already has four in his first three stages. It's safe to say you're the top American, you might even stay in the top twenty!"

"That would be great! I just tried to pay attention to the wind and to make the right sight corrections. I guess it paid off."

"I'll say! If Morgoloni hadn't been tripped up by the drug testing at the tryouts, you wouldn't even be here. Do you believe there are doping violations at the international level?"

Matt was exhausted. "I haven't thought about it. I made the team, I'm racing World Cups, and in two weeks I'll be at the Olympics. I'm just grateful to be here."

Vlad, who had reluctantly tolerated the interruption, reassumed control. "This boy has nothing left. You should please talk with our team leader, Stanley Reimer, who will arrange press conference with all American athletes after relay on Sunday. We thank you for your excellent reporting about biathlon in *Sports Illustrated,* but he must now go for dry clothes and warm drink."

Vlad smiled warmly and squeezed the woman's arm as if she were an old friend, then escorted Matt back to the waxing rooms, where he was mobbed by his teammates. The women hugged and kissed him in excitement. Even Oliver, who had finished earlier, seemed impressed by Matt's shooting. The radio crackled as Sergeant Jankowski, still in the coaches' box at the range, updated the wax room on the revised standings as the late finishers crossed the line. Matt had been listed on the big scoreboard in ninth place, but with each update he moved down the list.

"Wax room, this is the Sarge, over…."

Sandy reached for the radio, "This is the wax room, go ahead Sarge…."

"The last competitor has left the range. Johnson is the top shooter in the race with two minutes penalty! Looks like Popov and an Italian are next with three each. They are in a battle for the medals with the two Germans who won last week in Ruhpolding. If Johnson's with you in the wax room, nice going, Rookie, that was an impressive demonstration of keeping your cool and reading the wind! Range, out…."

Later, when the celebration calmed a little, Matt remembered to change out of his wet shirt. As he bent over his pack, cool hands slipped under his arms, long fingers caressed his bare chest, and he was drawn into a tight embrace. Trudy Wilson's lips brushed his ear and he smelled her perfumed hair. "Matt, you were awesome out there," she purred. "I'm sorry I teased you about falling asleep in Lake Placid. I think we should give it another try and celebrate your first top-twenty World Cup finish." Before Matt could respond, she gently explored his ear with her tongue.

Vlad rescued Matt by loudly reminding the athletes they should ski a cool-down lap. Someone suggested avoiding the crowds on the biathlon trails by touring a loop on the cross-country side. Soon, eight Americans were skating out of the Birkebeineren cross-country stadium on the '94 Olympic trail. Although they were physically spent from their races, the whole team had been energized by Matt's result. He had finished seventeenth, his first top-twenty result and his first World Cup points.

Later that evening, as the athletes filed into the dining room at the Birkebeineren Hotel, Matt was treated like a celebrity. Almost every member of the Norwegian team congratulated him. Dimitry Popov, who had nipped one of his German rivals to finish in second place, brushed off his own silver medal performance and teased Matt about his shooting. "Johnsonmatt, you will be very good biathlon man. With no penalty shooting, Johnsonmatt, *Ooo–Ess–Ahh* is in four place, only seven second from bronze medal!

"Johnsonmatt, you must have new Vostok rifle so you never miss targets. I can get for you in Novosibirsk, but for now, in friendship with America, Popov will change new, blue Vostok for old, tired Anschutz of you!"

The dining room erupted in laughter. Russians, Norwegians and Americans all hooted as the gregarious Siberian poked fun at his own equipment and complimented Matt's old rifle. Sergeant Jankowski was on his feet with a hurt look on his face, "Dimitry, you know that rifle had nothing to do with today's performance. Johnson's good shooting is a direct result of excellent coaching!" The other coaches in the room, including the Norwegians and Russians jumped to their feet and applauded. Popov nodded to the Sarge respectfully, and mumbled, *"Da...da...da...."*

After the meal, as the athletes left to wax skis, Matt was approached by Stan the Man, "Matt, great job today on the range! Best shooting in the race, damn, that's terrific! We can get some mileage out of that back home. The rifle and ammo companies are going to eat this up. Potentially, we're talking major sponsorship dollars here. I noticed Beverly Schmidt from *SI* caught you as you left the finish area. You gave her a few good quotes, I hope?"

"I don't know. I was totally whipped by then. She asked me something about Snake and if I thought there was doping here on the World Cup circuit."

"Aw, that bitch is just trying to dig up some dirt. You've got to remember, Matt, the interviews after the races are as important as the races themselves. They ain't going to give you any air time unless you do well, so when you do, you've got to be prepared to make the most of it. The American press loves a winner, and they don't give a shit about anybody else."

"The USOC and the corporate sponsors are interested in one thing — results. Aside from Sandy Stonington, there haven't been any to brag about in biathlon. It's a vicious cycle; nobody's interested in supporting the team until we have some promising results, but there's no chance for success against the Europeans unless we can generate adequate funding."

Matt was having trouble paying attention.

"You're probably wondering what all this has to do with you," Stan continued. "You don't have any sponsorship contracts, am I right?"

"The ski shop in Hanover sold me my Atomics at their cost."

"Hell, that's not a sponsorship, that's unloading last year's inventory. I didn't talk to you before because I was running ragged at the tryouts, and frankly Matt, because you didn't have any results worth promoting." At this point, Stanley put his arm around Matt's shoulder and whispered as if he were sharing a valuable secret. "Look, Matt, I'm in an ideal position to wear two hats. As the National Program Director for the Biathlon Federation, I'm in touch with dozens of major corporations.

My job's easier when I have some good results to work with, like yours today. Naturally, the suppliers are more eager to jump on board during the Olympic year. In a sport like biathlon, their only chance for TV air time is during the Olympics."

Stan was nudging Matt slowly from the dining room, his arm still around the athlete's shoulder. "Now, the second hat I wear is related to the first, but unofficial. Working with all these corporate honchos has given me the opportunity to act as an agent for promising athletes like yourself. I tell you what, Matt, it's absolutely criminal that our athlete support system in the States is so screwed up. Do you think there were any other racers who finished in the top twenty today who bought their own skis? Shit, no! In fact, most of the competitors who finished in the top half of the field were probably racing on skis that had been custom made for them! Matt, if you continue to improve, I can help you make a lot of money."

They talked their way from the dining room, through the lobby, and stopped near the rustic entrance to the hotel. "Before we talk any more about details, I want you to meet a friend of mine. He's staying downtown. I told him I'd bring you down for a beer after supper."

Matt hesitated, "Well...I...ah...was going to work on my skis...."

"No problem. This little conference will only take a few minutes. I'll have you back here by nine, guaranteed." Stan pushed through the heavy door without waiting for an answer, so Matt went for his coat.

It was a short drive in the frosty van from the Birkebeineren to the Rica Victoria in downtown Lillehammer. Stan chattered the whole time. Matt had never seen the team leader so energized, except perhaps at the press conference in Anchorage following the plane crash. The lobby of the Rica had crystal chandeliers and a carpet so thick Matt almost stumbled in his hiking boots. The furniture was a deep, rich leather. Brass fixtures reflected the light like burnished gold.

Stan led through the lobby to a dark, paneled lounge. A few customers sat on stools at the bar. Matt's eyes were slow to adjust from the sparkling glitter of the lobby.

"Way to go, Stanley, right on time!" A loud American voice overpowered the other conversations in the lounge. "Over here, Stan! An' this must be America's newest sharpshooter! Mike, isn't it?"

Stan was quick with the introductions. "Matt Johnson, I'd like you to meet, Boomer Ferguson. Boomer, this is Matt."

Boomer was wedged into a booth, his legs extending out into the aisle. He wore size twelve lizard-skin cowboy boots, blue jeans and a bright turquoise sweater with a rocket embroidered over the heart. Boomer's outfit was completed by a large, cream-colored cowboy hat.

Ferguson reached across the table to shake hands as Stan and Matt slid into the booth. "Damn, Matt, it's good to meet you! Stan's been telling me about you for quite awhile now, so I feel like we're already old friends. Somabitch, you musta felt great kickin' ass on the range today, huh?"

Matt was still disoriented by a king-size cowboy sitting in a bar in Lillehammer, Norway. "I wasn't thinking much about kicking ass, I was just trying to stay on top of the wind."

"Well, I guess you done a pretty damn good job at that!" Ferguson gave Stanley a conspiratorial wink. "What're you guys drinking? They got some beer here from Tromsø, way the hell up north. They probably make it from polar bear piss, but it ain't half bad. Hey, Lars!"

A young waiter in a starched, white shirt approached their table. "Lars, we're going to need some more of them midnight sun brewskis!"

"Three Mack-Øl's then?" the waiter responded without a trace of an accent.

Moments later he returned with three tall, golden beers. "Put them on the room as before, sir?"

"You got it, Lars! Number 402."

As the waiter turned to leave he said quietly to Matt, "Good shooting in the race today. My cousin, Frode Loeberg, used to race for the national team. Now he covers the World Cup for Norwegian Radio. He told me he's never seen better shooting in such difficult conditions."

"Thanks, I was lucky," Matt was surprised that a waiter in a Lillehammer hotel knew about his race.

"Hey, let's talk business." Boomer regained control of the conversation as the waiter left, "Matt you just got a great illustration of how you've become a marketable commodity. One o'clock this afternoon you finish a Biathlon World Cup with the best shooting of the day, and a couple of hours later even the waiters in Lillehammer know who you are!"

"I don't know how much Stan here told you, but we were at UMass together in the Sports Management program. I'm from Colorado and grew up alpine skiing, this Nordic shit is too much work. After school, I got into the ski business. I worked for a couple of different importers 'til I asked myself why the hell are we were sending all the profits back to France or Austria. So I formed my own company, Sno-Rocket Equipment. We started with recreational skis an' shit, then got into snowboarding, and now we're expanding into racing, Alpine and Nordic. We're looking for promising athletes like yourself, kids with the potential to win, to promote our products."

"To be honest, Mike, I mean, Matt; to be honest, we weren't really interested in biathlon because you guys just don't get any air time. But my ol' buddy Stan tells me you're a good prospect. So son, the long an' the short of it is, I'm here to offer you a contract with Sno-Rocket, the fastest growing name in the ski industry."

Matt did not respond immediately. His mind was spinning. Stanley filled the awkward pause, "Hey, Boomer, why don't you tell Matt what he gets?"

"Yeah, right. Well, of course you get new skis; ten, twenty pairs, whatever you need. Then we'll want you in Sno-Rocket warmups, racing suits an' all that shit, whenever it doesn't conflict with Olympic Committee rules. We'll give you a Sno-Rocket jacket like this," he picked up a garish red and turquoise parka, emblazoned with the Sno-Rocket logo and festooned with snaps, buckles and metal loops. "Flashy, ain't it? The snowboarders love it and they're setting the fashion trend for the whole damn ski industry. Then of course you'll get a pile of tee shirts, sweatshirts, pins, stickers, an' that stuff. Plenty of shit to give to your friends. We want you to spread the stuff around."

"But of course that's all fluff. The real meat of this agreement's the bucks, right? For the right to be the exclusive supplier of your ski equipment for the rest of this season, Sno-Rocket is prepared to pay you five thousand dollars!"

Both Boomer and Stan studied Matt expectantly. Matt wasn't sure how to respond. He was flattered by their attention. Five thousand dollars was twice what he could make in an entire summer, but he wasn't sure he wanted to give up his old Atomics, especially after they had been stone ground by Svensberget.

"Well, son, what do you think?" Boomer leaned forward across the table.

"I don't know. Everything's happening so fast. I mean, I've never even seen Sno-Rockets. I don't know about switching skis two weeks before the Olympics."

"Hey, no problem! Look, we're a marketing company, not a manufacturer. Our skis are made in a factory in northern Italy. Hell, that same plant pumps out skis for Rossignol, Fischer and Karhu!"

"What're you racing on now?"

"Atomics," Matt answered.

"Old, beat up Atomics he bought off the shelf from a neighborhood shop; not racing stock, no camber testing, and no access to the warehouse to pick 'em out," Stan added.

"Sheeiitt, you mean to tell me this kid finished seventeenth in a World Cup on boards he bought for himself at a ski shop? I'll tell you what, son, you woulda been in the top ten today if you'd been on our skis. But hey, I hear you about switching just before the Games, so what we do is take your ol' Atomics to the factory, which ain't but over the hill from Cortina anyways, and we just give 'em the Sno-Rocket paint job. We offered the same deal to Tommy Moe, who was nervous about switching from Dynastar."

"Is Tommy Moe skiing for you?" Matt asked.

"We're still talking, but I'm pretty sure he's going to come around."

"Just out of curiosity, how much do you offer a downhill gold medalist like Tommy Moe?" Matt asked. Boomer's downhome smile disappeared.

"Son, that's of no relevance to this discussion. As far as we're concerned, biathletes and Alpine skiers could be from different planets. But I can sweeten the pot for you a little. You get any air time at all on TV back in the States with Sno-Rocket's logo clearly visible, and it's worth a thousand bucks. You win a National Championships after the Games, an' it's another thousand. If you get really lucky and win a medal at the Olympics, that's a five thousand dollar bonus. I tell you what, son, there's not another biathlete in America being offered a package like this!"

"What about the next four years? I'm more committed that ever to train through the Olympics in Korea."

"Hey, that's great, son, but we're a results-driven company, you know what I mean? You keep racing like you did today, and you'll be on Sno-Rockets as long as you want, but we renew our contracts every year."

"Even with Tommy Moe?"

For the second time Boomer frowned. "Like I said before, we're still negotiating with Tommy Moe's people. Now do you want to represent our products or don't you?"

After an awkward silence, Stan spoke up, "Boomer's right, you know, Matt. There's nobody else on the team with a contract like this, not even any cross-country or Nordic combined skiers. Hell, even without an Olympic medal, you could finish this season with close to ten thousand bucks, and we all know a medal isn't as farfetched as it used to be. And remember, Matt, I'll be involved with selecting our starters at the Games. If we have corporate sponsors pumping big bucks into the ABF, are we going to let their athletes sit on the sidelines with the whole world watching? You want to guarantee a start next month in Italy, you'd better jump on Boomer's offer."

"This is all happening so fast. Could I think it over?"

"Sheeiitt, think it over all you want! But I'll be honest, son, we're interested in exposure at the Olympics, and right now it looks like you might be able to give it to us. But things change fast in this lash-up. Let's say today's race was a fluke, that Saturday you're back on the fourth page of the results…you see what I'm saying? And we're talking to other competitors all the time. As an American company, we'd obviously prefer to sponsor an American winner, but some of them Rooskies are real hungry, an' any given day you can count on one of 'em being on the podium. I could get three Russians for what I've just offered you, and in the process improve my chances of getting Sno-Rocket on the tube. You follow me?"

"Yeah, I see what you mean. Your top priority is to get Sno-Rockets on the tube during the Olympics, and you don't really care who does it for you. Thanks for the offer, I'll think about it."

Matt was pulling on his team jacket when he overheard Boomer whispering, "Stan, my boy. Thanks for bringing him down. Good kid. Now, Stanley do your job…." Then he roared, "Hey, Lars, how 'bout another beer over here!"

Saturday morning was much like Thursday, clear, cold and windy. The competition schedule had been reversed, the men starting at 1000 and the women at 1300.

On Matt's first approach to the range, which he later admitted he skied too hard, the spectators along the hill were chanting, "Matt…

Matt...Matt...." Because it was windy, he pulled into firing point number one, his pulse pounding and his chest heaving for air. As the sight picture settled between heart beats, his right elbow slipped on the glazed snow, and his first shot went into the berm four feet above the targets. But poise pulled him through. He shifted his elbows until they felt stable, then hit the remaining four targets in a brisk cadence.

His race wasn't spectacular, like Thursday's 20K, but at least it wasn't embarrassing. The unofficial results listed Matt as the third American, finishing in thirty-fourth place. Ragnar, probably inspired by being back in the old country, shot clean and finished ninth. Burl was twenty-eighth with two loops, and Oliver was thirty-ninth with two misses. Thomas and Heikki were seventy-second and eighty-ninth.

The men knew better than to add to the confusion in the wax room as the women and the coaches scrambled with last minute preparations. After offering a couple of insights about the trail, the guys left. Most headed to the bus for a ride to the hotel and a well-deserved rest in anticipation of the relay. Ragnar had so many friends in the crowd that he planned to watch the women's race from the trail. Matt wanted to see the women compete, but he wasn't anxious to stand out in the wind and cold all afternoon. He remembered the abandoned press booth he had discovered Thursday. As the early racers left the stadium and Matt sat in the warmth of the press booth, it occurred to him he had never before watched a Nordic skiing event in such comfort.

For more than an hour, Matt was engrossed in the women's race. Grete and Trudy shot well, and both appeared to have strong finishes. Sandy had trouble on the range, but pushed hard on the trail to make up for the penalties.

Predictably, the Russians, Belorussians and Germans dominated the top ten, although a Swede, a Finn and Michelle Meloche from Canada also made the list. Then the board cycled back to the top six, and Dybendahl, NOR, appeared in third place! Matt could hear the roar of the crowd. A World Cup bronze medal for Grete, and more important, the only Norwegian woman so far in the top ten! Surely this was the result she needed to make the Norwegian Olympic Team. As the scoreboard continued to scroll down through the results, Matt saw Trudy in nineteenth and Sandy in twenty-seventh. Gathering his gear, he anticipated how excited Grete and Trudy would be, and how Sandy would take it in stride. As he closed the door to the press booth, he realized that Sandy Stonington had skied four penalty loops and still finished in the top thirty.

There was little socializing Saturday night. Sunday's relays were the last international biathlon events before the Olympics, and the teams at the Birkebeineren were determined to leave for Italy on an optimistic note. Grete sought Matt out before supper and thanked him for his encouragement. Although the final selection would not be announced until Sunday evening, Ole Per Rognstad, the Norwegian team leader had told Grete to pack her bags for Italy.

Trudy was also ecstatic. She pointed out that it was the first time since before the '92 Olympics that another American had finished ahead of Sandy Stonington. For her part, Sandy was gracious and complimentary. In spite of her trouble on the range, twenty-seventh was not a disastrous result. Trudy was simply coming on strong.

From Matt's perspective, Trudy was coming on strong in more ways than one. After dinner, she cornered him in the hallway, "Looks like we have two top-twenty results to celebrate!" She pressed herself against him, pinning him to the wall. "I want you, Matt! We'll have a celebration you'll never forget. After the team meeting, send Thomas off to work on his skis. I guarantee you won't fall asleep this time!"

"Thanks, Trudy, but I think I'll pass. You're a knockout, but I'm not interested in being one more of your many conquests."

Her face transformed from feminine charm to disbelief, and then to anger. Her eyes flashed, and like a cornered cat, she lashed out. The open-handed slap caught Matt full on the cheek and brought water to his eyes. Satisfied that she hurt him, Trudy marched down the hall.

The team meeting resembled a military strategy session. Matt was unsure whether he would be selected to race or not. His anxiety diminished when Oliver announced that he wasn't feeling well and wanted to sit out the relay. Vlad assigned him to assist Andy in the wax room.

Aside from Oliver's withdrawal, Vlad's announcement of the relay teams held few surprises. The women's team would consist of Trudy scrambling, Kate Anderson, Jenny Lindstrom, and Sandy skiing the anchor leg. The men's team would consist of Heikki, Burl, Matt and Ragnar. Matt could feel his pulse jump as Vlad announced the team. He immediately felt a sense of duty and pride. He was no longer racing only for himself. He and his teammates represented the whole country. A lot of Americans were damned serious about how the United States stacked up against other nations. He just prayed he wouldn't screw up.

It was still clear and well below freezing, but the wind had disappeared by Sunday morning. The colorful flags in the stadium hung limp, occasionally luffing gently as if to rearrange themselves against the tall aluminum shafts. An hour before the start of the women's race, the stadium was packed with enthusiastic Norwegians, many with backpacks and small national flags. Some of the younger fans had painted their faces with the blue and white cross on the red field of the Norwegian national banner.

Matt watched only the start of the women's relay because he could feel himself getting nervous. Trudy fought for a good position, leaving the stadium among the top ten. Matt decided to cruise one of the cross-country loops, but a kilometer from the range, he could still hear the cheering.

By the time he returned to the wax room he had visualized his leg of the relay several times and was ready to race. The American women were happy with their result. Although they were not among the leading nations, they skied well, and all four had avoided the penalty loop. Trudy was especially enthusiastic. Her lead-off leg was only a few seconds slower than Sandy's anchor leg. It appeared that Trudy really was peaking for the Olympics.

Heikki got a good start in the men's race and was able to stay with the lead pack right into the range. He had to use a couple of extra shots, but he cleaned his targets and headed back to the trail not far behind. Matt could feel his adrenaline pumping, so he went back to the cross-country stadium to stretch.

He returned in time to see Burl shoot standing. The cowboy was hot! He shot five for five and left the range fighting it out with two other competitors for sixth place. Matt struggled to stay calm in the tag zone, but as the leaders approached for the exchange and the third leg racers jostled for position, Matt felt dangerously close to losing his breakfast. He saw Burl hammering stride for stride around the infield with the two other skiers. It was going to be a crowded tag! Watching the three finishers as they fought through the final 200 meters, Matt tried to anticipate where Burl would cross the line. Matt was jostled by the other athletes, then shoved roughly against the fence. Matt took his eyes off Burl and stared at the Bulgarian who had broken his pole in Ruhpolding. The Bulgarian and the other racer began to skate, in motion for the tag. Matt let them go. Burl saw Matt's strategy and coasted into the hand-off zone allowing the others to race ahead. As he overtook his teammate, Burl slapped Matt's shoulder. "Okay, Rookie, your turn to rock and roll!"

Matt skated out of the zone a few strides behind Bulgaria and France, confident he could catch them on the range, which he did by shooting clean prone. On the green loop the three athletes skied stride for stride: the Bulgarian leading, the Frenchman second, Matt following. They approached the range the second time in a train, encouraged by the crowd.

Matt ignored his rivals and concentrated on his own targets. He missed his fourth shot and had to reach for an extra round, but was relieved to notice the other skiers were also still shooting. It took Matt two extra shots to get the stubborn, fourth target, but when it dropped, he was already grabbing for his poles and racing toward the trail. The Bulgarian and the Frenchman were right behind, but the French racer bailed off at the penalty loop leaving only the Bulgarian clicking Matt's heels out of the stadium.

Matt pulled ahead on the gradual descents, but as soon as the trail began to climb, the Bulgarian was skiing up his tails. On the toughest climb of the loop, Matt skied to the edge of the groomed surface, giving the Bulgarian plenty of room to pass, but he stayed behind, dogging Matt's skis with every stride.

As Matt tucked the last descent before the climb to the stadium, he recognized the Bulgarian's strategy. The leaders were out of sight ahead. The Frenchman was thirty seconds back. Position, rather than time, was everything in a relay. Matt suspected the Bulgarian would make a move on the final hill to ensure that his anchorman would have a lead on Ragnar. His method was to hassle Matt early in the race, but stay behind, then catch the American napping in the final sprint.

Matt could feel his anger rising, but he forced himself to control his emotions as the trail climbed to the stadium. After clicking Matt's skis every step for half the hill, the Bulgarian suddenly yelled for the track. Matt skated to the right giving his rival plenty of room. With intense effort the Bulgarian pulled abreast, and Matt imagined they might thrash around the infield side by side. But with his next skating stride to the right, the Bulgarian lashed out with his ski as he had in Ruhpolding. Matt saw it coming this time, and snatched his left pole from the snow. The Bulgarian's ski slashed unobstructed over Matt's left ski, cracking him in the shin. The next instant, Matt planted his pole to keep from falling. The Bulgarian shifted his weight to his gliding ski and tried to recover the unweighted right ski, which had become locked behind Matt's pole. Instantly, the Bulgarian sprawled face-first in the snow. It happened so fast that Matt was astonished to be skating toward the finish alone. As he made the final turn to the tag zone, he saw the Bulgarian struggle to his feet with the Frenchman bearing down on him.

Matt's tag was unobstructed, and Ragnar sped from the stadium cheered on by enthusiastic spectators. Vlad was waiting in the finish pen and hustled Matt through the equipment check, then back toward the wax room.

"Hey, wait a minute, Vlad! I gotta find that damn Bulgarian!"

"This man from Bulgaria, he is not a sportsman! He has made this trick to break a pole many times, but the Technical Delegate cannot see him do it. Maybe today, in the stadium, they see what he tries. For now we staying away from Bulgaria team, you understand!"

"Vlad, that son of a bitch got me in Ruhpolding, and he tried to pull the same sleazy trick today!"

"I am sorry, Matt, but this is also biathlon. You learning very fast. I not make excuse for this man. I have never liked him. But it is impossible for you to imagine how he lives in his country. Biathlon is his job. It is how he supports his family. No good results, he is finished from National Team. No car, no apartment in Sofia, no foreign travel! For you Americans, biathlon is sport, as it should be; for this man, and many others, biathlon is everything!"

Ragnar, still inspired, shot clean and skied the race of his life. In a sprint to the finish he moved the Americans ahead of the Finns. The final standings placed the Germans first, the Russians second, a surprising Ukrainian team third, their best result since the breakup of the Soviet Union, the host Norwegians fourth, and a jubilant American team fifth.

There was a crowd at the wax room when the United States skiers returned from the stadium. Several Norwegian families waited to congratulate Ragnar. Mary Manheimer, Sergeant Jankowski, Gopher, Andy and Rosie straggled in from their assigned locations. And there were journalists, not just from Europe, but even reporters from the States!

Stan the Man basked in the limelight, as he cordially ushered the returning athletes into the wax room. He made certain the journalists had opportunities to snap photos of the proud team leader flanked by the two most photogenic members of the women's relay team, Trudy Wilson and Sandy Stonington.

With the door of the wax room closed and the men changing into dry clothes, Vlad spoke quietly about the race, "Boys, today you make me proud of my new country. We not winning a medal, this is true, but now you are all biathletes! Grandfather, I never would believe you have such speed left in those legs. Heikki, you are a real fighter in the start. Matt, even on your first trip to Europe, you keep your head in difficult competition. Burl, you shooting better every time you race.

"Thomas and Oliver, I not forgetting you two. Today you are alternates, but if someone can't race, I know you are ready. Finally, we are strong team! We have no medal today, but is okay. Now, for first time, I can say you are ready to win medal! Maybe this first medal will be at Olympic Games!"

There was cheering when Vlad finished. Ragnar claimed it was the most enthusiastic speech Vlad had given since he had assumed coaching duties after the '92 Albertville Olympics. Some of the athletes headed out to ski a cool-down loop, others loaded their gear on the bus for the ride to the hotel. Matt wanted to walk from the stadium to the edge of the plateau, then down to the hotel. It was a couple of miles, but it would be a good cool-down, he'd get a great view of Lillehammer, and most important, he'd have the opportunity to savor a final memory of his second World Cup.

Matt had assumed he would be walking to the village alone, but the road was clogged with Norwegian spectators: singing, laughing and reliving the excitement of the day. Several kids noticed the USA on Matt's jacket and asked for his autograph. Their parents asked where he lived in the States, whether he was friends with Ragnar, and how he liked Lillehammer. When finally he left the main road for the hotel, many in the river of spectators waved and wished him luck.

By the time Matt reached the Birkebeineren, the hotel was in turmoil. The Russians were packing their skis and rifles aboard a bus scheduled to take them to Oslo following the awards banquet. The lobby was thronged with athletes, biathlon fans, and journalists. Matt eased his way through the crowd and down the corridor to his room where Thomas was packing.

"Hey, Thomas, what's going on? The lobby's mobbed."

"Oh, that's right, you walked back. Well, a few minutes after our bus arrived from the stadium, Vlad got a message from the Competition

Jury. Bulgaria filed a protest against us, claiming obstruction. Vlad returned to the range to straighten it out. There's also a rumor that two of the Ukrainians never showed at doping control! The jury is trying to find out if they didn't get the word or what. I imagine Vlad will have the scoop when he gets back."

"Stan has scheduled another press conference. I think he's trying to capitalize on the controversies and banking on Vlad bringing back some answers. You've got just enough time for a shower before we have to be in the dining room all gussied up and smiling for the cameras."

The rustic dining room was packed when they joined their teammates and wove their way to the head table. Matt had to admit that as irritating as Stan the Man was most of the time, he could certainly pull together an impressive media event on short notice. As in Anchorage, Reimer had arranged a long head table on a raised platform, making certain the colorful ABF banner and the federation's major sponsors were prominently displayed.

Stan made the introductions and was optimistically summarizing the World Cup results when Vlad strode into the room. Stan explained that the coach was returning from an important meeting of the Competition Jury.

Vlad collapsed into a chair, tossing his gloves and ski hat on the table in front of him. From where he sat, Matt could see a silver stubble on the coach's leathery face. His graying hair, which had been covered by his ski hat since before dawn, was matted to his head.

"Coach Kobelev, did the jury uphold the protest?"

"What about the Ukrainians? Did they locate the two who skipped the drug test?"

"What do you think the United States Team's chances are for a medal in Italy?"

Stan lost control of the meeting.

"*Moment, moment!*" Vlad slowly stood behind the head table. "One at a time, please! First, I tell what I know of the jury meeting. The Bulgarians were foolish to protest in the men's relay. Because of skating, obstruction often takes place when one athlete overtakes another. Almost never is it, how do you say, intentional. However, this man who skis third for Bulgaria today, he has several times been involved in obstruction, usually out on the course where it is the word of one athlete against another."

"Many of you have seen the incident today on the final climb to the stadium. Race officials and even coaches from other nations also see this, but not one witness thought the American athlete intentionally obstructed the Bulgarian. The jury threw out the protest."

The room was filled with applause. Matt felt relieved but unnerved. It was frightening to consider that the protest, if upheld, would have disqualified the United States relay team.

Kobelev continued, "Perhaps you hear, two members of Ukraine men's relay team, which today finished third, never arrived at doping control. Even now, nobody knows where are these boys. The Competition Jury decided the team from Ukraine must be disqualified."

The assembled athletes and journalists were silent, absorbing the impact of Kobelev's revelation.

"Three hours after the race and nobody knows where these guys are?" asked a reporter.

"That is correct," Vlad answered.

"Coach Kobelev, in your estimation, what's going on here?"

Matt could see pain in Vlad's lined face as he responded to the reporter. "Please, you understand, right now, nobody know for sure. But I speak with my old friend, Ukrainian coach Yuri Medvedtsev. I believe Medvedtsev when he tells me he knows nothing of where are these boys. He knows only that Ukrainian Olympic Committee, because of money problems, makes very high standard for Olympic Team selection. The two boys who went to doping control as instructed, they have both qualified for Olympic Games. The boys who did not go to drug testing, they were very disappointed yesterday because their results in 20K and sprint were not enough for selection to Olympic Team."

"It is not always possible to have doping control after relay, even at World Cup. Medvedtsev is afraid his two boys did something against the rules, hoping the Ukrainian Olympic Committee would send a relay team even though they did not meet the standards for individuals. He is afraid they did not expect to be tested after the relay."

"Has this type of thing happened before?" Another voice from the audience shouted.

"Like many sports, biathlon has problems with athletes and coaches who want too badly to win."

"Does this mean the American team finished fourth?" The question was shouted from the back. Stanley and the athletes looked at Kobelev.

"Da...da, Norwegians third, United States fourth."

"Well, thank you very much for that update, Coach Kobelev," Stanley stood at the center of the table, determined to capitalize on the positive race results. "This means, of course, that both our men's and women's relay teams have finished fourth in the last international competition before the Winter Olympics! I think we have time for a few questions before we all have to leave for the awards banquet."

"Sandy..., you were ninth in the 15K at Ruhpolding and skied a fantastic anchor leg for the bronze medal there. Are you disappointed by your results here in Lillehammer, and does this change your goals for the Olympics?"

Sandy looked at the reporter, "First of all, I don't consider finishing fourth in a field of seventeen relay teams a failure. You may have noticed, it doesn't take much in this sport to change the results dramatically, miss one target by a couple of millimeters, and you're a dozen places back. My approach to the Olympics hasn't changed a bit. I'm confident I'm going to be in the hunt for the hardware."

As Sandy spoke, Matt noticed Trudy's photogenic smile appeared brittle.

"I say, Mr. Kobelev, Rodney Graham-Spencer, European Sports Desk for *USA. Today.* It appears you may be in a bit of a pickle when it comes to selecting who will participate in each of the Olympic events. How will you decide who races?"

Vlad smiled wistfully as he stood to answer the question. "In former Soviet Union this no problem, coach makes decision. But in United States, selection is not so easy. Some athletes train too hard for tryouts and never recover for most important races. No coach can predict how athletes will perform in big event like Olympic Games."

"On this team, all coaches meet and study results; tryouts in Anchorage, World Cups, maybe even we have a time trial in Italy. Then we pick best athletes for each event. First importance is best results for United States at Olympics. Second question, if possible, we try letting everyone race at least one event." Vlad scanned the audience then sat down.

"Sandy, Bev Schmidt, *Sports Illustrated,* have you recovered completely from the plane crash in Alaska, or does your eye still bother you?"

Sandy responded enthusiastically, "I haven't given it a thought since the swelling went down a couple of weeks ago." She ran a finger through the eyebrow, which almost concealed the vertical scar. "See, the eyebrow's almost grown back in."

A cameraman, balancing a bulky video unit on his shoulder, pushed forward through the tables, "Excuse me. Sorry. Sandy, can I get a closeup of that please?"

Standing in front of the head table, the cameraman ran tape as Sandy again mussed her scarred eyebrow with her finger. The other athletes watched with amusement. Then Matt spotted Trudy. Her face was deeply flushed. She appeared ready to explode.

"I got a question for the team leader," a confident drawl came from the back of the room. Matt saw the cream-colored western hat and casual stance of Boomer Ferguson. "It's no secret this here biathlon team's strapped for cash, and has been for years. Seems to me these kids are finally putting together some decent results. That helping you any with corporate sponsorships?"

Stanley smiled with such self-assurance that Matt was sure it had all been rehearsed. "You're exactly right! Our impressive results on this trip have generated interest in the team from several potential corporate sponsors. I'm currently negotiating with an airline, a prominent auto leasing company, and the most innovative winter sports company in America, Sno-Rocket. Of course it's a special bonus that our athletes will be peaking for their best results two weeks from now in the Italian Alps."

"Another question for Sandy…, Vickie Chang, *Women's Sport and Fitness.*" Stanley was irritated by the interruption when he was building momentum.

"Sandy, you'll turn thirty-five while you're in Antholz, will this be your last Olympic Games?"

Matt remembered Ms. Chang from the press conference in Anchorage, and the sparks that flew between her and Sandy. He was bracing for a feisty reply, when Trudy's chair clattered to the floor and she leapt to her feet.

"I've had it! Why is it always Sandy, Sandy, Sandy! Don't you people realize there are eleven other athletes on this team? What the hell do you think we're here for, to carry her bags?"

Stan was the first to react. He approached Trudy, but she twisted toward him, planted an outstretched palm on his chest and pushed him off the platform. "Stay away from me, you horny sleazebag!

"I've been gaining on Sandy for the past four years! Saturday I beat her fair and square, and all you want to know is what's wrong with Sandy? Well, I'll tell you! She's a middle-aged jock, who's probably been on testosterone and hGH since '92, and she's scared to death 'cause she knows I'm going to kick her ass at the Olympics!" Trudy glared at the stunned audience, before her face dissolved in tears and she bolted from the room.

The audience was in shock. Vlad rose and followed Trudy. Dazed from his fall, Stan was struggling back to his feet, "I'm all right, I'm not hurt. Don't worry, I'm okay."

The first journalist to recover was Vickie Chang, "Uh..., Sandy, it is obvious that Trudy's very upset, but she made some serious accusations."

Sandy struggled for control, "I've never seen her so upset. What she said about gaining on me since the '94 Olympics is true! I can understand why she's so frustrated; she hasn't gotten much recognition for that improvement."

"But that comment about taking hormone supplements to improve your performance; is there any truth to that?" Vickie Chang persisted.

"Hey, she lost it. We could all see that. It happens. I don't know if you folks understand the stress of making an Olympic Team, then knocking heads with the Europeans, and having the whole world watching. We all come unglued occasionally under that kind of pressure."

"But she accused you of taking performance enhancing drugs. Is that true?" Vicky Chang would not give up.

"I've been tested more than anyone else on this team: physiological tests, drug tests and gender tests! I have never failed one of those tests! I do not take hormones and I do not take drugs!" Matt could tell that Sandy was losing her composure.

Ms. Chang persisted, "Sandy, if you say you've never used drugs to improve performance, we have to believe you, until evidence turns up to the contrary. But if your teammate's accusation has any basis in fact, it's big news! Now, as a professional journalist, I must ask you again, Sandy Stonington, have you ever used performance enhancing drugs?"

The room was totally silent as the determined reporter and the experienced athlete stared at each other. Stanley had recovered enough to break the silence, "This is crazy. We're here to celebrate some great World Cup results...."

"Absolutely not," said Sandy, looking directly at Vickie Chang.

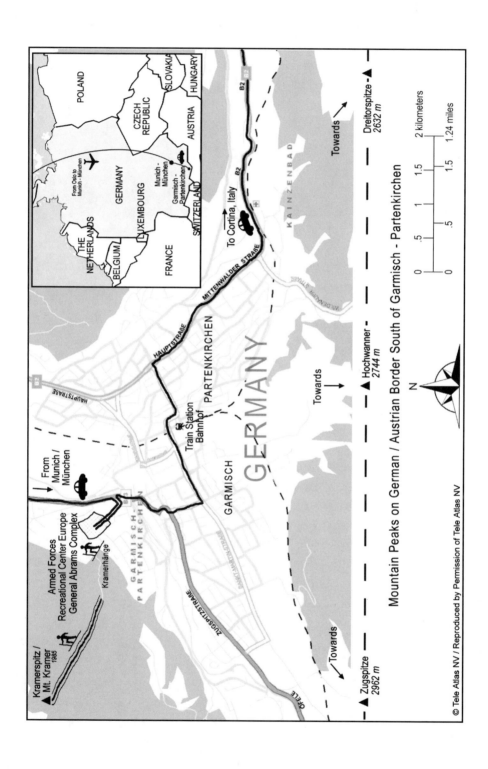

Mountain Peaks on German / Austrian Border South of Garmisch - Partenkirchen

© Tele Atlas NV / Reproduced by Permission of Tele Atlas NV

Team Building

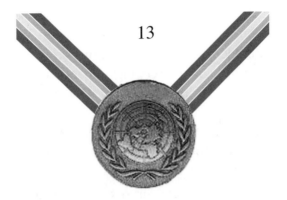

13

The United States Biathlon Team was in shambles. Members of the media sprinted from the press conference, eager to spread the news that America's most successful biathlete had been accused of illegal performance enhancement. Without speaking, the athletes boarded the bus in the dark the next morning. They were exhausted from the races and dreaded the fallout from the press conference. Trudy looked awful. Her face was splotchy, her eyes bloodshot, and she looked like she'd slept in her clothes. Once everyone was aboard, the driver slipped the bus into gear and pulled out of the Birkebeineren parking lot. Matt thought he heard one of the women stifle a sob. Amazing how quickly their fortunes could shift from flying high to chaos. There was no way to estimate the damage from Trudy's accusation.

　　　Matt almost felt at home when they deplaned in Munich, his third time through that modern terminal in as many weeks. This time they were met by American soldiers in camouflage fatigues, who helped load their gear into a faded green military bus. Matt couldn't help comparing the stiff vinyl seats to the German luxury coach which had taken them to

Ruhpolding three weeks earlier.

In less than two hours, they passed through the gates of a walled compound. Inside were tile-roofed, concrete buildings. A large wooden sign announced, Armed Forces Recreation Center Europe, General Abrams Complex.

As the athletes stepped from the bus and stretched, Stan Reimer hurried across the brown grass. "Good, you're here! We've got a team meeting in the conference room right now. Follow me."

"Hey, Stan, how about checking into our rooms and grabbing some lunch first? It's been a long morning." Gopher echoed the feelings of all the athletes.

"Nope, this meeting's important! Harrison Strideman, the Chief de Mission of the Olympic Team is waiting for us in the conference room. Let's go!"

There was grumbling, but everyone straggled across the lawn and followed Stan into the building. The white walls were decorated with framed posters of Alpine skiers in baggy pants. Stan held open a glass door as the athletes filed into a large conference room. An impressive table was positioned across one end of the room in front of rows of folding chairs.

A thin man, silver hair cropped in a severe crewcut, sat at the conference table engrossed in paperwork, which he studied through half-frame reading glasses. He wore a starched white shirt and a neatly knotted silk tie. The coat of his gray suit was draped over a chair next to him. He never looked up from his papers as the biathletes and their coaches trooped in and found seats.

"All right, do we have everyone? Find a seat, please." Stanley was in team leader mode again. "Uh..., Vlad, I'd like you and Sergeant Jankowski to sit up here with us. Thomas, Emily, Jenny, please move up so we don't have to shout." The athletes reluctantly moved forward, selecting chairs closer to the head table. With everyone settled, Stan moved behind the table, and spoke.

"Members of the Olympic Biathlon Team, it's my pleasure to introduce to you, Mr. Harrison Strideman, Chief de Mission of the United States Olympic Team at the Cortina Games."

For the first time since the athletes had entered, the lean, silver-haired man looked up from his reading. He scanned the audience, deliberately making eye contact with each athlete. After a long pause, he glanced at the Biathlon Team Leader and said, "Go ahead, Stanley."

"Right, Harrison…, I mean Mr. Strideman." Reimer was clearly ill at ease. "Well, where to begin? As you athletes have learned by now, I left Norway last night after the, ah…ah…press conference. I flew to Munich and got down here to Garmisch soon after breakfast. The USOC media offices, both here and back in Colorado Springs, have been swamped by requests for information and interviews as a result of our press conference in Lillehammer. I have been brainstorming with Mr. Strideman for the past four hours on how to keep this from becoming a media sideshow."

"We represent the United States of America, not only to all the folks back home, but to all the other nations on earth. We are one of the only American sports federations never to have won a medal in Olympic competition." The team leader plowed on, "Finally, it appeared we were on the verge of a breakthrough. Medals were a distinct possibility, and potential corporate sponsors were beginning to show interest in your success. Then we have this whole damn…, this…, this doping thing blow up in our faces!"

Stan seemed uncertain about how to proceed. Before the silence became uncomfortable, Harrison Strideman stretched a long arm over the back of the chair next to him and casually spoke in Stanley's direction.

"I'll take it from here, Stanley." He looked back at the athletes and waited for Stanley to be seated. Strideman remained in his chair. He gave the impression that he was having a quiet chat with a trusted associate, rather than addressing nineteen members of the Olympic Biathlon Team.

"I've been asked to lead the United States Olympic Team in Italy. As some of you may know, I'm a successful businessman. I competed in the equestrian events at the '68 Games in Mexico City, and I've been involved with the USOC ever since. I accepted this appointment because I see no reason why the United States shouldn't enjoy the same success at the Winter Olympics that we have had for decades in the Summer Games. As the leader of this delegation, I have one primary objective, to win medals. I don't believe this bullshit about moral victories or how wonderful it is simply to participate. The name of this game is to win!"

"Now, I'll have to confess that until I took your team leader's call last night, I didn't know a hell of a lot about your sport. Since then I've been briefed by the USOC staff, and I spent the morning with Mr. Reimer. I'm not impressed by what I've learned. To be painfully candid, I think you're a bunch of losers. In ten Winter Olympics, the top United States finish in biathlon is fourteenth! That's pathetic. If you were in business, you'd have been bankrupt and on the street decades ago."

"And as if dismal results are not enough of an embarrassment to the Olympic Committee, there's all this talk about drugs. First, you disqualify one of your top candidates at the Trials in Anchorage, and now your athletes are making headlines by accusing each other of illegal doping in front of the international press."

Trudy was on the verge of tears again.

"Folks, Opening Ceremonies are less than two weeks away, and I've already had all I can stomach of *biathlon*." The Chief de Mission continued. "I'm giving you until suppertime to iron out your internal problems and present an optimistic, unified Olympic Biathlon Team to the media. And if I were in your shoes, I'd be damned sure I brought home a few medals from Italy. Frankly, there are other sports lining up for a chance on the Olympic program, and we don't need the embarrassment of an obscure event that generates negative publicity but no medals."

In the silence that followed, Strideman glanced around the room, then nodded to Stanley and strode from the room. Vlad was the first to speak, "Athletes and friends…, okay, we have problem. But all teams have problems! I'm propose this. We are hungry and tired, so first we eat, unload bus and find rooms. Then, for training today we hike one of these beautiful mountains; everybody, a team! Finally, after dinner tonight we have meeting to settle these problems. From here we go to Antholz, and everyone agree, we must having good results at Olympic Games! *Da…? Harasho…?*"

After lunch they unloaded the bus and moved into their rooms. All the athletes were back in the parking lot in their training clothes by 1430 for the hike. They stretched without talking. Vlad watched the athletes for several minutes before he was satisfied, then he announced, *"Pashlee,* we go now!"

The heavy overcast skies of the morning had lifted, replaced by thin cirrus clouds. Vlad led the group out of the Abrams complex, through the surrounding neighborhood to the base of Mount Kramer, rising from sheer rock cliffs above the village. From the quiet street, Vlad found a path which climbed steadily up the foothills to the base of the cliffs. The athletes walked easily, while the other coaches and Dr. Manheimer struggled to keep pace with the tough Russian.

By 1615 they reached a broad plateau linking the rocky peak of Kramer to its neighboring summits. The view beyond Garmisch and Partenkirchen to the Austrian Alps was spectacular. They assembled for group photos with the snow-capped peaks in the background. It had been an exhausting day, with still another hour of vigorous hiking back to the military compound, yet no one wanted to leave. As Kobelev began ushering his flock back down the trail, the sun sank below a windblown cornice to the west. The clouds were painted the color of blood, bathing the snow-covered peaks to the south in a vivid, pink alpenglow. No one spoke. The colors intensified; deep red in the sky, pink fading to purple on the mountains. Then the lights of the villages below twinkled in the deepening shadow. It was the most dramatic display of natural color Matt had ever seen.

Finally Thomas broke the silence. "This is a sign, for sure!"

Matt was standing next to him, "What do you mean?"

"At home in Unalakleet, before the men head out to hunt whale or walrus they ask the elders to look for a sign. Sometimes the signs seem small, a dead gull on the beach, or a warm wind from the south. But these colors, with all of us on this ridge, two days before we head to the Olympics…, which direction is Antholz?"

Vlad pointed beyond the village of Partenkirchen toward snow-covered peaks still lit such a brilliant pink that they looked electric.

Thomas nodded, "It's a sign, all right. A very powerful sign."

By the time they reached the Abrams complex it was dark. Kobelev led them directly to the mess hall. Several USOC staff members decked out in colorful Olympic Team sweaters were eating together. A group of scruffy-looking teenagers moved through the cafeteria line, a sharp contrast to the military cooks dressed in crisp, white uniforms. Matt noticed the kids wore baggy pants that hung well below their hips. They had long, shaggy hair; one boy sported bushy dreadlocks dyed orange. Heikki Lahdenpera whispered to Matt, "The United States Olympic Snowboarding Team! And you know what? They're probably going to win six medals! Those kids are the best in the world!"

Before the biathletes finished eating, Stanley joined them. He pulled a chair next to Kobelev, and the two whispered for several minutes. Then Vlad stood and announced, "So..., we must attend informational meeting with USOC staff at 1930 in conference room. We should have short team meeting before, maybe 1900. Stan has arranged a room in the main building. We follow him there so soon as we finish."

The team meeting was productive. Sobbing, Trudy apologized for her remarks in Lillehammer, admitting she had been overcome by frustration and jealousy. One by one, each athlete stood and talked about what his or her teammates meant to them. When it was Matt's turn to speak, he thanked Thomas for his friendship and believing in him. Even Sandy was tearful as she thanked everyone for their support.

"I tell you something," said Vlad. "What happens here is more important than you know. Until now you are a collection of athletes in a very difficult sport. By facing this problem, you become a team.

"The athletes of the former Soviet state, they were not so much better than you, but they competed with strong support from each other. For many years it was Soviets against the world; very powerful motivation! When *any* Soviet athlete won, it was victory for whole team, victory for Soviet system. Just now, you become a team as powerful as any you will face in Italy. I am coaching biathlon for twenty years. I know this sport. I have coached many champions. I telling you, an Olympic medal is not impossible for this team!"

The meeting broke up in time for everyone to walk to the conference room, where the outfitting process would begin. As the biathletes entered, they saw members of the Olympic staff seated at the far end of the room. A middle-aged man with a friendly smile stood to welcome them. "Okay! The Biathlon Team's here! Come on up front and find the chair with your folder on it. Here's Coach Kobelev! You got everybody, Vlad?"

"*Da...da...,* we all here, Greg."

"That's great, Coach. I'm Greg Ingram, Director of International Games Preparation for the USOC. I head a crew of about forty USOC staff members and volunteers whose sole purpose in life for the next twenty-nine days is to do everything humanly possible to ensure your success at the Olympics. Our *only* mission is athlete support!"

"If you look at the first sheet in your folder you'll see the agenda for this meeting. Basically, we want to acquaint you with the folks who will be working for you in Italy. We'll try to keep it brief, but don't hesitate to ask questions. Since we've got a lot of material to cover tonight, I think we'll dive right in."

What followed was a parade of Games Preparation staff members who briefed the athletes on administrative records, medical coverage, and complimentary tickets. Matt was about to doze off when Ingram got his attention, "I know you're tired, but this is the most important information you will hear all evening. Alex McCall has been the USOC's chief of security since Albertville, following a twenty-year career with the White House Secret Service. Alex will outline our security concerns during the next four weeks."

The former Secret Service agent was tall, with thinning gray hair, and obviously fit. It was impossible to estimate the man's age; he could have been anywhere from his mid-forties to early sixties. As McCall placed a transparency of the Antholz athletes' village on an overhead projector, Ragnar leaned toward Matt and Thomas. "When you guys get a chance, look at his right thumb; big scar, thumbnail's all messed up. The rumor at Albertville was that McCall was closest to Squeaky Frome when she tried to assassinate Gerald Ford in Sacramento, back in '75. He stepped between Frome and the President and jammed his thumb under the hammer as she pulled the trigger!"

"First of all, let me add my congratulations for making the Olympic Team. I know I risk showing favoritism when I tell you, some of us believe you folks participate in the most challenging sport on the winter program. I don't ski, but I've spent my life around firearms, so I have great admiration for your skills on the shooting range."

"Now, most of the events of the next month will be inspiring and rewarding. But unfortunately, there is a darker side to the Olympics. You're too young to remember the massacre at the Munich Games in '72, but the fact is, there are still unbalanced extremists who see the Olympic Games as a televised opportunity to send their message to the world."

"I'm not trying to scare you, but it is important that you understand the seriousness of the situation. Since the disaster in Munich, security at the Olympics has been intensified dramatically. Some of these measures will seem inconvenient, but let me assure you they *are* necessary. If you think the pipe bomb in Atlanta's Centennial Park was a disaster, you'd be horrified by the plots that were disabled by the authorities *before* they caused any damage. Be assured, there *are* predators out there whose mission in life is to disrupt these Games in some dramatic fashion while the entire world watches."

McCall paused before continuing, "In your folders you'll find a pamphlet describing our security procedures. Please read it carefully. If you have any questions, track me down. Most of it is common sense. Wear your credentials at all times and never loan them to anyone else."

"We know you folks like to dry-fire your rifles in the evenings, so we've convinced the Italians to permit you to take your rifles to your rooms. However, you must store the ammunition in lockers at the security checkpoint. Make sure you comply with this! The housekeeping staff has been instructed to keep an eye out for bullets. If they find any in your room, you could be disqualified and sent home!"

"Another new procedure this year deals with casual clothing. Like Albertville in '92, these Winter Games involve more than half-a-dozen venues throughout a wide geographical region, so it's impossible to provide total security. In previous Games our teams have been proud to wear the United States insignia, identifying them as Americans from a mile away. L.L. Bean has done a terrific job outfitting the team this year, and as always, you'll have plenty of patriotic gear. But for the first time, at our suggestion, your wardrobe includes a subtle, understated winter coat. As a security precaution, we strongly suggest that when you leave the Olympic venues, if you go for a beer in downtown Cortina after a hockey game for example, wear the subdued, civilian coat. To be completely candid, it makes you less of a target for some crazy who may have slipped through our net."

"That about covers it. Chances are, if any of you have specific issues, they will be much more mundane; a stolen team jacket, a lost wallet, or a missing passport. We're here to help, but an ounce of prevention…, you know what I mean?"

"Finally, remember that you folks are our eyes and ears. If you see something out of the ordinary, let us know. Over the years there've been…, maybe half-a-dozen potentially life-threatening situations averted because an observant athlete or coach tipped us off in time. Thanks very much for your attention. Have a great Olympics."

Matt leaned over to Thomas, "Jesus, he makes it sound like we're going into combat!"

"From his perspective, we are," Thomas answered.

Greg Ingram was back on his feet. "Thanks, Alex. I know that sounded ominous, but it's important that you folks are well informed. Because of professionals like Alex, the three thousand security guards, and the four thousand Italian soldiers deployed during the Games, this briefing will probably be the last you hear about security."

The program continued by introducing Janet Keegan, the USOC's Athletes' Advisory Council liaison. Matt remembered seeing Janet's picture on the cover of *Sports Illustrated* after Barcelona where she'd won two golds and a bronze. She was followed by Larry Morain, the USOC's Director of Public Information, who gave the athletes a crash course in media relations.

It was late and the athletes were yawning when Ingram introduced Phil Shepard of L.L. Bean, the official supplier of the Olympic Team uniforms. What followed was an amazing fashion show — an extensive collection of competitive, parade and casual clothes. It was mind boggling. "How are we supposed to pack all this stuff?" Matt whispered to Thomas.

"After they issue all this stuff tomorrow, they give us big boxes to ship our old clothes home. Unreal, isn't it?"

The athletes applauded enthusiastically. Greg Ingram stood once again. "I think the entire USOC, and especially the Games Preparation Committee owes you biathletes a debt of thanks. Because of their success with Biathlon, L.L. Bean decided to outfit the entire Olympic delegation. In my view, Bean has done the best job of any company in recent memory."

"Now, as you can see from your agenda, we're approaching the end of tonight's orientation." Ingram looked down the table toward the woman who had spoken earlier about records and credentials. "Jennifer, would you let Mr. Strideman and the General know we are ready for them?" She quietly left the room. Matt glanced at Thomas. Neither of them was excited about the prospect of another confrontation with the Chief de Mission.

The door opened and an elderly, white haired man wearing a business suit limped into the conference room. His face was tanned and he wore the contented smile of someone who looked forward to every new day. He was followed by Harrison Strideman looking erect and severe.

The staff at the conference table jumped to their feet. The biathletes were slower to respond, although the coaches reacted almost as quickly as the USOC staff. The older man protested, "Oh, sit down, sit down for heaven's sake. You make it seem like we've got something important to say when you folks have already done all the hard work. Harrison, why don't you go first." He sat in a chair and everyone else followed his lead.

Greg Ingram, standing next to Harrison Strideman, appeared ill at ease for the first time all evening. "Ah…I understand that you folks met with Mr. Strideman this morning, so I'll dispense with the long introduction. You probably know that the United States Olympic Committee is a paid, professional staff headquartered in Colorado Springs, along with elected volunteers who oversee the Olympic philosophy and mission. Mr. Strideman is a former Olympic equestrian, a generous financial benefactor, and a long time USOC volunteer. He has been recognized for his contributions with the appointment of Chief de Mission for the Cortina Winter Olympic Team. Mr. Strideman….."

Strideman gave a canned speech, which he had apparently delivered many times, reminding the athletes that they represented the entire nation, that the whole world would be watching, and that their results and even their casual behavior could have important ramifications on future fund-raising efforts. He made only one oblique reference to the earlier press conference, adding that he wouldn't tolerate any further negative publicity from Biathlon.

Even after he sat down, Strideman scowled as Ingram introduced the final speaker. "It is with great pleasure that I present to you retired General Mac Moore, the president of the United States Olympic Committee. General Moore…." The staff clapped vigorously and the biathletes joined in, as the older gentleman stood.

"I know this is unconventional, but I'm going to excuse all of you except the athletes." Strideman looked bewildered. "That's right, Harrison! All you paper-pushers can head off to bed, I want a few words alone with these kids who'll be wearing the numbers."

There was shuffling and scraping of chairs as the USOC staff and the biathlon coaches left the room. Sergeant Jankowski was the last to leave, pulling the door closed behind him.

"There! Now we can talk. You know, being president of the USOC isn't what you think. Mostly I hobnob with a bunch of stuffed shirts from all over the world at fancy receptions, formal dinners and such. Not my cup of tea, really. Of course there are some benefits, like getting the last word at a meeting like this. And I get the best seat in the house at any sports event. Which will include some of your races, by the way."

"But I don't want to keep you kids up all night. Here's what's on my mind. I suspect you've had your fill of Harrison Strideman today. He's not a bad guy. He's done a hell of a job as a volunteer, putting the United States Olympic Committee on solid financial footing, and we all benefit from those efforts. I know, for example, that Biathlon's budget is quite a bit more generous this year than it was in Lillehammer. So we can't be too hard on Harrison. But sometimes it's easy for well-intentioned folks to get wrapped around the axle, if you know what I mean. They can lose sight of the big picture."

"I feel like I've got a real connection to you kids. Just over fifty years ago, a bunch of us, just about your age, were carrying rifles on skis only a few mountain ridges away from where you'll be competing. Totally different situation. I was in the Tenth Mountain Division. We were going up against the German Alpine Corps, and were they dug in! In some ways, it seems like yesterday...."

"Well, we finally beat 'em. But they fought like hell and we lost some damn fine men. Hell, most of us that made it back got shot up pretty good. In fact, a mortar round put an end to my skiing when I was twenty."

"Now you're all wondering why an old fart is rambling on about World War II? Well, I'm getting to that. Like I said before, Harrison Strideman's not a bad guy, but he doesn't have my perspective on these Olympic Games. When that French nobleman, de Coubertin, founded the modern Games over a hundred years ago, he was real clear about his purpose. Some of you have heard what he said, but I want to remind you. He said:

> The most important thing in the Olympic Games
> is not to win but to take part,
> just as the most important thing in life
> is not the triumph but the struggle.

"Now don't get me wrong, winning is important! But from my perspective, the Frenchman had it right. All anyone can ask is that you do your best. A medal may or may not be in the cards for Biathlon this time, though heaven knows I'd love to see it, and I don't know how much longer I'll be around. But if you kids just do your best as athletes and ambassadors, then you can be damned sure the folks back home will be proud."

"I envy you, being tucked away with the cross-country skiers up in Antholz. Cortina's going to be a nuthouse, you can be sure of that. Did you hear there'll be two thousand credentialed athletes and coaches at these Games, and more than seven thousand media people? You're lucky to be out of the traffic pattern."

"So you kids hang together up there. I know you've already had your share of challenges, like that plane crash in Alaska and the press conference in Norway. Well, you keep looking out for each other and you'll do fine. That's just how those of us in the Tenth got the Nazis on the run fifty years ago. I'll be up to watch you kids race, you can count on that. Okay, troop dismissed. Give 'em hell!"

The old soldier limped toward the door, and shook hands with each biathlete as they filed past. He asked their names, where they were from, and wished each of them good luck. As Matt and Thomas followed the others out of the Headquarters Building and across the frozen compound, they agreed that General Moore was a great choice to lead the United States Olympic Committee.

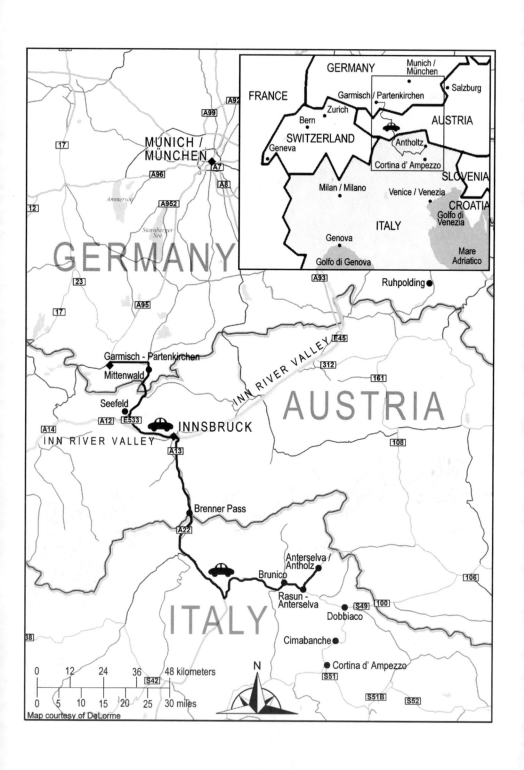

Map courtesy of DeLorme

On to Italy

14

Kobelev roused his team before breakfast for a morning run through Garmisch and Partenkirchen. Although they interfered with the morning traffic, the German commuters tolerated the inconvenience, recognizing the Olympic athletes.

After breakfast, the hectic processing schedule began. The women filed first through the tables of clothing, while the men went for identification photos and medical exams. After waiting in line for his official USOC mug shot, Matt stepped down the hall to meet with the medical staff. Eventually he was ushered into an examination room. The muscular doctor who had addressed them the night before was sitting at a desk, engrossed in a medical chart. He wore a white lab coat embroidered with, "Edward Porter, M.D.," and below that, "Harvard University Medical Center."

The doctor held out a huge hand, "I'm Ed Porter, and you're Matthew Johnson from Thetford!"

"You've heard of Thetford?"

"Sure. I wanted to play football at Dartmouth for Coach Blackman, but my dad and grandfather both went to Harvard. You know how that goes. I had friends at Dartmouth and visited often. Do the college kids still go skinny-dipping at the Union Village Dam?"

Matt smiled, "You bet. Some of the local kids, too."

"Well, Matt, I've looked over your chart and everything seems fine. Dr. Manheimer will be assigned to the Antholz athletes' village, so you kids will have top notch medical support up there. In addition, the Italians have established a polyclinic within the athletes' village. I've met the physician who'll be in charge, Dr. Luigi Clementi. He's a good man. Of course, if anything serious happens they'll get you right down to the hospital in Cortina. It's only twenty minutes by chopper. But you won't have to worry about that."

"No changes in your health since the physical last June, Matt? Why don't you strip down to your shorts and we'll take a quick look."

"I frost-nipped my toes in West Yellowstone in November."

"Hmmmm, I see.... They look okay now. Still sensitive to the cold?"

"Not for the past month or so."

"Good, let me just check you over." For several minutes Matt stood in his undershorts as the doctor looked down his throat, listened to his chest, and checked his blood pressure.

"You've got a good low pulse, even for an endurance athlete! Forty-two at this time of day, that's impressive!"

"We're about finished, I'll just check the rest of your folder.... Hmmm, you have type AB Negative blood with an interesting array of antigens. Matt, I don't want to alarm you, but this is potentially a serious situation. If you were in an accident, needed blood immediately, and the paramedics started giving you AB Negative, you could have a severe allergic reaction. I'll get an alert card laminated to hang on the chain with your credentials."

"Thanks, Dr. Porter."

"No problem. Good luck in the races."

The rest of the morning was consumed by meetings with the USOC's financial officer and the Media Relations staff. Everyone headed to the mess hall for lunch at noon. The women were impressive, wearing an assortment of new Olympic Team outfits.

As the biathletes ate, another group entered the mess hall. Leading the parade were five tiny girls in heavy makeup, followed by women in luxurious fur coats. The girls flitted like colorful songbirds, while the women in fur followed like a family of bears. Behind the first group came an assortment of men, laughing and joking. They were of varying heights, but they were all big.

"Damn!" Rosie blurted. "You know who those guys are? That's Willie Washington, the best wide receiver in the NFL! He caught the pass that won the Conference Championship for the Vikings last year. The other guy's Bubba Lane, an All-Pro linebacker for the Bills. He's got a career total of over a hundred sacks!"

Matt stared at the newcomers. The two pro football players were the biggest, toughest-looking men he had ever seen. Compared to the tiny girls, they looked like a different species. What are those guys doing here?" Matt asked.

"They're on the bobsled team! The old bobsledders don't like to admit it, but aside from the driver, the rest of the team is there to push like hell at the start, and for weight on the ride down. The Bobsled Federation finally got smart and went looking for athletes with tremendous leg speed and power, then taught 'em to push the sled, hop on, and keep their heads down."

"And the little girls are figure skaters?" Matt asked.

Sandy answered, "Right! The Asian-American is Stephanie Wang, she's the current World Champion and the favorite for the gold medal in Cortina. She's fourteen. The skaters usually travel with their mothers, a coach, a choreographer, and sometimes a sports psychologist. The fur coats are part of the uniform for the support crew."

The afternoon was like all of Matt's childhood Christmases rolled into one. The biathlon men moved from one uniforming station to the next, where they were given a staggering assortment of clothing. Matt and Thomas had to make two trips to haul their new clothes back to the barracks. Then they spent the hour before dinner writing their names in their new gear, and deciding which old clothes to box and ship home. Thomas reminded Matt to save some good trading items for athletes from other countries.

At dinner the biathletes modeled an assortment of L.L. Bean and USOC logos. As they finished their meal, Jankowski finally approached the head coach, "Vlad, you seem awfully quiet. What's wrong?"

"Nothing wrong, everything super!" The old Russian forced a smile.

"Something's eating you."

Vlad studied the rifle coach before responding, "Okay, you ask, I telling you. All this clothes is fantastic! I never have such nice things my whole life in Soviet Union. But I feeling bad when I think how much we are given, more than we need, for sure, and how little people from other countries have. My brother, he still lives in Novosibirsk, maybe he doesn't has one old winter coat. Today, they give me four! Maybe I am happy and sad at same time."

Matt was pleased the USOC had chartered one of the comfortable German tour buses to transport the team to Italy. The route took them through the mountains and then past the picturesque village of Mittenwald. When they arrived at the border, an Austrian official boarded the bus to check their passports. They drove on through the mountains until the hotels and ski lifts of Seefeld filled the valley to their right.

"Hey, Vlad, does this place bring back memories?" Burl shouted from the back. Vlad turned to face Burl and the other athletes, "Da... da.... In 1976 Seefeld was tiny village, not this...this big resort. But for Soviet athletes this place was, how shall I say it, beyond belief! The food, the friendly people, the shops full of wonderful clothes! If I don't have family in Novosibirsk, maybe I defected way back in '76."

"You won a medal that year, didn't you, Vlad?" Burl continued.

"Da, I have bronze in 20K and gold in relay. I should have gold in 20K also, but bad shooting. I'm not enough patient on the range. Anyway, I have good remembers from Seefeld, like you will have from Antholz."

Soon the bus was straining through its low gears as the driver gently eased down the dramatic switchbacks leading toward the broad Inn River Valley. There were groans from the athletes as they descended into a thick layer of brown smog which blanketed Innsbruck. Then the bus climbed again, as the driver headed south on A13.

At the height of land they stopped at the Italian frontier. Green, white and red Italian flags alternated poles with the colorful Italian Olympic banner. Huge billboards welcomed visitors in several languages to Cortina D'Ampezzo and the Italian Sud Tirol, host of the Winter Olympic Games. The Italian official in a glass booth spoke briefly with the driver, then passed them through with a nod of his head.

The highway descended past picturesque farming villages perched high on the shoulders of the the Alps. They headed east on a smaller road that fought for space on the valley floor with a turbulent river. Then the bus turned left and stopped at another checkpoint and Heikki announced that they had reached the Antholz Valley. Again, the Americans were waved through, this time by soldiers in camouflage fatigues. As the bus resumed its gradual climb up the valley, Matt noticed a parking lot filled with military trucks, jeeps and even a few ominous-looking armored personnel carriers.

The valley was a kilometer wide and dotted with sturdy farmhouses, while the steep slopes were thick with spruce and fir. The bus passed a collection of stucco buildings clustered around a fortress church. The snow-covered pastures surrounding the village reached up toward the dense forests. High into the pale blue sky, soared the jagged peaks of the Italian Alps. It was a valley created for an airline travel poster. The ground in Garmisch had been bare and frozen, but deep powder snow blanketed the village of Antholz.

Beyond the village, the bus turned off the main road and stopped at yet another gate. This time the driver rose from his seat and announced, *"Zo, velcomen til Antholz!"* Aside from the flags and banners lining the driveway, the athletes' village resembled a tastefully designed prison camp. The collection of buildings was surrounded by a double chain-link fence topped with coiled concertina wire. In the space between the fences, Matt saw soldiers with automatic weapons leading German shepherds on sturdy leashes.

The main entrance was guarded by an assortment of police and military personnel. Even before the Americans entered the building, they were besieged by officials begging for pins.

"Stanley, this is situation for team leader. You must help us," Vlad called to Reimer in mock alarm. Stanley made the tactical error of withdrawing a plastic bag heavy with USOC trading pins from his briefcase. Like voracious bees discovering a new source of nectar, the soldiers and *carabinarie* mobbed the American team leader. Soon all the security personnel at the main gate were proudly wearing the colorful United States pin, while a disheveled Stanley Reimer was left with an empty plastic bag. Vlad chuckled in Matt's ear, "First rule of changing pins, never show all you have!"

But Stan's distribution of pins did facilitate the biathletes' entry into the Olympic Village. One of the security people phoned the mayor of the village who arrived to welcome the American contingent. He explained that soldiers would unload the bus while the athletes were shown to their living quarters. After dinner they would be asked to return to the front gate, guide their baggage through the x-ray machines, then load it on a truck within the compound for delivery to their rooms.

As the soldiers began unloading the bus, the athletes handed their passports to a military officer, placed their day packs on the conveyer of the x-ray machine, and stood in line to be patted down by security police with electronic wands. When everyone had been passed through the checkpoint, the mayor led them down snow-packed walkways between rows of identical, prefabricated housing units, similar to double-wide mobile homes. Flags and banners were everywhere. Proudly, the mayor approached a unit flying the Stars and Stripes. He held open a door painted with USA in elaborate Tyrolean script. Inside, two young soldiers snapped to attention. The mayor introduced the Americans to their in-house guards, then walked the team down the carpeted central corridor.

Matt was pleasantly surprised. He had feared the worst when they began their journey through the collection of house trailers, but the rooms were comfortable. They were not large, but everyone was assigned a single. Space was maximized by clever built-in closets, drawers and bookcases. The walls of each small room displayed two decorative touches, a large, colorful Olympic poster, and a child's drawing of an Olympic scene. The mayor explained that school children from throughout the Sud Tirol submitted artwork to decorate the rooms of the Olympic athletes.

Midway down the trailer were the bathroom and shower facilities, one side of the hall for men, the other for women. Before he led them back to the lobby, the mayor suggested that his guests select their rooms and leave their backpacks. As they regrouped in the entrance, the mayor demonstrated a computer terminal, designated for the exclusive use of the American biathletes. Team members who had been in Albertville or Lillehammer grew excited.

"This is great," said Sandy, enthusiastically. "Each of us will be assigned an ID number, which is also our access code. All you have to do is type in your number then the menu lets you choose from a wide array of functions: start lists, results, weather forecasts, even interviews with medal winners. But the most fun is, you can communicate with anyone else who has an access code. You can wish Tommy Moe good luck before the downhill. If Burl gets the hots for some Czech figure skater, he just e-mails her! The computer can even translate from one language to another! Isn't that right, Burl?"

Burl grinned, "You bet, Sandy."

"The best part," Sandy continued, "is you can use the computer to handle the media. You just get the word out that you'll only respond to requests for interviews through e-mail. Then every morning you check your messages; decline the interviews you don't want, and schedule the ones that seem worth the time. It's great!"

The cafeteria could accommodate 200 people and was open around the clock. There were several serving lines featuring European food, North American food, and Asian food. There was also a pizza window and a short-order grill for hamburgers and french fries. Islands in the serving area offered a wide choice of breakfast cereals, fruit, breads, salads and desserts.

The heavy carved beams of the ceiling and the warm spruce-paneled walls were decorated with banners and large posters from earlier Olympics. Small national flags adorned every table. Although the dining room wasn't crowded, Matt tried to identify as many teams as he could from their warm-up jackets, and from the flags on the tables. The Americans were hungry, but there were so many choices, a few hesitated, unable to make a decision.

"Come on, Rookie! It may not be McDonald's, but it'll be the first burger we've had since we left Anchorage." There was no doubt where Burl was headed.

"Don't listen to him, Matt. You think the Russians and Scandinavians get so fast eating french fries and burgers? We have the fuel of champions — boiled potatoes, fish and cabbage!"

"Uh, thanks, Ragnar, but I had plenty of fish in Lillehammer. Since we're in Italy, maybe I'll try a pizza."

After dinner they went back to the main gate where their baggage was neatly stacked and guarded by two soldiers with assault rifles. The athletes and coaches began the long process of carrying their luggage, ski bags, rifles, and team equipment to the x-ray machine. Some of the larger boxes had to be opened and inspected before the officials permitted their entry. Once x-rayed, the baggage was taken within the fence and loaded on a small truck which hauled the gear to their building.

The entire process took two hours. Finally, when the athletes began unpacking, Vlad walked down the hall, announcing a short team meeting.

"I will keep short because already we have long day." Vlad looked tired as he addressed the team. "I am very happy with how things work out in Garmisch, and finally we in Antholz! For many years we are working for this. As we come closer to competition, we having more distractions, which does not help performance. So we are doing two things. First, I hand out to you very complete training and racing schedule for the next weeks," Vlad handed a stack of paper to Sandy who took one and passed them on.

"You all know we race only four athletes in each event," Vlad continued. "But it always happens, someone is sick and we must make substitution. So everyone follows this schedule and is ready to compete! Please remember also; training important for you, more important than press conferences, more important than meetings with corporate sponsors, more important than watching other events. You follow this schedule and you will do your best!"

"To help, we finish several projects tomorrow. We training in morning, then we must go to Cortina for credentials. After that, Stanley will arrange a press conference so USOC media man will be happy. Then we have dinner at Cortina Olympic Village and maybe you see how lucky we are to stay here in Antholz. Then we must have reception with Olympic corporate sponsors to make USOC officials happy. Maybe at this party we help Stanley raise more money for biathlon."

"Tomorrow is very long day, but when we return, we don't have to go to Cortina again 'til Opening Ceremony, more than one week. Congratulations! You make Olympic Team, you have too many Olympic clothes, and now you are living in Olympic athletes' village! Only one thing remains; do your best in Olympic competitions!"

Matt spent a few minutes unpacking and admiring his amazing array of new clothes. Studying the embroidered Olympic logo on one of his jackets, it struck him how dramatically his life had changed. He was a member of the United States Olympic Team!

His mind flashed back to his father's faded jungle hat. It was the only article of military clothing his father ever wore, and only in the woods, when he was hiking or camping. It was a sun-bleached olive drab, embroidered with captain's bars and aviator's wings. His father had talked about the hat only once. On a beautiful autumn afternoon the family had attended a Dartmouth–Harvard football game in Hanover. Filing into the stadium, Matt had asked his dad about the insignias on the army surplus field jackets then popular with the college students. Michael Johnson had identified the patches, but added gruffly that he didn't approve of college kids wearing military clothing, especially uniforms with unit insignias and name tapes.

"But you wear your jungle hat sometimes," Matt pointed out.

"I earned the right to wear that hat, and the insignias on it," his father growled.

As Matt tucked away his new clothes, he smiled, realizing that he was one of a select group who had earned the right to wear the interlocking Olympic rings. For the first time, he understood why his dad had been so defensive about the old jungle hat.

He had nearly finished unpacking when he discovered a photo of his mother, sister and himself, standing on the lawn at home, Smarts Mountain looming in the background. Now he recognized rebellion in Annie's posture and the sadness in his mother's eyes. Even during his father's wild mood swings, Matt's mother had kept the family on a steady course. She had taught elementary school for as long as Matt could remember, and cooked the meals, cleaned the house, did laundry, and cared for the garden each summer. Matt's mother simply ran the family…, until his dad died. Then his mom fell apart. Matt couldn't figure it out, in some ways it had to be easier now, but her strength and confidence evaporated with the loss of her husband. But then he reasoned, if Michael Johnson had killed himself she had a right to feel abandoned. After all, wasn't suicide the ultimate betrayal? I'll have to make it up to her somehow. If I do well here, she'll understand why I had to leave Vermont.

He taped the photo on the wall next to the twirling figure skater drawn by ten-year-old Gabriella Ferraro. As he slid under the heavy woolen blanket and turned out the light, it struck him that he was actually at the Olympics! He had never been more exhilarated or more frightened in his entire life.

After breakfast, they caught a bus for the short ride up the valley to the shooting range and the ski trails. Antholz had hosted major biathlon races for more than twenty years, and had developed one of the best competition venues in the world. Located in a high valley surrounded by peaks rising above 10,000 feet, Antholz always had good snow. The race course itself, next to a picturesque Alpine lake, the Antholzer See at 5,381 feet above sea level, was still below the maximum altitude limit of 1,800 meters for international competitions.

Like Lillehammer, Antholz had an uphill approach to the range, which made the shooting more challenging, but the winds in the Italian mountains were more predictable than those whirling through the rolling hills of Norway.

The trails were unique to Antholz. The biathlon course was designed with three concentric loops, the innermost 2.5K, the middle loop 3.75K and the outer loop 5K. Because the loops threaded their way through beautiful evergreens across the valley floor then veered slightly up the mountain walls, the innermost loop was relatively easy with enough climbs and descents to be interesting, but nothing terribly difficult. The outer loop, clawed its way up and down both sides of the valley and was a killer; long, steep climbs through spruce and larch forests, followed by wild, roller coaster descents across hillside pastures.

From the high point on the course, the trail slashed diagonally through a huge meadow and over three increasingly abrupt knolls, called The Rollers. As the Americans toured the course, Heikki warned Matt he would have to pre-jump the last two knolls or risk being launched into the air — not a comfortable prospect while carrying a rifle. The hill was fast and technical. Matt could imagine how treacherous it would be in icy conditions, but on their inspection tour, it was a blast!

When Matt and Thomas entered the range to shoot after inspecting the 5K loop, they were surprised to find the rifles silent. As the two American athletes approached the firing line, they saw all the coaches peering through their spotting scopes at a point high on the rugged cliffs above the targets. The Sarge motioned to his athletes.

"What are we looking at?" Matt asked, as he carefully put his eye to the lens, "Oh, wow! I see them, some kind of mountain goats on a sheer cliff. What are they?" Matt stepped back to give Thomas a look.

"Ibex," Jankowski answered. "Wild here in the Alps, and rare. The Italian coach pointed them out to the rest of us. They don't see them often."

After showering and grabbing a quick lunch, they boarded a bus for Cortina. Because they were headed for credentialing and then to a press conference, they all wore their awards uniform. The clear, cold day made the Alps even more dramatic, and the huge windows of the luxury bus gave the passengers a panoramic view of the countryside.

The new Olympic Complex was built on a hillside west of Cortina. Unlike the Antholz athletes' village, a temporary structure, the Cortina Olympic Complex was destined to become a hotel after the Games. There were two high-rise towers, one for the athletes, the second for the press, joined at the base by an expansive lobby and a shopping mall.

The bus deposited the Americans at the main gate, where they were met by an official hostess who led them to Credentialing in a bright, festive room with dozens of volunteers in distinctive sweaters.

After verifying the information on an official form, their photo was taken. Eventually each was handed a laminated, photo-identity card on a fine metal chain to wear around their neck until the Games were over.

Their next stop was a press conference. Stan the Man arranged the athletes on the stage of a small auditorium, saving a chair in the center for himself. Once the athletes were seated, Stan addressed the reporters. Again, Matt had to concede that Reimer was at his best when dealing with the media.

At first Matt was anxious, wondering what kind of questions the reporters would ask, but as his experienced teammates responded, he realized that the journalists were simply interested in each athlete's impressions and expectations. Matt described his excitement at the tryouts in Anchorage, the World Cups in Germany and Norway, and the mountain of clothing issued by the USOC. It amused him to see a roomful of reporters scribbling as they recorded his remarks.

As the media people ran out of questions, Stanley stepped in and wrapped up the session by inviting the journalists to Antholz to watch the races. He ushered the athletes back into the corridor and on to the dining hall. Their credentials were checked again as they entered the athletes' village.

The Cortina cafeteria was larger and more modern than its counterpart in Antholz. Here the athletes seemed to come in a variety of sizes. Matt recognized bobsledders, hockey players, and downhillers with thighs like tree trunks.

It was only a short drive into Cortina and the Hotel Cristallo. Stan addressed the athletes, "Okay, gang, you were great at the press conference. Even though we are still a week away from the Opening Ceremony, most Olympic sponsors are arranging receptions, meetings, and social events for their clients during the Games. This reception is the USOC's way to thank them for their support before the schedule gets too frantic.

"There are also potential donors here who want to meet Olympic athletes. Obviously, your enthusiasm and positive attitude could be very helpful. So let's go in there, mix and mingle, and tell these folks how much we appreciate their financial support. We'll regroup at nine o'clock. Remember, smile and be grateful."

The Hotel Cristallo out-sparkled the Rica Victoria in Lillehammer. The carpet was thicker, the crystal chandelier brighter, and the marble columns in the lobby more imposing than the aged wooden beams of the Norwegian hotel. The athletes were led to the banquet hall where the reception was underway. The huge room was crowded and voices rose in animated conversation. There were other American athletes, but Matt couldn't spot anyone he knew. There were dozens of older men and women; some in winter sports clothes, others in elegant evening wear. It seemed as if everyone held a drink, and a few smoked cigarettes.

Stan plowed confidently into the crowd, Oliver saw someone he knew from the ski industry, and Trudy, a marketing director's dream in her new Olympic uniform, was quickly welcomed into the first group of corporate executives she approached. The other athletes hung on the perimeter, observing, until they spotted a lavish refreshment table and quelled their nervousness with snacks. The coaches and a few of the veteran competitors eventually spotted other Olympians they knew, and were absorbed into those groups. The remaining biathletes awkwardly circled the room, too shy to introduce themselves to strangers. Dressed identically in their striking awards suits, Matt imagined they resembled a school of tropical fish circling a crowded aquarium.

More than once a well-intentioned older person attempted a rescue, "Well…hello there! Are you speed skaters?"

"No, sir…, we're biathletes."

"What'd you say? Bi…atha…what ?"

"We're members of the Biathlon Team, that's a combination of cross-country skiing and rifle marksmanship."

"Okay! Now I remember. You kids cross-country ski all over hell and gone, then stop and shoot at little targets. Seems like a damned tough way to get a trip to the Olympics, if you ask me!"

The biathletes glanced at each other, unsure of how to respond. The businessman's silver-haired wife filled the awkward lapse, "I'm sorry, but I just hate guns! There's too much shooting and too many guns in our country already."

Thomas tried to defuse the woman's fears, "I'm sure all the biathletes would agree with you, ma'am. That's why rifle safety is drilled into us until it's second nature. We see the rifle as a precise and expensive piece of sporting equipment; probably like a javelin thrower who doesn't view his javelin as a spear."

"Well, I can't help it, son, I hate guns! But I just love the figure skating. Those little girls are like delicate spring flowers, the music, the drama, it's like ballet." The woman seemed to be aiming a rebuke toward Kate Anderson, a big, strong, Montana ranch girl; definitely not a delicate spring flower.

"Well, this should be an exciting Olympics for you," Thomas continued, "From what we hear, Stephanie Wang has a good chance to win the gold medal."

The older woman brightened immediately, "Oh, isn't she wonderful! She's like a little china doll. Of course, she *should* win the gold, she's the current World Champion! But you know how those judges are at the Olympics. All those Communist countries gang up against our kids — it just isn't fair!"

"I guess that's one thing we don't have to worry about in our sport, it comes down to how fast you ski and how well you shoot; no judges." Heikki was trying to rescue Thomas. "How are you folks connected to the Olympic Committee?"

"Insurance," answered the weighty executive with pride. "We provide the USOC with the most comprehensive insurance package in the industry. We designed a group health plan for all the USOC's employees, we cover their facilities, and we insure all their vehicles. Hell, if one of you kids gets shot up there in the mountains, we've got you covered for disability, dismemberment, and death."

"Gee, that's great," responded Thomas.

"After that Tonya and Nancy fiasco in '94, we even developed a coverage for the USOC on the health of *potential* medal winners. Can you imagine the revenue the USOC would have lost if Nancy's knee had been banged up too badly to compete? We're talking millions!"

"Well, I've got to admit, I never thought about how important insurance was to the Olympics, but we athletes want you to know how grateful we are for your support." Heikki answered according to the guidelines.

"Hey, we're glad to do it! You kids are an inspiration."

"If you get the chance to come up to Antholz for a biathlon race, don't hesitate to give us a shout." Heikki held out his hand.

"Oh, I don't know if we'll risk it," the silver-haired wife chirped, "We've heard the road north is absolutely treacherous! Besides, we have tickets to all the figure skating events, and VIP passes to all their practices!"

"It sounds like you'll be getting your fill of figure skating!"

"Oh, I just can't get enough of it," the woman answered happily.

"Well, nice talking with you. We'd better find our teammates." When they were out of earshot from the insurance man and his wife, Heikki turned to the others, "I think if I had to watch every figure skating competition *and* practice, I'd shoot *myself,* and to hell with his disability coverage!"

They spotted Oliver lecturing a group of young businessmen who appeared to hang on the athlete's every word. Not far away, Trudy was surrounded by admiring, heavyset men with white hair and red faces. Thomas whispered to Matt, "I wonder if that insurance coverage extends to heart attacks at cocktail parties."

In the far corner of the room was a sizable group that seemed impenetrable. Dozens of people craned their necks to see toward the middle of the throng. At two-minute intervals, the harsh flash of a strobe light froze the people struggling for a closer look. As the biathletes eased into the crowd, the other guests, impressed by their Olympic uniforms, stepped aside. Drawn toward the center, Matt finally saw what was creating the stir.

An energetic photographer, draped with several flash cameras, was bobbing and weaving to achieve the perfect angle. His subject was a balding businessman sitting in front of a backdrop of the Olympic ice arena with Stephanie Wang on his lap. She was dressed in a gem-encrusted skating costume and was wearing her tiny, white figure skates. By the time Matt's eyes recovered from another flash, the little skater hopped nimbly to the carpet, and another corporate friend hoisted Stephanie to his lap. A new digital technology generated full color, eight by ten prints seconds after they were taken. Working at a small computer console, a technician inscribed each picture.

The technician's fingers flew over the keyboard, and a colorful photo emerged autographed in authentic cursive penmanship, "To my friend Wally, thanks for helping me achieve my Olympic dream! Love, Stephanie"

"Makes being an obscure biathlete look pretty good, doesn't it?" Thomas was smiling. "That poor kid probably can't go anywhere without people pestering her for her autograph or asking her to pose for pictures. Hey, it's almost time to make our escape! Let's swing by the food table again and stock up for the ride back to Antholz."

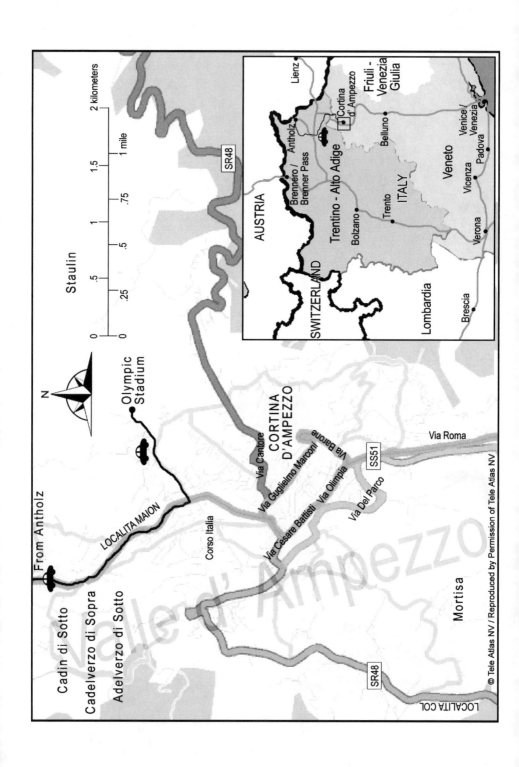

Let the Games Begin

15

Although Kobelev kept his sense of humor during the week before the Opening Ceremony, he displayed an intensity and discipline that Matt had not seen before. It seemed as if their coach had every moment planned, from the morning run, to studying technique videos and trail maps late into the evenings.

Because the first biathlon competition was not scheduled until the second week of the Games, Kobelev planned to work the athletes hard for ten days. He scheduled combination training in the mornings: short, fast, skiing loops with lots of shooting. After lunch and a short rest, they skied distance workouts until dark. Matt enjoyed the training. He liked the trails in Antholz even better than Ruhpolding or Lillehammer, and he was growing comfortable on the shooting range in spite of the uphill approach and an occasional crosswind.

Kobelev arranged time trials between the Americans and athletes from other nations. There was a relaxed approach to these competitions. None of the racers wanted to use up their best efforts, but they were anxious to test themselves in an international field on the Olympic course. The Americans were happy with their performances; Matt shot well and Sandy easily out-distanced the other women.

When the Norwegian team arrived, Matt was eager to see Grete, and she seemed happy to see him. They ate together in the cafeteria, occasionally sitting at the Norwegian table, at other times joining the Americans. Matt noticed Vlad had become an informal ambassador, enthusiastically greeting coaches and athletes from all the participating nations. He appeared to be friends with everyone.

Three days after they arrived in Antholz, Vlad was having lunch at the American table when Matt and Grete approached, carrying their trays. There was an awkward moment when Grete hesitated, unsure whether she should sit with the Americans. Matt glanced anxiously at the Norwegian table where several of their formidable cross-country skiers were eating. Vlad noticed their indecision, stood abruptly, and commanded them to sit. They watched the coach stride across the cafeteria and speak to the mayor of the athletes' village. Soon after Vlad returned, workers began circling the dining room, gathering the small national flags from the tables.

"The Olympics should bring people together, not keep them apart," Vlad explained. "We have no need of nationalism while we eat! From now on, sit where you want! We are all lovers of Nordic skiing. Get to know your colleagues from other countries!"

Vlad's initiative had an amazing effect. Within a day, athletes and coaches from all over the world were eating together in the dining hall and it became impossible to identify individual teams.

Aside from mealtimes, Matt's training schedule was so busy that he had little time to spend with Grete. They skied together twice when they both had over-distance workouts on their schedules. Matt was impressed by how fluid and graceful Grete was on the course. Sandy was powerful, she skied like a man; but Grete seemed to glide effortlessly over the snow.

The remote location of Antholz provided a pleasant isolation for the Nordic skiers. As the Opening Ceremony approached, more cross-country and biathlon teams arrived at the athletes' village, and the competitors mingled freely at mealtimes and in the shuttle buses to the Nordic stadiums.

Not surprisingly, the Russian biathletes were on a training schedule similar to the Americans, and Matt often rode to and from the range with Dimitry Popov. Although Popov was a medal contender, his attitude remained outgoing and friendly. Unlike his teammates, Popov embraced capitalism, and every bus ride was an opportunity to negotiate trades of all kinds, from commemorative pins to team uniforms.

On the ride down after an exhausting morning of training, Dimitry sat beside a severe, Russian cross-country skier who Matt recognized from the TV coverage of previous Olympics. He was Valeri Vassiliev, the aging veteran of the Russian Nordic dynasty. Vassiliev, along with an occasional Finn and a couple of Italians, was the only skier in six years of international competition to challenge the Norwegian stable of racehorses. With the breakup of the USSR, the Soviet Nordic machine was severely shaken, and among the men only Vassiliev consistently earned a position on the medal podium. Because he was almost forty years old, he was no longer expected to win the shorter races, but he was still a favorite in the 30K and 50K. In fact, the tougher the conditions, the more difficult the course, the better Vassiliev was likely to finish. His stature in Russia approached that of a god, eclipsing all former Soviet world record holders and Olympians. In fact, his summer training schedule was often published in the sports section of *Pravda,* and if he came down with the flu, it was a national calamity.

Sitting across the aisle from the two Russians, Matt noticed that Popov, usually so gregarious, was subdued and respectful next to Vassiliev. Matt imagined it would be like sitting next to Michael Jordan or Dan Marino. Popov caught his American friend staring at Vassiliev.

"Johnsonmatt, you have not met greatest Russian athlete of all time; winner of twenty-two Olympic and World Championship medals, forty-seven times National Champion, my friend, Valeri Vassiliev!"

Matt nodded to the Russian hero, who stared back with cold, gray eyes. Popov continued, "Valeri, this my America friend, Johnsonmatt. In Lillehammer World Cup two weeks ago, he has best shooting of everyone!"

Vassiliev leaned forward for a better look at Matt, "How many years have you?" His voice, like his eyes, betrayed no emotion.

"I'll be nineteen in the spring," Matt answered. He was tempted to add, "Sir" or "Your Majesty."

"I also eighteen at my first World Championships…, twenty years ago. I have racing in Ooo–Ess–Ahh., World Cup in Minnesota, also Anchorage. I very much like Anchorage."

"We had our tryouts for this Olympic Team in Anchorage, I liked it, too," Matt responded.

Popov seemed to relax. "Johnsonmatt, you have for Valeri the special Ooo–Ess–Ahh Olympic Biathlon pin?"

Matt rummaged through his pockets. Fortunately, he found one of the special biathlon pins Popov wanted and handed it over to Vassiliev. The experienced Russian took the pin, studied it carefully, and nodded as if the pin met his imperial standards.

"*Spaseeba*," he said.

Matt thought the idea was trading pins, but he was not about to embarrass Popov by asking Vassiliev for a Russian pin in return. Maybe when you got to be as good as Vassiliev, you didn't trade pins, you simply accepted the ones you wanted and rejected the rest.

Matt encountered Vassiliev three more times in the days before the Opening Ceremony. Twice, on bus rides down from the stadium, Matt nodded to the Russian, but the stone-faced Vassiliev showed no recognition. The third encounter occurred one afternoon while Matt and Grete were finishing a distance workout on the cross-country trails. They were skiing hard, twenty kilometers into a 25K workout, when a decisive grunt from behind warned them to yield the trail. They skated to the side as Vassiliev plowed past, head down and drenched with sweat in spite of the late afternoon chill. Matt and Grete watched in awe as the Russian pulled away with powerful strides that leveled the terrain.

On Wednesday, February 11, Janet Keegan scheduled a meeting in the small conference room of their housing unit. Since the team's arrival in Antholz, the athlete's rep had kept a low profile, sitting with the team at mealtimes and occasionally riding to the range to observe a workout.

"I'm sorry to take up your time, but this meeting is one of my obligations as your representative to the Athletes' Advisory Council. As you know, one athlete is selected to carry the flag and lead the United States delegation into the stadium during the Opening Ceremony. It's an honor, and it places that athlete in the national spotlight. So, our job here is, first of all, to determine if the biathlon team has a nominee, and secondly, to select a team captain to represent the team at tomorrow's meeting in Cortina."

There was silence when the swimmer finished speaking. Then Ragnar nominated Sandy, and the others eagerly agreed. At first, Sandy rejected the idea, but eventually they convinced her of the positive media attention it would generate for biathlon if she were selected to carry the flag, which seemed unlikely. Burl was elected to accompany Janet to

Cortina for the team captains' meeting, an assignment he didn't mind.

By Friday morning the Antholz athletes' village was filled to capacity. The Italians, French and Germans, who had all been training at higher altitude, finally moved in. Kobelev planned a killer interval workout in the morning and more combination training in the afternoon. When the American biathletes straggled into the dining hall for breakfast at 0715, they had already been out for a forty-five minute run.

It had started snowing Thursday evening and the passes between Cortina and Antholz were closed until dawn on Friday morning. Burl and Janet looked tired but happy when they joined the biathletes in the cafeteria.

Ragnar was the first to ask, "How'd the meeting go?"

"The selection of the flag bearer is supposed to be secret until the official announcement in Cortina at ten, but since we're so far out in the boondocks, it shouldn't matter if we tell you now. Sandy got it!"

"How did you manage that?" asked Ragnar.

Burl smiled at the swimmer. "Janet contacted a few athletes by e-mail before the meeting. The rest was luck. We rode to Cortina with the Cross-Country captain, and I had her convinced by the time we arrived. Luge and Bobsled supported Sandy right away — they know her from Lake Placid. Hockey didn't have a nominee of their own, so they fell in line after I made my presentation. Figure Skating couldn't decide on one candidate, so they were pushing for two skaters to carry the flag. That pissed everyone else off, and Sandy became the only logical choice."

It was clear that Sandy was not thrilled about her election. "Well, I guess it's good exposure for biathlon. Will there be more press conferences?" She looked at Janet Keegan.

"I'm afraid so. In fact, we have to head back to Cortina right away. I'll help you pack."

Kobelev remained inflexible with his training schedule for Saturday. Although the team had to be in their parade uniforms and on the bus by 1300, the Russian insisted on the routine morning run and a difficult combination workout at the range. They were not back to the Village until noon, leaving only an hour to shower, change, and eat lunch. Several athletes boarded the bus with bags of fruit and bread pilfered from the cafeteria because they hadn't had time to eat.

It was great fun to critique the parade uniforms of other countries;

the fluorescent colors and shiny fabrics of the Japanese and Koreans, the stylish topcoats and fedoras of the French and Italians, the Russian furs. Matt loved his L.L. Bean boots and the sheepskin coat, but he felt comical wearing the big Stetson. He had to admit it was a good choice though, when four athletes from other nations asked him if he would trade after the Opening Ceremony.

As they began their descent into the d'Ampezzo Valley, Matt could see the long line of buses snaking down the switchbacks below him. Soon after they reached the valley floor, they were waved through the narrow streets of Cortina by *carabinarie* and Italian soldiers, who barricaded all the intersecting roads. The village was thronged with spectators, many waving colorful flags. Skillfully the drivers threaded their huge vehicles through the historic streets. They emerged on the east edge of Cortina and climbed to the base of the Alpine runs.

The same village had hosted the Winter Olympics in 1956, but most of those competition venues had been completely rebuilt. The Italians had constructed a new jumping complex next to the final pitch of their most popular Alpine slope. On the other side of the ski jumping venue, they built the freestyle skiing complex — a broad, steep mogul run, and jumps for the aerial competitions.

During the fifteen days of the Games, the three stadiums would accommodate 90,000 spectators, but during the Opening and Closing Ceremonies, the seating would be reconfigured to create one huge arena facing the snow-covered hillside. As the bus edged closer Matt saw the outside of the stadium, bristling with flags.

The assembly area was teeming with athletes as Olympic hostesses in stylish overcoats guided the arrivals from Antholz to their national delegations. Matt noticed that the entire area was surrounded by a chain link fence and patrolled by armed soldiers with police dogs. Members of the USOC's Games Preparation Committee and several Athletes' Representatives, all equipped with hand held walkie-talkies, were mingling with the excited competitors, inspecting uniforms and answering questions. A crowd of kids bunched outside the fence, as close to the soldiers and dogs as they dared, waving and shouting to get the athletes' attention. One word was intelligible amid the jumble of Italian: "Autograph...autograph!"

When Greg Ingram moved among the Americans instructing them to line up, it was 1630. The athletes' reps assumed the role of sheep dogs, nipping at the heels of the athletes until the United States Team was organized into a broad column, six abreast. The Olympic Committee officials were decisive about the order of march, Figure Skating first, then Alpine Skiing, followed by Speed Skating. Matt suspected that the order was related to the international success of the sports. Biathlon was at the back of the delegation with Bobsled and Nordic Skiing.

Even after they lined up, there was more waiting. But then, without warning, the Italian girl bearing the placard "Amerika," led the huge delegation through the assembly area, and down a narrow street bordered by a barricade and military guards. Matt caught a glimpse of the Stars and Stripes beyond a sea of cowboy hats.

Even the soldiers along the fence seemed caught up in the excitement, smiling at the athletes and wishing them good luck. After another short march forward, the parade was dwarfed by the massive scaffolding of the stadium. Matt heard music from the ceremony, which was already underway inside the arena, and he got goosebumps from the amazing sound of ninety thousand people cheering.

A thin woman with a strained face, followed by an assistant, was bulldozing her way through the United States athletes. She wore a headset, and referred constantly to a clipboard. Her garish silver parka was trimmed in dark fur and embroidered with the unmistakable logo of the American Sports Broadcasting Network, a recently created television conglomerate that covered most major sporting events.

"Okay! Who do we have here...the Luge Team? Let's see," she studied her clipboard. "Duncan Kennedy, where's Duncan? I want you over here on my far left." The assistant repositioned the athletes so that Duncan Kennedy, winner of several World Cup events, would be marching on the outside of the formation.

"All right," she mumbled, studying the clipboard as she pushed her way through the sheepskin coats and Stetsons, "I think that's it for Luge." She glanced at the athletes. "You! Yeah, red hair! I want you behind Duncan!" The assistant grabbed a coat sleeve and quickly moved an attractive red-headed girl behind Kennedy.

"So this must be Bobsled!" The efficient woman looked up into the formidable, dark face of Bubba Lane. "Mr. Lane, I'd like you over here to my left, and Willie.... Where's Willie Washington? Oh there you are! Mr. Washington if you'd just march behind Mr. Lane." The young assistant was far more respectful repositioning the towering football players than he had been with the young luge riders.

"Thank you, gentlemen, that's great. Now who's left? Biathlon."

Referring to her clipboard, she studied the remaining rows of athletes. "Okay, you! That's right, the blonde girl. I want you over here behind Mr. Washington." The assistant was already tugging on Oliver's sleeve to move him from the edge of the parade to make room for Trudy.

"Hey, what difference does it make? Who the hell are you anyway?" Oliver complained.

The woman sprung around like a cat. "You got some kind of problem, fella? I'm the assistant producer of ASBN's world-wide coverage of the Opening Ceremony! We paid more than $450 million to televise these Games, and that gives me certain privileges! Now if you want to participate in this parade, get to the other side of the formation and shut up, or my assistant will escort you to the nearest medical aid tent."

"You can't get away with that!" Oliver lashed back.

She took a step closer to Wainwright and hissed, "If you want to march in this parade, get your ass over there right now, and quit wasting my time!"

He thought about it for an instant, but when the woman glanced authoritatively at her assistant, Oliver slipped out of line, and stepped to Trudy's former position. The woman resumed her inspection as if nothing had happened. When she spotted Thomas and Emily Livengood she barked, "Where are you two from?"

"Alaska," Thomas responded.

"Okay, good! I want her on the outside and you next to her, right here."

In another thirty seconds she had moved through the cross-country skiers, repositioning the most photogenic women to the outside column. Then, she charged back to the front of the delegation, chattering into the tiny microphone.

The column lurched ahead, gathered speed, and began marching into a tunnel. Suddenly like Alice stepping through the looking glass, they emerged into the brilliantly illuminated stadium. The gigantic arena was a jumble of colors; flags, banners, huge panels of fabric displayed on the snow-covered slopes, and an amazing variety of costumes. Matt's head and chest resonated with the amplified vibrations from the towering loudspeakers. When the announcer bellowed "AMERIKA, " a deafening roar from the crowd overwhelmed the music.

Although they had been instructed to march in step and stay in line, the athletes were so enthralled by the celebration surrounding them that it was easy to stumble in the snow. To Matt's left was the largest grandstand he had ever seen, packed with waving, cheering spectators. To his right was a broad, snow-covered expanse rising to the outrun of the jumps and the Alpine courses. The cheering was unbelievable. Everyone was caught up in the excitement, even the veteran football players, who waved their cowboy hats to the crowd.

In the infield were television crews, some walking backwards as the parade advanced, others operating remote cameras on long booms that towered over the passing delegation. One of the mobile crews jammed a big lens and bright lights at Trudy Wilson as she waved and blew kisses. Then they zoomed in on the two Alaskans. Never taking his eye from the viewfinder, a cameraman shouted, "SMILE!...WAVE!... You're supposed to be having FUN!"

Although the red, white and green colors of the host nation seemed to dominate, dozens of other flags were evident in the stands. They passed a section filled with Americans, screaming and waving the Stars and Stripes. As he made the turn at the far end of the arena, Matt caught a glimpse of Sandy Stonington, leading the huge delegation.

The pace slowed while athletes filed into the reserved seats in the grandstands. Matt watched other nations enter the stadium: Poland, Romania, Russia. He recognized Valeri Vassiliev carrying the Russian flag. Vassiliev had declined the leather harness other flag bearers used, and held the tall, heavy pole with its tricolored banner the way an alter boy might carry a tall candle down the aisle of a church.

The parade of nations continued, with the introduction of each new nation inspiring wild applause from the spectators. Finally, the host Italian team entered and the stadium shook with cheering and stamping feet. Before the Italian athletes had completed their circuit of the infield, some of the younger spectators started the Wave, and the undulating ritual of standing with arms stretched to the sky became a tribute that followed the home team on its march around the arena.

The Italian athletes took their places in the stands and the pageantry of the Opening Ceremony continued with the reading of the Olympic Oath. Manuela Di Centa, winner of five cross-country medals in Lillehammer, was introduced. Standing in front of nearly 100,000 spectators, Di Centa promised on behalf of all the participating athletes to compete fairly and honestly. She spoke in Italian but the announcer translated her words into French and English.

Then the strains of the Olympic Anthem filled the stadium and colored floodlights illuminated the sky as hundreds of doves were released, circled the arena then disappeared into the deepening dusk.

Accompanied by stirring music, six men dressed in the traditional costumes of the Sud Tirol emerged from the tunnel bearing a huge Olympic flag stretched between them. The lights in the arena were extinguished except for spotlights, which marked their progress across the snow to the tall flag pole between the ski jumps and the freestyle venue. The winter sky still glowed faintly above snow-capped peaks, as stars flittered overhead. The entire stadium was hushed as the flag was attached and majestically drawn to the top of the pole.

While a single spotlight dramatically illuminated the Olympic flag, a tiny twinkle of light swept across the slope high above the stadium. The announcer informed the gathering that the Olympic torch was arriving from the peaks of the Italian Alps, delivered by the nation's greatest Alpine champion, Gustav Thöni. The crowd chanted, "Gustavo…Gustavo…Gustavo…." as the former champion carved graceful turns across the mountain. When Thöni reached the end of the Alpine run, a spotlight revealed a second skier, on delicate cross-country equipment. The crowd began a new chant: "Maurilio…Maurilio…Maurilio…."

The second torch bearer was Maurilio De Zolt, several times an Olympic and World Cup 50K champion. Holding the torch high, the small powerful man skated effortlessly as the devoted crowd chanted his name. After circling the arena, De Zolt stopped in front of the towering twin cauldrons, commemorating the 1956 Olympics and the current Games.

De Zolt handed the torch to Eugenio Monti, the most admired bobsledder in history, and Italy's most successful Olympian. The silver-haired Monti bowed to the crowd and climbed the steep stairs to the lip of the lower cauldron. Again he bowed to his audience, and the huge crowd held its collective breath. Raising the torch high above his head, he tipped the flame over the edge of the cauldron. There was an instant of hushed expectancy, then golden flames danced around the edge of the cauldron and fire illuminated the winter sky. The mountains echoed with the roar of the spectators.

Monti descended and handed the torch to a young girl. She was an eleven-year-old figure skater from Bolzano, representing the youth of the world. She ran to the base of the taller cauldron, bowed to the spectators and jogged nimbly up the steep staircase. Bathed in the golden light of the lower cauldron, she faced the crowd and ignited the second flame, which rose into the sky with another roar from the crowd.

The stadium lights came on with a flourish of music and the President of the International Olympic Committee, Juan Antonio Samaranch, spoke first in Italian, then in thickly accented English, and finally in French. In a few simple sentences, he declared the Cortina Olympic Winter Games open.

What followed was a festival of costume, dancing and fireworks unlike anything Matt had ever seen. More than once he assumed they had seen the finale, only to have the music and fireworks intensify. When the announcer finally declared the end of the ceremony, no one wanted to leave. Hostesses urged the athletes from the grandstand toward the tunnel and parking lot beyond. The fences were lined with performers from the Ceremony; Tyroleans in their traditional costumes, dancers, and a colorful mob of children dressed as fuzzy teddy bears. The performers cheered for the athletes and the Olympians applauded the entertainers.

The biathletes had almost reached the waiting buses when a young man sprinted through the snow outside the fence. "Hey, any American team member! I'll give you a thousand dollars for your sheepskin coat!"

A few athletes looked through the fence at the entrepreneur. "No shit, honest! A thousand bucks for your coat! Come on, you got 'em for free, I'll give you a grand right now!"

"Are you serious?" Oliver stepped from the stream of athletes.

"Absolutely! That looks like the right size. I've got a thousand bucks right here."

"Hold on, I didn't say I'd take a thousand," Oliver responded. "You know damn well you can't get this coat anywhere else. There were only a couple hundred of 'em made. I'll sell it for two thousand!"

"Shit man, I don't have two thousand dollars! If I did I'd give it to you. I've GOT to have one of those coats! How about twelve-fifty?"

"No way," Oliver was toying with the guy. "These coats are great."

"I know, I know...." moaned the guy outside the fence, stumbling through the snow as he kept pace with Oliver. "Come on, take twelve-fifty. You've probably got a closet full of Olympic clothes at home."

"Fifteen hundred and you've got a deal!" Oliver responded.

"Shit man, that'll clean me out! The Games haven't even started. How am I going to eat?"

"That's why you brought your VISA card. Fifteen hundred or forget it!"

They were approaching the convoy of idling buses. The young man outside the fence realized he had run out of time. "Okay, okay… fifteen hundred. Here, come over to the fence!"

An Italian soldier, assault rifle slung over his shoulder, watched the transaction with amusement as the spectator pushed a roll of bills through the thick wire. Oliver counted the money, slipped off the heavy fleece coat, and tossed it over the fence. The young customer pulled it on, and beamed with satisfaction.

"Now don't be trying to use that coat to sneak into places you don't belong," warned Oliver. "The guards are on the lookout for people impersonating team members."

"Don't worry, I'll pack it away 'til I get home. I just had to have one of these coats!"

Matt watched Oliver's transaction, then hurried off in search of the bus.

"Dumbshit," Oliver grumbled. "No coat I'll ever own is worth fifteen hundred dollars. That chump will wake up tomorrow and realize he spent about twelve hundred too much for a coat he'll be able to order from L.L. Bean's catalog next fall."

Janet Keegan was waiting at the bus, checking a list as the athletes boarded. In the dimly lit interior they enthusiastically recapped the spectacular performance. The conversations faded when the bus pulled from the staging area and joined the convoy back to Antholz.

Matt wondered whether his mother and sister had watched the Opening Ceremony on television. He couldn't remember if it was scheduled for live broadcast, or would be delayed for prime time in the evening. Maybe his mother wouldn't watch at all. It had not been easy to call home from Europe, and when he did get through, the sadness and disappointment were evident in his mother's voice. Why was it so hard for her to accept his devotion to the Olympic dream? Hell, his father had been an Olympic hopeful when they married. In one way, Matt was completing a journey his father had started decades earlier. Maybe that was the problem. Maybe it wasn't Vietnam that destroyed his father at all, maybe it was the shattered Olympic dream. Matt's mother had been forced to live with that sad legacy for almost twenty years, and now it was beginning all over again.

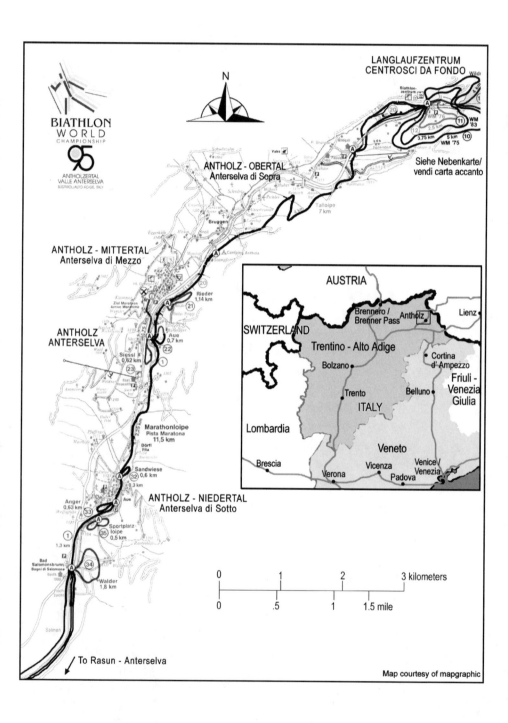

Good Shooting

16

On the morning following the Opening Ceremony when Kobelev roused his troops for their run, it was snowing hard. The biathletes were surprised that in spite of the weather, the road leading to the competition venue was already clogged with buses. The first Olympic event in Antholz was the women's cross-country 15K freestyle, and all of Italy seemed determined to see Manuela Di Centa duplicate her success in Lillehammer.

Approaching the race sites from the valley below, the biathlon range was on the left, the cross-country stadium to the right. There was a large cul-de-sac where buses stopped briefly to deposit or pick up passengers. Several arched wooden overpasses permitted spectators and competitors to cross from one side of the road to the other. The competition trails were a labyrinth of interwoven loops including dozens of tunnels and bridges. Although they were constantly within a few meters of each other, the cross-country courses and the biathlon courses were distinct, independent trails. Even more impressive was an extensive network of walking paths and bridges over the race courses, which allowed the spectators to venture beyond the start/finish stadiums and watch the athletes glide through the woods.

Although the range was crowded and the falling snow limited

visibility, the morning workout was productive. Matt's shooting was consistent, and he was finally feeling strong on the long climbs. The skis that Svensberget had stone-ground in Dombås skimmed over the new snow. After changing into a dry shirt, Matt was waiting for a shuttle when Grete and a couple of the American women suggested they run over to the cross-country venue and watch the finish of the woman's 15K.

The stadium was pandemonium. Spectators vaulted the railings and swarmed the finish area. In the midst of the mob, Manuela Di Centa was hoisted to the shoulders of two coaches, engulfed by a sea of adoring fans waving Italian flags. Matt had never witnessed such a celebration; the first Olympic victory of the Cortina Games was a gold medal for Italy!

The snow stopped Sunday night and Monday provided spectacular weather for the Men's 30K. As the biathletes were warming down after a tough series of intervals, Matt and Thomas cruised the five kilometer loop next to the 30K cross-country course. They cheered the four Americans in the race and admired the flawless technique of the Norwegians. Matt spotted Valeri Vassiliev, his skis slashing from side to side as he assaulted a long, difficult climb. The legendary champion looked pale, and a frothy beard of mucous hung from his chin.

"S'pose he's working hard?" Thomas asked, as the Russian plowed over the crest of the hill.

Later, Matt heard the results of the 30K: a Norwegian first, an Italian second, and a Finn third. Vassiliev had finished out of the hardware in eighth.

On Tuesday evening Kobelev called his team together for a meeting. After everyone was seated in the cramped conference room, the Russian began by covering a list of mundane items. Having defused some of the tension, he confronted a topic the athletes both anticipated and dreaded. "So…for the men's 20K the start order is Heikki Lahdenpera, Burl Palmer, Matt Johnson and Ragnar Haugen. In the women's 15K on Sunday our starters will be Paula Robbins, Kate Anderson, Trudy Wilson and Sandy Stonington.

"Okay! I believe we have done necessary preparations. Now with little bit of good luck, we have strong results in biathlon for United States. Oh! I'm almost forget! I speaking with Italian coach, Ubaldo Carrara. You know that often the Italians are first with waxing improvements. They are testing a new fluorocarbon glider that goes very well here, high in the

Alps." Kobelev grinned. "I convince Ubaldo that we can help him test this new wax, and if really it is faster, then we will be helping his team by pushing the Russians and the Germans farther back in results. So…Andy and I will testing this new wax through this week."

The next two days passed in a blur. After the team leaders' meeting on Wednesday, the start order was published and the athletes selected to compete in the distance events were given favored status on the shooting range, at the speed trap and even in the cafeteria line. When Matt remembered to check for messages on the computer terminal, he was overwhelmed by the requests for interviews. Thomas came to the rescue by offering to manage Matt's e-mail; he scheduled interviews after the 20K with six journalists, and rejected requests from others.

There were dozens of good luck wishes: one from his mom's fifth grade class; greetings from a man he'd never met at Wrangler Auto Leasing in Denver; and a note from the governor of Vermont, which read, "To Matt Johnson of Thetford. You make all Vermonters proud by your achievements. Ski fast and shoot straight."

On Thursday morning Kobelev and Jankowski concentrated their efforts on the four men scheduled to start on Friday.

"Well, Rookie, are you ready?" Jankowski asked.

"I guess so. The shooting's okay and I feel comfortable on my skis. I'm a little worried though. When I'm training it feels pretty much the same as always. I wonder if I'm psyched up enough."

"Whoa, Matthew!" Jankowski responded. "There are probably twenty athletes here who have the potential to win medals tomorrow. Most won't, because they'll get nervous and try too hard. They'll ski and shoot beyond their training, or they'll make mistakes. But the winners will compete as if it's just another race. If you're relaxed on the range and comfortable on your skis, you'll be happy with the result."

"Have you heard the weather forecast?" Vlad was smiling. "We have snow coming late tonight and on 'til tomorrow. In our testing, this Italian wax is very good. You give me your racing skis after dinner, the ones we stone-ground in Norway. I wax them for you."

"Thanks, Vlad. That would be great. They haven't felt super-fast yet, but Svensberget said they'd be best in new snow."

As Thomas and Matt entered the cafeteria, they met Grete and two of her teammates returning from their workout. The conversation drifted from the results of the day's cross-country races and the Norwegians standing, to the weather. The women reported that the approaching storm might dump a meter of snow before it blew itself out on Saturday.

Even before they finished eating, Matt was growing anxious. His time had been carefully scheduled for so long, he felt uneasy just sitting around chatting. He couldn't shake the sense that there was something else he should be doing. As the others finished their meals, Matt mentally reviewed his daily routine: he had already cleaned his rifle, he had left his skis in the wax room for Vlad…

"Earth to Matt, Earth to Matt, come in please!" Thomas's comment brought laughter from the Norwegians, and pulled Matt from his reverie.

"Sorry, I was thinking about what I've got to do before tomorrow," Matt explained.

"Yeah, like what?" Thomas demanded.

"That's just it, I feel like I'm forgetting something, but I guess all the important stuff is done."

"Let's go for a walk!" Grete suggested brightly.

Moments later Matt and Grete were headed out through the main gate on the path to Antholz Mittertal, a kilometer down the valley. The thick overcast had dropped even lower, and up at the Antholzer See, the biathlon range appeared to be socked in. In spite of the dreary weather, Grete's enthusiasm was captivating. As they walked past the neat Alpine farms and through the picturesque village, Grete deftly shifted the conversation away from the competition. For two hours they talked about their families and friends back home. They stopped at the fortress-like church in the center of the village. It was old and well cared for, but far more humble than the lavishly restored church in Ruhpolding.

As they climbed back to the athletes' village along another path at the edge of the valley, it began to snow.

"So, Matt Johnson, USA, do you like racing in a snow storm?" Grete asked as they approached the main gate.

"I love it! In Alaska, Thomas convinced me that any time the conditions are difficult, if you approach the competition with the right attitude, it's an advantage. I was skeptical at first, but I made the Olympic Team on a stormy day, and my best result in Europe was that windy day in Lillehammer. I hope it snows like hell tomorrow!"

Grete smiled, wrapped her arms around his broad shoulders, and kissed him. Vaguely aware of soldiers in the security building, he kissed her back. The two athletes were interrupted by clapping and whistling from the *carabinarie*. As they passed through the security screening, Matt's face was warm with embarrassment, but Grete joked with the soldiers.

Matt's wish was granted. When he left the housing unit at 0630 for his morning run, there was more than a foot of new snow on the ground, and it was still falling. He ran and stretched alone, then went to the cafeteria for breakfast. Vlad, Andy and Gopher were just leaving for the range. Matt had rarely seen Kobelev so excited.

"So, Matthew! You are ready, I can tell! This will be for you a good day, I think. Still snowing, some wind, a little altitude…this is biathlon, always different. And I tell you something; today nobody has faster skis than the Americans! This is true! Guarantee! We must go now but we looking for you at 0830."

After selecting his usual breakfast of oatmeal, toast, juice and yogurt, Matt joined his teammates. The three who were racing seemed less talkative than usual, lost in their own thoughts. The four competitors finished eating as Rosie Brown, Dr. Manheimer and several of the women arrived. There were wishes of "good luck" as the men left the cafeteria.

Back in his room, Matt changed into his racing uniform. He vacillated over minor decisions; should he wear his full-length polypro underwear, or was it warm enough to get by with the wind panel briefs? It was definitely too warm for the Swix earmuffs under his hat, but maybe he'd better bring them in his pack just to be safe? Should he put his Lycra racing bib on now and wear it to the range…?

"This is really dumb," he mumbled. "It's just another race, no big deal. I've got to stick to my normal routine." But he knew it wasn't just another race.

He joined silent biathletes from several countries and boarded the shuttle bus outside the main gate. There were polite nods of recognition, but none of the gregarious banter that usually greeted him. As the bus slowly climbed the valley, the heavy snow swirled, concealing the mountains and the road ahead.

When they disembarked at the stadium, Matt glanced across the firing line toward the targets. Although gusts of blowing snow occasionally obscured the black aiming circles, the targets never completely disappeared. Matt remembered Anchorage and suspected that the weather would be challenging enough to make the results unpredictable, but not bad enough to force a postponement.

He opened the door to the wax room and saw Vlad, Andy and Gopher, all wearing Darth Vader-type respirators as they feverishly worked on skis. Country Western music blared from a portable boom box as the three coaches ironed, scraped and brushed the expensive fluorocarbon gliders. When Andy spotted Matt in the doorway, he tossed down his scraper, grabbed a pair of Matt's Atomics, and pushed the athlete back out the door. Pulling his mask below his chin, Andy handed Matt the skis, "Sorry, Rookie, but the fluoros are thick in there. These boards are ready to go. Warm up on them, ride them through the speed trap a few times, and if you get a chance, follow some German or Italian down one of the hills. After you zero, check back here, we'll probably have others for you to test. Since you and Ragnar go out late, you guys can keep testing even after the race begins. Now go see the Sarge; he's set up on firing point twenty-two."

"Thanks for the waxing help, Andy."

"No sweat. You just have a great race out there today. Make us coaches look good!"

Zeroing went smoothly in spite of the storm. Although the bull was not the distinct, black dot that was visible in sunny weather, Matt easily centered the fuzzy target in his aperture.

"One more thing, Matt." Jankowski advised. "You're number sixty-eight, third seed, right? You'll be back there with the big boys. If Popov or one of those German studs comes blasting by you, don't forget they could be winning the whole goddamn race! Don't get discouraged; get tough and hang with 'em for a couple of kilometers. No need to save anything for tomorrow. If you ski yourself blind in the first 18K's and walk the last two, that's a hell of a lot better than cruising comfortably for 20K's and knowing for the rest of your life that you had something left at the finish line."

As Matt skated from the range through the start/finish area, he was surprised to see the grandstand filling with spectators in brightly colored parkas, nylon ponchos and even umbrellas to ward off the storm. Tyrolean music poured from the public address system, but the snow absorbed the shrill notes and the folk music seemed perfect for the high Alpine valley.

Matt was a kilometer out on the 3.75K loop before he noticed that his skis seemed exceptionally fast. He remembered Vlad's request and waited at the top of the first major descent letting three other competitors ski by.

Finally, the two German medal winners from Ruhpolding skated

easily up the hill. They nodded at Matt and pushed over the top. Matt gave
them enough of a lead so that he wouldn't be drafting, then coasted down
the trail after them. Before the racers reached the frozen lake, Matt was
forced to air check, standing up straight and spreading his arms wide to
increase wind resistance. Even this wasn't enough, so he threw his left ski
into a partial snowplow to keep from overtaking the Germans.

At the bottom of the hill, they turned and stared at the American.
Matt smiled and shrugged his shoulders. It wouldn't hurt to have two of
Germany's strongest thinking they had slow skis!

Back in the waxing room, Matt reported his results to Andy, who
hooted above the Clint Black song blaring from the boom box. Matt could
hear the announcer calling the names of the early racers so he searched
for a dry spot where he could be alone to focus on the race. He found a
covered stairwell leading to the timing center. As he stretched his lower
back, shoulders and neck, he rehearsed the upcoming race in his mind. He
saw himself coming into the range strong and poised, but for some reason,
he couldn't picture the result. Then he caught the image of his father
smiling — one of his rare signs of approval, when they shot together years
ago. He also heard the words of the USOC's Mac Moore, the old soldier,
"If you just do your best, that's all anybody can ask."

He walked back to the wax room where his Atomics were waiting
in the rack. Andy had autographed the skis with Magic Marker, and
Vlad had added something in Russian. As Matt rummaged through his
backpack for his Lycra racing bib, he felt a smooth, thin shaft. Mystified,
he withdrew the white oosik, the gift from Unalakleet. He realized it was
Thomas's way of wishing him luck. He carefully replaced it in the pack
and pulled on his racing bib.

He worked his way to the range to retrieve his rifle, and Jankowski
led him to the equipment check area. The organizers had plenty of
experienced volunteers, so the trigger weighing, ski and pole measurement,
and uniform inspection went quickly. As Matt slipped off his warmups
and stuffed them into a plastic bag, the Sarge reached over the fence and
punched him in the shoulder. "Rookie, just keep doing what you were
doing in Lillehammer and you're going to be happy."

"Okay, Sarge."

"And Matt, remember, it's supposed to be fun!"

"Thanks, Sarge. See you in a little while."

The start officials were friendly and efficient. They checked his
number against their start lists and asked in a heavy accent, "Johnson,

Matthew...Ooo–Ess–Ahh?"

"That's me."

"*Bonjourno,* Johnsonmatthew. *Buena veniete de Anterselva!* We wish you a good trip."

As the electronic tone beeped, racer number sixty-seven lunged from the starting gate, and Matt was guided into the narrow slot directly behind a delicate wand which separated him from the race course. He was aware that the rifle sounds from the range had become steady, though muffled by the falling snow. In earlier races he had been among the first competitors to shoot, but this time others would be nearly finished before he was even on the course. The traffic from the range, merging with the start lane was heavy. He realized that he'd need to be alert where the trails joined. An official gripped his shoulder, "*Attencion!*"

Matt watched the starting clock a few meters ahead of him. As the delicate arm of the clock jumped mechanically to five, the electronic tones sounded: beep...beep...beep...beep...beep...BEEEEEEPPP!

With a powerful thrust of his poles he was down the ramp and onto the broad trail leading out of the stadium. In a couple of strides he was at the junction. By hesitating an instant he slipped between four racers who were leaving the range. The early starters looked miserable, soaked from skiing through the falling snow and from lying in it on the range. He could see vapor rising from their backs as they skated out on the red loop.

A kilometer from the starting gate the trails split, and two of the racers skated left while Matt followed the others straight on. By the first climb, Matt was gasping for air and frightened by his thundering pulse. He had completed the first kilometer of the most important race of his life, and already he felt exhausted!

He recognized the sensation and reminded himself to settle down, relax, and to breathe. Matt slipped in behind another racer, and concentrated on getting a longer glide with each skating step. Within moments he felt back in control; in fact, he even had to check his speed to avoid clicking the skis of the racer ahead of him. Only then did Matt realize how easily he was gliding, because the racer he kept overtaking was one of the better Frenchmen.

Starting at number sixty-eight, Matt had anticipated being passed by some of the hotshots who were seeded behind him, and had prepared himself to hang with them for a short distance when they raced by; but he hadn't given much thought to tracking the early starters. As he skated behind the Frenchman, he fretted, aware his energy might simply be adrenaline from the start. Still, his skis were amazing in the falling snow and, with each abbreviated stride lagging behind the Frenchman, he was wasting precious seconds. He remembered Jankowski's advice and called, "Track."

The Frenchman stepped aside and Matt called, *"Merci"* as he skated by.

Before long, Matt was on the final climb into the shooting range. He glanced at the wind flags as he skated to one of the last prone firing positions. In one fluid motion he swung the rifle from his back, dropped to his knees, cradled the rifle as he attached the sling and inserted a magazine, then settled into a solid position. As he steadied the barrel on the target, he rechecked the number of his firing point and squinted again at the wind flags. No change from zeroing, steady from nine o'clock. The bull was fuzzy in his sights, but the picture looked good.... The rifle jumped against his shoulder. Concentrating on his follow-through, Matt could see only four black dots through the snow. The rifle settled on the second target and jumped again. He remembered his dad and the Sarge describing how world class shooters would "think" the shot off. He finally understood what they meant.

The last three shots went smoothly, and he couldn't help thinking that shooting was easy! Motivated by his success on the range, Matt charged onto the green loop. He powered through the tough climbs, overtook three other racers, and grinned to himself when he realized that they weren't early starters. At the high point of the course, he spotted Andy and Gopher, jumping and yelling despite their sodden parkas.

"You're doing great! Nice shooting and a fast ski time. How's the wax?"

Andy jogged up the hill as Matt hammered past.

"The wax is super! You guys really hit it!" An instant later Matt was accelerating down the far side of the hill and the American coaches were engulfed by the storm.

As he climbed through the forest on the south side of the valley, he wondered how he should take the rollers ahead of him. The snow was falling hard enough to accumulate on the trail, which meant the descents would be increasingly rutty. No doubt some of the early starters had fallen, leaving craters in the fresh snow. Matt thought he knew the trail well enough to take the downhill full bore, but visibility was limited, so he might not see a more cautious skier in time to avoid a collision.

He decided to play it safe, following the ruts as they disappeared into the white. The first bump came where Matt expected it, and he absorbed the rise with his knees, riding easily through the depression. Reaching forward to maintain stability, he crested the second rise and felt his stomach clutch as if he were riding a roller coaster. The speed pressed him into a low squat through the second depression, and he barely avoided a crater to the right of the tracks. At the crest of the third roll, his rifle floated above his back, weightless for an instant before he plunged into the third and deepest ravine. He fought to stay in the ruts, amazed by the speed of his skis despite the heavy snow.

As he was setting up for the hard left turn out of the pasture, a dark shape materialized through the falling snow. A fallen skier was sprawled across the trail ahead, a tangle of skis, poles and rifle. Matt yelled, "STAY DOWN!" tucked his knees to his chest, and held his breath. Miraculously the tips of his skis cleared the obstacle. As he settled into the rutted powder he fought to stay upright through the sweeping turn.

Even though Matt had been skiing at close to his physical limit since the start of the race, the near-disaster had elevated his pulse to a deafening pounding. More than a kilometer later, near the low point of the course, he remembered that he was approaching his first stage of offhand shooting. If he didn't get his pulse under control, he'd be lucky to hit the hillside! Climbing to the stadium, he concentrated on skiing smoothly and getting his breathing back to a reasonable level.

Gliding across the range to a vacant firing point, he was acutely aware of the throbbing in his ears. The spectators formed a wall of color through the falling snow. As quickly as the image registered, Matt ignored it and concentrated on loading his rifle, settling into position and checking the wind. It was still steady from the left, no correction necessary.

After the scare on the rollers, being back on the firing line was reassuring. His stance felt surprisingly solid, so he squeezed the first shot off. A hit! Bolt the rifle, breathe, relax, aim, squeeze.... A second hit! With his cadence established, the final three targets fell without hesitation. He threw the rifle on his back, snatched his poles, and skated out of the stadium.

Svensberget had been right, the old Atomics were like lightening. Matt hadn't been keeping track, but he knew he had passed several racers, even a few who had started in his group. He was energized by the shooting. He had a strange confidence, an intuition that if he didn't get in the way, he just couldn't miss.

The yellow loop was a breeze compared to the green; the climbs not as long, the descents not as challenging. He stormed the hills with joy rather than dread. He didn't hesitate when he drew in behind another competitor; he waited for a strategic moment and called, "Track."

He was overtaking a Japanese skier at the top of a hill when he heard the excited shouts of Mary Manheimer and Rosie Brown.

"Oh shit, there he is! Rookie, you're doing great! You're in the top...." Rosie's voice faded, absorbed by the snow.

The remainder of the yellow loop flew by and Matt was approaching the range for the third time. At the 100M sign he reminded himself, *Don't change a thing, just another race, don't think too much, just shoot 'em!* He felt strangely outside himself, an observer like the other spectators. Smooth, deliberate range procedure, good position, final wind check, natural point of aim, CRACK, the first target fell! Bolt the rifle, steady, CRACK, a second hit. Five shots, five hits through the curtain of falling snow. It seemed easy.

As he headed back into the woods Matt experienced both exhilaration and the heaviness brought on by fatigue. But he was on his final trip around the difficult blue loop. He knew he could hang tough for five kilometers of challenging skiing, only another fifteen minutes. He forced himself to concentrate as he fought up the difficult climbs. The adrenaline from the first loop had been expended long ago, now he was skiing on his training backlog and stamina. He remembered some of the stifling summer days on Smarts Mountain. He tried to convince himself that Smarts in the summer was far worse, but the deadening ache in his thighs and his shoulders undermined that argument.

As he approached the high point of the course, he spotted Andy again. Matt threw his weight on his poles, putting everything into the final strides of the climb. Andy ran alongside, "Sonofabitch, Matt, you're doing it! You've got a hell of a race going! Definitely top twenty, Matt! You're awesome!"

Matt was over the hill and tearing out of earshot, but Andy's encouragement was audible until he was absorbed by the storm. Matt was redlining it, pushing as hard as he could, knowing there wasn't any reserve. But he was also inspired as he continued to overtake competitors who appeared to be struggling. At first it was the less-experienced racers from Korea and Canada, but earlier on the blue loop he had passed a Swede and maybe a Czech.

As he pushed the limits of his strength, he focused on a racer barely visible ahead through the snow. Estimating the section of climb remaining before the trail pitched down into the rollers, Matt drove even harder to overtake the other skier, an Italian, before leaving the forest. The Sarge's parting advice rang in his ears, "Don't save anything, don't hold back."

Thighs burning from the climb, Matt tracked the Italian, then threw himself into several powerful double poles until he generated enough velocity to compress into a tight tuck. The Italian also had good skis, but Matt was in the lead by a stride and defiantly held his tuck to gain even more speed. As the first abrupt roll appeared through the blowing snow, Matt rose slightly and sucked his knees to his chest. The ruts were ragged in the new powder, but he kept his balance and rode through the compression to the second rise. Again he pre-jumped, and again he floated over the crest, settling into the second hollow. Although he was concentrating on setting up for the third and largest roll, Matt sensed the Italian was no longer on his heels.

That tiny lapse of focus made Matt's last pre-jump an instant late and he sailed into the air as the third ravine fell away beneath him. He had no hope of holding his tuck, but he fought to keep his hands and upper body forward, his arms flapping like giant wings as he struggled to keep his balance. The rutted, cratered snow rose to meet him. He landed heavily, crouched like a wrestler. Somehow he stayed on his feet! But before he could celebrate his good fortune, he had to negotiate the hard left turn out of the pasture. When he survived the turn unscathed, he cheered out loud! It was another shot of adrenaline. On the climb to the range for his final stage of shooting, he simply couldn't go fast enough. It was his day! In spite of the weather.... No! Because of the weather, he couldn't do anything wrong. His skis were like rockets, he was clean for three stages of shooting, and he had survived the rollers twice, at full throttle, in a blizzard!

Matt skated the length of the range feeling invincible. As the rifle trained on the first bull, he glimpsed the wind flags. A nagging internal voice made him pull his cheek away from the stock and study the wind again. Had it changed? Was it lighter on the far right of the range? Naw, his zero had been dead-on for the first three stages, why screw with it now? He settled back into position, took up slack on the trigger, waited until the wobble had a pattern, then...CRACK! He couldn't believe it was a miss! Steady now, don't panic. That sight correction! Should've listened to instinct. Cradling the rifle, he adjusted the windage knob, backing off the four clicks he had put on before the race. He carefully reestablished his standing position and shot the remaining targets, four for four. As he hammered out of the stadium for his final 2.5K loop, he thought he heard someone shout, "Thataway, Rookie! You're racing for the top ten!"

Matt would not remember much about the final loop. He didn't hit the wall in the conventional definition of running out of blood sugar, but he was pushing so hard that, had he hooked a tip and fallen, he couldn't have gotten back to his feet. He was vaguely aware of cheering, and people running alongside, urging him on. He might have heard Grete and the American women, but he was skiing with tunnel vision, everything except the trail immediately in front of him was badly out of focus. As he crossed the bridge over the road and fought his way up into the stadium, he was unable to remember if he had to shoot again, but officials directed him past the range toward the colorful banners of the finish line. It was confusing; flags everywhere, speakers blaring, a world of screaming people. Where was the line? Every second counts! Never let up, never....

"STOP, STOP! You finish! Racing over, you finish!" Matt was tackled by two volunteers who engulfed him in a heavy blanket. The cheering was deafening. He knew he had to clear equipment control, but he couldn't remember how to get his rifle off over his ski poles. The safety officers recognized his plight and checked the rifle as it hung on his back. A volunteer knelt to unfasten his skis. They guided him to the refreshment table, then ran to rescue another exhausted racer.

Matt stood in the falling snow, his thin uniform soaked through. He felt disoriented and stood only with the help of his ski poles. He studied the long table loaded with steaming tea, orange slices and cookies, but he couldn't comprehend their purpose. A smiling volunteer handed him a plastic bag. He tried to smile back, but he wasn't sure his face worked. When he still clung to his ski poles, she set the bag at his feet.

Surrounded by noise and confusion he struggled to understand what to do next, unaware that he was shivering violently. Then his eyes focused on a bearded man striding toward him, a broad smile animating the face and illuminating the eyes.

"Matthew Johnson, Ooo–Ess–Ahh, Olympic biathlonist!" Before Matt could respond, Vladimir Kobelev enveloped him in a massive hug, lifting him off the snow.

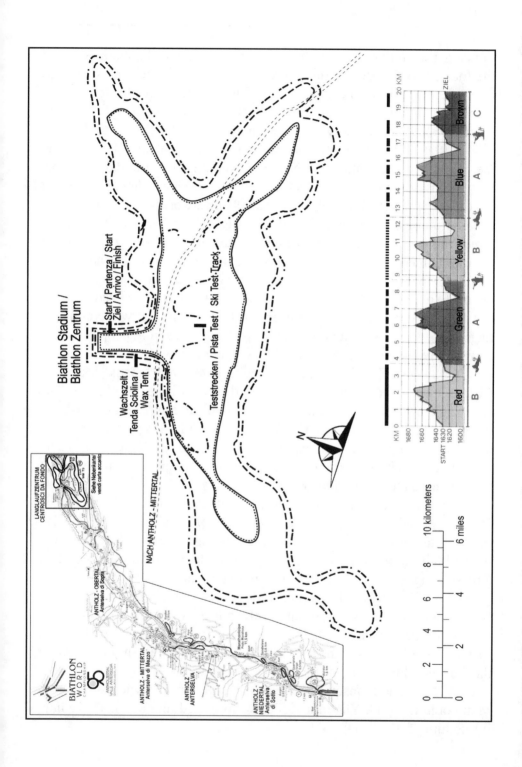

Biathlon Stadium /
Biathlon Zentrum

Start / Partenza / Start
Ziel / Arrivo / Finish

Wachszelt /
Tenda Sciolina /
Wax Tent

Teststrecken / Pista Test / Ski Test-Track

NACH ANTHOLZ - MITTERTAL

LANGLAUFZENTRUM
CENTROSCI DA FONDO

Siehe Nebenkarte/
vendi carta accanto

BIATHLON
W O R L D

ANTHOLZ - OBERTAL
Anterselva di Sopra

ANTHOLZ - MITTERTAL
Anterselva di Mezzo

ANTHOLZ
ANTERSELVA

ANTHOLZ -
NIEDERTAL
Anterselva
di Sotto

N

0   2   4   6   8   10 kilometers

0   2   4   6 miles

KM 0   1   2   3   4   5   6   7   8   9   10   11   12   13   14   15   16   17   18   19   20 KM

1680
1660
1640
START 1630
1620
1600

Red   Green   Yellow   Blue   Brown

B   A   B   A   C

ZIEL

America Wins a Medal

17

When Kobelev embraced his racer in the finish area, he noticed Matt's uncontrollable shivering and guided him to the medical building. The door was opened by a uniformed paramedic, revealing a room filled with bedraggled competitors and drenched coaches. The athletes were shivering like Matt, their faces pale, their lips blue. Two female medics were stripping an exhausted athlete of his soaking uniform and long underwear. He sat in a stupor, naked and trembling on the edge of a cot, as the women rubbed him vigorously with thick towels. Then they wrapped him in a heavy blanket, and handed him a cup of steaming broth. The athlete sipped the hot liquid while one of the medics gathered his wet clothing into a plastic bag. The other medic approached Vlad and Matt.

"So…Americans? May I see credential?"

Matt was stumped by the question, but Vlad displayed his laminated ID card, and after a brief search found Matt's credentials.

"*Grazie*," the woman took the ID and guided Matt to a cot. "We must to remove your clothings. Can you help?"

Matt nodded, but still hadn't figured out how to remove his ski poles. Vlad assisted and soon they had Matt stripped and were scrubbing him with dry towels until his skin grew bright pink. When they wrapped the coarse, woolen blanket around him, it actually felt good. He took a sip of the steaming broth, and could feel its warmth go right to his core. He held the hot cup reverently, beginning to comprehend what was going on around him as his shivering subsided.

A small man in a white lab coat led an athlete from the examining room. The athlete wore the warmups of the Italian Olympic Team, and a large bandage covered a shaved spot on the back of his head. As the athlete gathered his gear, he nodded to Vlad, then studied Matt, who was hunched over the cup of broth.

The Italian athlete approached Matt.

"Hello? You are American, yes? What number you have in this competition?"

"Sixty-eight."

The Italian looked confused.

"Six…eight…." Matt traced the numbers in the air, then reached into the plastic bag and withdrew his soaking Lycra bib.

"Ah, *sessanta-otto,*" the Italian smiled. "You overtake me at the big downhill on the blue! I am trying to keep with you, but you go too fast! I think maybe you are training with Tommy Moe!"

"I was lucky on that downhill, I thought I was a goner on the third bump. How's your head?"

"No problem!" The Italian smiled, "This good doctor, he makes me like new. But my rifle, that may not be so easy." The Italian grabbed the Anschutz Fortner, which had been lying amid the wet clothes, and held it up for inspection. The stock, stained with blood, was broken in half at the pistol grip. The carrying harness dangled uselessly from the splintered wood.

"That happened on the rollers?" Matt made the motion of waves with his hand.

"*Si, si,* I try to follow you and…*catastroph!*"

As the Italian gathered his belongings, the small man in the lab coat approached Matt, "Please, I am Dr. Luigi Clementi, head of medical support for the Antholz Olympic Village. Your name is…?"

"Matthew Johnson, USA."

"Ah ha! I have been to America, Columbia University School of Medicine, New York City! Now, Mr. Johnson, how you are feeling?"

"Better, thanks. I was cold when I finished, but I think I'm okay now."

"You mind, I take a quick look? My special interest is sport medicine so I must make this opportunity to examine Olympic athletes from around the world."

Dr. Clementi proceeded with a brief, but systematic physical exam. When he had finished he turned to Kobelev, "You are coach of this boy?"

"Da, da, sorry…yes, I am United States Biathlon Team coach. My name, Vladimir Kobelev."

"Mr. Kobelev, I believe your athlete, Johnson, like many others today, have early stage of hypothermia and dehydration. He will be okay, but maybe is best for him to rest tomorrow. Plenty of fluids, of course. If you wish, we can intravenously at the polyclinic in the Olympic Village."

"Thanks, but I feel better already!" Matt saw no reason for a needle when he could accomplish the same thing with soup and juice in the cafeteria.

"Okay! Change into you dry clothes and keep the blanket for bus down the valley. You can return it to polyclinic tomorrow, then I check you one more time." The doctor shook hands with Matt and Vlad, then moved into the adjoining room to examine his next patient.

It was not until three hours later, upon entering the cafeteria, that Matt learned the results of the race. He knew that Vlad was pleased, but the coach had been elusive about specific placings. Matt's teammates greeted him boisterously when he arrived at the housing unit. It obviously had been a good day for America, but finish order was not mentioned. After a hot shower and a change into warm clothes, Matt was recovered enough to attack the cafeteria. The women were still training, but Ragnar, Burl, Thomas and Matt headed to the dining hall together.

Inside the main entrance was a large bulletin board posted with start lists, announcements, and results. The four biathletes found the men's 20K standings and studied them intently. Before Matt found his own name, Burl pounded him on the back, and shouted, "Goddamn, Rookie, did you kick ass today! Will you look at this, seventh with one minute penalty! Shit, Matt, if you'd hit 'em all you'd a won the silver!"

"And how about this," Thomas added, "two other guys had one minute penalty, but nobody in the race shot better!"

"Damn, Johnson, that's really good biathlon. Congratulations!" Ragnar was uncharacteristically enthusiastic.

Matt thanked them and glanced at the results again. Popov was first with one minute penalty, Steinigen from Germany second, Zingerle from Italy third. Then another Russian, a Finn, a second German, and in seventh place, Matthew Johnson, United States.! He stared at the results as if in a dream. SEVENTH PLACE! In the Olympic Games! He checked again. Sure enough, if he'd hit them all, he would have finished four seconds ahead of Steinigen for the silver!

Then he remembered to find the placing of his teammates. Burl had ended up twenty-second, Ragnar thirty-first, and Heikki thirty-eighth. Burl was watching Matt study the results. "Even though you made the rest of us look bad, Rookie, it was still a damn good day for the Stars and Stripes! When was the last time we got all four Americans in the top half of the results at the Olympics? I'll tell you when! Never!"

"An' you know what else, look how we come out if you score all four racers from each team, you know, like a relay. I'll bet we're fourth or fifth behind the Russians, the Germans, the Italians and maybe the Finns. Damn, I can hardly wait for the relay. I honestly believe we've got a shot at a medal, I shit you not!"

The four Americans entered the dining hall and were immediately approached by athletes and coaches from other countries, who offered their congratulations. Even the food service people filling plates with spaghetti seemed to know the results. They pointed to each of the Americans and asked, "Johnson? Johnson?"

When Thomas and Burl pointed to Matt behind them in line, the Italians smiled, *"Buono, buono,"* pantomiming the act of shooting a rifle. After the four Americans found a table, there was a steady stream of athletes who stopped to offer congratulations. Matt was baffled. Seventh was fantastic, it was beyond his wildest dreams, but it was no big deal for a European biathlete.

"Hey, Burl," Matt asked his teammate, "I don't get it. I mean, I'm thrilled about finishing seventh, but I don't understand why all these Europeans are so excited. I could see them congratulating Popov, and Steinigen, and especially Zingerle since we're in his home town, but why all the fuss about some American finishing seventh?"

"Ah, welcome to Europe, my son!" Burl assumed the pose of an experienced veteran. "Matt, you just put together the best Olympic performance ever by an American biathlete. Through the years, three Americans have finished fourteenth, John Burritt in Squaw Valley back in 1960, Peter Karns in Sapporo, and Joan Smith last time in Lillehammer. You just smashed some kind of spooky barrier that kept us out of the top ten. And I think most of them know we're still amateurs in biathlon, we're not working for our Ph.D.'s in biathlon at some national sports institute, or being paid a comfortable military salary to train for biathlon full time. I'm sure it's different in the Summer Games, when we overpower the rest of the world in swimming and track, or even worse the goddamned Dream Team of NBA stars show up. But we've been underdogs in biathlon for so long that most of these Europeans admire a gutsy performance like yours."

"And you know something else, Matt? I'm not superstitious, but I think finishing better than fourteenth in the Olympics is a major breakthrough. I'm not saying we're about to kick the German's butts back to Ruhpolding, but you just wait...I've got a feeling you just opened the door."

There was a commotion at the entrance, and the first bus load of women biathletes poured into the dining room. The Americans bolted to where Matt and his teammates were seated, and showered them with enthusiastic praise. Each of the women hugged Matt, even shy Jenny Lindstrom and Emily Livengood. Trudy Wilson, purposely held back, but when she spotted Grete Dybendahl entering the dining room, Trudy embraced Matt and kissed him aggressively. Skillfully obscuring his view of the door, she whispered, "Matt, you're awesome! I thought Lillehammer was beginner's luck, but you're for real! I want you, Matt. You won't be sorry."

Whispering in Matt's ear, Trudy watched over his shoulder as Grete stopped and stared in confusion. Again Trudy pressed her lips to Matt's with an intensity that made him dizzy. She didn't release him until Grete's cheeks had flushed crimson and she'd stormed from the cafeteria.

"Finally! Where the hell have you been? I've been looking for you everywhere! We've got to get going or we'll be late. Go change into your award suit." Stanley Reimer was out of breath.

"Where're we going?" Matt asked the team leader, grateful to be rescued from Trudy.

"I've got a VIP van waiting! We're headed to Cortina as soon as you change. I set up a press conference for 1700, dinner with some suppliers at 1830, and I got tickets for the United States–Czech hockey game at 2030. Let's go!"

"I don't know, Stan. I was totally whipped after the race, maybe I'd better hang out here and recover."

"Are you crazy? And miss a chance like this! Honest to God, I've probably had a hundred requests for interviews since noon! Shit, you're not only the biggest thing ever to happen to United States Biathlon; you're the biggest United States story at the Olympics, at least for today. We can't afford to miss an opportunity like this. Now go change your clothes and let's get on the road."

"Uh, Stan, have you talked to Vlad about this?" Matt braced himself for an explosion.

"What the hell's Vlad got to do with it? Vlad's the coach. He takes care of the racing and training. I'm the team leader. I'm trying like hell to get funding and publicity for this sorry excuse for a National Team. Why is it you guys are always working against me? Now go change your clothes or we'll never make it to Cortina by five."

Matt looked at his teammates. Burl spoke up. "Stan, is all this VIP treatment just for the Rookie, or can we tag along? As long as we're back for the women's race tomorrow at eleven, I can't imagine Vlad would be too pissed off."

"Hell, I don't care if you all come, but let's get going!"

Ragnar and the women declined Stan's offer, but Matt, Burl and Thomas hustled off to change clothes, while Stan wrote a note to Vlad explaining the details of the expedition. Moments later they were in a comfortable Fiat minivan driven by a young Italian, who apparently had aspirations for the Grand Prix circuit. Though they arrived in Cortina in ample time for the press conference, they were dazed by their amusement park ride.

The press conference was a big success. Stan the Man was in his element, and skillfully guided the discussion so that it reflected well on the Biathlon Federation. When it became evident that most of the reporters were interested only in Matt, Stan drew Burl and Thomas into the discussion as well. Matt recognized several of the journalists from earlier press conferences in Anchorage, Lillehammer and Cortina.

Lester Morris, the sports reporter from the *Denver Post* directed questions to Burl, and Betty Moerlein from Anchorage was eager to get some quotes from Thomas. Vickie Chang asked the biathletes and Stanley Reimer to predict the outcome of the women's 15K event tomorrow.

Burl responded confidently, "Ms. Chang, you've seen enough international biathlon to know that predicting results is nothing more than guessing. But our training has been solid. It's no secret that our women have had stronger results internationally than the men. If I were you, Ms. Chang, I wouldn't miss tomorrow's race!"

Following the press conference, Stan instructed the driver to take them to the Hotel Cristallo. The guests in the ornate lobby exuded wealth: fur coats, heavy gold jewelry, and deeply tanned faces. Stanley led the athletes to a spacious dining room where a tuxedo-clad maitre d' guided them to a large table in the back. There were four men seated at the table, who rose eagerly as Stanley approached with his athletes. Matt remembered Boomer Ferguson from their meeting in Lillehammer. The colorful businessman looked even more out of place in the formal Italian dining room. Matt wondered if he ever took off his Stetson.

"Damn, son, I knew when we had that beer in Lillehammer that you have what it takes! You sure popped one hell of a race today. Even though you were outta the medals, that was damn good for your first Olympics. We gotta talk!"

"I thought you were going to buy yourself a couple of Russians." Matt responded.

Boomer's eyes narrowed, but Stanley Reimer interceded by seating the athletes between the businessmen and ordering a round of drinks. The meal was excellent and the athletes enjoyed talking biathlon to men who seemed sincerely interested in the sport. It was evident that Stanley was using the strong results and the young Olympians to lure the businessmen into sponsorship arrangements.

At eight o'clock Stanley began thanking his guests, explaining that he had to get his athletes to the hockey game. There were handshakes, wishes for more great results, and a couple of winks in Stanley's direction.

One of the businessmen, wearing a silver and turquoise bolo tie, took Matt aside to speak to him alone. "Son, my name's Calvin Worthington. I own a nationwide auto leasing business based in Denver."

"You sent me an e-mail message."

"That's right, just wanted to wish you kids good luck in your races. We've been considering a sponsorship of the Biathlon Team. Since our offices are in Colorado, most of us enjoy target shooting and hunting. I figure Wrangler Auto Leasing and the American Biathlon Federation would be a great match, but some of our PR people aren't so sure. They're afraid of a backlash about that whole firearms thing."

"Well, today, Matt, you helped me make a decision. I've always loved the Olympics, and I generally root for the underdog. I was so damn proud of how you hung in there through that storm! How you could even see those targets, I'll never know."

"We'll be working out the details with Stanley, but I hope you'll consider being Wrangler Auto Leasing's official spokesman. Fact is, you kids represent what I've strived for in my business: you work hard, you're straight shooters, and you're in it for the long haul!"

"I don't want you to miss your hockey game, but we probably won't get another chance to talk until the Games are over. We plan to sign on as a Gold Level sponsor through the next Winter Olympics in Korea. In addition to supplying all the team's ground transportation, we're going to put together a very favorable leasing arrangement for all your teammates and coaches. We'll also fund a victory schedule for the National Championships, the World Cups and the Olympics. We're thinking in the range of five, ten, and fifteen thousand dollars for bronze, silver and gold medals. In fact, if my people can work out the details with your team leader tomorrow, I'll put the schedule into effect for the remaining events of these Games!"

"One last thing, Matt. Stanley told me a little about your family. I was sorry to hear about your father. Stan said he flew choppers in Vietnam."

"He was a medevac pilot in the Delta."

"I was in the Navy. River boats out of Can Tho and Soc Trang in '69. I understand your mom's a teacher?"

"Yeah, elementary school, she's taught for twelve years."

"Well, look, Matt, here's what I can do. If you agree to be Wrangler's spokesman, we'll pay you for the time you put in for our company, and we'll get you the Ford of your choice. Whatever you want, Mustang convertible, Explorer, you name it. On top of that, we'll get your mom a new car, too! How's that sound?"

Matt was stunned.

"Hey, you must be exhausted. Don't worry about this now. You just keep up the great results in the next two races. When things quiet down after the Games, I'll be in touch. But you tell your teammates, my offer's good if any of you get into the medals here in Italy!"

The hockey game was terrific. The crowd was divided in its support of the Czechs and the Americans. The second period was as exciting as the first, with goals scored by both teams. For Matt, the action on the ice was matched by the thrill of spotting other American Olympians in the stands: Tommy Moe and Picabo Street, some of the speed skaters, two ski jumpers and three freestyle skiers. During the break between periods, Greg Ingram of the Games Preparation Committee and Phil Shepard of L.L. Bean congratulated the biathletes on their results.

At the end of the second period, an elegant Organizing Committee hostess passed a cream-colored note, embossed with the five interlocking rings, to Stanley who glanced at it, grinned, then showed it to his athletes.

Would you and your refugees from Antholz join me to watch the final period? My delightful hostess will show you the way.
Mac Moore, President, USOC

The Italian hostess ushered the biathletes to a richly carpeted executive suite furnished with comfortable leather armchairs overlooking center ice. General Moore broke away from a group of well-dressed guests and greeted the athletes warmly. He quizzed Matt at length about the course, wind conditions on the range, and the wax.

"God, I'm sorry I missed your race, but the road reports weren't promising and flying up in a chopper was out of the question. I hope you kids saved something for the upcoming races!"

"Hell, General we're just getting warmed up," Burl responded confidently.

"Thataboy! I'll get up there before the fireworks are all over. Now help yourselves to the food, then I want to introduce you to some interesting people before the third period starts."

After the refreshments and introductions to the four corporate dignitaries, the general guided the athletes to the leather chairs with the best view of the rink. Stanley and the other guests continued to talk near the buffet table, but General Moore and the biathletes were engrossed in the game, a cliffhanger that the Americans won in a shootout.

They thanked the general for his hospitality, then spent several minutes in the cold star-lit night searching for their van. It was nearly midnight before they headed back to Antholz. They were not even out of Cortina before Matt was snoring. He woke only briefly an hour later when Thomas guided him through the security check point and to his room.

"Here we are, Matt. Hey, nice going today! Burl's right, you really opened the door for the rest of us. Oh, by the way, where's your backpack?"

Matt pointed under the tiny desk as he fumbled with his award suit. "What do you need?" he yawned.

Thomas didn't answer, but withdrew the oosik from the pack. "Strong medicine," was all he said and slipped into the hall.

The following morning at breakfast, Rosie gave the men their assignments. Kobelev, Christensen and Gopher had already gone to the venue to set up the speed trap and test waxes for the women. Vlad had left specific instructions for everyone who was not racing. Matt's assignment was to assist the Sarge by recording range times. He remembered filling the same role in West Yellowstone. Trying to get everyone's range time and shooting score would be impossible at the Olympics, but Sergeant Jankowski reassured him they were primarily interested in the four American women.

The forest and mountains were blanketed in a thick layer of new snow and the sun was shinning brilliantly, ideal conditions for a biathlon race. Matt couldn't tell if there were more spectators because of the good weather, or if he simply hadn't been able to see the crowd through the falling snow on Friday. He highlighted the names of the four Americans on his start list so he wouldn't forget anyone in the excitement of the event.

As the women began to enter the range to shoot, the Sarge provided a running commentary, "Okay, watch this little Japanese girl on number four. She can't weigh more than eighty pounds! I'll bet that rifle she's hauling is fifteen percent of her body weight! They ought to give her a handicap. How do you think you'd ski if your rifle weighed twenty-five pounds?

"Now look at the Swede shooting on target nine. She'll hit 'em all, but she'll fumble picking up her poles. Did you see that? She always cleans her prone targets but loses fifteen seconds getting off the firing point.

"All right! Here comes Maria, the first Italian! Let's see if Maria can handle the pressure...." A powerful dark-haired woman wearing the garish Italian racing suit selected a firing point as the partisan crowd cheered. She dropped smoothly into position and loaded quickly. Her shots were followed by cheers and groans as she hit two and left three.

"Nope," the Sarge resumed, "not Maria's day today." Jankowski was just as philosophical about the American women; Paula Robbins and Kate Anderson had trouble, Trudy and Sandy shot clean in their first stages. Jankowski gave the coaches on the ski trail sight corrections over the radio. Matt concentrated on timing the women from the instant they placed their poles on the snow to the moment, after shooting, when they bent to retrieve them. He repeatedly glanced up when he caught sight of a Norwegian uniform, but he couldn't offer Grete any encouragement, because it was against the rules to communicate with the athletes from the coaches' box. He couldn't tell much about her skiing, but he was happy that she was shooting well.

After Sandy's second stage of prone, the Sarge had trouble controlling his excitement, "She's clean so far! Damn, five more good ones and she's got a chance for a medal!"

The chatter over the radio was intensifying. Vlad was cautioning Andy and Gopher to stay calm, "Just give splits! Don't tell places, and don't talk about shooting clean!"

Trudy was also doing well with only two penalties in the first three stages, but the focus was definitely on Sandy. When she hit the range for her final stage of standing, fire burned in her eyes. She never glanced at the coaches' box for reassurance; instead, she scowled at the targets with a fierce determination, then peeled her rifle off and in a heartbeat was in position and holding on the target. BANG! The report from the first shot came so fast that Matt flinched in surprise. Before he shifted his focus from Sandy to the target, she squeezed off her second shot. Two hits! Matt held his breath. The third shot was another hit!

Matt knew it was far from over, but she hit the first three with such assertiveness that he had a strong premonition that she was going to hit them all. BANG! Fourth shot, another hit! "She's going to do it, she's going to do it...."

BANG! The roar from the stadium echoing off the mountains confirmed that she had cleaned her targets. Jankowski babbled into the radio, almost incoherent with excitement. Moments later the word came back from Andy, "She's in fifth place past me, twelve seconds out of third!"

The next report came from Gopher who was stationed midway on the final loop where she had closed the gap to eight seconds! Vlad was so excited that he unintentionally depressed the transmit button on his radio as he ran alongside Sandy, yelling encouragement in a mixture of Russian and English. Other coaches on the range grinned at Jankowski as they overheard the jumbled transmission.

Racers charged up the final hill and sprinted into the stadium in a steady stream. The electronic scoreboard reshuffled after each competitor, the top six positions dominated by Russians and Germans. Matt strained to see across the road where the final 2.5K loop slanted down through the pasture. He saw Sandy in a tight tuck slicing across the field, her momentum carrying her up and over the arching overpass. Before she lost her speed, she drove her poles into the snow with fury.

As she charged the final hill, there was nothing graceful or delicate about her skiing; it was pure, ferocious power. Sandy's running time clicked away at the bottom of the scoreboard, like sand pouring through an hourglass. The top six names seemed permanent, their times forever imprinted on the scoreboard. The crowd was hushed as she crossed the range in long, powerful strides then turned the corner and lunged for the finish. Matt's upper body rocked along with each of her final double poles, three, two, one.... She actually accelerated through the finish line!

Like the eye of a hurricane, everything was still, thousands of spectators silently staring at the giant electronic board. Then the digital display flickered with revisions. The two Russians holding first and second place remained unchanged, but behind them in third, the letters registered STONINGTON–USA. The roar from the crowd was deafening. Matt stared at the Sarge in disbelief and saw tears filling the rifle coach's eyes. They both became aware of Andy's pleas over the radio, "Did she get it? Did she get it? Sarge, do you read me? Come in on the range!"

"Andy, this is the range. The big board's got her in third, four-tenths ahead of a German! Is there anyone still on the course who can bump her?"

"Negative, Sarge! I believe all the girls still out here had trouble shooting. Assuming there aren't any protests, I'd say she's won the bronze! Do you believe that? Over...."

Jankowski appeared to be in shock, unashamed of the tears coursing down his cheeks as he stared at the scoreboard. More racers struggled up the final hill, past the firing line and into the finish chute. Their names and nationalities were recorded, but the top six positions remained unchanged. Finally the announcer informed the stadium that the last competitor had completed the course.

Jankowski was mobbed by other coaches, bear hugged, thumped on the back, and kissed on each cheek. The Japanese shooting coach Hiroyuki Kodate pointed to the scoreboard, which also recorded each athlete's shooting penalties. With his finger, the short powerful Japanese man carefully traced four circles in the air reflecting Sandy's perfect score, zero misses in four stages of shooting. Finally Kodate bowed formally to Jankowski, who solemnly returned the gesture. Other coaches watched the ritual with delight, then applauded.

As Matt helped the Sarge pack up the spotting scope and the rest of the gear, he felt both electrified and numb at the same time. He was afraid to believe it, Sandy had won an Olympic medal! The first Olympic medal in the history of American Biathlon! Beyond that, she was the only American in thirty-eight years to shoot clean in the Olympic Games! Somehow Matt still couldn't suppress the fear that it was all a dream, that there had been a miscalculation, that another racer's time would be adjusted for some reason, moving Sandy out of the medals.

But the scoreboard remained unchanged, and the announcer signaled the conclusion of the women's 15K competition, reminding the spectators that the presentation of the medals would take place in the Antholz Mittertal village square at 1930. He also invited the spectators to return for both men's and women's sprints to be held on Wednesday, February 25.

For the first time all day, Matt was really aware of the beautiful weather: the bright sun, the blanket of fresh snow, the deep blue sky above majestic peaks. This was the way Nordic skiing was supposed to be; and best of all, Sandy won a medal!

The scene at the waxing trailer was chaos. Sandy, accompanied by Dr. Manheimer, had left for doping control and dozens of journalists were milling around, interviewing anyone in an American uniform. Jankowski, once he was recognized as the rifle coach, was immediately mobbed by eager reporters. The Sarge patiently responded to the shouted questions, but was obviously relieved when Stanley Reimer pushed his way through the crowd and took over.

Matt groaned at how lavishly Stan praised Sandy, but the reporters lapped it up. As Stan was hitting his stride, Sandy and Dr. Manheimer returned from doping control and were surrounded by media people. The video cameras rolled as Sandy was congratulated by her teammates and her coaches.

"Sandy, Sandy, how about a couple of comments on your race!" Several reporters echoed the same request.

"This is the most exciting race of my life. I knew I could compete, but putting it all together on the big day isn't easy. Today everything finally fell into place."

"Was there something in particular that inspired you?"

"Matt Johnson did. I figured if this kid could have such hot results on his first trip to Europe, there was no reason why I shouldn't after eight years on this team."

"Sandy, at what point did you suspect you had a chance for a medal?"

"I believe I can win every time I put on a racing bib. Today I skied fast and shot well, and it paid off. I've known for a long time that it was possible."

"You were less than thirty seconds behind the winner, Belova, and only about ten seconds behind Kulakova, both from Russia. Can you beat them in the future?"

"I've been ahead of Kulakova for the past two years in the World Cup standings, and I beat Belova in three pre-Olympic events this season. But the Russians really get up for the Olympics."

"Do you think there's more to their success at the Olympics than sophisticated training?" The question came from Vickie Chang, the persistent reporter from *Women's Sport and Fitness*.

"Ms. Chang, you were in Anchorage, so you know exactly what I think. I just had the race of my life on a day when it counted. I couldn't have shot any better, and I doubt I could have skied even ten seconds faster. I have no control over the other women in the race. I have to rely on the Organizing Committee and the IOC to keep the competition fair."

"What are you going to do with the money?" The question was shouted from the back of the group.

"What money?" Sandy shouted back.

"The USOC's Operation Gold money! A bronze medal's worth fifteen thousand dollars isn't it?"

Sandy smiled, "You know, I'd completely forgotten about that! To tell you the truth, I have no clue what I'll do with it. Ask me in April, I'll have it figured out by then."

Stan interrupted, inviting all the reporters to a press conference in the athlete's village following the medal presentation that evening.

Inside the waxing trailer the atmosphere was quite different. Kobelev, Christensen and Gopher, who had been up since well before dawn for more than a week, were quietly sipping German beer. The other women were organizing their gear and recounting the race when Sandy and Mary Manheimer entered. Kobelev stood and gave the medal winner a long embrace. Then he congratulated Trudy, Kate and Paula, who also had raced well. He thanked the assistant coaches and staff members who had all pitched in to support the effort.

"So…. Thanks to Sandy we finally have Olympic medal! This is very special because it is the first, and because she works so hard to win it. We must all celebrate this victory. The team made this possible, and the team is stronger because of Sandy's success. But this is not final goal, this is only a beginning! Sandy has won our first medal, but it will not be our last, maybe not even our last at these Games! Now Sandy shows it's possible, we have four more chances to win medals! Tonight after dinner we all attend medal ceremony and we celebrate Sandy's victory. Tomorrow, we get back to work to prepare for sprints and relays!"

In the cafeteria that evening the Americans were celebrities. Competitors and coaches from other teams kept stopping to congratulate Sandy. Dimitry Popov approached with the confidence of an international celebrity and hugged and kissed Sandy on both cheeks in Russian fashion, then congratulated Kobelev with obvious emotion. He apologized for his teammates, Belova and Kulakova, explaining they were too shy to congratulate her in person. Matt suspected that like many Russians, they were self-conscious about not speaking English.

It was less than a kilometer from the athletes' village down broad pathways through snow-covered pastures to Antholz Mittertal. In the cold evening air the smell of smoke from wood-burning stoves mingled with the scent of manure from nearby farms. Flags and torches lined the narrow streets, reminding Matt of his first World Cup in Ruhpolding. When the athletes reached the center of town, it was already filled with spectators enjoying the festivities. A Tyrolean band filled the village with music as flags of the participating nations waved from tall wooden poles surrounding the square. In front of the Rathaus a smaller version of Cortina's twin cauldrons held the Olympic flames and the winner's podium, decorated with red and white Tyrolean banners and evergreen branches.

The three athletes were led to the podium by young women in colorful local costumes, followed by three others bearing huge bouquets of flowers. The athletes were introduced by an announcer who effortlessly switched from Italian to German and finally to English. "First place in the women's 15K event, Svetlana Belova from Russia." As the Russian woman hopped nimbly to the top of the platform, the village was filled with cheers and the muffled sound of hundreds of mittened hands clapping in the cold mountain air.

"Second place, also from Russia, Lyudmila Kulakova!" More applause as the seasoned veteran stepped to the second level of the platform.

"And in third place, from the United States of America, Sandra Stonington!" The cheering was unmistakably louder than it had been for the Russian women. Matt felt a twinge of embarrassment, but it evaporated when he saw his teammate hop to her position on the podium. The three athletes were presented their Olympic medals and bouquets, then each was congratulated by the president of the World Biathlon Union. They stood at attention while the band played the Russian national anthem and the flags of the medal winners were slowly drawn high into the winter night. Even though the flag pole for the bronze medal winner was slightly shorter than the other two, Matt was overcome by a powerful belief that the most wonderful thing he could accomplish in sport would be to raise the American flag up one of those poles. As the music subsided, Belova reached down and drew the other two women to the top podium with her. The three Olympians smiled and waved as cameras whirred relentlessly.

After the ceremony, her teammates gathered around Sandy for a closer look at her medal. Then Stanley whisked her off to Cortina for more press conferences. Matt looked for Grete, but not finding her, he joined his teammates for the walk back to the athletes' village. After passing through security, Ragnar suggested that they swing by the cafeteria for a snack. Matt was the only taker, so they sat together in the quiet dining room reviewing the past two days. Matt asked his teammate a question that had been on his mind, "Ragnar, have you talked to Grete Dybendahl lately?"

Ragnar looked at Matt, "Grete...no, I don't talk to her for several days. But she was in the disco last night, dancing like crazy with that Frenchman, Rene Claudon."

A group of florid-faced Russian coaches entered the cafeteria and Matt was surprised to see Kobelev among them. The Russians were boisterous, a flagrant departure from their usual strict discipline.

"They've been into the vodka," Ragnar observed. Matt had never seen the coaches so gregarious. After helping themselves to heaping plates of food, the Russians retreated to a table on the far side of the dining room where their loud conversation was punctuated by outbursts of unrestrained laughter.

The two athletes were about to leave when another man entered the room and approached the jovial group. The new arrival was lean, with a narrow face and a prominent nose reminiscent of a predatory bird. He was pale and sallow, as if his whole life had been spent indoors. The mood of the group immediately changed, from celebratory to subdued. As one of the coaches pulled a chair from a nearby table for the newcomer, Kobelev stood. Matt noticed a transformation in his coach, in fact he was scowling. Then Kobelev mumbled something in Russian, and the hawk-like man snarled back. Kobelev shook his head as he strode from his former colleagues and out the door. It was as if the arrival of the lean man had destroyed the fellowship of the gathering as easily as a storm cloud blocked the sun.

"Who's that guy?" Matt asked Ragnar.

"Manfred Ullrich. He used to be sports doctor in East Germany, then for Russian biathlon team; but now, I think he works with Cross-Country."

"Looked like he and Vlad had met before."

"Ya, they don't like each other, I think," added Ragnar.

It was great to celebrate Sandy's success in the 15K, but only three days later, both men and women would race their sprint events. The difficult training was behind them, but Monday and Tuesday were still busy. Vlad, Andy and Gopher were working even harder to perfect the wax in the sprints. That meant an hour a day for each athlete riding skis through the speed trap.

On the positive side, at least from Matt's perspective, Sandy's medal had taken him out of the spotlight. By Tuesday morning he had responded to all his e-mail messages. Most of the reporters who had been so desperate for interviews on Friday night had moved on to other stories.

Monday night, Kobelev supervised a team meeting for both men and women. It was obvious that, having achieved the breakthrough medal, he expected better results from the entire team in the remaining four events. The sprints would be challenging logistically because the women began at 1000 and the men at 1300. That meant the important support functions — ski preparation, wax testing, zeroing, and providing splits during the races — had to be carefully scheduled.

The selection of who would race the sprints held no surprises. As a formality, Vlad asked, "So, everyone is feeling okay? Everybody is ready to race?"

Matt wondered whether the coach really expected an honest answer to his question. Since the men's 20K, Matt had been nursing a scratchy throat. After three days it wasn't any worse, but it hadn't gone away either.

Burl spoke up, "Ah, Vlad. I haven't felt a hundred percent since the 20K. I know you're going to be looking at the results of the sprints to choose the relay teams, but I think I'd race a better relay if I sat out the sprint."

"Burl, thank you for being honest. I also prefer that you are at your best for the relay on Saturday, so maybe Oliver races in the sprint?"

"I'm ready! My shooting's improved the past few days and I'm finally used to this altitude," Oliver added confidently.

"All right then, in the women's race we have Sandy, Trudy, Jenny and Emily; in the men's Matt, Ragnar, Heikki and Oliver. We have another meeting tomorrow night to hand out bibs and start lists. Burl and Thomas, check with me at breakfast and we discuss support jobs during the competitions."

Although Thomas showed no emotion, Matt knew he was tremendously disappointed. The four starters in the 20K had all performed better than expected, thereby earning a start in the sprints. When Burl withdrew himself, Oliver was next on the list. It appeared that Thomas wouldn't race at the Olympics.

By the time the others had filed out of the room, Matt had made up his mind.

"Vlad, can we talk for a minute?"

"*Da, da.* Andy, please you and Gopher wait in front room."

When they were alone Matt began, "Since the 20K, I've had a scratchy throat."

"You talked with Dr. Manheimer?"

"Not yet, it didn't seem bad enough to worry about. But if I rested through the sprint like Burl, I'd probably be stronger for the relay...and Thomas would get a chance to race."

Kobelev studied Matt before responding. "You know, sometimes I worry you Americans are too nice to be champions. When I was athlete in Soviet Union, never will I give my start position to rival team member. But you and Thomas help each other even at tryouts in Anchorage. Also

I must remember, you are young, maybe you don't recover so fast from a difficult 20K."

"Okay, I agree. You rest through sprint and prepare for relay. I cannot make official selection of relay team until after sprint on Wednesday, but you will race relay. I tell Thomas he is racing the sprint. Now please, you check with Dr. Manheimer about you throat."

"Thanks, Vlad."

"Da, da, harasho, we make good plan."

Tuesday morning at breakfast Thomas sat next to Matt.

"Vlad talked to me about the sprint last night. You really sick or just feeling sorry for me?"

"I've had a scratchy throat since the 20K. Dr. Manheimer said it's nothing serious, but I'd be stronger for the relay if I sat out the 10K. You just kick ass tomorrow so we can ski the relay together."

"Count on it, Rookie! I feel real good about racing tomorrow. I think the top twenty is a definite possibility."

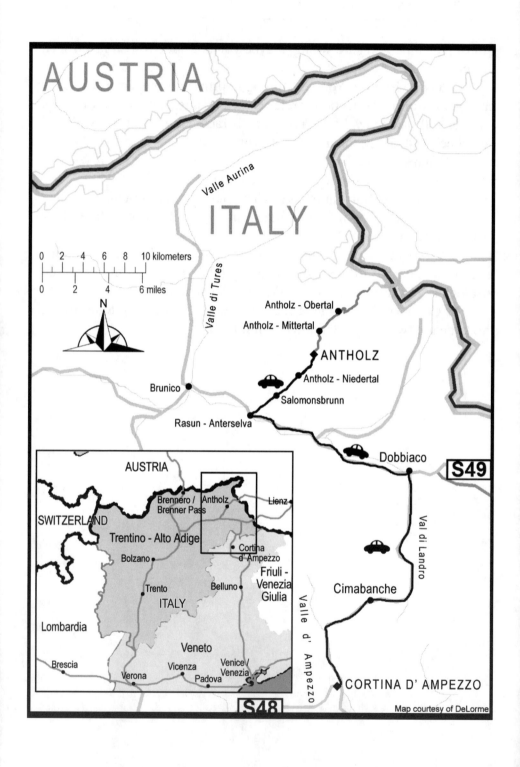

A Deadly Gamble

18

Wednesday, February 25. The weather was right out of the travel brochures for winter in the Italian Alps; sun, snow, and mild temperatures. Because the biathlon sprint races for women and men were both scheduled for the same day, the convoy of buses up the valley was impressive even at 7:30 in the morning. By the time the athletes arrived at the range the grandstands were filled with enthusiastic, flag-waving fans.

Both the women's race in the morning and the men's in the afternoon went smoothly. The Americans did well; four of the eight competitors registered a personal best performance in international competition. Trudy was thrilled to finish ahead of Sandy, who uncharacteristically had problems with her prone shooting. Jenny and Emily both finished in the top half of the field.

In the men's competition, Thomas Oksoktaruk was the surprise of the day, finishing in fourteenth place, the best American. Oliver broke into the top twenty-five for the first time in his career. Ragnar and Heikki both seemed a little flat, perhaps still fatigued from the 20K. Like the women, the four United States men finished in the top half of the results.

But there was an undercurrent of discouragement. Matt's performance in the distance event and Sandy's bronze medal had raised expectations. What would have been considered improved Olympic results only a few weeks ago, now appeared disappointing in light of Matt and Sandy's earlier races. This attitude was compounded by the American journalists who descended on Antholz like a cloud of insects, frustrated that they had missed the fireworks at the first two biathlon races. In their view, an Olympic event where America doesn't win a medal is a failure, and they weren't happy about enduring four hours on narrow mountain roads to watch United States athletes fail to make the top ten.

Kobelev was quick to put the results in perspective. He guided the reporters through the unofficial results, explaining what the sprints predicted about the relays. Finally, Kobelev reminded the media people that the two American men with the strongest 20K finishes had been sitting out the sprint, resting for the relay.

"Coach Kobelev, are you predicting medals for the Americans in the biathlon relays?" One of the reporters tried to pin Vlad down.

"You have results from distance and sprint races. I explain you how important is building a team, not just one or two champions. Even you who are not coaches can see, taken together four Americans doing very good against four athletes from other nations."

"We say, 'biathlon is biathlon.' It means anything can happen in this sport. This is why so exciting! Not possible to predict results, because so many variables. For almost forty years America has no chance for Olympic medals in biathlon. Now three days after winning first medal, everyone is disappointed we have no medals today. You see difference in this attitude? My advice, don't miss biathlon relays!"

Kobelev's comments had the desired effect, both on the press and on his own athletes. That evening in the team meeting, the members of the women's relay were announced: Paula, Kate, Trudy and Sandy. With only one day between events, the women would practice the relay format on the range and familiarize themselves with the tag zone for an hour on Thursday morning. Several of the women wanted to watch part of the final women's cross-country event, the 30K, but Kobelev squelched that idea. "Only one hour shooting and skiing today! Then you return to village for lunch and rest. You watch ladies' 30K on TV." It was obvious Kobelev's instructions were non-negotiable.

Vlad gave the men a day off on Thursday. It was so unexpected, the athletes were befuddled for a while, but after being secluded for nearly a month in Antholz, they quickly arranged an expedition to Cortina.

Gopher approached Stan the Man for logistical help, and after a call to Greg Ingram at the USOC office, the excursion took shape.

After their morning run, which Kobelev demanded even on their day off, the six athletes and Stanley piled into a van for the ride to Cortina. They drove directly to the stadium that had held the Opening Ceremony. The first run of the women's giant slalom was under way. Since the weather was warm and sunny, the biathletes hiked to a knoll where they could see most of the course. They cheered for all the racers, but loudest for the Americans and Canadians. In their official Olympic Team jackets, they were an immediate hit with other spectators, and during the lull between racers, some serious pin trading took place.

After the first run of the giant slalom, the biathletes walked past the outrun of the jumping complex to the freestyle stadium where the finals of the aerials were beginning. Matt was astounded by the complex convolutions the athletes performed in the air, and the incredible strength they demonstrated landing. Two Americans were in the hunt for medals, which added to the excitement.

There was a break in the action at noon and they went to the athletes' village cafeteria for lunch. After clearing security, Matt was reminded how much bigger and busier the Cortina village was than Antholz. Burl led them through the serving line, then headed straight for the tables bearing the small American flags. One was occupied by figure skaters and hockey players. The contrast was dramatic. The women skaters, kids actually, looked like cover girls for *Teen* magazine while the hockey players appeared to be survivors from a street brawl.

When Burl asked if the biathletes could join the table, they were welcomed by the skaters. Like the Nordic skiers in Antholz, the skaters had been concentrating on their own events, and were anxious to talk with athletes whose Olympic experience was different from their own.

As they finished their meals, Matt grabbed an opportunity he knew he'd never have again. "Stephanie, I hate to hassle you, but would you sign a couple of autographs?"

"Sure. Who are they for?"

Matt handed the skater a note pad and a pen. "The first one's for my sister Annie, she's the same age as you." Stephanie wrote a brief message on the page, signed her name, and turned to a new page. "The second is for Gabriella Ferraro."

"Who's she, a friend back home?" Stephanie asked as she wrote.

"Nope, she's the Italian girl who drew a picture of a figure skater on my wall back in Antholz. She'd be a lot more excited by your autograph than by mine."

"Oh, that's sweet. You're very thoughtful." She turned to a blank page and quickly wrote a third note.

"Thanks a lot. Good luck tomorrow night, we'll be watching it on TV in Antholz."

"Thanks, I enjoyed meeting you. Good luck in your last race."

As Stephanie left the cafeteria, Matt glanced at his note pad. The first page read:

Annie,
Your brother is cute!
Best wishes, Stephanie Wang

Matt felt himself blush. He glanced at the exit, but the figure skater had gone. He flipped the page and read:

For Gabriella Ferraro,
A friend on the United States Olympic Team told
me about your drawing of the figure skater.
Thanks for making our stay at the Olympics more
enjoyable.
Stephanie Wang, United States.

Then Matt turned to the third note. It read, simply:

Matt,
Love and Luck,
Stephanie

Next to her signature was a simple drawing, a quick swirl of the pen that she must have executed thousands of times. It clearly depicted a female figure skater in a high speed spin.

After lunch, Stanley led the biathletes to the speed skating arena for the finals of the women's 5000M. Even though no Americans were expected to win, they enjoyed the atmosphere of the indoor oval and were soon cheering for all the competitors. Stan bragged that he had also arranged tickets for an ice hockey game at 1830, so they left the speed skating for a quick supper before the hockey game. Outside, it had begun to snow. Their driver was concerned about reaching Antholz after the hockey game. The way it was snowing in Cortina, he said, the passes would be closed within an hour.

They held an informal team meeting in the parking lot. Oliver suggested spending the night in Cortina. Stan was confident the United States delegation would have beds available, because many Alpine skiers had already left for their next World Cup event.

"Staying here tonight is not the problem," offered Ragnar, "getting back to Antholz is the problem. If it snows all night, the roads could be closed 'til noon and we'd miss the women's relay. And if this is the big storm they've been predicting all week, we might not get back for our relay on Saturday! I say we load up now and try to make it before we get snowed in."

"I've been back and forth to Cortina since the start of the Games. They've had the passes open first thing in the morning after every storm," Stanley argued.

"Stan, I'd love to stay here tonight, but I have to agree with Ragnar. We've trained too long and too hard to risk missing our most important event. We'd better head over the mountain right now." Burl made it clear the discussion was over. There was a little grumbling from Oliver and Stanley, but they all piled into the van, and buckled up.

If they had delayed in Cortina fifteen minutes longer, they never would have made it. Even though the van was heavily loaded, had excellent tires, and was driven by an experienced volunteer, the wet snow was already eight inches deep when they reached Cimabanche, high above Cortina. The driver was aiming the van more than steering it, forced to maintain a speed that could plow through drifts, but not too fast to negotiate the frequent hairpin turns. Descending out of the Val di Landro to Dobbiaco, Matt assumed the snow would slacken, but the highway crews had been unable to keep up with the accumulation.

Finally, they reached the Antholz Valley and stopped at the guard post. After a typically animated Italian conversation between their driver and the commander, the Americans learned that several passes in the region had been closed due to avalanche danger. The soldiers had heard by radio that a hillside above Cortina had broken loose burying the road. There was no report of lost vehicles, but officials were predicting at least seventy-two hours to reopen the road.

Of more immediate concern was the road to the athletes' village. Because the walls of the Antholz Valley were steep and avalanches were common, that road had also been closed to traffic. After much negotiating, the Italian driver convinced the soldiers to allow the van through, but as a precaution, soldiers led the way in a tracked, armored personnel carrier. Matt had seen his share of snow storms, but this was a full blown blizzard. The APC, only a few meters ahead, was almost totally obscured by the swirling snow, but the wide, packed trenches left by its treads made it possible for the van to reach the village.

After thanking their driver, and supplying him with a generous supply of United States pins, the biathletes jogged through the drifts to the cafeteria. There was good-natured teasing and a rehash of the day's adventures as they ate, then they braved the blizzard to reach their housing unit. They had missed the team meeting for the women's relay, but Vlad quickly assigned the men tasks for the race.

By 2200 Matt was ready for bed. He wondered if Grete had been selected to race the relay. He considered walking to the Norwegian's building, but it was probably too late, especially the night before a race. He had tried several times over the past days to reach Grete, but they hadn't connected since before the 20K. At first he assumed they simply had conflicting training schedules, but after what Ragnar saw in the disco, he wasn't so sure. She was so vivacious and good looking, he'd be crazy to think other guys weren't also interested. Hell, what chance did he have when several medal winners were probably in hot pursuit.

Then Matt remembered the computer terminal in the lobby. He logged on to the e-mail program and sent Grete a message wishing her good luck in the relay, assuring her he'd be cheering for the Norwegian team as well as the Americans. He paused before closing, unable to decide how to sign off. "Sincerely" was too formal. "Your friend, Matt" might be true, but it sounded childish. He tentatively typed, "Love, Matt," and stared at the screen. The feelings he had for Grete were certainly more than friendship. He touched the screen in the box marked Send, and his letter disappeared. His final thoughts before drifting off to sleep were of Grete Dybendahl, her eyes flashing, golden hair flying, her face vibrant from the outdoors.

"Matt, Matt, wake up! You need to come with us, it's an emergency!" The whispered voice was insistent in the darkness.

"Huh? What's going on?" Matt mumbled, more asleep than awake.

"We have to talk, it's important," the voice continued.

"Who are you? This is crazy!"

"It's Mary Manheimer. There's a medical emergency and we have to talk to you. Now I'm going to turn on the light and step outside. I want you to get dressed. We've got to walk over to the polyclinic."

The light went on as she had warned, and Matt squinted against the painful brightness. As he fumbled into his clothes, his mind raced, a jumble of frightening images. Something terrible must have happened to his mother or his sister! He remembered Chuck Stevenson in the pouring rain, his father's mangled pickup truck, the flag-draped casket.

He stepped into the hall fully awake and frightened. When he saw Vlad and Stanley waiting with Dr. Manheimer, his heart started pounding. The old coach stepped forward, put a reassuring arm around Matt's shoulders and said, "We are sorry to wake you. There is an emergency, but don't worry, nothing bad happened to anyone you know."

"What's this all about, then?"

"We must go to medical clinic, then we explain everything. Come. It still snowing so we plow through deep snow for short way."

Moments later the Americans were shaking the snow from their team jackets in the waiting room of the polyclinic. They were greeted by the small balding Italian doctor Matt remembered from the 20K. A clock on the wall read 0324.

Hello! We meet again. My name is Dr. Luigi Clementi."

"I remember. What's this all about?" Matt asked.

"Thank you, Dr. Manheimer for acting so quick. Maybe you begin, *Signore* Kobelev."

"*Da, da...,*" Kobelev looked exhausted. "After midnight, I hear tapping on my door. I open to find old coaching comrade from Novosibirsk, Pavel Kashkarov. He is frightened, begging for my help. I followed Pavel to house of Russian team where he takes me to room of national hero, Valeri Vassiliev who is thrashing in his bed so violent, two other coaches, they cannot restrain him. I ask what is the problem, how do you say in English...epilepsy? These coaches, all very frightened. One reaches into

trash for small plastic bag with tube, and I understand what is happened…
blood doping.”

“‘Where is that damn doctor?’ I ask. ‘Gone…disappeared,’ they
tell me. One say he hears argument in Vassiliev’s room earlier. Then
after midnight he hears strange noises. He checked and found Vassiliev
thrashing and foaming from mouth.”

“I tell these Russian coaches only hope for Vassiliev is polyclinic.
They are terrible frightened, but finally agree, and we bring him here,
where Dr. Clementi races to save Valeri’s life.”

“Thank you, Coach Kobelev. I explain from here,” the Italian
doctor interjected.

“From examination of patient, and questions to Russian coaches,
with translation by Mr. Kobelev, I diagnose this athlete has acute
hematological shock, result from transfusion of mismatched red blood
cells. He is alive at this moment only because he is unusual strong human
being, but his liver and kidneys, already cease functioning. It is my opinion
this Vassiliev will die within hours unless he receives transfusion of proper
matched blood. Normally, this not life-threatening situation, except for
this storm. We cannot move him to the hospital in Bolzano. Also, we can’t
get proper blood here to Antholz before maybe tomorrow afternoon.”

“There is only one other possibility. I began to search the medical
records of volunteers, coaches and athletes here in Antholz. *Signore*
Johnson, your blood is maybe a match. As Chief of Medical Services, I
must to ask if you permit me a sample of your blood, which we can check
in our lab. If your blood is matching, I ask you to provide transfusion
which maybe saves the life of this Russian athlete.”

“Okay, Doc, you’ve done your job, now I have to do mine!”
Stanley Reimer spoke for the first time. “Matt, the reason this Vassiliev
is in trouble is because the Russians were engaged in blood doping. They
were cheating! They were trying to give him an unfair advantage in the
50K, and they screwed it up! If they hadn’t been attempting to cheat, their
national hero would be perfectly healthy right now.”

“And unfortunately,” Stan continued, “There’s a lot more to it than a
sick Russian. If you are a match and you agree to the transfusion, there’s no
way you can ski on our relay team. You’ll be wiped out, too weak to walk, let
alone ski.”

Matt looked at Dr. Manheimer for confirmation of Reimer’s
prediction. She nodded solemnly in agreement.

"By now," Stanley went on, "you understand how desperate the ABF is for funding. You were within a hairbreadth of an Olympic silver medal a week ago today! We desperately need a medal in the relay. Vlad could never admit this publicly, but our women have virtually no chance of placing higher than fourth. Our only realistic chance is with the men, and you're a key ingredient of that team. Without you, Matt, there's no chance of a medal! Am I right, Vlad?"

Kobelev gazed steadily at the team leader with obvious distaste, but remained silent. Reimer shifted his look from the athlete to the coach and repeated the question, "Do we have a reasonable chance of a medal in the relay if Johnson's not on the team?"

Kobelev shook his head slowly and muttered softly, *"Nyet...nyet,* no chance without Johnson."

"Thank you, Vlad," Stanley continued. "So you see, Matt, we've got a complicated situation here. Now maybe you can help this Russian through his medical emergency, although there are no guarantees; but in so doing you turn your back on your own teammates, the ABF, and the United States Olympic Committee. As a medical doctor, this Dr....Dr.... uh.... "

"Clementi," the compact Italian supplied.

"Right! Dr. Clementi's job is to do whatever it takes to save lives. My job as team leader is to do everything possible to ensure the success of the American team. I feel badly for this Vassiliev, but we can't throw away a possible American relay medal to bail him out. Besides, it's not like you're the only one who can save him!"

Matt looked quizzically at the Italian doctor.

"This is true. In my search through the records, I find two possible matches, you and a Canadian coach. Naturally, I first contact the coach. Unfortunately, when I explain about Vassiliev, this Canadian coach, he... he.... Well, he made the decision not to provide a transfusion."

Vlad filled in the missing details, "This is Ian MacTavish, formerly head coach of Canadian Cross-Country team. At Calgary Olympics in '88 he says in the press, the Soviet skiers are blood doping. The Soviet Olympic Committee makes protest and the Calgary Organizing Committee demands MacTavish apologize. He won't, so they fire him during Olympic Games!"

"Were the Russians blood doping at Calgary?" Matt couldn't resist asking.

Vlad sighed deeply and looked steadily at Matt. "I cannot say for certain. You understand, Biathlon and Cross-Country are separate federations under old Soviet system. But study the results and you see that Soviet skiers who race so well in Calgary were not so strong in early World Cup events. Also you should know that the team doctor for Soviet Cross-Country in 1988 is again doctor for Russian cross-country skiers. It is this same Manfred Ullrich who disappeared from Russian house last night."

"Vlad, do you think they were blood doping Vassiliev for the 50K?" Matt asked his coach.

"Yes. One reason I leave coaching in Russia is this Dr. Ullrich. After success in Calgary, he became Chief of Sports Medicine for all Soviet Nordic skiing, including Biathlon. I do not want to be part of his methods."

There was a pause in the discussion. Matt was confused. Dr. Manheimer broke the silence. "We have a complicated moral issue here. I won't review the whole thing, but one step seems logical. Matt, if you'll permit Dr. Clementi to draw a blood sample, we'll learn whether you are, in fact, an eligible donor. It might make the decision about the transfusion a moot point."

"As team leader, I must disagree, Dr. Manheimer," Stanley added firmly. "We are here in large part, thanks to the donations of average American families from across the country. They contributed their hard-earned money to provide our athletes the very best opportunity to win Olympic medals. That is our mission. I will not support any decision that diverts our attention from that mission. To be quite candid, the Russians got themselves into this problem, let them get themselves out of it."

Again the room was silent, except for the ticking of the clock on the wall, which now showed 0350. Matt studied the faces around him.

"Well, I'm not big on needles, but it probably makes sense to at least see if I'm a match. If I'm not, that's the end of it, right?" Matt looked to Dr. Manheimer for reassurance.

"That's right, Matt. If we take a sample now we should have an answer in a couple of hours, by breakfast at the latest."

"God damn it! I'm the team leader and I'm telling you we're not going to jeopardize our results!" Stan was prepared to make a stand.

"Stanley, this is not about race results or sponsorship dollars. This is about a man's life," Vlad was deadly serious. "I know Valeri Vassiliev.

He is not stupid and he is not a cheat! I cannot say the same for Manfred Ullrich. We do not know what happened."

"Oh, come on, Vlad! Are you trying to tell me that Vassiliev was blood doped against his will? That would be a neat trick, get a world class athlete to lie quietly for a couple of hours while he is being transfused with a unit of red blood cells against his will. Give me a break!"

"Stanley, you have no idea what it is like to live in Russia. You must believe me when I tell you Ullrich could easily put more pressure on Vassiliev than the athlete could resist."

"So what! The Canadian coach had the right attitude, the Russians got themselves into this mess by cheating, and we're under no obligation to bail them out, especially when it will jeopardize our performance."

Another silence, then Matt spoke. "I don't mind giving the blood sample. I've got a rare blood type. It probably won't match anyway, and that will be the end of it. If you take the sample now, will you know by breakfast?"

"That's right Matt, but I have to clarify one thing. Dr. Clementi and his assistants carefully screened the medical records of more than 1,200 people. You and MacTavish were the only two matches, precisely because you have the rare blood type. We suspect that you and Vassiliev are a match. The sample is to determine whether there are additional antigens or protein levels that could result in further hematological rejection. For Vassiliev in his present condition, that would mean certain death. We woke you, and Stan and Vlad, because we believe there is a good possibility of a match."

"So if I am a match, and I agree to the transfusion, there's no chance I could recover enough to race the relay?"

"None," Dr. Manheimer was unequivocal. "In fact, we'd probably keep you in the clinic for the remainder of the Games since you would be weak and quite susceptible to infections."

"And there is no guarantee that this transfusion will save Vassiliev?"

"That is correct," the Italian doctor interjected. "What we do know is that Vassiliev will be dead before the day is out if he does not receive a transfusion. The longer we debate, the more remote becomes his chance for survival."

"I don't believe this shit! We are not buying into this guilt trip, Dr. Clementi. These are the Olympic Games! We are here to compete, not to bail out cheats who were trying to gain an unfair advantage!" Stan reached for his coat, but nobody else moved.

"I don't see any harm in letting them take the blood sample," Matt said to the team leader.

"What the hell for! You're not getting tangled up in this, even if I have to call Harrison Strideman in Cortina to back me up!"

"I understand, but I'm going to provide the sample," responded Matt.

"All right, Johnson, want to play hard ball? I'm going to go call Strideman. We'll see what he has to say about this whole screwed up mess." Stanley grabbed his coat and stormed from the room.

"What do you think, Vlad?" Matt asked the tough old coach, who appeared on the verge of tears.

"This is very difficult decision. Even with transfusion Valeri may not survive. I truly believe you boys have the possibility for medal on Saturday, but who can say with biathlon? And so much happens before next Olympics. This must be your choice, Matt."

There was another long silence as the consequences of his decision swirled inside Matt's head. Finally, he spoke. "Let's take it one step at a time."

"I thank you on behalf of the Organizing Committee. Now, if you will come with me to the examining room," the Italian doctor was wasting no time.

"Okay, Dr. Clementi," Matt stood up, "but would you mind if Dr. Manheimer got the sample? She knows me, and...."

"Of course, of course. Dr. Manheimer...." He led them to a room off the main corridor. Clementi gave his American colleague a knowing glance when she asked her patient to lie back on the examination table. In seconds she found a vein on the inside of his elbow. Moments later, Matt was sitting up holding a cotton ball in the crook of his arm. As he stood to leave, Clementi shook his hand. "Thank you very much. We should have the results in two hours. We will find you. But please, you don't go to the race course before you hear from me?"

"Okay. I'll be in my room, or at the cafeteria having breakfast."

Back in his room Matt undressed and tried to sleep. He was exhausted, but he couldn't relax. His mind kept replaying images from his memory; trading pins on the bus with Vassiliev and watching the Russian champion push himself to the limit in the 30K. He also remembered the success of the American relay team in Lillehammer and the unrestrained joy that surrounded Sandy Stonington's bronze medal. Even though the men's relay team hadn't been announced, Matt assumed it might be Burl, Thomas, and probably Ragnar, in addition to himself.

At 6:00 he gave up trying to sleep, got dressed and went to breakfast. The only people in the cafeteria were women biathletes and their coaches. The conversation was meager because the competitors were barely awake, and anxious about their race. Matt saw Grete and smiled at her. She didn't respond, but he couldn't tell if she was still half asleep, or intentionally ignoring him. He sat with the American women.

"Gee, Matt, you look awful," Trudy was an expert on appearances. "Did you guys get plastered in Cortina last night?"

"Naw, nothing like that. We had a white-knuckle ride back through the storm, though. I didn't sleep well after that."

"Any advice from the hottest rookie on the circuit for a dark horse relay team?"

"Yeah, ski fast and shoot straight," Matt answered like a veteran.

"Right! Is that all, oh handsome youth, wise beyond your years?"

"That, and have fun!"

"Come on, girls. This kid's not going to reveal any of his secrets." Trudy stood and headed for the tray rack to dispose of her dirty dishes.

"Well, good luck," Matt said as the women gathered their gear.

"You're coming up later to watch, aren't you?" asked Kate Anderson.

"Yeah, I think so."

"What do you mean, you think so?" asked Sandy her voice sharp.

"I'll be there! Don't worry. Good luck."

Matt sat alone as he finished breakfast. He checked over his shoulder to see if Grete was still with her Norwegian teammates, but she was gone. Then he saw Oliver Wainwright striding toward him.

"I just talked with our fearless leader. He was babbling about some Russian blood doping screw up that you're getting roped into. What the hell's going on?"

Matt gave Oliver a brief overview.

"Jesus, Matt! Don't even think about it! After your seventh in the 20K, you've got to have an idea what a relay medal would be worth. Shit, if we only get the bronze, with the USOC's Operation Gold, ski company money, this car leasing agreement Stan signed yesterday, we're probably looking at fifteen to twenty thousand bucks, *apiece!"*

"And if Vassiliev really is in trouble, the Russian biathletes will be shitting their pants 'cause they're probably all on the same program. Hell, just being strung out about their national idol could take them out of medal contention in biathlon. Jesus, Matt, this is a heaven sent opportunity for us! This is a no-brainer, Matt."

Oliver was interrupted by a stumpy man in a Canadian team jacket. His clear blue eyes were set in a fair-skinned face burned painfully red by wind and cold.

"Which one a you's Johnson?"

"I am," Matt answered.

"I'm Ian MacTavish. I coach the Canadian cross-country skiers. I don't have much time to chitchat, but I gather you're the other guinea pig whose blood matches that sorry Russian cheat! Let me tell ye' something laddie, them Commies 'a been blood doping for years. Ye' can see it as plain as day, if ye' study the results. But the IOC's such a bunch of candy assed aristocrats, they're afraid to blow the whistle. So the East Germans and the Russians, an' all their naughty little neighbors just keep doping and winning! Hell, the few that get caught must be dumber than fence posts!"

"They been making a mockery of sport for years, laddie, and for the most part, they been getting away with it. Now finally, FINALLY, they screwed up good, an' the whole world's gonna see what they been up to. You can't bail 'em out this time, laddie! It'd be a crime. They cheat and win, so there's all the more motivation to keep on cheating."

"I tried to blow the whistle on 'em in Calgary, but nobody would listen. How many world class athletes have died since then, laddie? I'll tell ye', son, dozens and dozens; skaters in Holland, cyclists in France, swimmers in China, skiers in Russia. Losing their top dog at the Olympics, with the whole world watching just might make 'em throw out their whole crooked system! Don't you DARE bail 'em out! Hell, if Vassiliev pulls through, they'll cover it all up, like they have for years, and they'll keep on killing young athletes! You save Vassiliev and you can be damn sure you'll be murdering dozens of others!"

The fiery Scotsman scowled then turned and limped toward the exit. As he reached the door the rugged coach berated Mary Manheimer and Dr. Clementi. When the doctors recovered, they scanned the dining room. Matt knew they were looking for him, so he went to meet them.

Manheimer spoke first, "Dr. Clementi just finished the blood typing comparison. It's as close as we could hope for under the circumstances; not perfect, but certainly worth a try. It's possible we might begin the transfusion and Vassiliev's circulatory system would reject your blood, but by monitoring his vital signs, we would recognize such a rejection almost immediately."

Matt was trying to concentrate on Dr. Manheimer's words, but as they stood amid the breakfast traffic, they were joined by Ragnar, Burl and Thomas, all listening intently to the team doctor. Matt began to feel queasy. He had been hoping that the test would reveal that they were not a match.

"Matt, I imagine you've been wrestling with this decision since we first explained it to you. Vassiliev is slipping away while we talk. If there's any chance of saving his life, we must act now!" Matt had never seen Dr. Manheimer look so grave.

Oliver grabbed Matt's arm, "Johnson, it's their job to save him, not yours! We're the ones who've been busting our asses every goddamn day for the past six years for this chance! You can't let us down! Hell, it might be different if we had no chance to medal. Who gives a shit if we finish eighth or fourteenth? But for the first time in almost forty years, a bronze is a damn good bet, maybe even a silver if the Russians are rattled enough."

At the mention of the Russians, Matt glanced toward the table where the Russian team usually ate. They were all there, Dimitry Popov, his teammates and the legions of Russian coaches. In the morning light their faces looked grim. Some of the women had obviously been crying. And all eyes were were turned towards him.

NORTH
KOREA

3

47

47

47

1

48

2

◆ SEOUL

SOUTH
KOREA

3

20

◆ TAEJON

Kumsan ●

Kimch'on ○

34

34

25

Mt. Unjang ▲

Muju ▲

Minjuji ▲

TAEGU ◆

CHONJU ◆

Mt. Togyu ▲

▲ Mt. Kaya

25

26

NORYONG MOUNTAINS

SOBAEK MOUNTAINS

3

9

6

KWANGJU ◆

2

6

25

1

PUSAN ◆

N

0   25   50   75   100 kilometers

14

0   20   40   60 miles

Map courtesy of DeLorme

RUSSIA

MONGOLIA

CHINA

Khabarovsk ●

Vladivostok ●

Sapporo ●

Beijing ●

NORTH
KOREA

P'yongyang ●

JAPAN

Seoul ●

Chonju ● ▲ Muju

Tokyo ●

SOUTH
KOREA

Hangzhou ●

Nanchang ●

Ryukyu
Islands

T'aipei ●

North Pacific Ocean

TAIWAN

PHILIPPINES

Manila ●

A Medal of Honor

19

It was still snowing, but Olympic volunteers had shoveled narrow paths through the deepest drifts. Dr. Clementi led Dr. Manheimer and Matt single file from the dining hall to the polyclinic. The Italian doctor was opening the door when a voice called through the falling snow, "Hey, where do you think you're going! Wait! Matthew Johnson, DO NOT go in that building!"

The doctors frowned as the Italian held the door for the two Americans. Dr. Manheimer took Matt's elbow and ushered him into the clinic. Dr. Clementi followed and closed the door. They stood in the waiting room, anticipating a confrontation. Stanley Reimer burst in, winded and covered with snow.

"What...the hell...was the meaning of that? Coming in here...and closing the door...when I specifically told you...not to enter this building! How many times...do I have to tell you people...I'm the goddamned TEAM LEADER!"

"You'll have to keep reminding us until you start acting like one!" Dr. Manheimer stepped closer as Stan gasped for breath. "You listen to me, Stanley Reimer! You're way over your head in this situation. There is a young man who is dying and Matt Johnson is our only hope of saving him. We have explained the situation, and Matt has elected to help. It is not a question of the goddamn Olympic medal count, it is a question of doing the right thing. Now unless we get started immediately, nothing will save that athlete!"

"Just hold on a minute." Stanley pulled a cellular phone from his Olympic Team parka and jabbed the key pad violently with his index finger. "Harrison Strideman, please, this is Stanley Reimer in Antholz."

"Harrison, I'm at the polyclinic right now with Dr. Manheimer, the Italian doctor and Matt Johnson. Yes sir, that's right. Yes sir, I'd be happy to, here she is." He held the phone out to Dr. Manheimer. She took it and listened intently for what seemed to Matt an eternity. Finally, she said evenly, "I'm sorry, Mr. Strideman, but I can't do that. I took another oath when I began practicing medicine, and I'm afraid that supersedes any agreement I signed as a USOC volunteer. I understand. Certainly you can speak with him, he's not being taken hostage, you know."

She handed the phone to Matt, her eyes blazing with fury.

"Hello, Mr. Strideman, this is Matt Johnson."

"Matthew, my boy! I understand you folks have a ticklish situation up there in Antholz; snowed in, roads closed, and a Russian skier in rough shape. Now I've got to tell you something, son. Over the years I've come in contact with a hell of a lot of medical types. And you know what, Matt, they're all the same: overcautious! Hell, we train 'em that way, you know what I mean?"

"Yes sir."

"Matt, my guess is, this Russian will probably pull through whether he gets blood from you or not, you follow me? And on the other side of the issue, we've got to consider the future of the United States Biathlon Team. I understand it's popular with spectators here in Europe, but it's never caught on in the States, has it? To be candid, Matt, there are those in the USOC who see Biathlon as a black hole we just keep dumping money in, with no chance of a return. Hell, it's taken us thirty-eight years to get our first Olympic medal in biathlon! I'll tell you something Matt, we can't wait another thirty-eight years for Biathlon's next medal, you understand me, son?"

"Yes sir."

"We're getting requests all the time to consider new Olympic sports, everything from in-line skating to ballroom dancing. Every quadrennial we take a long, hard look at our expenditures and the successes of our teams. Frankly, Matt, Biathlon's in trouble. I'm not sure Stonington's bronze can save it. Now, I understand you boys have a decent shot at making the podium in the relay, and I suggest you do everything humanly possible to accomplish that goal, you follow me?"

"Yes sir."

"We understand each other then, Matt?"

"I'm not sure, Mr. Strideman, maybe I'd better review it just in case. You think Dr. Manheimer and Dr. Clementi have misdiagnosed Vassiliev's condition, and he's going to recover whether we do anything or not...."

"Now wait just a minute, young man...."

"Then you strongly implied that if we didn't win a medal in the relay, the USOC would withdraw funding for Biathlon. Is that about right?"

"You listen to me, you smartass little shit...."

Matt took the phone from his ear and depressed the off button with his thumb.

"We were cut off," he said handing the phone back to Stanley.

Capitalizing on the team leader's momentary confusion, the doctors led Matt down the hall. It was a typical, stark hospital room, two beds separated by a fabric screen. A young nurse in a crisp uniform sat in a chair at the foot of the far bed. As Clementi entered the room she rose and whispered to him.

Although his face felt cold, perspiration beaded on Matt's forehead. The hospital smells of disinfectants and rubbing alcohol flooded over him.

"Where's the bathroom?" he asked, his stomach churning violently. Dr. Manheimer guided him to a W.C. across the hall. Matt pulled the door closed and flipped up the toilet seat, as his breakfast surged from his stomach, and the tiny room was filled with the repugnant stench of vomit. He heaved until his stomach was empty, and even then he couldn't stop. He watched his breakfast swirl in the toilet bowl as bile burned his nostrils. He was trembling, so weak he couldn't stand.

Tentatively he reached for the handle and flushed the toilet. *Jesus, what am I going to do?* He wished there was someone he could talk to.

Grasping the rim of the toilet, Matt closed his eyes. In vivid detail he saw a picture his mother still kept on her dresser. It was a snapshot of his father, in his flight suit and helmet, leaning from the cockpit of his helicopter in Vietnam. He was smiling and flashing the photographer a thumbs-up sign. The sliding door of the chopper was brilliant white with a large red cross. Below the pilot's window had been stenciled,

Small Town Doc
We Make House Calls

From the moment in the Anchorage airport that Kobelev and Reimer told him he had made the Olympic Team, Matt had been driven to fulfill his father's dream. Now, miraculously a relay medal was a possibility, as it had been for his father in 1972. Matt knew it was too late for his dad, but if he could just bring home a medal, maybe his mother could see beyond the pain and frustration of the past twenty years and look ahead toward a better future.

But the image of Captain Johnson, medevac pilot, smiling from the olive drab helicopter with the big red cross wouldn't leave his mind. What would his dad do in his place? After all, he risked his life every time he flew that chopper, didn't he?

There was a knock at the door. "Matt, are you all right?" He could hear the concern in Mary Manheimer's voice.

"I'm okay, I'll be right there." He wobbled to his feet, splashed water on his face and rinsed out his mouth. When he opened the door to face the doctors, he was emotionally spent, but he had made his decision.

"Matt, are you sure you're okay?" Dr. Manheimer studied his face.

"I just lost my breakfast. I'm spooked by hospitals and I hate needles. I guess it got to me, but I'm okay now. Let's get on with it."

"Only if you're sure you're ready. At this point though, every minute is important. For now, let's just take off your boots, jacket and sweater. You understand, what we're attempting here is an emergency procedure."

"Because Vassiliev is going to die within hours unless this procedure is successful, we will be transfusing you directly. Dr. Clementi will monitor Vassiliev's vital signs, while I'll be watching yours. After I get the IV installed, it shouldn't hurt too much, although you'll feel a dull ache in your arm, and you'll get sleepy. Our objective is to give him enough blood to turn his vital signs around, but it's difficult to predict how much that will be. Do you understand, Matt?"

He nodded. "How long will it take? Are you going to be here through the whole thing?"

"You bet I'll be here. Harrison Strideman's already got my neck in a noose for involving you. If I left and anything happened to you, he'd make sure I never practiced medicine again. If Vassiliev rejects your blood, we'll know in a few minutes. If it's a good match, then it depends upon how quickly his organs absorb your blood. It could take several hours."

"Okay, Matt, give me your left arm. Now let's see…where was that good vein," She prodded and poked Matt's forearm.

"There we are…now, you'll feel a little stick…. Beautiful! Dr. Clementi, we're ready here when you are."

"Excellent!" came the voice from the other side of the screen as the Italian pushed the barrier aside. For the first time Matt could see the Russian champion lying in the bed next to him. Matt's breath caught in his throat. The person in the adjoining bed was gaunt, gray, and motionless. He bore absolutely no resemblance to the powerful Russian who had charged up the hill past Matt and Thomas a week earlier.

"Jesus," Matt whispered, "is he still alive?"

"Barely," answered Dr. Manheimer. "If this doesn't work, I doubt he will last another hour. Here, keep squeezing this." She placed a bright yellow tennis ball in Matt's left hand. He flexed his fingers and felt a dull ache in his arm.

"That's great! Keep it up, not fast, but steadily."

"Welcome back." Matt recognized Dr. Manheimer's voice, but when he tried to focus, the glare from the overhead light was too bright.

"I must have dozed off," he said, still disoriented.

"Is that what you call it?" There was a playfulness in the doctor's voice. "Actually, Matt you've been out for quite a while, but we thought you could use the sleep."

"What time is it?" he asked.

"It's six o'clock. The transfusion went on past lunch time."

"Wow! I've been out that long? How's Vassiliev doing?"

"So far, so good. He still could develop a rejection reaction, but at the moment all his vital signs are improving. We are not yet out of the woods on this one, but Dr. Clementi is hopeful Vassiliev will pull through."

"Great! Boy, do I feel whipped. I can't ever remember feeling so wasted, except maybe after that ski tour in Yellowstone."

"It's to be expected, considering what you've been through. We took every drop you could safely provide, almost three units. Once we were confident his body would accept your blood, it was a question of whether you could contribute enough to save him. You'll be very weak for several days. You won't feel much like training for a couple of weeks, and you won't be one hundred percent again for at least a month."

"So the Nationals are out?"

"I'm afraid so, but remember Matt, you saved another Olympian's life. You didn't have to, but you did. Oh, that reminds me, an Italian Olympic Committee official was here while you slept. They're in a diplomatic dilemma. They deeply appreciate your help in saving the life of a prominent athlete. But without a public confession from the Russians, the Italians are hesitant to publicize details of the emergency for fear the media will create an international scandal. Dr. Clementi has been strongly encouraged to issue a statement to the effect that both you and Vassiliev were stricken by a virulent stomach flu, and are expected to recover within a week."

"Clementi has not yet agreed to this. He feels strongly that you should be recognized for the sacrifice you made. At the same time, he doesn't want the gossipmongers in the press to give the Cortina Winter Games a black eye by speculating about a doping scandal."

"It's no big deal either way," said Matt. "I just hope they find that East German doctor! And I hope Vassiliev pulls through. It would be a bummer to miss the Olympic relay and the Nationals for nothing."

"Matt, even if the Russian doesn't survive, you didn't give up those races for nothing."

Although he felt weak, Matt was able to sit up in bed and eat bland soup and a plate of plain pasta. Not long after his dinner tray had been removed, he heard female voices in the hall. Sandy and the other American women peeked into his room. Seeing him sitting up in bed, they crowded around enthusiastically. He was captivated by their excitement. They related the highlights of the women's relay, in which they had finished an impressive fourth. The Russians won, the Norwegians were second, the French third, and the United States fourth, barely eight seconds back. Rather than feeling disappointed about missing a medal, the women were thrilled to be so close to the winners.

"So how about you, Rookie? This stomach flu must be wicked. You seemed fine last night. There are all sorts of rumors flying around the dining room. The big news is that Vassiliev, you know, the Russian cross-country stud, has been scratched from the 50K! Word is he's got the same stomach flu that hit you." Sandy glanced at Dr. Manheimer. The doctor remained stone-faced.

"Well Popov doesn't believe all this crap about stomach flu, and we don't either. So how're you doing Matt, really?" Sandy asked.

"I'm wiped out, that's all. Bummed by the timing of this, but that's life. How're the guys doing?"

"That's a different story," Trudy offered. "Stanley had them corralled for an hour after lunch. They looked like death after that. I think the coaches had trouble deciding who would start in your place. It finally came down to Oliver, Burl, Ragnar and Thomas. Heikki wasn't too happy about being left out."

"Yeah, and Stan the Man's on the warpath again." It was obvious Paula wasn't kidding.

"Vlad sends his greetings," Sandy added brightly. "He asked us for a detailed report on how you're doing. He says he probably won't make it over tonight, but he'll stop by after the race tomorrow."

Kate Anderson whispered something to Sandy, who glanced at her watch, and nodded. "Well, Rookie, we've got to head down to the village for the awards ceremony. Wouldn't want to seem like sore losers."

Dr. Manheimer remained in the room to check Matt over. She was pleased with his vital signs, and helped him walk the length of the hall. Matt felt as if he were ninety years old. Holding tightly to her arm, he struggled to suppress a sense of panic. How could shuffling down a corridor be so exhausting?

He was dozing later when Grete came in. "I look for you during the race, at the range, and on the hill in the forest, but you are nowhere. After the competition, Kobelev told me you are sick. I try to see you in the afternoon, but your doctor says come back in the evening. Matt, I am worried for you."

"I'm okay. Weak, that's all. Sorry I missed your race. Hey, let's see your medal!"

She withdrew the heavy silver medallion from her jacket. It was attached to a broad ribbon featuring the five colors of the Olympic rings. Matt was impressed by how heavy Grete's award felt in his hand.

"It's beautiful, Grete. Congratulations!"

"Thank you, Matt. You know how it is, other teams made some mistakes and we were lucky on the range. We could have easily been tenth. Anyway, I'm very happy to take home the silver. That's biathlon!

There was a pause as they studied each other. "Grete, I missed you. I kept looking for you last week. At first I thought you were concentrating on the races, like in Lillehammer, but then I began to wonder."

"Oh, Matt, I'm so sorry. There is a big misunderstanding. After the 20K I was very excited for you, but when I see you and Trudy in the dining hall, I think maybe you don't care about me anymore. Tonight at the awards I talk with Sandy and she explains to me everything."

She sat on the edge of the bed, leaned over and hugged him. "You must know there are rumors. Even the Russians are whispering that you saved the life of their hero, Vassiliev. It's not stomach flu, is it, Matt?"

"I'm not supposed to talk about it, Grete, but when the Games are over, I'll tell you everything. For now, I'm just glad you're here."

She swung her legs up on the hospital bed, and hugged him tightly. She moved her head to steal a glance at his face. His eyes were closed and he was sound asleep.

Matt was awakened by a nurse pulling back the window shades to reveal a bright sun sparkling on the snow like diamonds. The matronly woman chattered in Italian, unconcerned that Matt understood not a word. She left the room and returned moments later with breakfast. He finished everything on the tray.

Dr. Manheimer arrived after he had eaten. She conducted a brief examination, then announced it was time for more walking. They made several trips the length of the hall. Matt was encouraged that he felt a little stronger than he had the day before. They peeked into Vassiliev's room, and found that the Russian was awake, though apparently unable to sit up. Matt nodded, and thought the Russian nodded in response, but the movement was so slight it was impossible to be certain.

Back in Matt's room, Manheimer was excited. "Matt, I've got good news. I spoke with the mayor of the village, and he agreed to have a television moved into your room so you can watch the relay."

"Great! I don't think I've ever seen a biathlon race on TV. It will be strange watching a race I should be in."

As promised, a television was wheeled into Matt's room in time for the men's relay. The coverage was remarkable, with five cameras on the range and a dozen more out on the trail. Matt had anticipated the order of the American team, and the strategy seemed to be working. Burl led off, shot well and finished within sight of the leaders. Ragnar picked up a couple of positions with fast, accurate shooting.

Midway through the race, there were five teams within striking distance of the gold; Germany, Russia, Italy, the United States and a surprisingly strong team from Japan. Matt smiled at the closeup of Thomas waiting anxiously in the tag zone. Ragnar tagged Thomas cleanly, and the Alaskan headed out in fifth place. The Germans and the Russians were beginning to pull away from the other teams, but Thomas was holding his own with the Italians and the Japanese.

The coverage from the course showed Germany increasing its lead over Russia and Thomas hanging tough behind the Italian. The cameras zoomed in for close-ups as they struggled up the final hill and into the tag zone. Steinigen left the start area with thirty seconds over Popov from Russia.

"Will the Russian be able to catch the German?" Dr. Manheimer asked.

"The Germans have been tough, but Popov won the 20K! Hey, look at this!"

Charging up the hill like a man possessed was Thomas Oksoktaruk from the United States! Somehow the Alaskan had passed the Italian and put ten meters between them! The camera caught Oliver, looking over his shoulder in the tag zone. He looked terrified. Thomas slapped him on the butt, then collapsed in a heap. As Oliver skated from the stadium, Italy's anchorman raced in pursuit. Matt noticed a white bandage beneath the Italian's hat and remembered him from the first aid room.

"Can Oliver hold him off?" Concern was evident in Dr. Manheimer's voice.

"It'll be tough. That Italian would ski himself unconscious for a medal in front of this crowd. I think that shot of Oliver's face showed fear of failure rather than desire for victory. There's a big difference."

They watched the final leg of the relay with rapt concentration. As the leaders came in to shoot prone, it was clear that Popov had gained on Steinigen. Both athletes shot with astonishing speed, hit all their targets and bolted to the trail for the second loop. Matt was surprised that Oliver had held off the Italian. On the verge of panic, Oliver took an extra shot to hit his five targets, but the Italian had trouble with his magazine, dropped several bullets in the snow, and lost the opportunity Oliver had given him. Wainwright left the range with an even greater lead.

"I don't know.... If he shoots well standing, he might just pull this off," Matt commented without taking his eyes from the screen. Dr. Manheimer was too engrossed to answer.

Popov came in on Steinigen's heels to shoot standing. The Russian followed the German down the firing line and purposely set up on the adjacent firing point. They alternated shots, the crowd roaring at each hit. Steinigen hit his five and doubled over like a speed skater as he sped from the range. Popov rushed his last shot and missed. He glanced at the escaping German, smiled confidently, and reached for an extra bullet. He shot the extra round and hit! Poised and relaxed, Popov skated from the range adjusting his pole straps on his wrists.

"Has he given up on the gold?" Dr. Manheimer asked in disbelief.

"No, he's just cocky. But if the German has any speed in reserve, Popov's in trouble."

The cameras switched back to the shooting range where Oliver was approaching with the Italian clicking his heels. They coasted into firing points and slipped off their rifles. The Italian got the first hit, confirmed by a roar from the stadium. Oliver responded with a hit, but the Italian's second shot came back instantly. Oliver rushed and missed. A third hit for the Italian. Wainwright forced his third, another miss.

Dr. Manheimer groaned and shook her head.

"Remember," Matt whispered, still staring a the screen, "he's got three extra bullets. It isn't over yet."

The camera picked up three more racers approaching the range, the Japanese, a Norwegian, and a Czech.

"Now it gets dicey," Matt said, thinking aloud.

The Italian sprinted from the firing line, his targets clean. Oliver reached for an extra round, three bulls still visible down range. The Japanese skier and the Norwegian began firing. Oliver's first extra shot was a miss. Manheimer groaned again and held her hands to her face. Oliver reached for the second extra bullet, loaded and fired. A hit! He fumbled for the last bullet, loaded, hesitated then dropped the rifle to his knees and took a deep breath. The Norwegian cleaned his targets and skated from the firing line as Oliver looked on helplessly. He brought the rifle to his shoulder, paused and fired. Another miss! He had used all eight bullets and left two targets untouched. Like a man in a dream, he swung the rifle to his back and skated to the penalty loop.

Both the Japanese skier and the Czech had also left targets, so Oliver was not alone on the loop, but any hope of a bronze medal had evaporated. The television coverage switched from the range to the trail, where Popov was gaining on Steinigen. As the German crested the high point of the yellow loop, he glanced back at his pursuer.

"That's it! Did you see him look back?" Matt was so excited he almost shouted. "Steinigen's not thinking about the finish line, he's worried about Popov catching him! Watch this!"

Popov continued to gain on the struggling German. They fought up the final hill together, but in the sprint to the line, the feisty Russian pulled ahead by a stride. The packed stadium screamed in appreciation for the dramatic battle. Then the compact Italian skated into view for the bronze medal. He raised his arms in victory, whipping the partisan crowd into a frenzy.

The three medal winners were shaking hands in the finish area when the Norwegian coasted across the line in fourth. Moments later the compact Japanese skier skated across the range and toward the timers for fifth place. Then the camera picked up Oliver Wainwright, staggering up the final hill. In the background, the Czech skier was closing.

"Oliver's got to kick it if he wants to hold on to sixth," Matt told the doctor. As if Matt had prior knowledge of the outcome, the Czech gained on the American as they pushed to the finish. Oliver appeared to be in a trance, he staggered to the line like a robot. The Czech stepped to a parallel lane and with a few smooth strides overtook Wainwright for sixth place.

"What a race! I'm exhausted. We were third until Oliver's last standing! How do you suppose Oliver will handle it?" Dr. Manheimer asked.

"He'll be pretty bummed out," Matt predicted.

As the TV camera panned the finish area, Popov was on the shoulders of his teammates as the Italians sprayed the grandstand with champagne. Oliver was surrounded by reporters and cameramen. The picture zoomed to his face, creased with fatigue and discouragement. The commentator shouted his questions above the din of loudspeakers and cheering.

"Mr. Wainwright, Mr. Wainwright, a comment about your race, please? After the strong performances earlier in the Games, was there a great deal of pressure on you Yanks today in the relay?"

The camera caught the conflict on Oliver's face, a mixture of defiance and desperation. Matt sensed he was on the verge of total collapse.

"It wasn't my fault!" Oliver sobbed into the camera, "Look at the start list! Every other team put their strongest out last, but that asshole Kobelev sent our hotshots out first just to make me look bad...."

"Well, Mr. Wainwright, I'm sure our viewers can understand your frustration. Have you Yanks ever been so close to a medal in the relay before?"

"We weren't close to a medal today! Don't you understand? It looked good for two laps because we raced our fastest people first. Now I get all the blame for losing the goddamn bronze and it wasn't my fault! Shit, even with two penalty loops I had a faster leg than the Eskimo!"

"Well, actually, Mr. Wainwright, the final leg of the American relay was nearly two minutes slower than the other three. Of course, those are unofficial times at the moment."

"Whatever.... That bastard Kobelev knew we didn't have a chance for a medal and just wanted to make me look bad."

"Well, thank you for speaking with us, Mr. Wainwright. This is James Bedford Jones for EuroSport, with an obviously disappointed American biathlete, Oliver Wainwright, at the final biathlon competition of these Olympic Games. Now back to you in the studio, Elizabeth...."

Matt had more visitors during the afternoon. Kobelev stopped in, as promised. Always the coach, he hauled Matt out of bed to walk the corridor. Vlad was happy to see that Matt was gaining strength, but Matt could tell the burly Russian was emotionally spent. He had expended maximum effort through six biathlon competitions, and he was running on empty.

After a while Kobelev wandered to Vassiliev's room where Matt could hear the two conversing quietly in Russian. When he returned, he appeared on the verge of tears, "Matthew, with the help of these doctors you save Russia's greatest Nordic skier. Valeri does not have words to tell you how much he is grateful, also his family. If you racing today, Matt, maybe we have a medal, who knows? But saving the life of another athlete...." The coach studied the floor for a time, then cleared his throat, "So...I must do packing, clean wax room, and keep your teammates from shooting Oliver." He smiled. "Please, you must rest! On Monday we by bus several hours to Munich, then airplane to Washington, DC, and finally home. You must rest."

Later Burl, Thomas and the women stopped to visit. Both Thomas and Burl were happy with their relay legs and philosophical about the final result. The women had been trading uniforms and looked like a random assortment of international athletes. Trudy wore a Russian mahogany-colored fur hat which contrasted beautifully with her blonde hair and blue eyes. Paula Robbins twirled around showing off her stylish wool overcoat, part of the Italian's Opening Ceremony outfit. Kate was thrilled with her elegant Swiss warmup suit, and Emily Livengood grinned in a chaotically colorful Korean parka.

"You're going to hate us, Matt, but we've got to run," Burl said, slightly embarrassed. "I can't believe she can actually pull it off, but Janet Keegan said she could get us tickets for the figure skating tonight! Gopher arranged transportation, so we're headed down to Cortina. If you don't have anything better to do, watch for us on the tube."

Sandy was the last to leave. "They needed you out there today, Rookie," she said quietly.

"Yeah, I saw it on TV."

"Is Vassiliev going to make it?"

"Dr. Clementi says things look promising."

"That's good. I suppose it's unrealistic to hope they've learned a lesson about blood doping. We'll have to wait and see. I've got to go, but I wanted you to know, you've got what it takes for this sport. It may seem crazy with these Games not even over, but you should start thinking about Korea. Trust me, four years will be gone in a flash. With your savvy on the range and more experience on the skis, you could be a legitimate medal contender at the next Olympics. It's not too early to make a plan." Then Sandy leaned over the hospital bed and gave Matt a quick hug.

Grete came by after dinner. She smuggled in ice cream, which she had pilfered from the dining room. She was vivacious as always, but Matt sensed a serious undercurrent. When he asked, she admitted she was dreading the end of the Games. Matt had never considered what would happen after the Closing Ceremony.

On the final day of the Olympics most of the attention would be on the men's slalom in Cortina, and the men's 50K cross-country in Antholz. Then, the athletes and coaches would congregate one last time for the Closing Ceremony. Early Monday morning most of the teams would leave, and by evening the Cortina Games would be only a memory.

Grete looked sad. Matt realized he had no idea when he'd see her again. He reached out and drew her into a strong embrace.

"Oh, Matt, I love you." She squeezed him tightly, his pulse jumped and his mind became a jumble of emotions. Before he could speak, a clamor in the corridor startled them both.

"Johnsonmatt! *Gidyeah myha droog Amerikanski biathlonist,* Johnsonmatt?"

They heard footsteps in the corridor and doors opening. Grete hopped off the bed and peeked into the hall. An instant later, Dimitry Popov and his three relay teammates were standing at the foot of Matt's bed.

"So, my friend, *harasho?* All is good?"

"Yeah, Dimitry, *harasho.* I'm a weak puppy, but I'll be over that in a few days. How's Vassiliev?"

"Valeri is also good. No more competition. Maybe he becomes trainer for young skiers. But Matt, sorry, my English is no good. We are coming for thank you for saving Russia sports champion. Even he makes serious mistake at Olympic Games, still you give away your chance in relay to help Vassiliev. Johnsonmatt, you are true sportsman!"

Popov unzipped his team jacket, revealing the heavy gold medal he had just received for the biathlon relay. His three teammates stood behind him; taller but equally as fit. With broad cheekbones and deep-set eyes, they all looked very Russian. Then Popov slipped the ribbon over his head, stepped to Matt's bedside, and formally placed the gold medal around Matt's neck. The Russian glanced at his teammates, who smiled back, and pronounced with conviction, *"Harasho!"*

Matt was stunned. He could feel the weight of the medal on his chest. There was a glow of friendship and gratitude on the faces of the four Russian Olympians. Grete's eyes filled with tears.

"Dimitry, I…I…can't. I mean, this is an Olympic gold medal! I couldn't take your gold medal." Matt held the heavy medallion in his hand and began to slide the ribbon back over his head.

"*Nyet, nyet!* You must! This is small gift from Popov, from these champion biathlon racers," he pointed to his teammates, "and from Russian people. We cannot repay what you give to Russia Olympic Team. You understand?"

Before Matt could protest further, Popov grabbed Matt by his shoulders and kissed him repeatedly on both cheeks. Then Popov stepped back and his relay teammates duplicated the ritual. When they had finished, they watched as Matt self-consciously studied the gold medal.

Popov broke the silence, "So! *Harasho?* Johnsonmatt, you are now Olympic gold medalist in biathlon! In Russia this very important!"

"I don't know, Dimitry. I appreciate it, but this is too much. You keep your gold medal." Again Matt tried to slip the the ribbon over his head.

"*Nyet!* No problem. This gold medal for my America friend." With a golden smile, Popov withdrew the 20K medal from his pocket. "Anyway, I have plenty gold medals!"

Matt felt stronger on Sunday. He walked the corridor several times by himself without getting dizzy. He stopped in Vassiliev's doorway and found the Russian sitting up for the first time. Vassiliev motioned Matt into the room, and they greeted each other tentatively. Vassiliev's English was not a good as Popov's, but with hand gestures they could understand each other. Matt was alarmed by the weakness of the former champion.

"Hey, they brought me a TV yesterday. I could roll it in here and we could watch the 50K."

"*Da...da...*I like very much see 50K!"

Soon Matt had the TV set up in Vassiliev's room and together they watched the most prestigious race in Nordic skiing. At first Valeri made brief comments about every athlete: those who were medal contenders, those who had promise for the future, and those who had passed their prime. The TV coverage was tremendous, switching from one camera location to another along the course. Eventually, the Russian's comments tailed off. Matt noticed the silence and saw tears coursing down the face of the former champion. Matt pointed at the television, asking in sign language if the Russian had seen enough. Vassiliev nodded, so Matt turned the set off and returned to his room.

Thomas stopped by to assure Matt his gear would be packed and ready for departure in the morning. He didn't stay long because the buses to the Closing Ceremony were departing at 1630.

By 1830, Matt was famished. He was about to ask the nurse for supper when Grete burst in with two covered trays from the athletes' dining room, full course meals made especially for the final night of the Games.

"Hey, the buses left for the Closing Ceremony hours ago. Why aren't you in Cortina?"

"I prefer to be here! Maybe we get a better look on television."

They enjoyed their meal together and then went to Vassiliev's room to watch the Closing Ceremony on EuroSport. It was a spectacular celebration, and the cameras found many of the outstanding personalities of the Games. Popov led the Russians into the stadium, and Vassiliev smiled as the biathlete strained to carry their flag one-handed. The camera also found Sandy Stonington, smiling and waving as she marched into the arena. Stephanie Wang carried the American flag, but she was dwarfed by the heavy banner. As a camera followed her past the grandstand, a rugged hockey player swept the tiny skater and the national flag to his shoulders. The crowd loved it!

When the Olympic flame was extinguished, the three athletes high in the Antholz Valley were silent, sensing even over television, the emotional significance of the moment. Grete reached for Matt's fingers in the darkened room. He squeezed her hand as President Samaranch declared the Cortina Olympic Games closed. The stadium responded with a groan of disappointment. But then, the IOC leader called upon the youth of the world to reassemble four years hence, for the Games of the Korean Winter Olympics.

"You will compete in Muju?" Vassiliev asked his guests.

"Maybe. But four years is a long time," answered Grete.

"And you?" Vassiliev looked at Matt.

"I hope so. I've learned a lot on this trip."

Matt Johnson's story continues in

THE HEROES OF MUJU

The forthcoming sequel to

A MEDAL OF HONOR

Night Ambush

1

Matt hunkered down. He had to become invisible. The persistent drizzle had soaked through his camouflage fatigues and he struggled against the urge to shiver uncontrollably. Hours earlier, as the platoon had advanced unopposed to the summit of a small rise, the decision had been made to set up a perimeter for the night. The four rifle squads were assigned two-hour rotations on guard duty, shallow defensive positions were established, and the coordinates of the hilltop were radioed back to artillery fire control. Those G.I.'s not actually on perimeter duty quietly broke open MRE's, knowing it might be their only opportunity to eat for several hours.

At midnight, when the fourth squad took its turn on the line, Matt was assigned a listening post 150 meters out beyond the perimeter, beside a well established trail. It was assumed that if the enemy attacked during the night, they would probably advance along the trail before spreading out for a final assault on the hill. The listening post would provide a crucial, early warning of the enemy's approach, but it was a terrifying assignment. The soldier manning the listening post out beyond the defensive perimeter could easily be overrun by the enemy or just as easily be shot by his trigger happy buddies, as he scrambled back to friendly lines.

At least the rain muffled the rustling of the fallen leaves and dead grass, as Matt cradled his M-16 in his elbows and low-crawled across the open field in front of the platoon to the tree line beyond. Once he reached the forest, he whistled softly to attract the attention of the sentry he had been sent to relieve. No response. Matt advanced cautiously, afraid of surprising the other soldier. He whistled again. Silence.

The bitter taste of bile rose in Matt's throat. Where the hell was the kid he was supposed to replace? Matt worried that he might have crawled off course in the dark and was now looking in the wrong place. With his pulse pounding in his ears, he advanced deeper into the trees. In a low crouch, he moved through the wet bushes in the darkness until he tripped and fell headlong, into a shallow ditch.

"What the f...."

"Shhhhhh, I'm here to relieve you."

"Shit, I must'a fell asleep. Which way's back?"

"Over there. You remember the password, when you reach the wire?"

"Yeh, I got it. Thanks for spelling me. This duty sucks."

"Yeh, well don't surprise 'em going in. See you in the morning."

"Roger that."

Within seconds the other soldier disappeared in the wet blackness. Like a blind man, Matt groped around for a tree trunk to sit against, hoping he was facing in the general direction of the trail. As his breathing and heart rate steadied, he became aware of the forest around him. The rain in the trees, which had intensified from a light drizzle to a steady rain, drowned out all other forest sounds. He flipped off the safety on his M-16, realizing that an entire enemy company could file past him down the trail, and he'd never even hear them.

For several minutes, he stared into the darkness and strained to distinguish the slightest variation in the symphony of precipitation pouring through the canopy around him. Eventually he relaxed slightly, and his thoughts began to wander. He smiled to himself, marveling at how dramatically his circumstances had changed. What was it, less than five months earlier, he had attended the Olympic Team Banquet in Washington, D.C.?

The lavish conference center had been festooned with flags, banners and the interlocking five rings. The huge hall was crowded with Winter Olympians, fresh from the Winter Olympic Games in Cortina, Italy, as well as the Washington elite in tuxedos and ball gowns, clamoring to be seen, and photographed with America's latest, athletic heroes.

Predictably, the gold medalists had been the center of attention. Tiny figure skater, Stephanie Wang was engulfed by a sea of enthusiastic admirers. The hockey players, Alpine skiers and jumpers were also surrounded by clusters of adoring fans. Certainly, had Sandy Stonington been there, America's first Olympic medalist in biathlon would have received plenty of notice. But as soon as the competitive season had ended, Sandy had made it clear that she was finished with public appearances. She had packed her gear, including the bronze medal, and headed for her cabin, overlooking Lake Ontario. Without a celebrity in their midst, the biathletes assumed their customary positions, on the periphery of the party, self-consciously chatting with each other.

Following the dinner, the obligatory speeches, and an inspirational film, which highlighted the dramatic achievements of America's athletes at the Games, the assembled guests filed into an adjacent ballroom where a terrific band quickly had the floor filled with dancing couples. Matt tried to get into the mood of the evening by asking his teammates to dance. Paula Robbins was an enthusiastic, almost acrobatic dancer, and they elbowed and jostled through the crush until her old cross country team buddies lured her away.

Emily Livengood, her eyes in the partial squint of a perpetual smile, was soaking in the spectacle from the security of a corner.

Both geographically and culturally, she was a long way from her home in Anaktuvuk Pass, Alaska. At first, she resisted Matt's efforts to lead her onto the floor, but she eventually relented, and they danced a couple of numbers on the edge of the crowd.

But even as Matt danced with the shy Alaskan, his thoughts wandered to his Norwegian sweetheart, Grete Dybendahl. So much had happened during the past months; it was still a whirlwind. The one constant through the endless travel, the exhausting competitive schedule, and the emotional turmoil of the Olympics, had been Grete. Matt's initial fascination, then attraction to Grete had evolved during the winter into a deep desire to be with her. After the Closing Ceremony, when he had returned to the States to recuperate, Grete had finished out the World Cup schedule with the Norwegian team. They stayed in touch by e-mail and occasional phone calls, but as the weeks passed, Matt ached to be with Grete.

They counted the days until the national teams of several countries, including America and Norway, convened on Dachstein Glacier in Austria, for the first, on-snow training camp of the post-Olympic season. Their reunion was a joyful, passionate roller coaster ride. Romantic entanglements between athletes of different nations were not new on the World Cup circuit, but Grete and Matt became so inseparable at Dachstein that they endured plenty of good-natured ribbing from the other athletes. Their parting at the conclusion of the camp was the most difficult Matt had ever experienced.

Although it was clear the band would play as long as there were Olympians and dignitaries willing to dance, Matt escaped to his hotel room at the first convenient opportunity. He shared the suite with Burl Palmer, his teammate from Wyoming, but Matt suspected the cowboy would be charming some of the nation's young beauties until dawn. Dancing had lost its charm for Matt without Grete, but he had also been intrigued by the offer Gopher, the team's manager, had whispered to him after dinner. Apparently, the President was inviting a select group of Olympians to join him for a run before breakfast, the following morning. Matt had agreed to be biathlon's representative, and he wanted to get a decent night's sleep before the Presidential workout.

The six-thirty call woke Matt from a sound sleep, but he washed, pulled on his warmups and running shoes, and made it to the lobby in fifteen minutes. He was surprised by the large number of Olympians who had been invited, most of them medal winners.

A lean, serious man in a dark suit, glanced at his watch, and asked the assembled athletes to follow him. Outside, at the hotel's entrance, idled a line of gleaming, black SUV's. The athletes quickly piled into the vehicles, and the motorcade sped away.

"Does the President run every morning?" A hockey player asked the dark suit riding shotgun in the front seat.

"Pretty much, when his schedule permits."

"Does he have a regular, morning loop?"

"Nope, we mix it up. Can't establish any predictable patterns."

"According to the media, he's a pretty decent runner," a hung over Alpine skier said, with a hint of anxiety.

"You'll see for yourself in a couple of minutes," answered the suit, for the first time, turning to smile at the athletes.

Moments later, the motorcade stopped at temporary barricades blocking Ohio Drive to Hains Point, next to the Potomac River. As the athletes took in their surroundings, another black SUV arrived, and several men in warmups hopped out. The President of the United States, his hair whiter, and his face more deeply lined than Matt had expected, strode confidently toward the athletes.

"I hope you kids had a good time last night. If I'm lucky, most of you did more celebrating than sleeping, and I won't embarrass myself on this little run. This loop's only about four miles, but it's all the time I can carve out of the schedule most days. Okay, let's go."

He nodded to the Secret Service officers, then headed down the road in a brisk jog. A couple dozen, slightly baffled, Winter Olympians scampered after him. By the halfway point, many of the athletes had fallen off the pace, but eight or ten Nordic skiers and speed skaters ran easily with the President and his guards. The President impressed the athletes by conversing with them as they ran.

When they returned to barricades, the President shook hands with each Olympian, then headed back to his vehicle. As he was about to duck into the back seat, he turned and called,

"Hey, I almost forgot, is Johnson, the biathlete in this group?"

Matt was stunned, but managed to raise his hand,

"Yes sir, I'm Matt Johnson."

The President motioned Matt over, while asking his Secret Service detail to wait. He put a sweaty arm around Matt's shoulder and guided him behind the vehicles.

"I got a personal call awhile back from President Pribilov of Russia. He filled me in on what happened up in the mountains there in Italy. You probably know, I love sports, and I've suspected for years that those Eastern Bloc bastards have been cheating. I have to admit, if I'd been there in Antholz, and known what was going on, I probably would have encouraged you to go for the medal."

"But I've got to tell you, son, President Pribilov sounded mighty grateful. He apologized for not being able to thank you and the United States publicly, but he assured me he would take action to root out the cheaters in Russia's sports organizations. He also said he wanted to thank you personally if you would visit him in Moscow."

Matt listened in disbelief. He didn't know how to respond. The President sensed his confusion,

"We'll let all this Olympic hype blow over, then I'll have someone at State, or maybe the USOC arrange the trip. This is too good an opportunity to pass up. The public may never know about the choice you had to make over there, but I can assure you, son, I'm grateful for the improved rapport with the Russians you might have stimulated."

That conversation, just he and the President of the United States, had occurred in April. Now it was August, and Matt was hungry, dead tired and soaking wet in the pitch dark, fighting desperately to stay awake and to keep his teeth from chattering. He thought he heard something nearby, but the persistent rain drowned out all other sounds. Then he glimpsed something off to his right. He swung the rifle off his lap, but too late. A vice-like, perfect hammer lock yanked him violently from the ground and cut off his air supply. The M-16 fell away as he clawed at the powerful forearm which was choking him. Struggling frantically, Matt smelled alcohol as his assailant whispered menacingly in his ear,

"Welcome to the real world, Whaleshit. You are now a prisoner of war!"

To order additional copies of

A MEDAL OF HONOR

Contact:

Discover History LLC

P.O. Box 527, Bronxville, NY 10708

Fax: 914-793-8166

Phone 914-337-9636

Phone: 1-866-343-4757

Book: $19.95   Shipping/Handling $4.95

Visit us on the web at:

www.discoverhistory.net

The United States Biathlon Association

The US Biathlon Association exists to support and encourage the development of biathlon in the United States and to prepare athletes for international competition, including the Olympic Winter Games.

Founded in 1980, USBA works with Biathlon Clubs and Regional Centers around the country to organize training and competition at the grass roots level and staffs and finances the US Biathlon National Team, Development Team and Junior Team.

The US Biathlon Association is recognized by the International Biathlon Union and the Unites States Olympic Committee as the National Federation for Biathlon in the United States and is an IRS recognized 501 c (3) non-profit organization. There is an annual meeting of the membership each year and the USBA Board of Directors meets twice a year. Between meetings the Executive Committee meets on an as needed basis.

Help us grow as an association in supporting our members, clubs, and national team athletes. Become a member, renew annually (by 10/31), and recruit others!

Membership benefits include:
☐ Subscription to the electronic USBA newsletter (if we have your e-mail address)
☐ Membership Card & small gift
☐ Insurance coverage at all sanctioned races and sanctioned training events.

If someone has already used the Membership forms on the following pages, you can find them on the internet at our web site:

www.usbiathlon.org

You can also call or write to use at :

US Biathlon Association,
29 Ethan Allen Ave., #4,
Colchester, VT 05446,

1-800-BIATHLON,

339

US Biathlon Association Membership Application

Please print legibly, fill out both side of this form and read and sign the liability release form on the following pages. Membership cannot be processed without the proper signatures on the back.

Name _____

M ☐ F ☐ / Jr ☐ Sr ☐ DOB __ / __ / _____

Address _____

City _____ State _____ Zip . _____

Phone (_____) _____ _____

E-mail _____ @ _____

Name on Card _____

MC/Visa # _____ Exp. __ / __

Signature . _____

Must Check a "Membership" & "Election" Category on the next page

"Membership" Categories (please check one)

☐ $50 Biathlon Competitor-winter & summer athletes (E or F)
☐ $25 Jr.Biathlon Competitor-(under 21 yrs. By 30 Dec.) (E or F)
☐ $50 USBA General Supporter (I)
☐ $50 Family-(1 Parent(I) + 2 Junior Biathlon Competitors (E or F)) or
　　(1 Parent(I) + 1 Senior Biathlon Competitor (E or F))
☐ $50 Biathlon Coach/Official/Cert Trainer/Tech Delegate (G)
☐ $50 Amateur Sports & Biathlon Organizations/clubs (A or B)
☐ $50 Current/Past USBA BOD Officer (D)
☐ $1000 USBA Lifetime Membership (H)
☐ $1000 Corporate/Partnership/Organizations Membership (C)
☐ $10.00 Member for a Day:

race date: __ / __ / __
race location: _____

Biathlon Club Affiliation: (name of biathlon club you are a member of)

_____

"Election" Category Declaration (check only one)

Organizational Members:(the club, Org. or Corp. it self not the individual members)

☐ Group A – Regional Amateur Biathlon Club/Organizations
☐ Group B – National Amateur Sports Organizations- conduct National or International Biathlon programs or races
☐ Group C – Corporations, Partnerships & Organizations which are interested in development of Biathlon in USA.

Individual Members:(the "person/human" it self)

☐ Group D – Present/Past elected USBA BOD Officers
☐ Group E – Within past 10 yrs. Named Former USBA Olympic or Winter Sr.World Champ Team Member or alternate (see USOC By-Laws Chapter XII, §12.3, re: athlete representatives)
☐ Group F – Current and former Biathlon Competitors NOT in group E
☐ Group G – Present Biathlon Coach, Certified Trainer, Licensed Official or Technical Delegate
☐ Group H – USBA Lifetime Member
☐ Group I – USBA Supporter

United States Biathlon Association Inc. is a Not for Profit IRC 501(C)(3)

☐ I would like to help the USBA more! Enclosed is an additional contribution of $ _____

☐ I would like to help aspiring junior athletes. Enclosed is a contribution to the Walter Williams, Jr. Development Fund $ (Every year one top Jr. Male & Female each receive $1,000.00 award)

☐ Please do not share my name or information with any other organizations.
☐ I would not like e-mail notification of information, newsletter, events, or press releases.

Make Checks Payable to: Or Pay by MasterCard or Visa!
US Biathlon Association, 29 Ethan Allen Ave., #4, Colchester, VT 05446,

1-800-BIATHLON,

341

United States Biathlon Association
Assumption of Risk and Release From Liability
(Read carefully before signing)

I know and understand that biathlon in its various forms, as well as preparation for participation in, coaching, volunteering, officiating and relatedactivities in winter biathlon, summer biathlon and roller ski biathlon competitions and clinics (all of which are hereinafter collectively referred to as "Activities"), involve many **RISKS, DANGERS AND HAZARDS**. These risks, dangers and hazards include, but are not limited to, changing weather and snow conditions, variations in steepness or terrain, natural and man-made obstacles and structures, equipment failure, collisions with objects or structures, being struck by skier/riders or equipment, and exceeding my own abilities. I further understand that biathlon training and competitions involve performance at the limits of one's abilities, and therefore are more hazardous than recreational skiing or roller blades. I understand that **INJURIES OF ALL TYPES ARE COMMON AND ORDINARY OCCURANCE.** I know that the risk of SEVERE INJURY and even DEATH exists in all training and competitions. I also know that personal training, coaching, instruction, supervision and enforcement of rules by the United States Biathlon Association, its subsidiaries, affiliates, officers, directors, volunteers, employees, coaches, contractors and representatives, clubs, competition organizers and sponsors (hereinafter the term "USBA" shall be used to refer to all such persons and entities collectively) do not and cannot guarantee my safety. With full knowledge and understanding of the **RISK OF SEVERE INJURY AND DEATH** involved in biathlon training and competition, **I FREELY AND VOLUNTARILY ACCEPT AND FULLY ASSUME THE RISK THAT I MAY SUFFER TEMPORARY, PERMANENT OR EVEN FATAL INJURIES**, even if I follow the instructions or advise of USBA.

In partial consideration of USBA's acceptance of my membership application, and in spite of the risk of severe or permanent injury, or even death, the undersigned (hereinafter the "Member") agrees to:

1. Member agrees never to utilize any venue, course or facility for any training, practice or competition without first conducting his/her own thorough visual inspection of the venue, course or facility.

2. Member hereby unconditionally **WAIVES AND RELEASES ANY AND ALL CLAIMS, AND AGREES TO HOLD HARMLESS, DEFEND, AND INDEMNIFY USBA (as defined above) FROM ANY CLAIMS**, present or future, to Member or his/her property, or to any other person or property, for any loss, damage, expense, or injury (including death), suffered by any person from or in connection with member's participation in and Activities in which USBA is involved in any way, due to any cause whatsoever, **INCLUDING NEGLEGENCE** and /or breach of express or implied warranty on the part of USBA. Member's sole remedy in the event of any injury shall be compensation for medical expenses under the USBA secondary accident insurance program.

3. Member hereby **RELIEVES USBA OF ANY DUTY TO PROTECT MEMBER FROM HARM** in connection with any Activities in which USBA is involved in any way.

4. Member authorizes USBA to obtain medical care for, or transport him/her to a medical facility or hospital if, in the opinion of USBA, medical attention is required and Member is unable to make such decisions for himself/herself. Member agrees to pay all costs associated with such medical care and related transportation and shall indemnify USBA of and from any such costs.

5. The Agreement shall be construed in accordance with, and governed by substantive laws of, The State of Vermont, without reference to principles governing choice of conflicts of laws. In addition, Member agree that all lawsuits for personal injury or related loss against USBA must be maintained in state courts sitting in Chittenden County, Vermont for federal district courts sitting in the District of Vermont, and member consents and agrees that jurisdiction and venue for such proceedings shall lie exclusively with such courts. In the event any portion of this release is found to be unenforceable, the remaining terms shall be fully enforceable.

HAVING CAREFULLY READ THE FOREGOING AND UNDERSTANDING IT TO BE A LEGALLY BINDING RELEASE AND INDEMNITY AGREEMENT, *MEMBER SIGNIFIES THEIR ASSENT TO THE ABOVE TERMS BY SIGNING BELOW:

*For Clubs, Organizations or Corporations this must be the OFFICIAL LEGAL REPRESENTATIVE who signs on behalf of the organizations BOARD OF DIRECTORS (usually SECRETARY, PRESIDENT OR VICE PRESIDENT)

Signature: _____

Date of Birth: _____/_____/_____

Print Name: _____Title:_____

Date Signed: _____/_____/_____

SIGNATURE OF PARENT OR GUARDIAN REQUIRED BELOW FOR ALL MINOR MEMBERS

As the parent or guardian of the minor Member named above, I hereby make and enter into each and every agreement, representation, waiver and release described above on behalf of myself, the Member, and any other parent of guardian of the Member, intending that they be binding on me, the Member , and our respective heirs, executors, administrators and assigns, I intend to give up my right, the Member's rights, and the rights of any other parent or guardian to maintain any claim or suite against USBA arising our of the Member's participation in any Activities involving USBA in any way. I believe and represent that **I HAVE LEGAL AUTHORITY TO MAKE THESE AGREEMENTS, REPRESENTATIONS, WAIVERS AND RELEASES, AND I AGREE TO DEFEND AND INDEMNIFY USBA** from and against any and all liability arising out of any lack of authority on my part to legally bind the Member, or any unenforceability for any reason the above agreements, representations, waivers and releases made by or on behalf of the Member.

Parent or Guardian Signature: _____

Print Parent or Guardian Name: _____

Date: _____/_____/_____

About the Author

John Morton has had the amazing good fortune to have participated in seven Winter Olympic Games as an athlete, a coach, the U.S. Biathlon Team Leader, and most recently at Salt Lake, as Chief of Course for the Biathlon events.

After eleven years as Head Coach of Men's Skiing at Dartmouth College, he wrote *Don't Look Back*, a comprehensive guide to cross-country skiing. He is a commentator for Vermont Public Radio, and designs Nordic trails from his home in rural Vermont.